THE HIGH KING

GORDON ANTHONY

Part I - The Usurper

Chapter I

Lying on his belly, Greumaich used his elbows to wriggle forwards to where he would have a better view. As he hauled himself through the rough bracken, a sharp twig poked into his thigh, bringing an involuntary curse to his lips. Brushing the offending sliver away with his left hand, he squirmed to the very edge of the trees.

"Do you see anything?" Morcarrus asked in his nasal, whining voice.

"I'd have said so if I did," Greumaich snapped in reply. "Now keep quiet like I told you."

Morcarrus grunted angrily, settling back down into the shadows of the undergrowth. He muttered softly for a few moments before falling silent when Greumaich awkwardly twisted round to shoot him a warning glare.

Greumaich did not need to guess what Morcarrus had been grumbling about. The surly bandit's complaints were always the same, focusing on how he, Morcarrus, would do things differently. It did not matter what they were doing, Morcarrus would snipe away at Greumaich's decisions, undermining his authority. If it were not for the fact that Morcarrus was one of the best fighters in the gang, Greumaich would have disposed of him long ago. As it was, a confrontation was probably coming soon.

Greumaich wondered whether it would be better to deal with Morcarrus before the man plucked up the courage to challenge him. Yes, he thought to himself, as soon as this latest venture was over, he would call Morcarrus out and kill him so that everyone would see who was in charge. That, thought Greumaich, was how to deal with problems.

He rubbed his hand over his shaven head, smiled to himself, then settled down to watch. Morcarrus would have to wait just a little longer before getting what he deserved. First, they had a job to do.

It was the sort of task Greumaich and his men were good at. The man who had hired them had come bringing rings, brooches and other trinkets, and had also presented Greumaich with a fine sword, a weapon that was the mark of a chieftain. Greumaich, who had never owned a sword before, had been impressed, especially when the mysterious visitor had promised more wealth if the gang did what he wanted.

The bandit leader, though, was not blinded by the riches on offer. He had been suspicious of the stranger and his motives. When the man had first arrived at their camp, Greumaich had thought he might be a druid because of the long, grey robe he wore but, although the stranger had behaved in that arrogant, self-confident way that druids always exhibited, he was young for a druid, still in his mid-forties, and his hair had not been shaved from the front of his head, nor had he worn a beard. Greumaich suspected he was a nobleman of some sort but the man had refused to divulge any information about himself.

Greumaich, who had not become the leader of his small band of bandits by being reckless, had remained cautious and, although his suspicion was partly allayed by the sight of the reward, he wondered why anyone should offer such treasure just to arrange the death of one man.

"You are paying us to do what we would do anyway?" he had asked the man.

"I want to be absolutely sure that you will complete the task," the stranger had replied.

"This man you want killed," Greumaich had remarked warily, "will have a war band, will he not?"

"A small escort," the stranger had answered dismissively.

"That could make it difficult."

"That is why you are being paid so much," the man had reminded him. "But you only need to kill the one man and bring me his head as proof of his death. Once he is dead, you need not concern yourself with the other men. Kill them or leave them, as you please. They are of no importance."

Greumaich had not enquired who the victim was, nor why this stranger wanted him dead. He did not care about such things. The chance for more plunder was always welcome and to be paid to carry out a raid on travellers was more than Greumaich could usually hope for. He and his men lived a nomadic life, wandering the rugged hills, taking food from isolated farms, stealing cattle or

2

attacking small villages. Food, silver and women kept Greumaich's men happy.

They had been wary of coming so far south, into the lands of the Caledones, but they had been able to carry out a couple of successful raids and had managed to avoid the war bands that had been sent after them. Greumaich, though, was no fool. He knew that the Caledones were a powerful tribe. If he caused too much trouble they would surely hunt him down, so he had decided to go back north for a while, perhaps until the following year. There was no point in taking unnecessary risks.

Then the man dressed as a druid had found him and offered him a chance for one more raid. It was too good an opportunity to pass up but, even so, Greumaich was wary.

"Is there anything else I should know?" he had asked.

The stranger had answered, "He will also have women with him. Two of them will be fair-haired, a mother and daughter. Capture them alive and be sure not to harm them. If there are other women in the party, you may do as you please with them but I want the two fair-haired ones alive."

"We may not be able to do that," Greumaich had frowned. "It depends on how many men there are."

"There will be no more than a dozen. Probably fewer. And your reward will be doubled if you bring the women to me alive and unharmed."

Greumaich's greed was sparked by the mention of the reward but it did not overcome his natural caution.

"A dozen is still a lot," he frowned.

The false druid had smiled, although there was no humour in his eyes.

"So ambush them," he had suggested. "I know the perfect place."

Which was why, two days later, Greumaich and the fifteen men of his raiding party were hidden in the bushes at the edge of a small woodland, waiting for the travellers to appear. The stranger had been right about one thing, Greumaich thought. This was an ideal place for an ambush. The trackway the travellers would follow ran along the higher ground, avoiding the swamps and marshes of the valley floors, but here, the narrow path dipped into a low saddle of land between two hills. Not only that, there was a wide, open space of grass beside a pool of fresh water, surrounded

3

by stands of tall trees. It was an inviting place to stop, especially for weary travellers.

Greumaich and his men waited all morning, surrounded by the click and buzz of insects. They took water from the tiny stream that meandered through the wood on its way to feed the watering hole, they chewed on salted beef they had stolen from a farm some days earlier, and they lay quietly, cowed to virtual silence by Greumaich's harsh threats.

It was a long, boring morning. From overhead came the cry of an eagle as it soared high above in a clear, blue sky, but nothing else moved.

Greumaich wished he could lie out in the warm sunshine instead of lurking in the shadows, but when the first rider appeared on the ridge, silhouetted against the skyline, he instantly forgot all thoughts of comfort. Hissing a warning to his men to remain hidden, he peered up at the hilltop.

More riders followed, the horses walking at a leisurely pace as they picked their way down the slope towards the grassy resting place. Greumaich saw heads turning, arms pointing and knew they were discussing whether to stop here for a rest. He knew they would. The nearest village was several hours' walk away, so the travellers must have been riding all morning.

Morcarrus wriggled forwards, his long-handled axe gripped in his right hand. He edged through the bracken until he was beside Greumaich.

"How many?" he asked.

"Eighteen," Greumaich whispered in reply. "But there are four women and a couple of children. A dozen men."

"That's a lot to take on," Morcarrus grimaced, his voice a little hesitant.

Greumaich hissed, "What's wrong? Are you afraid to do some real fighting? Or is cutting the throats of farmers more to your liking?"

Morcarrus bridled at the accusation.

"You've done your share of murdering," he retorted.

"Maybe so. But this time we need to earn our pay."

"It will be hard-earned," Morcarrus grumbled sourly. "Some of them are wearing armour."

Greumaich looked again. The riders were closer now, close enough to pick out details. He swore softly when he saw that nine of the warriors were indeed wearing long tunics of chainmail.

4

Each of them carried a spear in his right hand and wore a small shield on his left arm. They also wore swords at their left hips. Worse, they rode with the casual ease of men who knew how to use the weapons. But armour? The mysterious druid who had paid them to carry out this ambush had not known about that. Or perhaps he had deliberately not mentioned it.

Most men prided themselves on fighting with only their skill and their painted symbols to protect them. Greumaich himself had an outline of a rampaging bear tattooed on his chest. Having his skin pricked by the artist's sharp needles had been painful but Greumaich was immensely proud of the result. The image was a perfect match for his own build and temperament. He commanded this band of murderers and brigands because he was bigger, tougher and meaner than anyone else. Even Morcarrus, for all his bravado, was afraid of Greumaich.

But these travellers were wearing armour. That changed everything. Greumaich had expected to face an escort of warriors, men who could be intimidated by his size and by the ferocity of his attack. Watching the approaching riders, he recognised that they were not at all like the men of most tribes.

For an instant he considered calling off the attack and telling his men to slip away into the woods to allow the travellers to pass. The idea faded almost as soon as it occurred to him. The druid had promised that they would be well rewarded for success. More importantly, Greumaich could imagine Morcarrus' comments if he refused to fight and merely slunk away like a coward. He would lose all authority if he ran away.

"If they are afraid to fight without wearing that protection, they can't be much good," he said softly.

Morcarrus raised an eyebrow at the obvious lie.

"Is that what I tell the lads?"

"Damn right."

Greumaich scowled as he considered his options. The stranger only wanted one man killed but leaving the others alive would leave Greumaich and his gang vulnerable to pursuit. They did not possess horses and any survivors among the travellers could hunt them down on horseback. Yet tackling nine armoured warriors would inevitably result in his own men suffering some casualties because men in chainmail were hard to kill.

5

He sighed inwardly. He had only two choices; to kill the entire war band or to abandon all thoughts of the reward and sneak away, leaving them unmolested.

When he thought about it like that, it was no choice at all.

"We'll wait until they have stopped and are eating and resting," he decided. "If we catch them off guard, we can kill most of them before they know they are under attack."

"We could still lose a few men," Morcarrus pointed out.

"Which leaves a bigger share of the loot for the rest of us," Greumaich told him with a wolfish smile that concealed his own concerns.

Morcarrus returned a grin of his own.

"As you say," he nodded.

"And remind the lads that we need the two blonde women alive."

Morcarrus nodded again then, his eyes scanning the ambush site, exhaled a long, slow breath of admiration and awe.

"I wondered about that," he murmured. "But now I know why he wants them. Take a look at that one."

Greumaich followed Morcarrus' gaze. He saw that one of the riders was a young woman, probably not yet twenty years old. She had long, blonde hair that shone like a beacon in the bright, mid-day sun. The tight fit of her travelling clothes, a grey, woollen tunic and leather leggings, showed him that her figure matched the perfection of her face. He felt a stirring of desire as he imagined laying his hands on her and ripping away those clothes.

"She warrants fighting nine men for," he agreed softly. "But the druid wants her unharmed."

"We won't hurt her," Morcarrus said with a salacious grin.

"Nobody is to touch her," Greumaich hissed.

Morcarrus shrugged but Greumaich was not fooled. He would need to keep an eye on the burly axeman. Then he relaxed when he decided he would have a perfect excuse to kill Morcarrus if the man disobeyed the instruction and tried to rape the blonde woman. That would solve all his problems.

He turned his head so that Morcarrus would not see his expression but the axeman was still studying the riders as they slowly trotted into the open area of grass beside the pool.

"So which one is the leader?" Morcarrus asked casually.

"The big one. That's what our mystery druid said. He'll be the biggest one there. He has dark hair and will probably have a bloody great sword on his back."

The two of them watched while the riders reined in their mounts near the pool and dismounted. Greumaich could see that there were four women in the group. Two, including the blonde beauty, were young. One was older, but still attractive, with blonde hair that matched the golden locks of the young woman he had been admiring.

"That will be the mother," he whispered. "We've to take her alive too."

"Fine looking woman," Morcarrus commented admiringly. "Not like the one behind her."

Greumaich looked to where the axeman had indicated a fourth woman. She was tall, skinny, and angular. She was nothing much to look at but then, Greumaich had fifteen men who needed to be kept amused. They could not afford to be too fussy.

He watched as the skinny woman lifted a small girl from her horse while she chatted to the slim, fresh-faced man who had been riding alongside her.

Greumaich's eyes wandered again, seeking out the blonde girl. By all the Gods, she was gorgeous. He began to wish the stranger had not insisted that the blonde women should not be touched. The younger one was certainly enough to fire the desires of any man and Greumaich could hardly take his eyes off her.

Morcarrus nudged his arm, interrupting his daydream.

"That must be him," Morcarrus said, pointing with a nod of his head.

Greumaich mentally scolded himself. The women were a distraction. Tearing his eyes from the girl, he looked to where Morcarrus had pointed. He felt a jolt of surprise as one of the biggest men he had ever seen appeared from among the jumble of horses and people. The man was giving orders, pointing out where he wanted sentries posted.

Damn, thought Greumaich. Sentries? But at least that meant there were two men who would be isolated from the crowd.

He looked at the big man again. He was older than Greumaich had expected, his long, dark hair tinged with grey at the temples, but he carried himself like a fighting man, light on his feet. On his back, just as the druid had predicted, was a huge longsword in a shining scabbard of silver and gold. He was tall,

7

more than a head taller than most of his companions, and broad across the shoulders. His muscles seemed to bulge and strain beneath his shirt and sleeveless leather tunic. He would be no easy man to kill, Greumaich thought. At least, not in a fair fight, which Greumaich had no intention of allowing.

"You and I will take him down while the lads take care of the rest of them," he told Morcarrus.

Instead of agreeing, the axeman swore again.

"What is it now?" Greumaich asked.

"I know him," Morcarrus replied with uncharacteristic anxiety. "Holy Dis! Nobody said it was him we were supposed to kill."

"What are you talking about?" Greumaich snapped, surprised at the hint of awe in Morcarrus' voice. "Who is he?"

"You mean you don't know?"

"I wouldn't bloody ask if I knew, would I? Who is he?"

Morcarrus face was grim as he replied, "It's Calgacus."

Chapter II

Calgacus stretched the muscles of his back and legs. It had been a long, if uneventful, ride that morning and he was glad of a chance to rest for a while. In his youth he could have ridden for days with barely a stop but he was fifty years old now and, although he was still more than capable of holding his own with the young men of his village in most things, he privately acknowledged that he grew tired more quickly these days.

He was also more cautious than he used to be. This seemed an isolated spot but even here, far from any known enemies, he insisted that two of the men stood watch.

His wife, Beatha, said, "Let them have a rest, Cal."

In response, he gave her a dark look.

"You can never be too careful," he muttered.

Beatha shook her head but she was smiling at him.

"You worry too much," she told him.

"I have a lot to worry about," was his gruff reply.

"You do not like having us accompany you, do you?"

Calgacus shrugged, "It's different when there are women and children to consider."

"You can hardly expect us to stay behind," Beatha protested. "We are going to a wedding, after all."

"I am not likely to forget that," he replied as his eyes scanned the company, making sure that he knew where everyone was.

This was an argument he had lost before, so he knew there was no point in going over the same ground again. His daughter, golden-haired Fallar, his youngest child, who had once been a happy, laughing baby, was to be married. He was taking her to the west, to the home of Coel, the mightiest King of the Caledones. Her marriage to Coel's grandson would seal an alliance between their tribes and would ensure that the Caledones would fight under Calgacus' command when they faced the inevitable Roman invasion.

This journey was important. Calgacus would have preferred to make it quickly but if Fallar was to be married, Beatha must accompany her. That was not open to debate.

There were two other women in the party. Emmelia, Calgacus' niece, the daughter of his long-dead sister, had insisted on travelling with them. Calgacus did not mind that, for Emmelia was a resourceful, intelligent woman, but she would not leave her two young children, so they were also making the journey, accompanied by Emmelia's husband, the quietly-spoken, inoffensive Caedmon.

"You should treat this as a family holiday," Beatha told him happily.

"Travelling in another tribe's land can be dangerous," Calgacus frowned.

"This marriage was your idea," Beatha reminded him. "You want this alliance."

"Yes, I do. But I did not force her into it. I would never do that."

"I know," smiled Beatha, placing her hand on his arm. "But she needs a husband. Most girls her age have been married for a few years and it's past time she wed. Not to mention that there have already been several fights over her at home."

"I know."

"And she says she likes Tuathal, even if he is a rather serious young man."

"She hardly knows him."

Beatha gave a soft laugh as she told him, "Stop worrying. It is a hand-fasting. She can always divorce him in a year's time if she is not happy with him."

The prospect of a failed marriage and the resultant collapse of his planned alliance was not something Calgacus wished to contemplate but he was saved from further argument when Runt sauntered over to them.

"Is everything all right?" the little man asked.

"Everything is fine, Liscus," Beatha assured him.

"This is a nice spot," Runt observed. "I'm surprised there's no farm or village here."

"It's probably a nightmare when the winter snows come," Calgacus grunted.

"Cheer up, you miserable sod," Runt chided amiably.

Beatha laughed, "That's what I told him."

10

Calgacus scowled at the two of them.

"I *am* being cheerful," he growled.

Runt grinned happily. He had been Calgacus' friend and companion since childhood. His diminutive stature, which had given rise to his nickname, made him look tiny when he stood beside Calgacus but the difference in height had no bearing on their relationship. They were as close as two men could be.

"How long will we stay here?" Runt asked.

"Long enough to get something to eat," Calgacus replied.

Runt nodded. His hair was thinning now, so he wore a soft, woollen cap to protect his balding head from the sun. He also wore a sleeveless, sheepskin jerkin over his shirt, despite the day's warmth. Strapped around his waist was a broad belt from which hung two Roman short swords, one at either side. People who did not know him often laughed at what they thought was an affectation but Runt was able to use either hand with equal skill and had carried twin swords for the past thirty years. Yet his smile and humour could be as disarming as his skill with weapons.

"I'd better go and see how Tegan is getting on," he said, giving a brief wave of his hand.

Calgacus watched Runt head towards the small pool of water where the women and children were spreading blankets on the grass. Tegan was the fourth woman in the party, a young, dark-haired girl who was now Runt's wife. Calgacus saw her sit down on a patterned blanket, tugging open the shoulder fastenings of her dress so that she could feed the baby girl she held in her arms.

Calgacus looked away.

Beatha, who had noticed where he had been looking, asked softly, "What is wrong?"

"Nothing."

"Cal," she stated, "we have been together too long for you to lie to me successfully. Something is bothering you."

Calgacus sighed, "It's Tegan."

"What about her? She's a nice girl."

"I know she is."

"I hope you are not jealous because Liscus has a young wife while you are stuck with me."

"Of course not!" he protested. "You should know that."

"I do," Beatha smiled soothingly.

She looked at him thoughtfully as she added, "It's the baby, isn't it?"

11

He nodded. Tegan's daughter, Sorcha, had been born nine months after he and Runt had rescued the dark-haired girl from the aftermath of a disastrous rebellion against Rome. Tegan's tribe, the Ordovices, lived far to the south, but Calgacus had travelled to join them because the man who led the revolt, a young chieftain named Brennus, had been making the seemingly outrageous claim that he was Calgacus' son.

Brennus was dead now but his young wife, Tegan, had accompanied Runt back to the North where she had soon agreed to marry him.

Beatha guessed, "You are worried because you don't know who the child's father is."

Calgacus gave a curt nod.

"She might be my granddaughter, the child of Brennus."

"Or she might be Liscus' daughter," said Beatha. "For what it is worth, even Tegan does not know who the father is. But it does not matter. Liscus will be her father and we will all care for her. She is one of us."

Calgacus gave his wife a weak smile as he acknowledged, "You are right. As always."

"So stop fretting over it. Try to be nice to Tegan."

"I am always nice to her," he protested.

Beatha smiled indulgently.

"Then try to smile when you speak to her. Come over and talk to her."

"In a moment. I must check on the men and horses."

Beatha regarded him closely before sighing, "All right. But don't be long."

"I won't."

She stood up on her toes to plant a soft kiss on his cheek before going to join the rest of the family near the pool. Calgacus watched her go, admiring her elegant poise. She was, he knew, like a calm haven in the storms that often assailed him. Sometimes, he thought she was the strong one in their relationship.

He shook his head, pushing thoughts of family and friends aside to concentrate on his warriors. Looking around, he quickly checked that two of the men were posted as sentries, that others were watering the horses at the pool and that the rest were breaking out some of the food they had brought with them.

He exchanged a few words with Adelligus, who commanded their small escort. Adelligus was Runt's son from an

12

earlier marriage, although there was little resemblance between the two men, except that Adelligus had the same rakish good looks his father had once been famous for. In Adelligus' case, his looks were enhanced by the scar on his cheek, a memento from a bloody skirmish they had fought against the Romans and their Brigante allies; the same fight in which Calgacus' son, Brennus, had been killed.

Adelligus had proved himself that day. The young man took after his father in his fighting prowess, which was why he was the commander of their escort despite his youth. Then again, Calgacus could not help reflecting, at twenty years of age, Adelligus was older than his step-mother, Tegan.

Calgacus shook off his preoccupation with Runt's convoluted family arrangements and asked Adelligus, "Any problems?"

"None at all," the young man replied.

Calgacus gave him a studied look. Adelligus, who had inherited Runt's habitual good humour, had been unusually solemn during their slow trek across the country. Calgacus had put that down to the young man taking his responsibilities seriously but he thought Adelligus seemed a little distracted. Then again, he reflected, he was more than a little preoccupied himself. There was a lot riding on this mission and perhaps his own anxiety was spreading to those around him. Beatha had often told him that the young warriors were nervous about living up to his high standards.

"You are too tough on them," she would say. "They are already the best trained warriors in any tribe and yet you drive them hard all the time."

"The Romans will drive them harder," he would argue.

But she probably had a point and he decided to show Adelligus a more companionable side.

"It's a hot day," he said. "We can rest up here for a while. Keep your eyes open but let the lads relax a little."

Adelligus gave a nod of thanks. Offering Calgacus a hunk of salted pork, he said, "We'll get the rest dished out in a moment, then we'll re-fill the waterskins."

Calgacus took a bite from the tough, chewy meat. Doing his best to appear friendly, he said, "We should reach Coel's home tomorrow evening."

Adelligus nodded but his eyes moved to look beyond Calgacus and his eyebrows arched in undisguised admiration.

13

Calgacus turned to see his daughter, golden-haired Fallar, moving away from the others, heading towards the trees that lay some fifty paces beyond the pool. As usual, she was walking with a sway of her hips that was designed to attract men's attention. Once again, it had worked. Calgacus noticed that the other soldiers had momentarily stopped what they were doing so that they could admire her.

With a resigned sigh, he said to Adelligus, "I'd better see where she's off to."

"I'll go with her if you want," Adelligus offered.

"No. You see to the food. I'll get her."

Adelligus' mouth tightened but he did not argue, although his eyes quickly flicked back to watch Fallar as soon as Calgacus had turned away.

Calgacus muttered low curses as he strode after his daughter. The sooner she was married to Coel's grandson, the better, he thought to himself. He knew about the fights among the young men of their village. He suspected that Fallar encouraged them by constantly teasing her admirers, but when he had confronted her about it she had laughed and said, "Don't worry, Father. None of them will ever do anything. They are all too afraid of you."

It had not helped Calgacus' mood when Beatha had laughed, "She can always beat you, Cal."

He knew it was true. When it came to his daughter, Calgacus could never be angry for long. He knew it and, from the way she took constant advantage of his indulgence, so did Fallar. Grimly, he wondered whether her prospective husband, Tuathal, knew what he was letting himself in for.

He caught up with her twenty paces from the trees.

"Where are you going?" he asked.

"To answer a call of nature," she replied archly. "Is that all right with you?"

Her impudent smile stopped him in his tracks. Other members of their group had been using a low screen of bushes a little way downstream as a makeshift latrine area but Fallar, as so often, had decided to do things differently.

"Just be quick," he managed to say. "And don't go too far into the trees."

"You don't need to wait for me," she told him. "I am not a child."

"I'll wait."

"Really, Father, sometimes you are very embarrassing."

"I'll wait," he repeated insistently.

She turned away but he grabbed at her arm. She whirled on him, half laughing, half angry.

"What is it now?" she demanded.

"Get behind me for a moment," he hissed urgently, hauling her back.

Almost stumbling, she stepped back, pushing at his hand in an attempt to escape his grip.

"What is wrong?" she wanted to know.

"I thought I saw something," he replied as he scanned the shadow-dappled trees with his eyes narrowed.

"A fox," she suggested impatiently. "Let go of my arm."

He released his hold but held out his arm, blocking her path.

"Stay here," he commanded.

His eyes were fixed on the gloom beneath the trees. Something had alerted his senses to danger but he had not yet identified what it was. A moving shadow or a whisper of sound that should not have been there? He did not know but his instinct warned him that something was out of place.

Before he could put his finger on what troubled him, he heard a roar from within the tangled undergrowth. Shadows suddenly transformed into men who rose from cover, spears and axes in hand. As they charged towards Calgacus, he heard the bellowed command.

"Kill him! And grab the girl!"

Fallar screamed.

Pushing her away with his left hand, Calgacus yelled at her to run. He had no time to see whether she obeyed because the charging bandits had surged out of the woodland and were almost on him. His right hand whipped over his shoulder, gripped the leather-bound hilt of his sword and pulled the blade free of the scabbard in a fluid, well-practised sweep. The familiar, rasping sound as the blade slid free was drowned by his war cry.

"Camulos!"

His shout echoed across the valley as he called on the war god to aid him. The shout would also bring his warriors running but he knew that they were too far away to give him any

15

immediate aid. Knowing that to stand still was to die, he leaped forwards to meet the charging mob, swinging his sword with a two-handed grip.

A huge, shaven-headed man with the image of a standing bear etched on his massive chest was running at him, a sword held high. Beside the swordsman was a wild-eyed, shock-haired man wielding a long-handled axe. The rest of the bandits carried an assortment of spears, axes or long hunting knives. Calgacus charged to his left, cutting away from the two leaders to attack the group of men who were strung out to their right. These men, although they were yelling wildly, had hung back slightly, content to let their leaders do the killing. Calgacus hoped they would not have the stomach to face a man armed with a longsword.

Bellowing his defiance, he flailed his sword, knocking aside a spear, then rammed his shoulder into the spearman, sending him reeling into his neighbour. Still moving, Calgacus hacked right. He felt the satisfying thud of the sword gouging into flesh, heard a man scream in agony, then he tugged the blade free, swept it left to drive away another spearman and leaped through the gap he had carved.

He spun round, his back now to the trees. Beyond the milling bandits he saw Fallar running hard. Runt had already reached her, his two swords drawn, while Adelligus and the others were dashing past the horses towards the fight. They were coming, but it would take time for them to reach him. Time that he knew he must create for himself.

To his left he caught a glimpse of another brigand going down with a spear impaled in his thigh. Part of Calgacus' mind registered that one of his sentries was attacking the bandits' left flank but the man was too far away to join him.

He saw all this in an instant, while he was still moving. He had caught his attackers by surprise but they were turning to face him. Some of them were clearly shocked, nervous of moving within the reach of his sword. He attacked again, giving them no time to rally.

Three men made tentative moves towards him but they jumped back fearfully when he swept his sword at them. One jabbed a spear half-heartedly but Calgacus batted it away with his sword, then rolled his wrists to send a powerful thrust at the man's belly. The bandit lost his footing as he tried to back away. He fell to the ground, blocking another man's attack.

A roar of fury cut through the chaos as the shaven man with the bear tattoo barged through the melee. He ran at Calgacus, swinging his sword, intent on using his massive bulk to drive Calgacus to the ground.

Calgacus stepped to his left, swung his sword to drive away a spearman, then hurriedly blocked the swordsman's attack. The shaven man stumbled past but Calgacus was unable to deliver a killing blow because the man with the axe was coming for him. He jumped back, just managing to avoid the heavy axehead as it swept down to thump harmlessly into the turf.

In an instant, the huge swordsman was attacking him again. The man's snarling face mirrored the fierce image of the bear on his barrel chest. He was built like a bear, too, Calgacus thought, but his attacks were clumsy as he tried to use the sword like a club to bludgeon Calgacus to the ground.

Calgacus, who had trained as a swordsman since his youth, blocked the blow easily then delivered a dazzlingly fast counter-attack that almost caught the big man's shoulder.

Calgacus laughed aloud as the bandit reeled backwards. The man had a sword but it was obvious that he was not accustomed to fighting with it.

The other raiders had momentarily stalled their attacks, waiting for the shaven man to defeat Calgacus and nervous of Runt and the other armoured men rushing towards them.

But Calgacus was still alone and virtually surrounded. A spear jabbed at him but he knocked it aside and swung his blade to drive the assailant away.

"Come on then, you yellow bastards!" he mocked. "Who wants to die next?"

The man with the axe snarled a coarse insult as he sent a sweeping blow towards Calgacus' legs, but there were so many bandits crowding around Calgacus that there was little room to swing an axe properly. Calgacus stepped away, allowing the axe to pass him harmlessly.

The shaven man roared, "Kill the bastard! Get behind him. He can't fight us all."

"Not brave enough to fight me on your own?" Calgacus taunted.

He was dimly aware of another fight beyond the range of his vision. Men were screaming, some in pain, some in triumph.

17

He could not see what was happening but he guessed Runt and the others must be battling some of the bandits.

The shaven man knew it, too. He swung his sword again but Calgacus side-stepped, allowing the blade to flash past him.

The swordsman roared in frustration.

"Kill him and let's get out of here!" he bellowed. "Leave the others but this one must die! I want his head!"

He made as if to run at Calgacus but the deadly blade of Calgacus' sword dissuaded him.

Some of the bandits dutifully spread out, circling to either side, and the shaven man grinned malevolently.

"We've got you now," he told Calgacus.

Calgacus waited, his head turning in an effort to watch for attacks that might come from any direction.

"Camulos!"

The cry came from half a dozen throats as spears flew, punching bandits from their feet.

The shaven man turned in alarm, a look of fury on his face. Most of his surviving followers decided that they had had enough. They ran for the shelter of the trees.

The axeman had turned to face the new threat. He hefted his weapon, ready to strike, but Calgacus saw him stagger back, arms flailing, the axe dropping from his hands. The man fell to reveal Runt who was already moving to attack the shaven-headed swordsman with the bloodied blades of his twin swords.

"He's mine!" Calgacus roared.

The shaven man tried to run but Calgacus intercepted him. He easily blocked the man's clumsy blow, then swung his sword at the brigand's head. He tried to turn the blade so that the flat would strike the man down, disabling him but keeping him alive, but the big bandit turned unexpectedly and the edge of the massive killing blade smashed into the side of his head. He went down with barely a sound, his skull shattered.

Calgacus whirled round, ready to face another attack, but there was none. Adelligus and the other warriors had arrived. They were pursuing the remaining bandits, chasing them into the trees. Calgacus watched approvingly as Adelligus called the men back, preventing them from running into the dangerous shadows where they could be ambushed.

Runt, his voice full of concern, asked, "Are you all right?"

"Not even a scratch," Calgacus replied. "Is Fallar safe?"

18

"She's fine. The girl can run like the wind."

Calgacus nodded his relief. He was breathing heavily now, his heart pounding in his chest. His legs felt weak as the exhilaration of the fight was replaced by the realisation of how close to death he had come.

"Thank you, Liscus. You arrived just in time."

"Too late for poor Dullocorvus," Runt grimaced, gesturing to where a mail-clad body lay surrounded by dead and wounded bandits.

Calgacus swore. Dullocorvus had died trying to save him. The lad had been only nineteen years old, little more than a boy in Calgacus' eyes.

"Why on earth would they attack a well-armed party like us?" Runt wondered.

Calgacus recalled the words he had heard the bandit chief shout.

Grimly, he said, "I think somebody is trying to kill me."

Chapter III

Coel of the Caledones was generally regarded as the most powerful King of that large tribe. He was certainly acknowledged as the most astute and influential. Approaching seventy years of age, his hair had turned silver and his limbs had lost most of what strength they had ever possessed, but his eyes, his ears and his mind were as sharp as any. These, Calgacus knew, were Coel's main weapons. The old King had gained, and maintained, his position by virtue of his cunning rather than his strength.

He was a small man, almost wizened in appearance, who dressed plainly and wore no ostentatious jewellery. Calgacus always thought that Coel had the appearance of a servant or slave rather than a chieftain, but appearances were deceptive where the old King was concerned. As soon as he spoke, his authority was evident in the way people hurried to obey his commands.

Coel's home was a broch, a massive, round tower of stone that sat on a hilltop overlooking a long sea-loch. Clustered round the foot of the hill were the homes and workshops of his people, a sprawling village that was, in turn, surrounded by meadows and ploughed fields.

The broch was ostensibly designed for defence but Calgacus knew that it could not possibly house the hundreds of people who lived and worked in the immediate vicinity. Its main purpose, he guessed, was to show everyone that the man who lived here was a person of power and importance.

Yet for all his power, Coel did not sit within his tower to have his visitors brought to him. Instead, in a gesture of welcome and respect, he came down to the main door and waited outside as Calgacus and his small party approached. He was wearing a plain tunic and trousers but he stood out from the crowd by virtue of his commanding manner. He stepped forwards to clasp Calgacus' forearm as soon as the big warrior dismounted.

"Welcome, my friend," the old King smiled.

Calgacus returned the greeting although he would never have described Coel as a friend. The man may have been an ally but Calgacus knew that he was far too devious to ever be a true friend.

Mustering as much good grace as he could, Calgacus made the introductions.

Coel's smile was almost a leer as he greeted Beatha and Fallar, but grew more polite when he welcomed Emmelia and her husband, Caedmon. Emmelia pretended not to notice. Her angular face, with its prominent nose, would never be described as pretty by anyone except Caedmon, although her features lit up when she presented her eight-year-old son, Morcant, and her three-year-old daughter, Bonduca, to the old King.

Coel ruffled Morcant's hair and beamed cordially at little Bonduca.

"You are very welcome here," he told them.

"You know my friend, Liscus, of course," Calgacus reminded him.

Coel clasped Runt's hand.

"Of course. Welcome to my home."

"And this is Tegan," Calgacus added, remembering to smile.

Tegan, slim and dark-haired, clutched at her baby as she gave the King a hesitant smile.

Coel's leer returned as he looked Tegan up and down while formally greeting her. Then his gaze swept past the armed escort of warriors and a slight frown wrinkled his aged brow.

"Where is the rest of your party?" he asked.

"You see it all," Calgacus replied.

"You brought no slaves or servants with you?"

"I keep no slaves," Calgacus replied. "All my people are free. As for servants, we get along fine doing things for ourselves."

Coel gave an exaggerated shake of his head as he laughed, "You are a singular man, Calgacus. But I am glad you have brought your women and children to this special occasion. Children are a blessing to us all. Now you must come to meet mine."

Turning to a group of men who stood deferentially behind him, Coel introduced his own family and advisors who were waiting to meet their guests.

"Broichan, you know already," the King began as he gestured towards the most senior of his advisors.

Broichan the druid was tall, spindly, with long, grey hair trailing down the back of his head while the front part of his skull was shaved clean. He possessed a luxurious beard but the most striking thing about him was the intensity of his dark eyes which glared out at the world from beneath tangled eyebrows. Those eyes studied Calgacus with a disapproving look, although he gave a polite, if formal, greeting.

In turn, Calgacus acknowledged the druid with a curt nod. He had spent most of his life opposing druids and their arcane ways and Broichan, whom he had met twice before, seemed to him typical of the greybeards and their fixation with prayer and sacrifice which rarely seemed to do any good. As a young man, Calgacus had encountered an elderly hermit who had shown him that the druids, for all their ancient lore and professed wisdom, kept the common people in a state of unthinking belief in order to maintain a privileged position among the tribes. The power of the druids had been greatly diminished since the Romans had destroyed the centre of their cult years earlier but a few still lingered in the wild northern regions where they sought to re-establish their former hegemony.

Calgacus had met one or two druids he respected and liked but Broichan struck him as being of the old school and the antipathy between them was palpable. Coel, clearly understanding this, quickly moved on to introduce the other men who stood patiently in line beside the druid.

There were five of them. Coel introduced the first two as his sons, Crixus and Drust. They were both middle-aged. Crixus was small and, like his father, rather nondescript. Drust, in contrast, was taller and more burly, with a weathered face and a squat nose that had clearly been broken at some point in the past. Both men were polite but wary, as men sometimes are when meeting strangers.

Calgacus' immediate reaction on meeting them was that neither of them was overly confident. Drust, in particular, seemed almost timid, as if he was afraid that his father might scold him like a child, while Crixus' face bore an expression of surly resentment.

"And these two young men are Crixus' sons," continued Coel as he introduced a pair of identical twins. "Their names are Eudaf and Eurgain, although I confess I still struggle to tell which is which."

Both young men grinned at the jest. The twins were in their early twenties, bright-eyed, good-looking and cheerful. They smiled amiably, especially at Fallar.

The last man also paid considerable attention to Fallar. Like Eudaf and Eurgain, he was young, with a handsome, if rather serious, face. He wore a torc of gold around his neck and gold rings on his fingers.

"This, as you know, is my other grandson, Tuathal."

Coel's voice was thick with undisguised pride as he introduced the last man in the line.

"Welcome to our home," Tuathal said politely. "I am glad you made it here safely."

Dutifully, he clasped the men's hands with a firm grip and greeted each of the women with a formal embrace.

Fallar gave Tuathal a tentative smile. This was the young man she was to marry and she seemed unusually shy now that she had arrived for their wedding, as if the realisation of what she had agreed to do had only just struck her.

Coel, quick as ever to smooth over any potential difficulties, waved to some of his retainers who hurried to take the horses.

The King said, "I have had a house set aside for your warriors. Your horses will be cared for. But you and your families will stay with me."

Adelligus and the warriors went with their guides, while Calgacus and the rest of his party followed Coel into the dark gloom of the broch.

Passing through the door in single file, they climbed the stone stairway of broad, flat steps that wound up between the massively thick inner and outer walls of the circular tower, their way lit by burning torches set in brackets on the walls.

At ground level, the broch provided a wide, circular space for storage and also acted as a sanctuary for people and animals who might need shelter in times of danger. Above the lower space, a floor of solid oak beams provided a second level which served as Coel's main hall.

"Sleeping quarters have been prepared for you on the level above," Coel explained. "But first, come and eat. We can talk over a meal."

This large room was where Coel would normally entertain his household warriors. As a King, he provided them with shelter

23

and food in exchange for their loyalty. Today, though, most of the room had been cleared, leaving only one wide, wooden table, flanked by long benches, sitting in the centre of the circular chamber. Only a handful of guards were admitted as Coel ushered his guests inside.

"Please sit," he invited, waving everyone towards the table where food and drink were being placed.

Serving girls laid out platters of dark bread, slices of roasted lamb and salted beef, along with several types of fish, clams and mussels, and a variety of birds' eggs. The season was early for fruit or vegetables but Coel's cooks had found some roots and boiled seaweed to accompany the meat. While the diners filled their plates, the servants poured dark beer into large, silver goblets for the adults and thrice-brewed small beer into clay mugs for the children.

Despite Coel's generous hospitality, an awkward atmosphere hung over the table. Apart from the twins, Eudaf and Eurgain, none of Coel's family seemed inclined to say very much. Again, Calgacus had the impression that they were afraid of incurring Coel's displeasure. Drust concentrated on his food and drink, while Crixus wore the expression of a man who wished he could be somewhere else. His eyes constantly flickered towards Calgacus but he looked away nervously as soon as Calgacus returned his gaze.

Calgacus' own party waited for him to take the lead. Even Beatha, who was normally happy in any company, was more reticent than usual, as if she sensed that something was not quite right.

Calgacus wondered whether it was merely the uncertainty of meeting people who would soon be related by marriage. They all knew that the union between Fallar and Tuathal was a business arrangement rather than a love match. The young couple sat facing each other across the table, while their families sat around them, wondering what to say.

Coel eventually broke the silence.

"My men tell me you had some trouble on the way here. What happened?"

"We were attacked by bandits," Calgacus replied. "One of my men was killed, although it could have been a lot worse."

Briefly, he outlined what had happened, adding that he thought the attack had been an attempt on his life.

24

"You are sure of that?" Coel asked. He seemed tense, as if the news had some importance. "They were not merely bandits who chose to attack the wrong victims?"

Almost apologetically, Crixus interrupted, "What my father is hinting at is that I have been chasing a gang of raiders for the past three weeks. They've plundered a couple of farms and killed a few of our kindred. From your description of the leader, it sounds like the same group. There cannot be two brigands matching that description."

"The leader is dead," Calgacus informed them. "That was a shame because I wanted to question him. Fortunately, some of the others were still alive. I spoke to them."

He paused, looking meaningfully at the druid, Broichan, as he went on, "They all said that a man had come to their leader, Greumaich, and had paid him to have me killed."

Broichan returned Calgacus' stare with cold, expressionless eyes.

"You believe I know something of this?" he sneered, barely making any attempt to conceal his hostility.

"They told me that the man who spoke to Greumaich was a druid," Calgacus replied icily.

Broichan blew air out of his mouth in a dismissive snort.

"It was not I. Why would I do such a thing?"

"I know it was not you," Calgacus replied. "The bandits I interrogated said the druid was younger, a small man. He wore a hooded cloak, so only Greumaich saw him clearly, but they were quite certain that he was not an old man."

"There are very few druids in this area that I know of," observed Coel.

Broichan said, "That is true, but Calgacus' disrespect for druids is well known."

The corners of his mouth twitched in what might have been a mocking smile as he added, "Perhaps you have upset someone. It would not be the first time."

"I don't know," Calgacus admitted. "But someone wants me dead."

Runt muttered, "Someone is always trying to kill you, Cal. It is not that unusual."

The twins laughed. Eudaf, or perhaps it was Eurgain, said, "It sounds like a magnificent fight. I wish we had been there to see it. One man against sixteen."

25

Beatha put in, "It was terrifying."

She laid a hand on Calgacus' arm as she added, "But Cal was magnificent."

Crixus, his eyes still unable to hold Calgacus' gaze, asked, "What of the bandits? What has happened to them? Are they all dead?"

Calgacus' face took on a grim expression as he answered, "Six were killed, including the leader. Three were wounded so badly they could not walk. The others escaped."

Crixus clucked his tongue.

"That is a shame. We will need to track them down in case they raid any more farms. I presume you killed the wounded?"

"No. We left them."

Crixus' eyebrows rose in surprised disappointment as he asked, "Why?"

Calgacus stared back at him as he responded, "I have an aversion to killing men who are helpless. I would prefer that the Gods decide their fate."

Crixus frowned. Cautiously, he ventured, "They may well attack and kill others."

"Unless their friends go back for them, they will more likely bleed or starve to death," Calgacus replied dismissively. "But I will not kill an unarmed, defenceless man."

He paused. Then, with an angry glance towards Broichan, he added pointedly, "I leave that sort of thing to the druids."

Broichan glared at him but was prevented from arguing by Emmelia, who quickly interjected, "That is not the main issue here. Somebody ordered Calgacus' death. It occurs to me that the man who arranged the attack may not have been a druid at all. Perhaps it was someone who simply dressed in a druid's robe."

"Why would anyone do that?" Broichan wanted to know.

He spoke harshly, clearly still annoyed by Calgacus' barbed comment.

"To disguise their true identity," Emmelia replied. "One thing is clear, though. Whoever this man was, he was wealthy enough to pay the bandits handsomely."

She looked around the table, gazing intently at each face, gauging their reaction. Drust studied his mug of beer, while Crixus lowered his eyes. As Emmelia scanned the others, Tuathal frowned uncertainly and the twins exchanged puzzled looks.

Broichan snapped at her, "Stop that!"

Emmelia gave him an innocent smile as she asked, "Stop what?"

"You have some training," the druid accused. "You are seeking to read us."

Emmelia shrugged, "I am no druid."

Broichan was about to say something more but Coel thumped his palm on the table.

"Enough of this!" he commanded sharply. "Nobody here would have done such a thing. Besides, I believe I know who ordered the attack."

The room fell silent as all eyes went to him.

Calgacus asked, "Who was it?"

"It is a long story," Coel explained. "But you are quite correct. Somebody wants you dead."

Chapter IV

Coel sat back, taking a deep breath.

"There is much to tell you," he began. "I know you came here expecting a wedding celebration, but there are other, more pressing matters that we must discuss."

Calgacus sat very still, struggling to maintain a calm expression. Even though the marriage alliance had been his idea, he had harboured reservations about this trip because he had always been wary of Coel's cunning. The man had a reputation for extorting agreements from less powerful tribes and Calgacus' own people were a very small group of refugees who had fled to the north to escape the ever-expanding Roman Empire. Although they retained their own identity, they were nominally members of the tribe of the Boresti but the Boresti were themselves a relatively small clan who lacked much influence. Only Calgacus' reputation as a War Leader gave him any standing among the other tribes and he knew that, lacking a sizeable war host of his own, he had very little leverage against any demands Coel might make. He could only hope that those demands were not too onerous.

Calgacus' eyes quickly scanned the men sitting opposite him. They had been on edge ever since he had arrived and he realised that their unease must be because they knew what Coel was about to reveal to him.

Drust's eyes were still downcast, refusing to meet his gaze, and Crixus shifted uncomfortably. The twins seemed perplexed but Tuathal sat up expectantly, his eyes bright.

Giving Coel a hard glare, he demanded, "What other matters?"

Speaking calmly but firmly, Coel explained, "Suffice to say that there have been other attempts to kill people."

He waved a hand towards his grandson, Tuathal, as he went on, "Twice, we have thwarted attempts to poison Tuathal and once an arrow from a hunting bow missed him by a hair's breadth. The culprit, whoever it was, escaped."

Tuathal was not abashed at being the new focus of attention. He gave Fallar a confident smile as he assured her, "I was not harmed. I have been lucky so far."

"You think there will be more attempts on your life?" Emmelia asked.

She was alert and eager, her blue eyes sparkling. Calgacus smiled to himself when he saw how she suddenly seemed to dominate the gathering. It was true that Emmelia was no druid but she had spent many years studying under the old hermit, Myrddin. Her quick wits and intelligence, combined with what she had learned from the old man, made her formidable when she put her mind to something. Quite apart from her family connection, part of the reason Calgacus had been happy for her to accompany them was because he wanted her support in his dealings with Coel and Broichan.

Tuathal gave a slight shrug as if to suggest that he did not care whether his life was in danger but Coel answered Emmelia's question.

"It seems more than likely. Perhaps I should tell you Tuathal's story."

"Please do," Emmelia invited.

Coel looked intently at Calgacus as he enquired, "What do you know about the island of Eriu?"

"Not a great deal. I know it lies across the sea to the west and is reputed to be a large place, but I have never been there."

Coel confirmed, "It is indeed a large island; the furthest west of all the lands. Its people are much like us. We often trade with them."

"I take it this has something to do with the attempts on Tuathal's life?"

Coel nodded and cleared his throat.

"I am no bard," he explained, "so I will keep this short. My daughter, Eithne, was wed to the High King of Eriu, a man named Fiacha Finnolach. She was pregnant with her first child when there was a rebellion. Four of the sub-kings of Eriu rose up and overthrew Finnolach. He was killed but Eithne escaped. She made her way back across the sea and came home to me."

Coel smiled benignly at Tuathal as he went on, "Her child was born here but Eithne died. She was my only daughter but she has been gone now for many years."

29

His eyes, usually so hard and unreadable, seemed suddenly sad and nostalgic.

"I miss her," he confessed quietly.

Everyone was respectfully silent while the old man remembered his daughter. Only Tuathal seemed impatient for the King to continue.

Softly, the young man prompted, "Grandfather?"

Coel raised his head again. When he looked around the table, his eyes were once again hard with determination.

Speaking with an air of authority, he continued, "I have always wanted Tuathal to return to Eriu to reclaim his father's position as High King."

He paused, his thin lips twitching in apparent irritation before he went on, "Unfortunately, it seems that others have heard of my wishes. I believe that Elim mac Conrach, the usurper who seized the rule of Eriu from Tuathal's father, has heard of my intentions. He has decided to remove any threat by sending assassins to kill Tuathal."

"He has waited rather a long time," Emmelia remarked with a hint of scepticism.

"Elim is an arrogant man," Coel responded insistently. "He had nothing to fear from a boy but Tuathal is a grown man now. I do not know the mind of the Usurper but it might be that he has grown more fearful that his dynasty may be threatened."

Emmelia accepted the explanation but still objected, "Assuming you are correct, assassins should be easy to spot. Surely you would know when strangers arrive."

Bristling at her questioning, Coel shot back, "As I said, we have many dealings with the people of Eriu. Ships are always crossing the sea between here and there. Strangers are commonplace."

Calgacus glanced at Fallar. Her face had grown pale and she was chewing her lower lip as she regarded Tuathal with a worried look.

Turning back to Coel, Calgacus asked, "So what do you intend to do about it?"

Before Coel could answer, Emmelia interrupted, "First, tell us what this has to do with the attempt on Calgacus' life."

"The two questions are linked," Coel replied. "I intended to send Tuathal to Eriu with an army at his back. I have been in touch with some of his cousins from his father's family. They will support him. I want him to kill Elim and become High King, as is his right."

"That is folly!" exclaimed Calgacus. "We have a war against Rome. We cannot afford to send an army to Eriu, or anywhere else!"

"Hear me out!" Coel barked abrasively.

Calgacus took a deep breath as Beatha placed a warning hand on his arm. Gruffly, he nodded, "Very well. Go on."

Coel stared at him for a moment but then resumed his story.

"It was a long-held dream of mine to see Tuathal restored. I thought perhaps to wait until Elim mac Conrach died but things have changed. I know that he has heard of my plans. There are many in Eriu who would like to see him overthrown and who have sent me messages. The Usurper is a violent, ruthless man. I have been warned that he intends to remove any threat to his rule by having Tuathal killed."

Calgacus was growing increasingly uneasy as he listened to Coel's explanation. There was, he could tell, something more to this than rivalry between kings and a dispute over dynastic succession.

He said, "Assassination is a threat faced by many powerful chieftains. This is unfortunate but it should not distract us from facing our main threat. The Romans will come against us soon. They are pushing further north each year."

"There is more you should know," Coel told him. "I fear that Elim mac Conrach must have learned of our own plans to unite our families. I suspect that he feared you would accompany Tuathal to Eriu as his War Leader."

Coel gave a small smile as he added, "Your fame in that regard has, I fear, made you a target for Elim's assassins."

Beatha's fingers dug anxiously into Calgacus' arm but he kept his gaze on the old King as he growled, "I have a feeling you are about to propose a solution that I will not like."

Coel's eyes flicked to Broichan who responded to the signal by explaining, "It was my suggestion, but it is the only solution we can see."

Calgacus felt his muscles tense. He was sure that any suggestion of Broichan's was bound to be one that he disliked.

"Just tell me," he rasped.

31

Broichan gave a humourless smile as he explained, "It is very simple. We should do what Elim fears most. You and Tuathal should sail to Eriu. Coel can provide several hundred warriors and more will join you when you land. Elim the Usurper is very unpopular. He already faces rebellion from one of his former allies, Eochaid of Leinster. It is clear that Elim is losing support. Now is the time to take advantage of that fact. All you need do is march to Tara, the seat of the High King, defeat him and put Tuathal in his place."

"You make it sound so simple," Calgacus remarked drily, not bothering to hide his sarcasm. "There is one big flaw with that plan."

Broichan's wicked smile broadened.

"The Romans?" he enquired.

Calgacus nodded, "Exactly. We are supposed to be building an alliance to oppose them when they march north. That must be our only priority."

"That has not changed," Coel stated reassuringly. "That is still my intention."

"So we cannot afford to waste time by starting a war in Eriu," Calgacus insisted.

He felt his temper rising, suspecting that he was being manoeuvred into a situation he would find difficult to escape.

Broichan's face barely changed its expression as the druid countered, "For one thing, that war has already begun although, as yet, you and Tuathal are the only combatants on our side. If we do nothing, the High King will eventually succeed in having you both killed."

"He can try," Calgacus growled. "I am not that easy to kill."

Beatha squeezed his arm again as she whispered, "Cal, Fallar would be in danger, too."

Broichan gave a slight nod of agreement. He went on, "For another thing, the Romans are no threat this year. Their advance has halted. There is plenty of time for you to complete this mission and still be ready to face them when they come further north."

Calgacus' eyes narrowed.

"You cannot be sure of what the Romans will do," he challenged.

"On the contrary," Broichan replied confidently. "Crixus has been to see for himself. As part of our plans for an alliance, he has visited the southern tribes. He has seen the Romans and heard of their problems."

Everyone looked at Crixus. He shifted uncomfortably, then ran a hand over his face, rubbing at his nose.

"It is true," he announced gravely. "The Romans have been sorely tested in conquering the Brigantes. They fought the Novantae and the Selgovae, who have both submitted, but the Romans have decided to remain where they are. They are building forts and supply bases but they will not advance any further this year. Everyone says so."

"Everyone could be wrong," Calgacus argued.

Crixus shook his head.

"There has been some sort of disaster in the Romans' homeland," he explained. "They say two of their cities were destroyed when a mountain exploded."

Broichan interjected, "There can be no doubt that the gods are displeased with the new Emperor of Rome. The omens are quite clear. As a result, the Legions are paralysed. They will not attack us this year."

Calgacus wondered which gods had displayed such clear evidence of their displeasure. Despite thirty years of sacrifices, the druids had never been able to gain sufficient divine support to halt the inexorable Roman advance. That, though, was a minor consideration. Another, far more compelling, thought filled his mind.

"Then we should attack them!" he exclaimed. "We can pin them into their forts. Surround them. This is our chance to defeat them!"

Speaking calmly, Coel asked, "But what if Elim mac Conrach should send more assassins to kill you and Tuathal while you are busy fighting the Romans? What if he kills your daughter to prevent her giving Tuathal an heir? What happens to our alliance then?"

"Those are risks worth facing if it means defeating Rome," Calgacus insisted.

Broichan offered, "In normal circumstances I would agree with you but there is more you must know. Elim has a sorceress. She can cast spells and curses against us. If we do not destroy her and her master, all our plans are doomed to failure."

33

His words brought soft whispers of concern and muttered prayers for protection from most of the people seated at the table. Only Emmelia laughed.

"She cannot do that," she declared. "Nobody can."

"What do you know of her powers?" Broichan challenged irritably.

"Enough to know that a curse will only work if the person who has been cursed knows about it."

Broichan shot her a scowl that suggested he was more annoyed at her divulging trade secrets than at her scepticism.

He rasped, "Magic is not to be taken lightly."

"I take it very seriously," Emmelia assured him. "But it is an art which can be mastered, just like any skill. Anyone can do it."

"Nonsense!" Broichan spluttered, his craggy face flushed with anger as he glared at her.

Emmelia was unaffected by the druid's outburst. In answer, she calmly reached out to pick a small gull's egg from a nearby plate. She tossed it up in front of her face, catching it easily when it fell, then threw it again, higher this time. A third time she threw, sending the egg high into the gloom above her head, catching it deftly when it tumbled back down. Then she waved her left hand.

"Watch!" she commanded.

With a flourish, she threw again. All eyes looked up to follow the egg but this time it did not reappear from the high shadows.

Emmelia folded her hands in front of her, smiling at the perplexed expressions on the faces of the men opposite her who were gaping in amazement because they had seen the egg vanish into thin air above her head.

Only her husband, Caedmon, who had seen this trick before, was smiling. After a few moments, Emmelia reached down to her son, Morcant.

"What have you got in your ear?" she asked him.

Her hand went to his ear. When she pulled it away, she was holding the missing egg which she calmly replaced on the plate in front of her.

Morcant and young Bonduca giggled. Most of the adults gaped in astonishment. Eudaf and Eurgain thumped their palms on the table in applause.

"You are very skilled," Broichan conceded grudgingly. "But tricks like that will not defeat Elim's witch."

"Of course not," Emmelia agreed. "But neither should anyone fear her tricks. That is all they will be. No mortal can perform true magic."

Coel said, "So you are saying that Tuathal and Calgacus need not fear Elim's witch?"

"I am saying they need not fear her curses," Emmelia corrected.

Calgacus put in, "Whatever the truth, I have not agreed to go to Eriu, witch or no witch. I have no intentions of going anywhere except to fight the Romans."

"You must go!" Coel blurted insistently. "Now is the only time. If we delay, Elim will send more killers. You, your daughter and Tuathal are all at risk. Besides which, he can send war bands to raid our shores so that we will be forced to fight him as well as the Romans. We must remove him. Now."

Calgacus was about to make an angry retort but Beatha squeezed his arm again, warning him to keep his temper in check. He glared angrily at Coel, hating the man for his foolishness.

Coel's own face was set hard, his eyes blazing a challenge.

The King said, "If you wish to build an alliance against Rome, I must insist that you do this for me, if not for yourself."

He paused for a moment, then went on, "In the meantime, your family will remain here as my guests."

A sliver of ice sliced through Calgacus' body when he heard that implicit threat.

"What are you saying?" he rasped.

Coel's voice was as hard as iron as he replied, "I am saying that if you wish to keep your family safe, you will do my bidding in this."

Calgacus knew he was trapped. In his youth he had faced druids and rulers who were far more deadly than Broichan or Coel. The young Calgacus would have faced them down, would have resorted to violence if necessary. But he was no longer young. He had friends and family to consider; friends and family who would be held hostage by Coel to ensure that Calgacus did what the old King wanted.

Somehow, he found his voice.

"We are supposed to be allies," he said hoarsely.

35

"And so we are," replied Coel. "And so we will be. After you have defeated the Usurper and placed Tuathal as High King."

Calgacus sighed. He was trapped. He had brought his family into a snare from which there was only one escape.

Hating himself for giving in to the old King's demands, he said, "Tell me more about this High King."

Chapter V

The rebellion in Eriu had not lasted long. By the middle of spring, it was all but over. The only thing that was yet to be decided was how it would end. It was an ending that Domnan knew would come very soon.

He awoke to the trumpeting of horns which sounded their strident warnings in the dim light of early dawn, drowning out the birdsong and the crowing of cockerels. In answer to the insistent call of the horns, men rushed to the wall, clutching at spears or swords, cursing as they ran, attempting to cover their fear with coarse swearing and loud voices. In the roundhouses, frightened women comforted their children or dug holes in the earth floor to bury any precious treasure in case the High King's army came to plunder their homes.

Domnan, youngest and only surviving son of the King of Leinster, dressed quickly and fastened his sword belt. The heavy weapon was still too large for him and it threatened to become tangled in his legs but he was determined to wear it. Somehow, having the sword made him feel older than his fifteen years.

Hurrying outside, he joined the warriors as they clustered on the rampart. He gripped the hilt of his sword as if the weapon was a lifeline, the only thing that could keep him alive. Yet in his heart he knew that there was very little that could save him now. Only the strength of the wall that blocked the peninsula stood between him and death. It was a strong wall but Domnan did not truly believe that it would be strong enough.

His father stood near the gates, a dozen anxious warriors guarding him. They made way for Domnan, shuffling aside to allow him to join the King.

Eochaid Ainchenn was nearly seventy years of age. He had been King of Leinster for more than thirty of those years but his rule had weighed heavily on him. His thinning hair was entirely grey, his limbs had lost much of their strength, and his face was thin and wrinkled by age. He turned weary eyes on Domnan as the boy approached.

"The High King has come," Eochaid said in a cracked, throaty whisper.

Domnan raised his sword slightly, keen to show his readiness.

"We shall fight," he declared, although his face was pale and his voice was not as confident as his words.

Eochaid shook his head.

"The fighting is done, my son. I have no wish to see more men die. The Morrigan will be disappointed today."

Domnan frowned. The Morrigan, the bloodthirsty goddess of war and death, roamed battlefields, taking the souls of fallen warriors. She had taken many during the past year, including all of Domnan's brothers. Domnan had expected her to come for him before the day was over but his father's words made his heart leap. Whether the feeling that gripped him was relief that he might live or dismay that they would all be dishonoured, he could not tell. All he knew was that warriors should fight to the death.

Struggling to grasp all the implications of his father's words, Domnan gasped, "You cannot surrender!"

"I fear that I must," Eochaid replied.

He lifted a thin, almost skeletal hand, killing Domnan's protests.

The King continued, "We do not have the strength to win this war, my son. We have suffered too many defeats, lost too many of our best warriors. Most of my under-kings are dead or have abandoned us. So I will go on my knees to the High King and beg for his mercy. He may grant it; he may not. Either way, Leinster will submit to him."

"We should resist," Domnan insisted. "This is a strong fortress. The approach is narrow and the wall is high. We can hold out until the other kings—"

"The other kings cannot help us now," Eochaid interrupted. "The High King's witch has cast her spells over them and none will join our cause. As for holding out, we may be able to defend the approach but the High King has more than enough warriors to swamp even the bravest defence. And if he decides not to waste their lives, he can simply starve us out. Either way, our people will be slaughtered or enslaved."

Domnan's emotions whirled. He was angry that they had been defeated, frustrated that there was nothing he could do, yet he could not deny that a part of him was relieved that there would be

38

no battle. With all three of his brothers having been killed in the recent fighting, he knew he would be required to take their place in the front rank of what remained of his father's war band. In his heart, Domnan knew he would not survive if they faced the High King's army. At fifteen years of age, he was a warrior in name only. He had never fought, had never drawn his sword in anger. He knew in his heart that he would be no match for the fierce warriors who followed the High King.

Yet he was not convinced that surrender would save him. Domnan was young but he was old enough to know that the High King, Elim mac Conrach, would almost certainly take bloody vengeance for their rebellion. Domnan sensed the same concern among the warriors who stood protectively around him. If they were going to die, it would be better to die fighting than to be bound, hobbled and beheaded.

Domnan looked despairingly at his father.

"Then we are lost?"

Eochaid gave him a smile that momentarily transformed the taut, pale skin of his careworn face.

He said, "For the moment, but not completely. The High King will have his day today but there is another way for us to see him overthrown."

Domnan's eyes blazed with desperate eagerness as he asked, "What way? Tell me, Father. How can we defeat him?"

Eochaid gestured to the east, across the tops of the thatched roofs of the homes and workshops of the wide settlement that lay behind the protective wall.

"There is a boat waiting for you down in the bay. You should go now, while there is still time."

"Go where?" Domnan asked, feeling a rising sense of dread and loss at the thought of leaving his father to face the High King's wrath alone.

"You must cross the sea to the lands of the Pritani. Find help and return with an army at your back."

"The Pritani will not help," Domnan spat sourly. "You have told me often enough that they have troubles of their own."

Eochaid smiled again, a conspiratorial smile that hinted at defiance tempered by desperation.

He confided, "No, my son. Do not go to any of the tribes of the Pritani. You should go to the Romans."

For a moment, Domnan struggled to grasp his father's intention, then he frowned uncertainly.

"You want me to bring an army of Romans here?" he asked doubtfully. "I have heard that they are harsh masters."

"They cannot be any more harsh than the High King," Eochaid replied grimly. "Yes, we will be forced to submit to the Romans, but if we befriend them, they will allow us some freedoms. You and I will be client kings but at least we will still be kings. Above all, Elim, the High King, will be dead."

Eochaid reached out to place his hands on Domnan's shoulders. Speaking earnestly, he explained, "This is our only chance, my son. Go now and bring us allies who are powerful enough to defeat the High King and his witch."

Domnan inclined his head in a bow.

"I will do as you ask, Father. But I will not leave until I know what the High King intends to do to you."

After a moment's hesitation, Eochaid nodded, "Very well. But go quickly as soon as you learn what my fate is. If I live, I will need you to bring me the help we require. If I die, you will be King and must fetch help so that you can avenge me. The people of Leinster are relying on you."

Domnan felt the weight of his father's words heavy on his young shoulders. He wanted to protest that he was not ready for such responsibility but a shout from one of the warriors alerted him to movement beyond the walls.

Everyone turned to gaze out across the palisade. Someone uttered a soft groan of despair at the sight that met their eyes. A host of warriors was marching steadily towards them, banners flying, sharp spearpoints glinting as they caught the first rays of the morning sun.

"Around two thousand of them," Eochaid estimated.

He glanced along the wall, reminding himself of just how few defenders lined the ramparts. The wall was not the fortress's only defence because the narrow approach to the peninsula on which it stood could be held by twenty good men manning the narrowest part. But Eochaid's war band had been virtually destroyed in the earlier fighting and the men who remained were the old, the timid and the unblooded youngsters like Domnan. They could not hope to resist the battle-hardened men of the High King's war host.

But the enemy did not attack. They halted on the mainland, some four hundred paces from the wall.

"What are they doing?" Domnan asked anxiously.

"An emissary will come," Eochaid told him. "Or perhaps the High King himself. He will demand our surrender. I will not disappoint him."

Eochaid called down to the men who stood behind the gateway, telling them to be ready to remove the great beam that barred the gates so that he could go out to meet whoever approached. He saw movement among the High King's army, caught a glimpse of men on horseback and others on chariots. One of them would be Elim mac Conrach, the High King himself.

A chariot detached itself from the host and came slowly towards the wall, accompanied by a rider bearing a long, leaf-covered branch.

"You were right, Father," Domnan observed.

"Now we will learn our fate," Eochaid breathed softly. He turned to his son and said, "Stay out of sight. I will tell them you are dead."

He clasped Domnan's hands as he went on, "Farewell, my son. Always remember that I am proud of you. Whatever happens, the fate of our people is in your hands."

Domnan's reply caught in his throat. He raised his father's hands to his lips to kiss them. Then he nodded, blinking away the tears that stung his eyes. He felt ashamed of those tears. He was a warrior of Leinster. He should not cry like a child.

Slowly, the King made his way down to the gates, waving back the warriors who offered to accompany him. When the huge doors were swung back, creaking loudly on their hinges, Eochaid Ainchenn walked out to meet his enemies.

Eochaid walked to the end of the narrow neck of land that connected his home to the mainland, then waited for the chariot to approach him. He ignored the rider bearing the branch of peace, concentrating on the two people in the chariot.

One was Elim, driving the two war ponies almost as expertly as a trained charioteer. The High King was a big, powerful man but now running to fat. His long hair was grey, almost silver in the early sunlight, but that only served to make him appear more imposing. The aggressive thrust of his prominent

41

chin and the wild gleam in his eyes were enough to make anyone tremble under his gaze.

Eochaid knew the High King of old. They had been allies once, perhaps even friends; as far as a man like Elim could ever have friends, that was. But the years had wrought their changes and whatever friendship there had once been had cooled, gradually turning to enmity. Elim mac Conrach was too ambitious, too ruthless and too violent to have friends; he desired subjects, not equals.

In the years since Elim had seized the rule of Eriu from Fiacha Finnolach, Eochaid had suffered so many injustices at the High King's hands that he had eventually decided to depose him. He had known it was a great risk but he had also recognised that Elim was jealous and suspicious of him. Sooner or later, a confrontation had been inevitable, so Eochaid had decided to strike before Elim made the first move.

He had failed. The rebellion had been a disaster. The other sub-kings had not joined him and his army had been routed. Three of his sons were dead and now Elim would demand his revenge.

Yet Eochaid was resigned to whatever fate Elim had in store for him. He was not afraid of the High King's anger, nor of his desire for retribution. Eochaid was past caring about such things. But when he saw who stood on the chariot alongside the High King, he felt his resolve falter.

She was tall, with long curls of red hair that seemed to glow like fire when the sunlight caught them as it did now. Her appearance was striking but her features, which might have been considered pretty, were marred by a large, red-pink blotch which covered the left side of her face from her forehead to her jawline. The unsightly blemish was both terrifying and fascinating, a clear sign that this woman had been marked by the Gods. Yet it was her eyes that drew Eochaid's attention. Green and bright, they seemed to bore into him. He swallowed nervously, forcing himself to stand erect as the chariot wheeled to a halt only a few paces from him.

The woman stared at him, her face expressionless. Eochaid knew that she called herself a sorceress. Most people called her a witch.

Elim stood alongside her, his expression triumphant, his chin thrust forwards, his small eyes burning with anticipation. In spite of his resolve, Eochaid felt his legs grow weak when he looked up at the High King. He knew Elim was a cruel man who delighted in confrontation and revelled in humiliating people. Eochaid had seen him reduce a clumsy warrior to tears by the ferocity of his anger. What would he do now that Eochaid had raised an armed revolt against him?

Swallowing his fear, Eochaid held himself upright, reminding himself that he was a King, not a slave.

The High King looped the long reins over the front edge of his ornately decorated chariot. The ponies, strong, agile beasts with their coats immaculately groomed and their manes neatly braided, stood obediently still. The High King turned to face Eochaid. He did not dismount from the chariot's platform but stood there, looming over his beaten foe.

His lips curled in a sneer as he asked, "Well, Eochaid? Do you still desire to fight me, or are you here to offer your surrender?"

The King of Leinster bowed his head.

"I submit to your mercy, High King. I was wrong to oppose you and I ask that you forgive me."

It was the sorceress who replied. Her voice was harsh.

"Why should the High King show any mercy to you, Eochaid Ainchenn? You rebelled against his authority out of a desire for personal gain."

Eochaid felt a stirring of anger at the way she addressed him. He answered, "I did no more than the High King once did himself, when he was Elim of Ulster. He will remember that I helped him overthrow Fiacha Finnolach."

Ignoring the jibe, the witch retorted, "You rebelled against the High King and you lost. There is a high price to be paid for failure."

Eochaid was appalled at the ferocity of her anger. She regarded him as if he had personally attacked her and she sounded as if she would gladly see him torn to pieces by wild dogs.

Turning his gaze to Elim, Eochaid said, "I have already paid. My army was defeated, with three of my sons killed in the battle. My fourth son is also dead. Many of my sub-kings have been killed. Elim mac Conrach, I ask you for mercy in recognition of our past friendship and of the loss I have suffered for my foolishness."

"But what am I to do with you, Eochaid?" Elim asked. "If I allow you to live, you will simply begin plotting against me as soon as I turn my back on you."

"You should make an example of him," the witch urged.

"But if I execute him, who would be King of Leinster?" Elim mused. "If I place one of my own sons on the throne, the people will be resentful."

"They are resentful already," the sorceress pointed out.

Elim waved a hand at the woman.

"Be silent, Scota. I am the High King. I rule the whole island of Eriu. That rule is difficult enough without creating more enemies."

Eochaid could see that Elim was enjoying himself. He suspected that the High King had already decided his fate and that the two of them were acting out a rehearsed conversation that was designed to torment him. The High King was not usually averse to putting his enemies' heads on poles but Eochaid felt a glimmer of hope when he heard Elim's words. Still, he tried not to let them see that he had any expectations of anything other than death. He knew that Elim was perfectly capable of raising his hopes only to dash them. Elim enjoyed watching the distress that such tactics inflicted on his victims.

Eochaid lowered his eyes, waiting for the decision.

Elim looked down at him. After a long silence, he ordered, "In five days' time, you will come to Tara. When you get there, you will crawl on your hands and knees and swear loyalty to me. You will bring three hundred head of cattle as tribute and you will hand over your sons' wives and children as hostages. Those are my terms. Accept them or I will destroy your home and kill or enslave every person I find there."

Eochaid did not hesitate.

"I accept your terms, High King."

He lowered his head once more, so that they would not see the relief on his face. Humiliation and the giving of hostages would keep his people alive.

Scota, the sorceress, gave him a look that suggested she was suspicious of the ease with which he had agreed, but Elim barked a triumphant laugh.

"Five days, Eochaid," the High King warned.

Then he tugged the chariot's reins free, preparing to drive back to his army.

Scota continued to stare at the King of Leinster.

"If you break your oath, I will curse you," she promised.

44

Elim flicked the reins, sending the ponies into a canter. The chariot lurched forwards, leaving Eochaid alone in the early morning sunlight. Despite its warmth, he shivered.

But he had won. He lived and his son would bring an army to Eriu which even the High King could not defeat.

Chapter VI

Domnan picked his way down the treacherous path that led from the settlement to the rock-strewn bay. The small boat that awaited him rocked gently as he and two of his father's warriors stepped aboard.

In moments, the sailors untied the mooring ropes, pushed the boat away from the small, wooden dock and raised the tiny sail. Slowly, weaving a cautious route between the rocks and tiny islets that made the bay so dangerous, they set sail for the north-east.

Domnan felt some trepidation about the task he had been charged with but he was buoyed up by the knowledge that his father still lived. The tribute that Elim had demanded was high but it could be met. Eochaid may have to grovel before the High King but at least he would live. That knowledge sustained Domnan as the sea breeze clawed at his face. Soon, the High King would learn what it meant to humiliate the King of Leinster.

Domnan knew little about the Romans but he had heard stories brought across the sea by refugees from among the tribes of the Pritani. Everyone said that the Romans were invincible in battle and always eager for conquest. How could they refuse the opportunity to add Eriu to their empire? Eochaid would claim the High Kingship, ruling the land as an ally of Rome, which meant that, one day, Domnan would be High King. An alliance with Rome would mean paying some tribute but that was a small price to pay for gaining a victory over Elim mac Conrach.

Domnan smiled to himself as the boat ploughed its way across the waves, pushed on by the westerly wind. The day, which had started so badly, was becoming one of promise.

Five days later, Eochaid Ainchenn, King of Leinster, arrived at the sacred hill of Tara. Three hundred head of cattle had been driven across the land to be delivered to the High King as tribute. Eochaid also delivered the wives and children of his dead sons as hostages.

Accompanied by his sorceress and a score of fierce-looking warriors, Elim walked down from his own fortified settlement which lay some distance to the east of Tara. He nodded approvingly at the dust being raised by the milling cattle before turning his attention to Eochaid.

"You have come, then," he grunted. He seemed disappointed.

"As I promised."

Elim's stony gaze regarded Eochaid for a long, silent moment. Then the High King said, "I will go to the *Lia Fail*. You will crawl there to meet me."

He smiled as he added, "But I am feeling generous today, so your sons' wives and your grandchildren may walk behind you."

"Thank you," replied Eochaid helplessly.

Elim waved to his warriors to follow at the rear of the train then turned away and began striding towards the entrance to the long processional way that led to the sacred enclosure. He went alone, without a care in the world, confident that nobody would dare disobey his commands.

Scota stood beside Eochaid. When the High King's back was turned, her expression became less fierce. Eochaid thought that her green eyes even seemed to show a hint of sympathy.

"You must crawl," she reminded him brusquely.

Slowly, Eochaid lowered his aged bones to the ground. On his hands and knees, he crawled after the High King. Jeers and catcalls came from the people who had gathered to watch his humiliation. He ignored them. Someone threw a clod of earth which struck his shoulder but Scota angrily shouted at the crowd that it was the High King's place to dispense justice, not theirs. There was some angry muttering but no more missiles were thrown.

"Thank you," Eochaid said to the witch.

Scota did not reply but she took a position beside him, walking slowly to keep pace with his laboured progress. Behind him, he could hear the shuffling of feet as the women and children who would be Elim's hostages followed his ignominious journey.

It was then that Scota added to his misery.

"You are a fool," she told him.

He could almost taste the scorn in her voice.

"I am paying for my folly," he replied.

"We may all pay for your folly," she muttered as if she were disgusted at him.

47

He continued to crawl along the well-trodden pathway of hard earth and trampled grass, ignoring the aching protests from his hands and knees.

"What do you mean?" he asked her.

"What did you think you were going to accomplish?" she sneered.

"I was attempting to rid Eriu of a tyrant," he retorted, not caring that his words marked him as a traitor to the High King.

"A noble sentiment, I am sure," Scota sneered. "And who would replace him if you had succeeded? Did you think the other Kings would acknowledge you as High King?"

Eochaid had no answer to her question but she did not appear to notice his silence as she went on, "The other Kings would have reacted like a pack of wild dogs scrabbling over the carcass of a dead goat. You would have plunged Eriu into more years of conflict."

Eochaid's face grew red as his anger added to the strain of crawling along the processional way.

He snapped, "Does that justify doing nothing in the face of evil?"

"Bringing a greater evil is no solution," she shot back. "And have a care what you say. Your words are not those of a penitent."

Eochaid muttered, "I am an old man. There is little Elim can do to me now. I have lost all my sons and my war host has been virtually destroyed. What is left for me?"

"Life," Scota told him. "You should be grateful that the High King has not demanded more from you. My advice to you is to grovel as much as he requires and then to return to Leinster and maintain the peace."

Reluctantly, Eochaid sighed, "I have no choice in the matter, so I will do as you say."

"Good. Be sure that you keep your word. And if you should hear any rumours that others might be planning to do something foolish, I expect you to inform me. I will be watching you closely, Eochaid of Leinster."

He could hear the implied threat but made no response. He was growing tired now; his hands and knees were scraped, his arms and legs aching with the effort of crawling up the slope of the hill of Tara. Thankfully, his weariness prevented him revealing Domnan's mission. It would have been gratifying to see the shock and fear on Scota's face if she learned that the Legions of Rome would soon put an end to Elim mac Conrach but Eochaid decided he would keep that pleasure for a later date. For now, he decided, he would follow her advice and do the High King's bidding. Later, when Domnan returned with an army at his back, Eochaid would take his revenge.

His long, agonising crawl up the avenue continued. He scrambled slowly into the wide enclosure of Tara, passed the ancient mounds and dragged himself to the broad summit until he came to where Elim stood beside the standing stone of the *Lia Fail*, the Stone of Destiny. Almost exhausted, Eochaid collapsed at Elim's feet.

"I think he understands the error of his ways," Scota told the High King in a voice that had resumed its hard edge.

Elim ignored her.

"Get him up!" he barked to his warriors.

Hands grabbed at Eochaid. Two big men hauled him roughly to his feet. He staggered and would have fallen if their vice-like grips had not sustained him. Reeling, he saw the terrified faces of his daughters-in-law and grandchildren who had followed him and a spark of fear ignited in his heart.

He watched, horrified, as the screaming began.

The warriors who had followed them to the hill drew their long knives and quickly surrounded the three women and their children.

Eochaid saw arms thrusting, heard the screams of terror, and he saw the blood as bodies began to fall to the ground.

In anguished desperation, he shot a look at Scota but she, like him, was watching with an expression of horror on her marred face and he understood that she had not expected this slaughter.

He whirled his head, looking for the High King.

"What are you doing?" he yelled. "We surrendered to you! You gave your word!"

Elim responded with a quizzical look as if he did not understand the question. Then he shrugged, "I changed my mind. I will install one of my sons as King of Leinster. After all, your sons are dead. There will be nobody to succeed you, so you may as well die now."

Eochaid felt his legs collapse. Only the iron grip of the two men who held him kept him upright. He watched as Elim drew his sword. He could not struggle. There was no point. Resignedly, he waited for death.

"May the Dagda curse you," he spat at Elim.

The High King's eyes blazed furiously, the dark pupils like pools of ebony malice. His air of detached amusement vanished to be replaced by a rage that was so sudden and fierce that even the men holding Eochaid flinched.

"You betrayed me!" Elim shouted. His anger burned so hotly that Eochaid expected to see flecks of spittle flying from the corners of his mouth but, in spite of his rage, Elim did not lose control of himself. It was almost as if the display of fury was an act, a device he used like a physical force to intimidate his helpless victim.

He prodded Eochaid's chest with his finger as he punched out each word.

"I am the High King! Me! Not you or anyone else."

Eochaid remained calm in the face of Elim's aggression. He knew now that he would not leave this place alive. He had no time left for anger or fear.

He said, "You are High King now but not, I hope, for much longer. One day soon you will meet your match. I have seen it in my dreams."

"You lie!" Elim yelled. "You lie!"

With his left hand he grabbed Eochaid by the throat as if he intended to throttle him but his right hand still held his sword. With an incoherent scream of rage, Elim thrust the blade into Eochaid's belly.

Eochaid groaned and fell to the ground in a pool of blood as the two warriors released their grip on his arms.

Still Elim was not satisfied. Furiously, he hacked down with his sword, mutilating Eochaid's dying body. Blood spattered his arms and legs as he chopped and cut in a frenzy of rage that lasted long after all life had left the ruined corpse.

At last he stood straight, the manic gleam in his eyes fading.

"Take him away," he ordered the men, adding with a wave of his bloodied sword towards the bodies of the dead women and children, "And dispose of those others."

Scota had quickly overcome her shock at the brutal murder of the women and children. Now, with her face impassive, she said, "You did the right thing, Lord."

50

"Of course I did. There is only one way to deal with traitors. Now everyone else will think twice before they consider opposing me."

"Only fools would dare such a thing," she assured him.

His eyes narrowed as he regarded her suspiciously.

"Did you hear what he said? About his dreams?"

She shrugged, "I heard. He lied. You will remain High King for many years to come."

"Are you sure of that?" he demanded.

Most people would have quailed under the intensity of Elim's questioning but Scota remained calm.

She answered, "The future is difficult to read but some things are certain and can be seen by those who possess the power. Eochaid will not be the last to oppose you but you will prevail."

Far from being satisfied, Elim pounced on her words.

"Who else is plotting against me?" he demanded.

Scota spread her hands in a gesture of helplessness.

"I cannot say with any certainty."

"Then find out!" he barked.

He pushed his face forwards, so close that she could smell the stink of his breath. In a low, menacing whisper he snarled, "You are supposed to be a sorceress. Use your magic to unmask the traitors. Do you hear me?"

"I hear you, High King."

Scota closed her eyes, waiting for his next outburst, but he turned his back on her and she heard him moving away. When she opened her eyes again, he was stalking away down the hill.

She breathed deeply, summoning her reserves of strength. She served the High King because she knew the alternatives were worse but she had no illusions about his capacity for cruelty and vindictiveness. Her own position was a favoured one but she understood implicitly that her continued safety depended on her usefulness.

Elim had been correct about one thing; the unexpected brutality of the murder of Eochaid and his family served as a potent reminder of the risks of making an error of judgement. Scota vowed that she would not give the High King any excuse to doubt her.

"I hear you, High King," she repeated softly to herself. "With the Gods' help, I will reveal the traitors soon."

51

Chapter VII

"We don't have a choice," Runt muttered darkly. "Coel's trapped us and he knows it."

Angrily, Calgacus slammed his right fist into the palm of his left hand. He looked around at the grim faces of his companions who had gathered in one of the small chambers on the upper floor of the broch. A sliver of bright daylight filtered in through a narrow window in the thick walls but even that was insufficient to dispel all the shadows in the room or the gloom that hung over what should have been a joyous wedding party.

Calgacus shivered. He was accustomed to living in wooden roundhouses, so being surrounded by thick, cold stone, high in a tower felt alien to him; even more strange than the times he had spent in Roman buildings of brick and plaster. The strangeness of his surroundings did nothing to improve his dark mood.

"Does anyone have any ideas?" he asked.

A dull, heavy silence fell over the chamber as everyone exchanged looks, waiting for someone else to speak first.

At length, Emmelia ventured, "I hate to say it, but I think Liscus is correct."

"Surely Coel would not really harm us," Beatha protested.

Calgacus growled, "Coel would cut out his sons' hearts if he thought he would get his own way as a result."

Emmelia added, "One of them might do the same to him. They obviously hate him."

"Yes," Calgacus agreed, "I noticed that. It's pretty clear that Tuathal is his favourite. He seems to have put all his hopes on the boy."

Beatha said, "That boy is a young man, and potentially the High King of Eriu."

"Only if I agree to help him," Calgacus grumbled.

"I don't see how you can avoid it," Runt muttered. "He has our families as hostages."

Beatha argued, "Coel must know that the other tribes would not trust him if he does anything to us."

"The other tribes don't trust him anyway," Calgacus informed her. "That is why it has been so difficult to build an alliance."

Caedmon put in, "He must know that he cannot defeat the Romans without an alliance. Even the Caledones cannot stand on their own."

Emmelia gave her husband a weak smile as she said, "He knows that. I suspect he has more than half a mind to submit to Rome when the time comes. Either that or he will hope that Tuathal, as High King of Eriu, can send warriors to aid him."

"Broichan wouldn't agree to a deal with Rome," Calgacus asserted. "He may be devious but he's a druid. He knows he can't befriend Rome."

"Then why is he helping Coel?" Caedmon asked.

Calgacus shrugged, "I don't know. I can't figure that out."

Emmelia suggested, "The obvious answer is that he genuinely believes Elim mac Conrach is a threat."

She paused, then added, "Not that it really matters. Our problem remains the same."

"Can we not escape?" Fallar asked anxiously.

Runt shook his head as he explained, "There is only one door out of this place and it is well guarded. Even if we could all get outside, we'd still need to find the horses and also reach Adelligus and the others."

Another bleak silence fell over the room. After a long look at each of them, Calgacus sighed, "Then I suppose I will need to go to Eriu and kill this High King."

"I am glad you have made the right decision," Coel said when Calgacus returned to the great chamber to give the King his answer.

"It's not as if I had much of a choice," Calgacus growled. "You should know that I dislike being forced into this. Allies should not treat one another this way."

Coel's face was hard and impassive as he replied, "We will still be allies. Nothing has changed. Your daughter will be married to Tuathal as soon as he becomes High King."

"That will be up to her," Calgacus retorted sharply.

Coel shrugged, "You misunderstand my motives, Calgacus. I need your help with this. I have vowed to see Tuathal restored to his rightful place before I die. With the Romans threatening us and Elim the Usurper sending assassins, I cannot afford to wait any longer. We must make the attempt now. I know it is hazardous but your presence will make the difference; I know it will. So, I need you to do this for me, but you need my help to face the Romans. We will help each other. That is how allies should act."

"Allies should not threaten each other's families," Calgacus replied coldly. "I warn you, Coel, if you harm any of them while I am away, I will kill you as soon as I return. That is a promise."

"If you reinstate Tuathal as High King, they will not be harmed," Coel countered with equal coldness.

"And if I fail?" Calgacus asked.

"If you fail," Coel replied, "I fear we are all doomed."

The old King's response was hardly encouraging but Calgacus knew he was in no position to argue. With a sigh, he said, "Very well, let us get this done as quickly as we can. We need to make plans."

Still iron-faced, Coel told him, "Everything is in hand. I have called for volunteers from among my warriors. I want only the best men for this venture and many have answered the call. More boats are coming, too. The muster will be complete in three days."

Calgacus realised that Coel had been planning this venture for a long time. The King had made his preparations knowing that Calgacus would have no choice but to accede to his demands. Bitterly, Calgacus wondered whether the offer of a marriage alliance had been nothing more than a ruse to trick him into bringing his family to the Caledones' stronghold. Ruse or not, he had certainly blundered straight into Coel's trap.

He shook off the thought. What was done could not be undone. Now, he must see this through.

"How many men?" he demanded testily.

"We have boats enough for at least six hundred," Coel informed him.

"That's not enough," Calgacus retorted instantly. "You can't conquer an entire land with six hundred men. Not even the Romans can do that."

"More will join you when you arrive in Eriu," Coel told him, dismissing his objection. "Tuathal will have his army."

Shaking his head, Calgacus asked, "What about provisions?"

"Ready to be loaded," was the instant reply.

"Horses. We will need horses."

"You will get them when you reach Eriu. Tuathal's cousins have been informed of your coming. They will meet you. They will bring an army to join you."

Calgacus felt that he was being swept along by events. Coel had arranged everything.

He asked, "What makes you think the men of Eriu will follow my commands?"

"They will follow Tuathal," Coel informed him. "He is the rightful High King. Your role is to advise him, to ensure that he defeats Elim mac Conrach. Make no mistake, though; Tuathal leads this expedition."

Calgacus growled, "As long as he does as I tell him."

"He knows your reputation."

Calgacus felt his temper rising. Wanting to escape the old King's presence, he said, "Then I suppose I had better take a look at your boats. I would also like to know more about Eriu. I want to know what we can expect to face."

"Broichan will tell you whatever you want to know," Coel told him.

Calgacus needed to get out of the chamber. Coel's grand home, with its massively thick walls of stone surrounding him, felt like a prison. It *was* a prison. He would be allowed to leave, but his family would remain until he did what Coel wanted. He felt angry, betrayed and, above all, sick to the very core of his being. Giving Coel a curt nod, he turned and stalked out.

Broichan joined Calgacus and Runt as they looked down at the small pebble-lined bay on the shores of the sea loch below the broch.

"As you can see," the druid said, "everything is well in hand."

Calgacus merely grunted an acknowledgement. He could see that there were already half a dozen small, wooden-hulled sailing ships moored in the bay. These would form the core of the flotilla that Coel was gathering. Clustered on the beach were more than thirty of the long, sea-going curraghs that were favoured by raiding parties. These vessels had lightweight, wooden frames which were covered by waterproofed animal hides. The largest of them had seven wooden benches to accommodate fourteen oarsmen, with a steersman at the stern and a small perch for a lookout at the pointed prow.

Calgacus had seen such boats before. He knew they were ideal for travelling far inland up shallow rivers and that they were often used in coastal waters, but he had not expected Coel's fleet to consist of so many lightweight vessels. He eyed them sceptically.

"You expect us to cross the sea in those?" he asked the druid.

"Of course. They are very strong. As long as you avoid deep water in a storm, they are perfectly capable of crossing to Eriu."

Calgacus was no seaman. He hated the feeling of having nothing but water below him. On the few occasions he had ventured to sea, he had experienced rough weather and storms that had made his stomach heave. On one occasion he had been shipwrecked. He would never admit it, but the prospect of another sea voyage filled him with dread.

Giving the shallow-draughted curraghs a disdainful look, he declared, "I'll travel in one of the sailing boats."

"As you please," shrugged Broichan. "The King has commanded that you depart in three days. By that time, all of his warriors and ships will be ready."

"If the weather holds," Calgacus countered.

"Do not seek to avoid this," Broichan warned brusquely. "You must go to Eriu. Elim and his witch are a threat to us all."

"I know what I need to do," Calgacus responded in a surly growl. "But I don't have to like it."

"You will succeed," Broichan told him. "The warriors who will accompany you are among the best of the Caledones. The King selected them personally."

Calgacus could not dispute that. He had seen some of the men who had come to join the expedition. More were arriving each day. They came in their war bands, sometimes only six or seven in a group, sometimes as many as thirty. They were tough men, coarse and rough, happy to pit their strength against anyone and always eager for adventure, especially if there was the prospect of plunder. They came with their spears and their long knives, their faces and bodies already daubed with blue paint or decorated by tattoos.

56

"They'll do," was Calgacus' grudging comment. "Now tell me about Eriu. I want to understand what we are up against, and what the situation is. Coel said we can expect help when we get there."

Broichan nodded, "Tuathal has cousins in Eriu. They have sent messengers giving assurances that the men of Ulster are ready to rise up against Elim mac Conrach."

"How many men will they bring?"

Broichan hesitated before saying, "As many as they can."

"Wonderful," Runt muttered sarcastically.

Calgacus asked, "More importantly, how many men can the High King call on to oppose us?"

Broichan shrugged, "A few thousand, perhaps. But most of them will be levied from the general population. He will only have a few hundred trained warriors."

Calgacus suspected that the druid had no real idea of the true situation in Eriu. The greybeard's answers were too vague to be reliable.

"What about his sorceress? How do we counter her?"

Again Broichan gave a slight shrug as he admitted, "I only know what I have heard from others, although I believe she is skilled in divination and prophecy. She is said to be a shape-shifter and a necromancer."

Seeing the look of concern on Calgacus' face, the druid added, "I suspect some of the tales may be exaggerated but whatever she can do, she can be slain by a sword or spear."

Calgacus did not press the point. He decided that, where magic and witchcraft were concerned, Emmelia would be able to advise him better than Broichan.

Frustrated, he asked, "All right. Then tell me about Eriu itself. Can we expect any help from the other sub-kings? Who are they and where are they?"

Using the tip of his staff, Broichan sketched out a crude map, drawing a lop-sided rectangle on a patch of dry earth.

"This is Eriu," the druid explained.

Tapping the top right corner of the diagram, he said, "You will land here, in the part they call Ulster. It is the closest to us and is also where you will find the most support."

Runt put in, "I heard that Elim was King of Ulster before he became High King. Doesn't that mean he will have the support of the people there?"

Broichan shook his head dismissively.

"Tuathal's father was also from Ulster," he explained. "Many of the people remember him fondly and most are now opposed to Elim."

Calgacus felt the druid's explanation was too glib to be relied upon but the old man did not allow them any further interruptions. Concentrating on his diagram, he drew rough lines with his stick, dividing the map into four sections.

Tapping the lower right partition, he continued, "This is Leinster. The King of that place recently rebelled against Elim. We have heard that his army was destroyed but we do not know what has happened to the King himself. However, in view of Elim's reputation, it is more than likely that he is dead."

"So who rules there now?"

Broichan gave yet another slight shrug.

"Elim has two sons. He may have placed one of them as the new King, or installed a puppet King from among the nobles of Leinster. In either case, it is doubtful whether the new ruler will be able to bring many men to face you. He will be busy enough controlling his new kingdom. In fact, it is likely that the men of Leinster will rise up and join you as soon as they learn of Tuathal's arrival."

"You don't know that for certain," Calgacus objected.

Broichan ignored him. He tapped the lower left portion of the map and went on, "This is Munster. The King there is a subject of the High King, of course, but he is too far away to become involved if you act quickly. You can discount Munster."

He switched to the upper left section before Calgacus could raise any objection to his assessment.

"The final kingdom is Connacht," Broichan intoned. "This is potentially the greatest threat. We are unsure of how the King of Connacht will react. With luck, he will join you, but we feel it would be best to defeat Elim before the King of Connacht becomes aware that you are even in Eriu."

"With luck?" Calgacus challenged. "People who rely on luck rarely achieve anything."

Scowling, Broichan tapped the map near the intersection of the kingdoms he had named as Ulster and Leinster.

"You will not need to rely on luck," he said acerbically. "The High King's home is here at Tara. All you need to do is get there quickly, kill him and put Tuathal in his place."

"Then we should land further south," Calgacus argued. "That gives us less distance to travel overland."

"No," Broichan replied emphatically. "Tuathal's cousins are in the northern part of Ulster. That is where you must join them. Besides, the further south you sail, the more chance there is of running in to Roman war galleys."

Calgacus reluctantly conceded the point but he remained unhappy.

"This is not much of a plan," he complained bitterly. "There are too many unknown factors."

"Coel has faith in you," Broichan informed him.

"But what about you?" Calgacus demanded. "What do you get out of this, Broichan? You know it is the Romans who are our real enemy."

The druid's stony expression did not alter. He hesitated slightly, as if debating whether to reveal his thinking but, after a moment, he confided, "I think you misjudge me, Calgacus. I know only too well that the Romans are the real threat to our safety. But building an alliance is proving difficult, as you know. This expedition can help us."

"How?"

"If Elim lives, he can attack us. We cannot afford to fight him while we face the greater threat of Rome. But if he dies and Tuathal replaces him, the warriors of Eriu will become our allies. That will greatly increase our strength."

Calgacus nodded thoughtfully.

"Perhaps. But this is a huge gamble we are taking."

Broichan gave a slight nod but was not prepared to agree fully.

"Not doing this is a greater risk," he argued. "Our hopes rest on the strength of the Caledones. You need Coel if you wish to defeat Rome. Coel wants Tuathal to become High King of Eriu. It has become something of an obsession for him. If you go against him, you will never gain your alliance."

Broichan gave Calgacus an intense look as he added, "Coel is a stubborn man. He is used to getting his own way. But you should bear in mind that, if you help him, he will be in your debt."

"I won't let him forget that," Calgacus promised.

"Do you believe him?" Runt asked as he and Calgacus trudged their way back to the broch.

"Broichan?" Calgacus shrugged. "He's a devious bastard but he's not stupid. He knows he needs us as much as we need Coel, so he wouldn't deliberately send us into a trap. It's just that he doesn't have a clue how to fight a war."

"He helped Coel set this trap for us," Runt pointed out.

"Probably because he knows we need Coel's cooperation against Rome and he reckons this is the best way to achieve that. I don't agree with him but I can understand his reasoning."

"Are you forgetting it was a druid who set that gang of bandits on us?" Runt asked.

"No, but I don't see what Broichan has to gain from our deaths."

"I wouldn't trust a druid if he told me the stars come out at night," muttered Runt.

Grimly, Calgacus laughed, "At least he hasn't tried to sacrifice anyone yet."

"Don't give him any ideas," Runt advised sourly.

"I don't think he'll try anything like that," Calgacus replied. "But it would probably be best if Adelligus and the lads stayed here just in case."

After a moment's consideration, Runt nodded, "He won't be happy about staying behind but I think you are right. If we don't come back, the women and children will need somebody to look out for them."

"Tell him to get them home safely if anything happens to us."

"The wedding is off then?" Runt asked.

"That's up to Fallar," Calgacus shrugged. "But even the prospect of being High Queen of Eriu doesn't seem to interest her. She's frightened and all she wants is to go home."

"She's not the only one," Runt murmured. "But Coel has us by the balls and he's squeezing hard."

"I should never have trusted him," Calgacus sighed. "I didn't realise he was so determined to see Tuathal as High King. It's as if he's obsessed."

"Not like you, then," Runt grinned.

"What do you mean? I'm not obsessed."

"No," Runt agreed. "You have hardly mentioned the Romans all morning."

"That's different!" protested Calgacus.

"If you say so."

Calgacus frowned but did not argue. Opposing Rome had been the main focus of his life for as long as he could remember and he supposed his constant warnings might seem like an obsession to some people.

Runt asked, "Do you think it would be worth speaking to Tuathal and trying to persuade him not to go through with this? I think he's out beyond the village, chatting to the war bands."

Calgacus shook his head.

"No. He's a smart lad but his head is full of daft ideas Coel has put there. He won't change his mind."

"Obsessed?" Runt suggested archly.

"He thinks it is his destiny to become High King," Calgacus sighed. "But I can't blame him for that. It's Coel who is the problem."

Runt remarked, "If you ask me, the whole family are a few arrows short of a quiver. To be honest, I'm almost looking forward to getting away from them for a while."

Chapter VIII

Crixus was in a contemplative mood as he slowly rode across the heather-clad hills. Deep in thought, he let his attention wander, trusting to his horse to keep its footing and his men to keep their eyes alert in the search for the bandits.

He had always known that leaving his own homestead to visit his father at the great broch would be an ordeal and so it had proved. The old man's bitterness towards him had not lessened over the years and it had been difficult to refrain from talking back when his father treated him like a disobedient child.

It has always been thus, Crixus recalled bitterly. Growing up with Coel as a father had been difficult at best. The old man had lavished most of his affection on his only daughter, relegating Crixus and Drust to the fringes of his attention. Drust, physically powerful but mentally weak, had accepted his role with typical, dull acceptance, finding solace in alcohol by the time he was fourteen years old.

Crixus had never fallen so far. He had always been the one to argue, always been the one who was mocked, derided and beaten by their father whenever he made what the King regarded as insolent remarks. Yet Crixus had continued to defy his father in small ways and, when the opportunity arose to demonstrate his independence, he had seized it.

Arilla had been beautiful but she was the daughter of a lowly slave, as low-born as a young woman could be. Crixus could have bought her and kept her in his household, marrying a more suitable wife and taking Arilla to his bed when the notion took him. Instead, he had freed her and married her before his father could prevent the hand-fasting. He had done it more to annoy the old man as anything else and it had worked. From that day on, Crixus was even more of an outcast from his father's affections than he had ever been.

Arilla was long dead now, a stillborn daughter killing her in childbirth only a year after the twins had been born. Crixus had not married again, refusing to accept any of the matches his father occasionally suggested and declining to elevate any of his slaves to a lofty position.

He had concentrated on the twins, raising them almost as if they were his friends rather than his sons. Their bonds were close but even Crixus acknowledged that the boys were more outgoing and friendly than he had ever been.

That was almost enough to make their grandfather accept them despite their mother's lowly birth. Yet Coel still favoured Tuathal over Eudaf and Eurgain, a fact which only served to add to Crixus' resentment against his father.

Sulking in the sanctuary of his own homestead, Crixus had based his hopes on the fact that Coel could not live forever. When he passed away, Crixus would be the prime candidate to succeed him as the leading King of the Caledones. It would require the approval of the tribe's chieftains but Crixus was confident he would be able to bribe or threaten enough of them to ensure they would proclaim him King.

The problem was that Coel continued to live. Crixus was a patient man but even he was becoming increasingly irritated by the old goat's continued good health.

His concerns had grown as Tuathal came to manhood. Coel favoured the boy so much that Crixus was worried he might nominate Tuathal as his successor. When Crixus heard of the marriage plans to tie Tuathal to Calgacus, that concern had grown.

And then he had learned of Coel's real plan. He had talked about it for years, of course, but Crixus had always scoffed at the improbability of being able to install Tuathal as High King of Eriu. Now, it seemed, Coel and Tuathal were intent on making the attempt.

That suited Crixus perfectly because it would remove Tuathal as a threat to his own position as heir apparent to the rule of the Caledones. That was why he had supported his father's plan and why he had encouraged his sons to ask that one of them should accompany Tuathal. The family needed to be seen to be backing the venture and there was, naturally, no chance that Crixus would be sent to Eriu. Coel had always viewed him as incompetent and untrustworthy which, on this occasion, suited Crixus' plans since it would allow him to consolidate his own position.

Yet remaining at the broch and seeing his father every day was proving intolerable, so he had decided to venture out and track down the survivors of the bandit gang who had attacked Calgacus.

Taking thirty horsemen as well as two houndmasters and their hunting dogs, he was glad to leave the intrigues and deceptions of his family behind for a few days.

"There they are!"

The shout jerked him from his reverie and he looked up to where one of his men was pointing.

"After them!" he roared.

The horses broke into a fast canter, spreading out to form a long line, blocking their quarry's escape. The hounds barked eagerly, straining at the leashes of their handlers who ran awkwardly, vainly trying to keep pace with Crixus' thirty riders.

Crixus peered ahead at the small band of figures plodding along the hillside. He was sure it was the brigands they had been hunting. There were six ragged men, one of them hobbling badly because of his injured leg. It must be them.

At last, he had found them.

Crixus had begun his search by taking his hunting party to the spot where the bandits had ambushed Calgacus. The corpses of the dead brigands lay where they had fallen but a mound of earth near the small pool showed where Calgacus' fallen warrior had been buried.

Crixus surveyed the scene with distaste. Foxes and carrion birds had mutilated the abandoned bodies, and the sickly smell of death and rotting meat hung heavy in the air. Trying to ignore the stench, Crixus walked his horse slowly into the midst of the carnage, checking the bodies as he went. He smiled in satisfaction when he saw the huge bulk of a man with a shaved head and a chest tattoo. There was no doubt about it. Greumaich's raiding days were ended.

Incredibly, one of the bandits who had been wounded was still alive. Unable to walk because of dreadful wounds to both legs, he had dragged himself to the side of the pool so that he could drink. He had bound his own wounds to prevent himself bleeding to death but he was weak from hunger and loss of blood. He called out for help when he heard the riders arrive.

Crixus waved a hand to his men.

"Search the woods," he commanded. Then he dismounted and walked over to the wounded brigand.

"Help me," the man begged, his voice weak and desperate.

"Where are your companions?" Crixus demanded.

"Gone. All gone. The yellow bastards left me here to die."

64

"Where have they gone? Which way?"

"North. They're going home to the land of the Creones."

The wounded man held out an arm in supplication.

"Please. I need food."

In response, Crixus drew his sword.

"You attacked some of our farms. You killed and you raped our people. Those crimes cannot go unpunished."

The wounded man said nothing.

Crixus continued, "Calgacus should have killed you after your attack on him failed."

He clucked his tongue as he added, "Never mind. I will finish the job."

The bandit's face contorted into a mask of hatred.

"Bastard!" he hissed.

That was his final word before Crixus' sword plunged into his chest.

They found one more dead brigand in the woods but there was also a trail of blood, dark spots spattered on the ground. The dogs soon had the scent.

In the next valley they came across another corpse. The bandit had been too badly hurt to go any further and had simply lain down to die. The dog handlers let the hounds sniff the earth until one of the beasts let out a howl and the hunt was on again.

Now they had found the six survivors of the raiding party and Crixus grinned to himself as he anticipated what would happen next.

He waved to the dog handlers.

"Release the hounds!"

Shouting encouragement, the handlers slipped the leashes, allowing the huge hunting dogs to run free.

The bandits heard the baying and barking of the hounds. They began to run but there was nowhere to hide, no sanctuary in sight. They had been caught in open ground, with only the heather-clad hillside stretching in all directions. The limping man quickly fell behind as the other five brigands ran for their lives.

"Kill them all!" Crixus yelled.

His men pushed their horses into a gallop. They thundered across the hillside, whooping and yelling with the thrill of the chase. One horse went down screaming as it lost its footing on the uneven surface beneath the covering of heather but the others pounded on, disregarding the danger.

The dogs, bounding ahead of the horsemen, reached the wounded man who was trailing behind his companions. Snarling, they hurled themselves at him, bringing him down. His screams of terror echoed across the hillside but the dogs were well trained. Once they had him on the ground, they surrounded him, then backed away, growling and yapping but leaving the kill to their masters.

A horseman reined in, leaned from his saddle and hacked down at the injured man until the screaming ceased. Then the rider clapped his heels to his horse and was off again. The dogs bayed as they ran after him.

There was no fight. The raiders were exhausted, stumbling and staggering wildly as they tried in vain to escape. One by one they were hunted down and killed. Crixus allowed his men to take their heads as trophies but left the bodies for the crows.

He sat in his saddle, watching as the corpses were decapitated, feeling immensely pleased with himself. Greumaich's raiding party had been wiped out. Such was the price of failure.

Two days later, Crixus returned in triumph just in time to see the expedition to Eriu set off. He rode down to the shore of the bay where hundreds of people had gathered to see the men depart.

Dismounting, he made his way to the front of the crowd where he noticed Calgacus' wife, Beatha, standing beside her daughter. The two blonde women really were beauties, he thought. The sight of Fallar's statuesque figure was enough to excite any man, and seeing her sent a tingle of anticipation through Crixus' body although the sensation vanished when he caught sight of Calgacus himself standing beside Coel, Broichan and Tuathal.

They all looked up as Crixus strode towards them. Coel gave his son a disapproving look and Crixus steeled himself for another confrontation. Let the old man rant, he thought. Soon enough, Crixus' own plans would come to fruition. He could endure another scolding.

"Well?" the old King asked expectantly.

Crixus felt the familiar irritation he always experienced when he spoke to his aged father but he swallowed down his annoyance as he replied, "We caught them. They are all dead."

"What about the druid who hired them?" Calgacus asked. "Did you discover who he was?"

Crixus faltered slightly under the big man's questioning gaze.

"No," he admitted.

"Did you even ask them?" Coel demanded in a disparaging voice.

"We killed them all," Crixus replied angrily. "That is what you wanted."

Coel rolled his eyes in exasperation.

"We will talk about this later," he said, dismissing Crixus.

"I did what you wanted!" Crixus shouted.

Coel waved an angry hand to silence the protest.

"Enough! I said we will discuss it later."

Dismissed like a recalcitrant child, Crixus clenched his teeth together, struggling to keep his temper in check. Standing on the fringes of the gathering, he watched with mounting anger as Coel embraced Tuathal before nodding a farewell to Calgacus.

Taking several deep breaths, Crixus calmed himself. Now was not the time to confront Coel. Let the old man have his way today. There would be a reckoning soon enough. He watched closely as Calgacus and his little companion hugged their families before climbing aboard one of the larger sailing boats that was moored at a tiny, wooden landing stage at the side of the loch.

"Good riddance," he muttered under his breath.

Then he saw his sons, Eudaf and Eurgain, walking towards him. He relaxed and smiled as he turned to meet them.

"Did you find them?" Eudaf asked.

"They are all dead," Crixus confirmed.

"That is something, at least," observed Eurgain.

"What about you two?" Crixus enquired. "Which of you is going with Tuathal?"

"I am," said Eudaf.

"We wrestled for it," Eurgain explained. "Eudaf won. Only just."

He was smiling as he said it, no trace of rancour in his voice at being defeated by his twin brother.

Crixus embraced Eudaf.

"May the Gods watch over you," he whispered in his son's ear. "I will pray for your success. Be careful."

"And you, Father," Eudaf replied quietly.

Crixus released his son, clapping him on the shoulder.

"Go! Before they leave without you."

Eudaf pushed through the crowd, following Calgacus and Runt into the boat. As soon as he had clambered aboard, Tuathal followed. He was the last man to board.

Crixus watched as Broichan sacrificed a goat, a young kid, allowing the blood to drip into the water, then the sails were being hoisted, oars splashed, the men in the long curraghs were shoving out into the deep water, and the fleet began to slowly edge its way into the loch, heading towards the western sea.

On the shore, there were tears, anxious faces and shouts of encouragement. Women lifted their children to let them see the great fleet leaving for Eriu. Everyone was waving, even old Coel.

Everyone except Crixus.

Sitting on a low bench, Calgacus looked back towards the shore, keeping his eyes on Beatha and Fallar for as long as he could.

Beside him, Runt said confidently, "We'll see them again."

Calgacus nodded grimly as he replied, "I hope you are right."

"Adelligus will take care of them," Runt assured him.

"Let's hope he doesn't need to," grunted Calgacus.

"He isn't best pleased about being left behind," said Runt.

"I'm not best pleased about having to leave," Calgacus muttered.

"You are in a cheerful mood, aren't you?" Runt scolded.

"I don't like being on the water," Calgacus complained.

"I know. But you don't like not getting your own way, either. I can see this is going to be a really enjoyable voyage."

Calgacus grimaced. Already, the rocking motion of the boat was causing his stomach to protest. Placing his hands on the bench beside him, he gripped tightly and tried to ignore the queasy feeling in his belly.

Runt grinned, "I've just thought of something else that's good about this trip."

"What is that?"

"Well, we may have a dangerous sea voyage, unreliable allies, a powerful King and a witch to contend with, but at least we don't need to worry about the Romans."

68

Chapter IX

"Good morning, Publius."

The Governor's voice was disconcertingly cheerful for such an early hour.

"Good morning, Sir."

"Another busy day ahead of us, I fear."

"Yes, Sir."

Publius Cornelius Tacitus almost voiced the opinion that every day was a busy day but he managed to restrain himself. The Governor, Gnaeus Julius Agricola, may have been Tacitus' father-in-law but he was also his commanding officer. When on duty, Agricola was a stickler for proper discipline and respect.

As usual, Agricola wasted no time in getting down to business. Quickly finishing the last crumbs of his meagre breakfast, he announced, "I want to inspect the work on the bridge this morning, then check on our supply levels. It is always a good idea to let the Quartermasters know we are keeping an eye on them. I also want to speak to the Auxiliary cavalry, to check on the state of their mounts. It won't be a formal inspection but I'd like to keep them on their toes. Then I'd better visit the infirmary to see the men there. After that, I propose visiting a few more of the local chieftains. I need to keep reminding them that they have agreed to be loyal subjects of the Empire and that they will be well paid for supplying us with grain."

"Very good, Sir. Do you wish to sign your correspondence first? The secretaries have prepared the various letters you dictated yesterday."

"Yes, have them brought in. Is there anything else?"

"Yes, Sir. Another barbarian arrived late last night, asking to speak to you. He is very young and I would have sent him away, except that he said he has travelled all the way from Hibernia to find us. From what I can gather, he claims to be a prince who is seeking our help to defeat his enemies."

"Another one?" Agricola sighed with a hint of weary impatience. "I've heard that tale a hundred times since I came to Britannia."

"I know, Sir. These barbarians do squabble amongst themselves."

"Indeed they do," Agricola agreed.

He paused, frowned pensively, then gave Tacitus an enquiring look as he asked, "Hibernia, you say?"

"Yes, Sir."

"Very well. I shall sign my letters first, then you can have him brought to me. Send word to the Legates to join me for that."

"Very good, Sir."

Tacitus left the large command tent. Outside, six secretaries waited expectantly, scrolls and writing tablets clutched tightly in their hands. He signalled to them to go in. Then he summoned one of Agricola's freedmen and sent him to ask the Legates to come to the Governor's tent.

"And tell the Duty Centurion to bring that barbarian who came in last night."

"Yes, Sir."

When the freedman had scurried off, Tacitus let out a soft sigh as he contemplated the day ahead. Inspections, visits, letters and more inspections. After two years as Agricola's aide, he still struggled to keep up with everything. He also knew that there would be many more matters to be dealt with during the course of the day. There would be petitions and requests from the soldiers, problems with supplies and with discipline, reports from patrols, and meetings with the senior officers, not to mention the inevitable small raids by hostile barbarians. Most of the locals had been bribed or cowed into submission but there were always some hotheads who were ready to cause trouble. Life on the borders of the Empire was never quiet.

As if that were not enough, there would be matters from elsewhere in the province to be dealt with. Every day, letters and reports from all over Britannia arrived at this northern command base. Every letter had to be read, logged and responded to. Of course, the secretaries did most of the actual work but the Governor's aide was required to check through the letters, seek the Governor's instructions where necessary, and then review the replies before presenting them to the Governor for his signature. The duties, it seemed to Tacitus, were never-ending.

Taking guilty advantage of a few moments' respite, Tacitus gazed around the huge camp. The scale of the place was impressive even by Roman standards because the Governor had decided to turn this camp into a permanent forward base for the conquest of the northern part of Britannia.

The soldiers of two Legions, along with several Auxiliary units, were gathered here. The walls and ditches were enormous, the interior crammed with tents. More permanent structures were being erected, so the daily noise of an army camp was augmented by the hammering of nails and the sawing of wood, accompanied by the cries of the engineers as they manoeuvred blocks of stone or massive wooden frames into place. They were building workshops, forges, ovens, an infirmary, a command post, barracks for the soldiers, stables for the horses, latrines, a bath house, storerooms and granaries. The Romans had arrived and they were stamping their mark on the landscape.

It was, Tacitus acknowledged, a dramatic landscape to mark. As usual with Roman bases, it was situated on good, level ground with plenty of trees nearby to provide building materials and fuel. A great many trees had been felled over the previous autumn and winter because the engineers insisted that timber felled in spring or summer was no use for building.

"Too much sap rising," one of them had explained to Tacitus. "You can't build properly with wood like that."

Now, though, the engineers were building with a speed and efficiency that only Romans could achieve.

It was not only inside the camp that construction work was being undertaken. A river flowed nearby, broad enough for small supply ships to bring food and raw materials. There was a usable ford but the engineers were already building a bridge, while the legionaries were busy constructing a road that would allow yet more supplies, plus any reinforcement that may be needed, to travel overland quickly.

More than all this activity, what made this place distinctive, what set it apart from other forts Tacitus had seen, were the three hills that towered over the camp. They were the only hills of any significance for many miles around, standing proud and dominating the local landscape. The barbarians had a settlement spread across the slopes of one of the hills but Agricola had demanded that they remove themselves so that he could place a watchtower on the summit. Not that the settlement prevented the building of the watchtower, but it would not do for barbarians to be able to block the route from the hilltop to the camp. The savages had gone unwillingly but their chieftains had been bribed with gifts of cloth, wine and silver and had been shown the power of the Legions, a combination of reward and threat that had been sufficient to ensure their grudging cooperation.

Tacitus looked up at the hills, the green of their slopes stark against the bright blue of the early morning sky. Trimontium, the soldiers had begun calling this place as soon as they arrived. Trimontium; *The Three Mountains*. The Governor liked the name for its Roman simplicity, so it had quickly become official. This would be the forward base from where the next stage of the northward expansion of the Empire would be launched.

"Impressive, aren't they?"

Tacitus turned to see an officer smiling at him. Beneath his crested helmet, the man's face was tanned by years of soldiering, his dark hair cut short in the Roman fashion although, for all his outward appearance of being a true Roman, Tacitus recognised him as a commander of an Auxiliary unit.

"Hello, Macrinus. Yes, they are rather imposing."

Julius Macrinus was a veteran soldier and Tacitus was slightly in awe of his brisk efficiency. The man had an easy self-confidence and a commanding manner that Tacitus rather envied.

"I have my daily rosters," Macrinus reported, handing over a small bundle of writing tablets. "Bloody waste of time if you ask me. I spend half my time writing reports."

"The Army thrives on bureaucracy," Tacitus told him with a wry smile as he accepted the writing tablets.

He knew Macrinus did not need to bring the rosters personally, so he suspected the man had some other reason for coming to the Governor's tent. The Auxiliary Centurion's next words confirmed that suspicion.

"My lads are growing bored," Macrinus complained. "Is there any word on when the campaign will resume?"

"I don't think much will happen this year," Tacitus replied.

Macrinus gave a grim laugh.

"We're going to sit on our backsides all year?"

"The Governor is consolidating what we have gained," Tacitus explained. "The campaign against the Brigantes took longer than he had hoped."

"Aye, there was some tough fighting, right enough," Macrinus agreed.

"You should know. Your men were in the thick of it."

Macrinus smiled, "We certainly were. Tough bastards, the Brigantes, but we beat them in the end."

Tacitus nodded. The Brigantes, a powerful and numerous tribe, had been fighting the Romans for several years in a long, brutal war that had gradually sapped the strength of the tribe. Agricola, building on the campaigns of his predecessors, had finally subdued them after twelve months of determined and methodical violence.

"I thought your men would welcome a period of rest," Tacitus observed.

Macrinus grinned, "They are Germans. They enjoy fighting."

"There are bound to be more hostile tribes to the north," Tacitus said. "But our supply lines are now becoming stretched. The Governor wants to prepare properly before moving on."

"That's sensible," Macrinus agreed. "How is the work progressing?"

"We are building storehouses further south," Tacitus informed him. "The Imperial fleet will be able to keep the army supplied when we resume our advance."

"It makes a pleasant change to have a Governor who knows what he is doing," Macrinus observed.

Tacitus wondered whether Macrinus was trying to flatter the Governor, knowing that Tacitus was Agricola's son-in-law, but he decided the man's comment was probably genuine. Macrinus was the type who would not hesitate to criticise if he disagreed with what the senior officers were doing. The Auxiliary commander, who had been a soldier for more years than Tacitus had lived, clearly approved of the Governor's precautions.

Unfortunately, all these preparations took time to organise. Some generals would have pushed on regardless but Agricola was always solicitous of his soldiers' welfare. He would not ask them to march into unknown territory without being certain that they would be adequately supplied.

"There's a great deal still to do," Tacitus explained. "We really don't know very much about the tribes who live to the north."

"Assume they are hostile," Macrinus advised with a grim laugh.

Tacitus shrugged, "Some may submit without a fight. The Governor has sent scouts, emissaries and spies to discover what lies north of here, and galleys from the Imperial Navy are mapping the coastal areas. We won't go in blindly."

Macrinus nodded, "I understand. But the lads will grow restless if they have nothing to do all year except build roads and dig ditches."

"They will need to be patient," Tacitus commented. "Collating and evaluating all of the information will take a considerable amount of time. All things considered, I expect to be based at Trimontium for several months."

"Maybe the Governor will let me take a few men to scout out the land," said Macrinus hopefully.

"Perhaps. Personally, I intend to use the time to write up my journal."

"You're keeping a journal?"

"Yes. When I return to Rome, I intend to devote my time to writing, to giving the people of Rome an account of my father-in-law's exploits in Britannia."

"Very laudable," Macrinus remarked, although his tone suggested that he had no real interest in such things.

For his part, Tacitus was grateful to his father-in-law for providing him with a senior military position on this campaign. The young Roman knew in his heart that, unlike men such as Macrinus, he was not a born soldier. He was diligent and efficient, but the military life did not really suit him. It was something to be endured until he was able to devote himself to study and to writing.

He would never confide in someone like Macrinus but he hoped that his writings would be a way to repay Agricola by setting the Governor's name down in history for eternity.

Trying to make light of his literary pretensions, Tacitus said, "Mind you, I sometimes wonder whether my account will be believed. This is such a strange island, people might not believe the truth of what we have seen."

"You think so?"

"Oh, yes. Before I came here, I read a book written by a man named Pytheas. I don't suppose you've heard of him?"

Macrinus shook his head.

"No."

"He was a Greek navigator and mathematician. He claimed to have visited the various islands of Britannia two hundred years ago."

"Really?"

Macrinus appeared genuinely surprised.

"That is what he wrote in his book. The trouble is, he has often been accused of inventing his account. Men who spent their entire lives in Rome declared that it was impossible for human beings to survive this far north because of the extreme cold."

Macrinus laughed, "I know a few soldiers who would agree with that. Last winter was a hard one."

"I know, but we are here, despite what the experts predicted."

"I don't have much time for armchair experts," said Macrinus.

"It wasn't just that," Tacitus explained. "Pytheas told tales of endless forests, of treacherous marshes and bogs, of snow and ice, and places where the sun does not set for months at a time."

"I've seen most of those things, right enough," Macrinus agreed. "I'm not so sure about the sun not setting, though. That sounds a bit far-fetched."

"Perhaps, but you must have noticed how the daylight lasts longer the further north we go. Who knows? Perhaps if we travel far enough, the sun will stay in the sky permanently."

"That would be a sight to see," agreed Macrinus dubiously.

"Pytheas has been correct about so many things," Tacitus continued as he warmed to his theme. "For example, he mentioned how the inhabitants of these northern lands only reaped the top of their corn, leaving the stems as fodder for their livestock. I always thought that sounded strange and barbaric, yet I've seen it for myself. Now I understand that it is not so strange after all. It provides easy fodder for the cattle who also fertilised the fields for next year's crop."

Macrinus gave him an amused smile as he said, "If you don't mind me saying so, Sir, you think too much. Most of us don't concern ourselves about such things."

Tacitus acknowledged the truth of the soldier's statement with a smile of his own. "Not all men are soldiers," he shrugged. "I just hope that my own journal is not derided the way Pytheas' was."

"I'm sure it won't be," Macrinus commented politely.

"Rome is not a forgiving place, Macrinus."

"I wouldn't know. I've never been there."

The veteran officer's face clouded as he asked, "Have you heard any recent news from Italy?"

Tacitus frowned, wondering how much to reveal. The recent news from the Imperial city had not been good. Emperor Vespasian had died the previous summer, to be succeeded by his elder son, Titus. After the turmoil that had preceded Vespasian's rise to power, his long reign had been one of stability and prosperity, but Titus was something of an enigma. As a young man, he had earned himself a poor reputation but Tacitus had heard from friends in Rome that Titus had the makings of a great man. From all accounts, it seemed that he was doing his utmost to emulate, or even outshine, his father in matters of common sense, kindness and generosity.

But after a promising beginning, marked by the inauguration of the enormous, stone amphitheatre that had finally been completed, things had gone very badly wrong.

"The news I heard wasn't good," Macrinus observed. "Vesuvius, I mean."

Tacitus nodded. Everyone had heard of the disaster.

"Yes, that sounds awful. Two cities destroyed, covered by the lava and ash. It is scarcely believable. Pompeii and Herculaneum both obliterated. It's dreadful to think about."

"Not a good omen for the new Emperor," Macrinus said evenly.

One of Tacitus' friends, a young man named Pliny, had actually witnessed the dreadful events at Pompeii from his home across the bay. He had written to Tacitus, telling him about the event, describing the awful day when Mount Vesuvius had erupted so furiously, burying the city from sight while its deadly, black cloud had turned day into night.

Pompeii had not fully recovered from the effects of an earthquake several years previously. It would never recover now, for it was said to have utterly disappeared under thick layers of rock and ash.

Not only was it a disaster on an almost unimaginable scale, it was, as Macrinus had pointed out, a dreadful portent to mark the new Emperor's reign. Tacitus knew that Agricola was daily expecting some command from the Emperor to halt his march northwards in case the destruction of Pompeii was a warning from the Gods of more disasters to come.

Not wishing to divulge too much to Macrinus, he said, "I suppose that is another reason for us to be cautious this year."

"True enough," Macrinus agreed. "Only a fool would disregard such an obvious warning from the Gods."

Tacitus nodded briefly. He knew that Agricola was desperate to complete the conquest of Britannia but the Governor was too good a Roman, and too good a soldier, to take any risks when the portents were so grim and when his supply lines were so stretched. Whatever his personal inclination, the Governor was determined to do the job properly, even at the cost of his own glory. Only Tacitus knew how much that irked Agricola.

Their conversation was interrupted when the secretaries scuttled out of the Governor's tent, carrying the freshly-signed letters.

"You must excuse me," Tacitus said to Macrinus. "Duty calls."

"Of course. Just remember, if the Governor needs any fighting done this year, my lads are always ready."

"I won't forget," Tacitus promised.

With a wave of his hand, Macrinus wandered off through the camp. Tacitus sighed. It was time to speak to the barbarian visitor.

On cue, the Legates arrived, followed by their escort of soldiers, lictors and freedmen. Shaking off the gloom invoked by thoughts of the disaster of Vesuvius, Tacitus greeted the two men cordially but with the respect due to men of senatorial rank.

"Good morning, Tacitus," smiled Marcus Licinius Spurius, commander of the Ninth *Hispana*.

Spurious was a dark-haired, fresh-faced man in his early thirties, newly appointed as Legate of the Ninth. Having served under Agricola for only a few months, he was still nervous when he was in the Governor's company, as if he were afraid he would never master the skills of soldiering as well as Agricola. Spurius' main problem was that he usually attempted to over-compensate for his lack of self-confidence. This, Tacitus knew, irritated the Governor because Spurius was a competent soldier and a good administrator. Unfortunately, he tended to make poor judgements out of a desire to impress. As he greeted Tacitus, he betrayed his usual fault by speaking just a shade too loudly.

"Another barbarian supplicant?" he asked.

"Yes, Sir. I'm afraid so."

"We should just put him with the others," Spurius grumbled, referring to a group of around half a dozen barbarian chieftains who were being held in the camp under open arrest because the Governor wanted them kept close at hand where he could keep an eye on them.

The other Legate, Silvanus, suggested, "Perhaps we should hear what he has to say first."

Spurius shrugged, indicating that he felt the barbarian's story would mean little to him and that it would be unlikely to alter his opinion. Still, he did not argue with his counterpart.

Gaius Marius Silvanus, who commanded the Second *Adiutrix*, was older than Spurius, more self-confident and more experienced, having spent some years serving in Syria where he had been a military Tribune during the great Jewish Revolt. He was a stern disciplinarian who was feared by his officers and loved by his soldiers. *Adiutrix* was a relatively new Legion, formed only ten years previously by the Emperor Vespasian, but under Silvanus' command it had performed well in the recent conquest of Brigantia.

Tacitus saw some soldiers escorting the barbarian visitor towards them, so he ushered the two Legates into the Governor's tent where they took seats beside Agricola. Once the Legates were settled, the barbarian was led in by two armed legionaries who took up positions behind him as he stood before the Governor. Another man, an interpreter, stood beside him.

The barbarian prince looked absurdly young and understandably anxious at being in the Governor's presence.

Tacitus studied the barbarian, noting his young, earnest face, his travel-worn clothing and the expression of tiredness mixed with apprehension as he presented himself. Despite his youth, though, the gold jewellery he wore confirmed that he was from a noble family.

Agricola began by asking the interpreter, "Do you have his story?"

"Yes, Sir. The language this man speaks is similar to that of the Britons."

"Proceed," Agricola commanded, gesturing for the interpreter to continue.

"Yes, Sir. His name is Domnan mac Eochaid. He is the son of a King in the island of Eriu which lies across the western sea."

"Do you mean Hibernia?"

"Indeed, Sir. That is the place. The natives call it Eriu."

Agricola nodded. He had seen the coast of Hibernia as a distant smudge on the horizon the previous year. A third Legion, the Twentieth *Valeria Victrix*, was pushing up the western side of Britannia, its route running parallel to the eastern advance. They had met some resistance from the local inhabitants, so Agricola had personally overseen the previous year's campaign. Resistance had been swiftly crushed but when he had reached the western coast, Agricola had been intrigued by the distant sight of Hibernia.

Agricola gestured to the interpreter to continue.

Haltingly, stopping several times to seek clarification from the young man named Domnan, the interpreter relayed his story to the Roman commanders. When he was done, Agricola leaned back slightly before looking enquiringly at the Legates.

"Well, Gentlemen? What do you think?"

Spurius, who never failed to judge the Governor incorrectly, answered, "It sounds risky, Sir. We don't have enough ships to transport many men across the sea and we are not sure how large the place is. Besides, we have enough on our hands here."

"From what little I know of Hibernia," Agricola responded thoughtfully, "it is much like the rest of Britannia. It should not be too difficult to conquer if we have willing allies."

Spurius fell into an embarrassed silence.

More in tune with the Governor's thinking, Silvanus offered, "It is not as if we are doing much else at the moment. But it would need to be a quick campaign."

"Yes, it would," Agricola agreed. "But unlike the rest of the Britons, it sounds as if Hibernia is more or less united under one ruler. If that is true, all we need do is defeat this High King, then install Domnan's father as our loyal ally and the entire island will be ours. A small expeditionary force ought to be capable of achieving that."

Tacitus smiled to himself. He could see that his father-in-law was tempted. A new ally meant, in reality, a new subject who would pay taxes to Rome. Adding Hibernia to the province of Britannia would also enhance the Governor's military reputation. With his plans for marching north necessarily delayed, Hibernia offered a chance to achieve a quick victory before any messenger from Rome could arrive with orders for the army to withdraw to the south.

Agricola thought for a moment.

"It would be a sideshow, but I think it might be worth a little risk. If what this fellow says is true, there are three kings who could join us in overthrowing this so-called High King. If the gods smile on us, we could win over the whole place without too much effort."

"It's worth a gamble," Silvanus agreed. "Although I'm not sure how many men we could spare."

"You could each spare one Cohort," Agricola suggested, speaking in such a way that neither man could offer any objection.

"The junior Cohort?" Silvanus countered.

Agricola gave a soft laugh. A Legion's junior Cohort was composed of the least experienced men.

"Very well, the junior Cohort from each Legion. That should spur both sets of men on, to prove that they are better than the men from the other Legion. But we should send some Auxiliaries as well."

He glanced at Tacitus and asked, "Which units are available, Publius?"

"Julius Macrinus has two Cohorts and some cavalry, Sir. I happen to know that he is very keen to see some more action."

"Excellent!" Agricola declared. "Macrinus is a good man. One of the best soldiers we have, and he's always ready for a fight. This sort of thing will suit him well."

Spurius sounded slightly shocked as he asked, "You are not proposing that he commands legionary troops, Sir?"

"Of course not. But he is the sort of man who could advise a less experienced commander."

"So who will command this expedition?" Silvanus asked.

Agricola gave a soft smile as he looked to Tacitus.

"I think it is about time young Publius here gained some experience of command, don't you?"

Tacitus felt himself flush slightly at the attention he was receiving.

"Me, Sir?"

"Why not?"

Tacitus cleared his throat nervously before responding, "Well, Sir, I am honoured, of course, but there are many men in the army who are more qualified than I."

Agricola insisted, "All the more reason for you to get some experience. Don't worry, this will be very straightforward. You will have two thousand men, with Macrinus to advise you. He's as good a soldier as any Roman. Besides, this mission may involve negotiation and diplomacy as much as fighting. If you can persuade the other chieftains to join you, things would be even easier. You know how to impress the barbarians when it comes to negotiations. Between the two of you, you should be able to bring the three sub-kings over to us, dispose of the High King and be back before winter. One quick battle and the place should be ours."

"With respect, Sir," interposed Spurius, "it may not be as simple as that."

Agricola said, "In which case we pull out quickly."

He looked at Tacitus as he added, "Do you hear, Publius? If it does not go as planned, you pull your men out. I don't want to be dragged into a lengthy campaign."

"Yes, Sir. I understand."

"I can assist with the planning if that would help," Silvanus offered.

"Thank you, Gaius. That is an excellent idea. But I want it done quickly."

Agricola turned back to the interpreter. He could see the worried frown on Domnan's face. The young man had no idea what they had been talking about but he brightened, offering profuse thanks when he heard the Governor's decision. Agricola waved him away, ending the audience.

It was all that Tacitus could do to retain a solemn expression but he managed it because he was a Roman. It was his duty to serve the Empire. Anyone who aspired to a position of respect in Rome knew that military experience was essential for a successful political career. Now his father-in-law had handed him an opportunity that few men were ever granted; the chance to bring an entire island within Roman control.

It had seemed a daunting prospect when the Governor had offered him the command but the more Tacitus thought about it, the more he wanted to seize this opportunity. As the Governor had said, it should be simple. The barbarians were always squabbling among themselves and from listening to Domnan's story, Hibernia sounded almost as bad as the rest of Britannia. If three sub-kings were prepared to join with Rome, victory should be little more than a formality.

Spurius and Silvanus said their farewells. When they had gone, Agricola asked Tacitus, "Well, Publius? What do you think?"

"It is a great honour, Sir. I will not let you down."

"I know, but don't do anything foolish. Things can always go wrong. You know what stories barbarians can tell. If the situation should prove more difficult than this Domnan of Leinster has told us, I don't want you losing two thousand men. Hibernia is not our main objective, so don't take any reckless chances. We lose nothing if you come back without a victory."

"Except pride."

"Spoken like a true Roman," Agricola smiled. "But losing a little prestige is better than losing four Cohorts. Besides, if it does not turn out well, we can always blame our allies or the Auxiliaries."

"I understand, Sir. But we gain a great deal if I am successful."

"We do indeed. This refugee prince gives us a perfect excuse to expand the borders of the Empire."

Tacitus nodded in agreement. Domnan's fortuitous arrival had provided him with a chance to achieve greatness. When the Gods presented such an opportunity, only a fool would turn it down.

Chapter X

Despite Calgacus' fears, the sea crossing was mercifully uneventful. The fleet followed the coast southwards for a day, stopping for the night on a remote beach, then setting off at first light the following day. They continued southwards all morning and for the better part of the afternoon, hugging the shallow waters to avoid the maelstrom where the winds and currents from the great western ocean met the more sheltered seas that were bounded by Eriu and Britannia. Late in the afternoon, they turned westwards, battling against the prevailing breeze, towards the dark line of the coast of Eriu.

Calgacus clung grimly to the side of the boat, fighting to keep his stomach settled. The sailors assured him that the sea was calm, a claim that, in Calgacus' opinion, belied the buffeting of the deep swell beneath the keel. He closed his eyes, letting the sea breeze cool his face, gritted his teeth and waited.

He constantly dreaded hearing the warning cry that a Roman galley had been sighted but luck was with them. Apart from a few small fishing boats, the sea was empty.

Late in the evening, the boat eventually tacked its way towards the far shore and the steersman guided them southwards until they reached a long stretch of sandy beach.

"This is it!" Tuathal called.

The steersman headed inshore and the boat ground onto the sand, its prow digging a furrow on the beach while the stern bobbed on the lapping waves. Two sailors lifted a heavy, stone block which was attached to a thick, horsehair rope that had been looped through a large hole drilled through the centre of the stone. They heaved the anchor over the stern to keep the ship in place.

"I will go first!" Tuathal announced as he clambered over the side, jumping down to splash into the shallow water.

"Time to get our feet wet," Runt observed jovially.

Calgacus and Runt joined the other warriors as they climbed over the side of the boat which rocked alarmingly at the movement. Then they dropped knee-deep into the cold water. Calgacus gasped at the shock but ploughed his way towards the beach, following Tuathal who had hurried to reach the shore before anyone else. The Prince trudged from the water onto the dry sand where he fell to his knees then ostentatiously bent down to kiss the earth. The warriors cheered him.

Calgacus dripped his way ashore, shaking his legs and tugging at his sodden trousers which clung clammily to his legs. The damp smell of salt filled his nostrils.

"We are here!" Tuathal declared as Eudaf helped him back to his feet.

"Thank the Gods for that," Calgacus muttered.

He stamped his feet on the sand as if to reassure himself that he was on dry land once more.

Looking around, he frowned, "Now let's hope the rest of them make it."

Eudaf, smiling broadly, said, "Of course they will. It is Tuathal's destiny."

Calgacus gave the young man a disparaging look but said nothing. Instead, he turned to look back out to sea. Another sailing boat was disgorging its cargo of warriors onto the beach. More sails were close but the ragged fleet of curraghs was still a long way from shore. Calgacus could only wonder at the tiredness the men must be feeling, having driven their long paddles into the water all day without any opportunity to rest. Some of the larger curraghs had small sails but most of them relied entirely on the strength of the rowers.

Runt said, "They won't take long to get here."

"Good. The sooner we have everyone ashore, the better."

The few men who had waded to the beach were milling around, waiting for some instructions.

Calgacus, acutely aware that these were warriors of the Caledones rather than his own men, said to Tuathal, "We should post lookouts. Also, send some men to find fresh water and any food they can. And we need wood for fires."

Tuathal nodded, "I will see to it."

He walked away, with Eudaf following closely on his heels.

Runt clicked his tongue approvingly as he watched Tuathal walk along the beach, giving his orders.

"He's got some promise," he said to Calgacus.

84

"Yes," Calgacus admitted. "But he's still full of grand ideas that Coel has drummed into him. I hope the reality doesn't come as too much of a shock for him."

"Cheer up," Runt encouraged. "Things are going well so far."

Shaking his head, Calgacus said, "It's not that."

"Then what is bothering you now?"

"You mean apart from the fact that Coel is holding our families hostage?"

Runt forced a weak smile as he sighed, "I hadn't forgotten that, Cal. But there is nothing we can do about it. We will just have to make the best of this and get back to them as soon as we can."

"I know. But this whole thing doesn't feel right."

"What do you mean?"

Frowning, Calgacus confessed, "It's just that I've spent my whole life fighting against the Romans. That's because they came to conquer us, to take away our land and our freedom. I know it is right to oppose them. And when I've fought against other Pritani, it's because they attacked me first. But now what am I doing? Crossing the sea to conquer some people I don't even know. It feels wrong."

"Don't start getting soft, Cal," Runt warned. "I don't like it any more than you do but this is war. The High King sent men to kill you. We can't afford to forget that."

"Don't worry. I'll do what needs to be done. I just wish there was another way."

Runt suggested, "Maybe Coel should have sent an assassin instead of an army. If all we need to do is kill Elim, one man could do the job more easily than a thousand."

Calgacus shook his head.

"You're right, except that Tuathal needs to be seen to defeat him in order to claim the title of High King. Which means that hundreds will probably die instead of one."

"I take it you have a plan?"

"Not yet. I need to hear what the locals can tell us. Tuathal's cousins are supposed to be meeting us. I hope they get here soon."

The invasion force trickled ashore in small numbers throughout the long, summer evening and the previously deserted foreshore

85

slowly came alive with the sound of chatter, laughter and curses, accompanied by the dull thuds of axes chopping wood.

And still the men came ashore. One by one, the curraghs ploughed their way onto the sand. The men unloaded their supplies before lifting the lightweight boats and carrying them up the beach. Climbing through the long, sharp-edged grass onto the foreshore, they turned the boats over, propping them against paddles which they wedged as uprights to make crude shelters for the night.

A little way inland from the beach, Tuathal's men lit fires to cook an evening meal. Calgacus prowled the camp, checking that sentries had been posted, reluctantly conceding that Tuathal had everything in hand. They had found a stream of fresh water which allowed the warriors to boil up some gruel in the small, iron pots they had brought with them.

Their arrival appeared to have gone completely unnoticed because the countryside remained deserted. Not a single person seemed to have witnessed the arrival of the invasion force and Calgacus could not help voicing his concerns over the absence of the expected reception.

Tuathal, his face alive with delight, assured him, "My cousins will be here soon."

"I hope so," Calgacus replied.

He remained anxious until, towards evening, a sentry called out a warning of chariots approaching from the west. They all turned to see two of the speedy vehicles cresting a low rise, their outline clear against the orange of the setting sun. Calgacus, Runt, Tuathal and Eudaf went to meet them.

The chariots raced down the gentle slope, each one pulled by two war ponies. As they drew near, the driver of the lead vehicle jumped up from the open front of the platform, vaulted onto the long, wooden pole and ran nimbly along the shaft between the two ponies. With the chariot still racing at top speed, he performed a little dance before turning back to resume his place on the platform and seize the reins once more.

"He's good," Runt observed.

"He's showing off," retorted Calgacus, although he could not help but admire the driver's skill and bravery. It took a confident man to balance on a wooden pole that was bouncing and swaying in time to the movements of the ponies who were harnessed to it.

In a rumble of iron-rimmed wheels, the thudding of hoofs and a jingle of decorated harness, the chariots wheeled, turning so that they faced away from Tuathal's army. The drivers relaxed, looping their reins over the corner posts while the two passengers stepped down from the riding platforms.

Calgacus groaned when he saw the first man.

"Another bloody druid," he muttered sourly.

"He's a bit young for a druid," Runt remarked.

Calgacus looked again. The man advancing to greet them wore a long, grey robe that fell to just above his booted feet. Around his waist was a broad belt from which hung several small, leather pouches. His heavy, hooded cloak was fastened by a bronze brooch. Even in the fading light, Calgacus could see that his attire was unmistakeably that of a druid. Yet he also realised that Runt was correct; the man was young, in his early twenties at most, with a clean-shaven face and a mop of unruly hair. If he was a druid as Calgacus suspected, he must have been a novice because his head was not shaved at all.

The youthful druid's companion was taller, broader and dressed as a warrior, with a leather, sleeveless jerkin and carrying a sword at his left hip. His arms were bare, revealing massive biceps and corded muscles, all of which were covered in dark tattoos.

Tuathal stepped forwards, one hand raised, his palm towards the strangers.

"Welcome to our camp," he announced formally. "I am Tuathal, son of Fiacha Finnolach."

The young druid beamed happily.

"We have been expecting you," he said in a light, cheerful voice. "I am Findmall. This is my brother, Fiacha Cassan. Our mother was sister to your father."

Tuathal immediately stepped close to embrace the two men.

"Welcome, Cousins," he said.

Smiling broadly, he introduced the others.

Calgacus asked the newcomers, "Have you brought any more men with you? We were expecting an army to join us."

The question came out rather more brusquely than he had intended and he saw Tuathal frown slightly at the rude greeting but if Findmall was offended, he did not show it.

Waving an arm back towards the west, he declared, "We have more than six hundred men, all of them ready and willing to fight against Elim mac Conrach, the Usurper. They will be here very soon."

"Six hundred?" Calgacus complained. "Is that all?"

"More will join us as we go," Findmall assured him airily.

Calgacus was about to vent his frustration but Tuathal interrupted him by calmly saying, "This is a good start. Our army has doubled in size at a single stroke."

Smiling at the two men of Eriu, he added, "They are all welcome."

Calgacus remained tense, watching until the dark mass of Findmall's army appeared at the top of the distant ridge. The new arrivals cheered loudly then swarmed down the slope towards Tuathal's camp.

Calgacus studied them nervously, fearing a trap. He glanced back to make sure that Tuathal's warriors were alert but he was acutely aware that he and his companions were exposed in the open.

"You are not a very trusting man, are you?" a voice asked in his ear.

Startled, Calgacus turned to see that Fiacha Cassan, the warrior, was standing close beside him. Calgacus had not heard him approach.

"It pays to be cautious," he responded defensively.

"You are expecting treachery," Fiacha Cassan observed in an amused voice.

"I have been tricked before by people who claimed to be my friend."

"More fool you, then," was Fiacha Cassan's mocking reply.

Tuathal interrupted, "Come, Cousins, show me your army. Let me speak to the men so that I can thank them for coming."

Calgacus was about to advise against this when Fiacha Cassan laughed aloud.

"You really are a very suspicious old man, aren't you?" he chuckled.

Calgacus gave him a dark look. Still wary, he followed Tuathal while Findmall led the young man into the heart of his army. Calgacus was mindful that his own family were virtual hostages. If anything happened to Tuathal, they might suffer at Coel's hands, so he stayed close to the young prince, watching for any signs of betrayal. Tuathal, though, seemed oblivious to any possibility of danger. His expression was innocent and trusting as he greeted the warriors cheerfully, speaking to them, asking questions, telling them they were the best of men and that soon they would defeat the Usurper.

The men of Eriu cheered him, proclaiming him High King and swearing that they would present him with Elim's head. Tuathal was obviously delighted, while Eudaf's always happy face bore an almost idiotic grin of sheer pleasure.

"Are you satisfied, old man?" Fiacha Cassan asked Calgacus.

"They seem like good lads," Calgacus agreed.

"The finest fighting men in the world," Fiacha Cassan declared proudly.

Privately, Calgacus thought that the men of the newly arrived army were much like any other warriors. They were proud, boastful, eager to show off their prowess and even more eager for plunder. Long-haired, unwashed and loud, they carried the usual assortment of spears and swords. In one area, though, they could be a great help.

"At least you have horses," Calgacus conceded.

"The finest in the world," Fiacha Cassan agreed.

Two hundred of the men were mounted on small, sturdy horses, while around twenty of the chieftains and wealthier warriors rode in ornate chariots. Tuathal now had his cavalry.

The men of Eriu set about making their own fires. Some of them swapped food and drink with Tuathal's Caledones. They also exchanged stories, jokes and boasts.

Calgacus, unable to shake off his dark mood, worried that the meetings might result in squabbles or fights, but Tuathal delivered a short speech, urging the warriors of both camps to keep the peace as they were with friends who shared a common goal. To Calgacus' ears, the young man's words sounded naive and impossibly optimistic but the men listened intently before settling down happily alongside their new allies.

"The lad has a way about him," Runt observed.

As the sky turned dark and the first stars began to appear, men gathered round their fires. By the time it was fully dark, nearly twelve hundred armed men were camped on this lonely shore.

Tuathal's quest to become High King was under way.

Chapter XI

The fire crackled, sending sparks wafting up into the night air like darting fireflies. Six men sat round the flames; Calgacus with Runt, Tuathal with Eudaf, who was still smiling and grinning amiably, and Findmall with his brother, Fiacha Cassan, who watched everyone with a constant mocking smile playing on his lips.

"We are glad you have come at last," Findmall told them. "The land has been beset by evils these past twenty years. Famine and plague have tormented the people of Eriu and it is all because Elim the Usurper is High King."

"Things will change soon," Tuathal assured the young druid gravely.

Calgacus held up his knife which had a piece of toasted bread he had been holding to the fire.

"There doesn't seem to be much sign of famine," he pointed out. "Your warriors all have heavy packs."

Findmall gave him a happy grin as he responded, "You are not a man for stories, then?"

"Not really," Calgacus admitted.

"That is a great pity," Findmall sighed. "Stories are what people believe. It is well known that famine and plague are rife when a bad King rules. Elim is a bad King, therefore there must be famine. Don't you see?"

"You'll have a hard job convincing people of that if they have plenty of food," Calgacus countered.

"Not at all. Many people barely have enough to eat. And if they do, then I tell them that the famine is in the next village, or perhaps a bit further away."

He shot Calgacus a searching look as he added, "Anyway, you have your own stories. I have heard them. They say you have a magic sword."

"So they say," Calgacus grunted unenthusiastically.

Findmall laughed but Fiacha Cassan's eyes sparked with interest.

"May I see this magic sword?" the warrior asked.

Calgacus hesitated, then lifted his sword from the ground where he had laid it beside him. The glittering scabbard reflected the light of the fire, sending shimmering streaks of orange and dull red along the length of the polished, metal casing.

Fiacha Cassan accepted it almost reverently. He admired the gleaming scabbard, then gripped the long hilt, clasping his fingers reverently around the tightly bound leather grip. Slowly, he drew the long blade free.

"Mind you don't cut yourself," Calgacus muttered.

Fiacha Cassan ignored the jibe. He held the massive blade upright, placing his left palm flat against the metal. With a graceful, fluid move, he rose to his feet, stepped a few paces from the fire and began to test the weight of the sword. He swung it from left to right, then back. Faster and faster his arm moved, sending the blade slashing through the air in intricate patterns. He gripped the hilt in two hands, then in one, then switched from right to left and back again, tossing the sword as if its weight were nothing.

The blade sang through the night air in a dazzling, constantly moving display of speed and grace. Fiacha Cassan whirled, dancing lightly on the balls of his feet, cutting and slashing at imaginary foes. Then he threw the sword high, sending it cartwheeling end over end. It rose high, seeming to hang in the dark sky for an instant before tumbling back down. As it fell, he stepped back before flashing his arm out to grab the long, leather-bound grip. For a moment he stood perfectly still. Then, without a word, he returned to the fire, sheathed the sword and handed it back to Calgacus.

Calgacus was impressed. He knew that Runt could perform such tricks with his short swords but he had never seen anyone do what Fiacha Cassan had just done so effortlessly with a massive longsword.

He took the blade from Fiacha Cassan with a nod. The warrior was smiling, evidently pleased with himself.

Proudly, Findmall declared, "My brother is the greatest warrior in the land."

"That was very impressive," Calgacus agreed.

"Could you do the same?" Fiacha Cassan asked, his eyes flashing a challenge.

"No," Calgacus confessed. "But then, I use my sword for killing, not for showing off."

Fiacha Cassan laughed, although his humour sounded a little forced.

"Well said, old man. Perhaps soon, you and I will fight Elim mac Conrach. Then you can show me how you use your sword. It is a fine blade. I felt its magic."

Calgacus told him, "The magic is not in the sword. It is in the skill of the person who wields it."

"I know that," Fiacha Cassan agreed amiably. "I felt it."

Runt gave a soft chuckle but Calgacus did not respond to the boast. Humility was not a trait that most warriors would betray and Fiacha Cassan was clearly no exception. Where he differed from most others Calgacus had met, was that he obviously possessed the skill to match his boasts.

Findmall asked, "How can we lose? We have the greatest warrior, the greatest War Leader and we have our own High King."

"We can lose if we are overconfident," Calgacus warned.

"We can lose if we are too timid," Fiacha Cassan countered.

Calgacus nodded, "I agree. But I would like to know what we are up against. It is not wise to rush against an enemy without knowing his strengths."

Turning to Findmall, he said, "We have around twelve hundred men. How many can Elim mac Conrach command?"

Findmall put a hand to his mouth, giving a slight cough, as if he had hoped that he would not be asked this question.

"Well," he recounted, "he can easily call on two or three thousand. Given time, he can get six or seven thousand and if the other kings come to help him, then we might be faced by as many as twenty thousand."

Runt gave a sardonic laugh as he mockingly asked, "Is that all? How can we lose?"

Calgacus noticed that Tuathal's face was even more serious than usual. Resisting the temptation to mention his earlier warnings, he said, "Then we need to defeat Elim before he has time to gather his full force. We need to isolate him."

Findmall commented, "If I may say so, you do not sound confident."

"That's because, even at best, we will be outnumbered at least two to one unless we can find a way to make Elim divide his forces. Those are not good odds."

"You are the great War Leader," Findmall reminded him. "We rely on you to devise a stratagem."

Calgacus gave a derisory snort to show what he thought of that. Then he said, "I want to win this war as much as any of you. But there are other considerations apart from Elim's army. What can you tell me about his witch woman?"

Findmall scratched his chin thoughtfully.

"To mention her name would be dangerous," he informed them. "It might draw her attention to us."

"She really has such power?" Calgacus asked.

He recalled Emmelia's assurances about the limitations of magic, but the threat of sorcery evoked a secret, primal fear in spite of what his rational mind told him.

"Oh, yes," Findmall confirmed. "Her powers are infamous. She can turn men into beasts. She can control the weather and she can bend anyone to her will."

Calgacus felt the threat of dark magic claw at his belly but he had learned long ago that what people believed was not always the truth. Like his niece, Emmelia, he had learned from the old hermit, Myrddin, to question such beliefs.

"You have seen her do these things?" he asked.

"Not personally," Findmall conceded. "But I have heard about her from others."

"Then we should stick to facts, not stories," Calgacus insisted firmly.

"You should not dismiss such stories," Findmall protested. "The witch's power is well known."

"Perhaps it is," Calgacus replied, "but I am sure we have all heard tales of magic. I have often listened to bards sing of cauldrons that will not cook food for cowards, or magical rings that give protection against illness, or magical cloaks that conceal a man from the eyes of his enemies, but I am old enough and cynical enough to say that I have never seen such a thing for myself."

After a deliberate pause, he indicated his own sword and added, "I have even heard people sing of magical swords and I know those tales are false."

Findmall was disappointed by Calgacus' reaction.

"But what are facts?" he asked. "The truth depends on who sees it."

Calgacus had heard such arguments before. Findmall's words reminded him of old Maddoc, a long-dead druid who had once told him that there are many truths. He could no longer restrain his curiosity.

"Are you a druid?" he demanded.

The smile returned to Findmall's face as he replied, "Ah, the answer to that would be both yes and no."

"He's a druid, all right," murmured Runt to nobody in particular.

Calgacus protested, "That is no answer at all."

Findmall shrugged as he explained, "Things are not the same here as in your land. We call ourselves druids but we are not like the old greybeards you know. Some of them came here after their home was destroyed by the Romans. They were strange men, claiming they could talk to the Gods and demanding sacrifices of human blood."

"That sounds like them, right enough," Runt muttered darkly.

Findmall continued, "They did not last long. We know that druids have no more luck than any man in persuading the Gods to do anything. We are more like teachers, healers, guides and keepers of legends. For example, I can recite the list of Tuathal's ancestors going back forty generations."

"Another time, perhaps," Calgacus put in bluntly. "Is there anything else you can do that might be useful to us?"

"I can pull a tooth if need be," Findmall told him happily.

Everyone else laughed but Calgacus frowned. He did not enjoy being the butt of other people's jokes and he felt more out of place than ever when confronted by Findmall's constant levity. Fighting to keep his impatience under control, he rubbed his fingers against his forehead.

"Just tell me about this witch," he said sharply.

"Well, if you are sure I can't pull any of your teeth, I suppose I could tell you a story," Findmall smiled.

"As long as you keep it short and to the point."

"That is an unfair restriction to place on any teller of tales," Findmall complained, "but I will do my best, seeing as you are not a man who enjoys stories."

He straightened his shoulders, took a deep breath, and began.

"There is a story from long ago," he proclaimed, lapsing into a lilting, storyteller's dramatic voice. "It is a tale from many generations in the past, the tale of a Princess who lived in a land

94

far way to the south, where the sun burns hot all year round. It was a land where they build great burial mounds of stone, as tall as mountains.

"Some say this Princess was banished for plotting against her father; others say there was a war; still others say her father was assassinated. Whatever happened, the Princess was forced to flee from her home in fear for her life. Taking her sons and a band of loyal followers, she travelled for many years, sailing west along the coast of the hot lands, then overland to the north. Years and years the journey took her, but she never found a place that pleased her, never found a home that could replace what she had lost.

"She knew she could never return home, so she took to the sea once more, sailing north until she landed on the blessed island of Eriu. Here she decided to stay, although others were here before her. Still, her people are hardy and they refused to leave, fighting many battles in their quest to find a permanent home. Her descendants are still here."

Findmall paused for a brief instant. Then, as if he was plucking up the courage to leap into a fast-flowing river, he continued softly, "The Princess was named Scota, and her people call themselves the Scotti. They are fierce warriors, wanderers who move from place to place, never welcomed but refusing to leave Eriu until they find a proper home."

Findmall paused again. Everyone waited for him to continue but he closed his eyes as if he had come to the end of his tale.

Eventually, Calgacus prompted, "What has this to do with the sorceress?"

Reluctantly, Findmall informed him, "The Scotti now serve Elim, the High King. They are deadly in war."

After another long pause, he went on, "They are ruled by a Queen, a woman who is said to be the re-incarnation of the original Princess. She shares the name of her ancient ancestor. She is a Queen who commands dark powers."

"Elim's witch?"

"Aye, Elim's witch."

"What do you think?" Runt asked as he and Calgacus wrapped themselves in their cloaks in the shelter of a grass-topped sand dune.

"I think the whole thing is mad," Calgacus replied with a disheartened grunt. "I can't see any way we can win this war. I don't know the land, I don't know my enemy and I sure as damn don't know my allies."

Runt grinned, "You'll think of something. You always do."

Calgacus gave another disparaging snort.

"Let me sleep on it," he sighed. "We can decide what to do in the morning."

He lay down, wrapping his cloak tightly around his body. Disdaining the warmth of the fires, he and Runt had returned to the upper reaches of the beach. Other men had done the same, seeking out sheltered spots where they could lie on the soft sand in preference to the hard earth of the foreshore. After a few moments of blundering around in the darkness, the two friends found a narrow sand gully where they could lie in relative comfort, shielded from the sea breeze by high, grass-topped dunes.

Calgacus lay awake for a long time, gazing up at the stars and listening to the gentle lapping of the waves against the shore. No matter how often he told himself this mission was necessary, his doubts persisted, preventing him from finding sleep.

Questions chased one another through his mind. How could they overcome an army of thousands with the few men that they had? Was Elim's witch nothing more than a skilled trickster like Emmelia? Was Elim a bad King? Above all, was Calgacus justified in leading this war? He was tormented by the thought that he was playing the part of an invader.

As he slowly drifted into dreams, vivid images flashed across his mind. He saw Beatha and Fallar imprisoned in Coel's stone tower, waiting for him to rescue them. Then Emmelia was there, waving her hands in a battle of magic against the druid, Broichan. The druid vanished but Emmelia transformed into another woman, an indistinct shadow against a dark background. She was laughing at him. He could hear no words but he knew that it was Elim's witch. She was taunting him, telling him that she was searching for him, that she would use her magic to defeat him.

Calgacus tried to escape but he was helpless, unable to move. Then he saw the sorceress standing tall above him, a dagger in her hand, the sharp blade glinting in the cold starlight.

He could do nothing to defend himself, could not even cry out. Her magic had transfixed him, frozen him where he lay. He watched in petrified horror as she raised the blade, preparing to strike.

He woke with a sudden start, crying out as a terrifying sensation of falling assailed him. He felt that he had tumbled from a high perch and was plummeting to the ground which lay far below him. The sensation ended with a lurch almost as soon as it had begun. The sand, soft but firm, was beneath him, just as it should be.

But the memory of the dream was still strong. Fear gripped him, making him believe that Elim's witch was still standing there in the darkness with her deadly knife poised to strike. Instinctively, he rolled onto his side, trying to move away. Even as he did so, he felt a burning sensation across the back of his left arm, a hot slash that flashed just below his shoulder.

He cried out as the fiery pain lanced through him. Still confused, still caught between his dreams and the waking reality, he rolled again, trying to escape whatever it was that had burned him. He dreaded looking round to see Elim's witch pursuing him, knife in hand, so he rolled away as quickly as he could in case she had leaped from his dream into the waking world.

He tasted sand. It burned his eyes, forcing him to close them. Where was he? He could not think.

Then he heard Runt shouting a challenge, followed by the sound of feet thumping away across the sand. Long grass rustled as someone scrambled frantically through the dunes.

"Cal! Are you all right?"

He could hear Runt struggling towards him, his feet sinking into the soft sand.

Calgacus wiped sand from his face and spat to clear the hard grains from his mouth. "What happened?" he asked, although the answer was already forming in his mind.

"Someone attacked you. He had a knife."

Runt's voice told of his fear.

"By Toutatis, you were lucky. You could be dead."

Calgacus' mind snapped into focus with cold clarity.

"Get after him!"

He pushed himself up, feeling the pain in his arm. It was accompanied by the warm, sticky sensation of blood. He ignored it.

"Where's my sword?" he demanded as he scrabbled in the darkness.

"Here!"

Runt scooped up the long blade and tossed it to him. By the time Calgacus had caught it, Runt was already running after the assassin.

Calgacus followed, his feet sliding and slipping on the treacherous sand as he tried to run. All around, men were waking up, demanding to know what was happening. Calgacus did not answer. He hauled himself to the top of a dune and leaped onto the firm grass beyond.

With solid ground beneath his feet he broke into a run, holding his scabbarded sword in his right hand while his left arm continued to throb in protest.

Runt was ahead of him, arms pumping as he charged into the camp but the night was filled with the light of hundreds of small fires, dazzlingly bright after the darkness of the beach. Runt stopped, blinking, peering blindly into the night.

A shout from their left brought more cries of alarm. Runt dashed off in that direction with Calgacus pounding after him.

"Assassin!"

The cry went up from ahead. It was quickly echoed as more and more men leaped to their feet, picking up their weapons as they shrugged away sleep.

Calgacus dodged round several fires, blundering into men who were milling around helplessly, not knowing what was going on. Cursing and pushing, he shoved his way after Runt.

"He went that way!" a voice shouted.

It was Eudaf, excited, breathless and more than a little shaken.

Calgacus skidded to a halt beside the young man. Runt was there, bending over, hands on his knees as he tried to gulp air into his lungs.

Tuathal was on his feet, sword in hand, his head twisting this way and that as he sought out the source of the uproar.

"What happened?" he demanded.

Excitedly, Eudaf blurted, "A man with a knife. He came running past."

He held up his left arm, revealing a streaming wound on his forearm.

"The bastard slashed me when I tried to stop him."

Calgacus stared into the night. The camp was in turmoil. He felt his side ache with the effort of running and his arm was wet with blood.

"Whoever it was, he is well hidden now," he muttered angrily. "It could be anyone."

Runt, still gasping for breath, panted, "Sorry, Cal. I couldn't catch him. I'm not as fast as I used to be."

"You were never that fast," Calgacus told him.

"I didn't see you overtaking me," Runt retorted.

He tried to laugh but it sounded more like a wheeze. Then his face grew serious and he gasped, "You're hurt!"

Tuathal exclaimed, "By the Gods! You've been cut."

"It's just a flesh wound," Calgacus assured them. "Lucky for me, I woke up just in time."

Then he looked Tuathal in the eye and said, "But you know what this means."

Tuathal nodded. The look on his face was one of horror and disbelief as he said, "Elim's assassins are in our camp."

Chapter XII

Nobody had managed to get a good look at the man with the knife. Calgacus had barely seen him at all, only glimpsing a shadowy figure that might have been part of his dream, and none of the others could agree on what they had seen.

Runt admitted, "I didn't get a good look at him. All I can say is that he seemed to be of average build."

Eudaf shook his head.

"I thought he was tall and thin," he ventured. "Taller than me, anyway."

The only thing they agreed on was that the assassin had been wearing a hooded cloak, which, as Runt wryly pointed out, narrowed the suspects down to around twelve hundred.

"We must find this killer," Tuathal declared.

The attack had clearly shocked him. He paced up and down, frustrated that the assassin had vanished.

"How?" Calgacus asked.

He sat on a tussock of grass, wincing while Findmall stitched his wound with a curved needle.

Tuathal stopped pacing long enough to give a helpless shrug.

"I don't know," he admitted.

Calgacus breathed in sharply as the needle finished another stitch.

Findmall told him, "It's not too bad. Just a flesh wound, as you said. You were very lucky. Still, I will put a poultice on it to prevent it turning bad."

Calgacus nodded gratefully. Even seemingly trivial injuries could cause death if evil spirits entered the wound. But his own cut had been relatively shallow and, while it had bled freely, Findmall had stitched it up quickly enough once he had wiped away the blood and washed out the tiny grains of sand.

Eudaf's wound had been more serious, a deep gash across the top of his forearm that bled profusely. Findmall had washed it and stitched it, then smeared it with honey before bandaging Eudaf's arm with some cloth torn from Calgacus' shirt. The shirt was ruined anyway, the left arm stained dark with Calgacus' blood. His cloak was in better condition although there was a long tear in it where the dagger had caught him. Runt was busy repairing the hole while Findmall sewed Calgacus' wound.

Findmall placed a small poultice on Calgacus' upper arm, then tied another strip of cloth to hold it in place.

"That will do you," he declared.

Calgacus stood, awkwardly slipping on his leather jerkin.

"Thank you," he said to Findmall.

"It's my pleasure," the young druid replied. "Are you sure your teeth are all in working order? I could easily pull one if you like."

"My teeth are fine. And we have more important things to talk about."

Tuathal agreed. Resuming his pacing, he frowned, "If there is an assassin in the camp, he will surely try again."

Calgacus nodded, "He may lie low for a while but I think you are right. I suppose he will probably go after you or me. Neither of us should go anywhere alone. Especially you."

"I will watch over Tuathal," Eudaf volunteered.

"Good. But choose another four men you can trust. Make sure that at least two of them are awake and nearby at all times. If Tuathal dies, this whole expedition becomes pointless."

Eudaf nodded, "It will be as you say."

Speaking in a matter-of-fact tone, as if the subject of his death was of no great concern, Tuathal said, "I mean no disrespect, Calgacus, but I am puzzled as to why the killer did not try to come after me first. As you say, if he kills me, there is no point in the rest of you being here."

Calgacus shrugged, "Perhaps because I was an easier target. I was on the beach, away from the fires. You were in the middle of the camp."

"And I was awake," added Eudaf, radiating pride that his presence had probably saved Tuathal.

"So if we cannot find who it was, what do we do now?" Tuathal asked.

"Whatever we do, we must do it quickly," advised Calgacus. "Unless the assassin is one of the men we brought over the sea with us, it means that Elim has at least one spy in our camp. Do you know what that means?"

Tuathal nodded grimly.

101

"It means that Elim knows we are here."

Calgacus nodded approvingly. Tuathal may have been young but he was clearly able to grasp things quickly.

Glancing at Findmall, he said, "This means the Usurper has spies among your men."

"I cannot believe that," Findmall protested.

Tuathal waved the matter aside.

"It does not matter."

Turning to Calgacus, he asked, "If Elim knows we are here, how can we surprise him?"

Calgacus was pleased at Tuathal's determination not to be diverted from the important issue.

He answered, "We must do something to draw him out. Get him to come after us so that we can fight him in a place of our choosing. If we can do something to goad him, he may come after us with a small force, before he has had time to gather a large army."

"That sounds sensible. But how do we do that?"

Recalling the methods the Romans had used for years, Calgacus explained, "The best tactic is to pillage his lands. Destroy farms, attack villages. Provoke him by showing that he cannot keep his own people safe."

"Then that is what we shall do," Tuathal decided.

"Wait," Calgacus cautioned. "There is one problem with that plan. The Romans do this because they care nothing for the people whose farms and homes are destroyed. But those who will suffer are the very people who will be your subjects once you are High King."

Tuathal frowned, "They are Elim's subjects now but I see what you mean."

He considered the problem briefly, then continued, "I will give them a choice. If they join us, they can live. If they refuse, they will suffer the consequences."

Speaking firmly, Calgacus responded, "A warrior should not murder innocent people who cannot fight back."

Tuathal gave Calgacus a defiant stare as he replied, "There are times when a King must be ruthless. My grandfather taught me that."

"Your grandfather is not here," Calgacus told him. "You must be your own man. Remember, once you make an enemy, they are your enemy for life."

"A King always has enemies," Tuathal countered sharply. "My grandfather taught me that, too. We will do as I have said. Those who do not join us will be treated as enemies. That is my decision. So, we must act quickly. We shall march towards Tara and draw Elim out by plundering his lands."

Findmall interrupted, "There is something else we could do."

He paused, waiting for Tuathal's nod of encouragement before going on, "We should capture Emain Macha."

Frowning, Calgacus asked, "Who, or what, is Emain Macha?"

Findmall explained, "Emain Macha is the traditional home of the kings of Ulster. Elim's son, Fergus, governs this part of Eriu from there. If we seize Emain Macha and kill Elim's son, the Usurper will come after us as if all the demons of the spirit world were chasing him."

"You might have mentioned this before now," Calgacus said reprovingly.

"You didn't ask," Findmall replied airily.

Calgacus rolled his eyes in exasperation.

"I am asking now. How far is this place?"

"For an army on foot, no more than five days' march, Perhaps four if we set a quick pace."

"And how many men does Elim's son have there?"

Findmall scratched his head as he shrugged, "Not more than a dozen in his household, I think. Although he will be able to call on many more from the surrounding countryside."

Calgacus said, "But if Elim knows we are here, he may be there with his entire army."

"Which means we can beat him all the sooner," Fiacha Cassan asserted.

"No," Calgacus corrected. "It means we may have to fight him before we are ready."

"We are ready now," declared Fiacha Cassan.

"No, we are not," Calgacus stated forcefully, becoming annoyed at Fiacha Cassan's boastful overconfidence. "If we simply turn up hoping to win, we may well lose. We need to plan our battle to make sure that we win."

Tuathal insisted, "Whatever Elim is doing, we cannot sit here. We must do something before he makes his move. We will march to Emain Macha."

Calgacus nodded, "I want to go ahead, to check out the lie of the land."

He turned to Findmall and asked, "May I use your chariot?"

It had been many years since Calgacus had ridden in a chariot. He stood on the platform, his legs slightly apart, his left hand gripping the upper, curved rim of one of the side struts. Findmall stood on his right, mirroring Calgacus' pose, while the driver, a small, dark-haired man with a mouth full of yellowing teeth, stood in front of them, urging the ponies on. Like most expert chariot drivers, he was slightly built, with thin, although deceptively strong, limbs. He also possessed the driver's powers of intense concentration, with his eyes constantly scanning the ground ahead, flicking the reins, calling encouragement to his ponies in a series of strange clicks and unintelligible shouts.

Urged on by the driver's skill, the chariot hurtled across the ground at a dizzying speed. The wind whipped through Calgacus' long hair, stinging his eyes and fluttering his cloak behind him. Despite his concerns over what lay ahead, he could not help but enjoy the sensation. This was how his own people had traditionally gone to war. He knew that chariots were outdated in warfare but the thrill of charging across the land was an experience that brought back many good memories.

When Calgacus was a boy, his brother, Togodumnus, the King of the Catuvellauni, had often allowed Calgacus to ride alongside him when he practised the art of war, hurling spears from a moving chariot, then dismounting when the driver pulled the ponies to a bone-jarring halt, before leaping back aboard at the very moment that the driver flicked the chariot into motion again.

Calgacus glanced to his left, to where a second chariot bore Runt and Fiacha Cassan. Runt, too, was smiling happily. He gave Calgacus a wave as if to say that he had not had such fun for a long time.

Beyond Runt were more chariots and behind them a hundred mounted warriors, led by Tuathal who had decided that he, too, wished to see Emain Macha for himself. Calgacus had tried to dissuade him, telling him that he should remain with the bulk of the army but Tuathal had been adamant. He had issued orders for the footmen to follow as quickly as they could, leaving half of the cavalry with them.

"If Elim has spies in our war host," he had said, "it would be better for me to outpace them."

"Unless the spy is one of the mounted warriors," Calgacus had pointed out.

"Ah, but there are proportionally fewer of them, so there is a greater chance that the assassin will be left behind."

Calgacus could not argue with the young man's logic, so now they were racing inland, hoping to reach Emain Macha before Elim mac Conrach could hear word of their approach.

The chariots led the way, hurtling across the landscape, their four-spoked, iron-rimmed wheels leaving twin trails in the grass behind them.

The countryside in this part of Eriu was good for chariots, with low, rolling hills, gentle slopes and long, wide valleys. They could travel quickly over such terrain but rougher going did not slow them unduly. The chariot bounced a little more when they crossed uneven ground but the bed of complex rope webbing that supported the central section of their platforms absorbed most of the shocks, allowing the vehicles to maintain a fast pace without causing the passengers too much discomfort.

Their route meandered as the drivers avoided low areas of marshy, boggy ground and skirted round woodlands but still they made excellent time. While the main force of their army might take four days to reach Emain Macha, this fast-moving advance guard would be there before nightfall.

Findmall chatted incessantly as they rode. Calgacus had decided to ride with him rather than his bellicose brother because he thought that Findmall might provide better company and more useful information. Findmall, though, was rather vague about Emain Macha and what it might contain. All that Calgacus could glean was that Fergus, the nominal sub-King of Ulster, had a home within the ramparts of the fort but that most of his people lived in a village that lay outside the walls.

Calgacus knew that they must take this fort. It lay between them and Tara so to by-pass it would leave an enemy force behind them. However small that force might be, it had the potential to cause problems for them. Besides which, Findmall's suggestion that killing Fergus would draw Elim to battle was probably a wise one. Calgacus recognised the strategic advantage that would give, but once again a part of him felt less than comfortable that another stranger must die for the sake of Tuathal's ambitions. He pushed those concerns aside because he grudgingly conceded that to kill Elim while leaving his son alive would only prolong the war, turning it into a blood feud.

He hated himself for going along with the plan because he knew it was precisely what old Coel would have done. Yet the fact remained that, if Tuathal wanted a quick end to this campaign, Fergus must die.

Calgacus was unable to dwell on these dark thoughts because Findmall continued to talk throughout the long journey. It was evident that the young druid had a love for the land they were passing through. He extolled the virtues of the fertile soil, the health and vitality of the cattle, the honesty and hard work of the people.

"All of Eriu is wonderful," Findmall pronounced proudly, "but Ulster is by far the greatest of the kingdoms."

Calgacus was slightly puzzled by the druid's description of the various kingdoms as settled regions, each with their own King. Calgacus belonged to a world where a tribe inhabited a certain part of the land but the territory they controlled depended very much on the strength of the chieftain and his war band. Borders constantly fluctuated and although towns, rivers, forests and mountains usually had names, most territories were simply referred to as belonging to a particular people. Yet here in Eriu, if Findmall was to be believed, the kingdoms appeared to be more or less fixed and the people belonged to the land; the very opposite of what Calgacus was accustomed to.

Findmall's other stories concerned the various Gods. He regaled Calgacus with tales of the Dagda, chief among the Gods, of the Morrigan and her sister Macha, of Lugh, Giobniu and Angus Og. Like the Gods that Calgacus was familiar with, each of these deities had their own particular attributes but, unlike the Gods of the Pritani, the Gods that Findmall spoke of behaved more or less like ordinary, if rather unruly, people.

Findmall recounted several stories of how the various Gods had visited the human realm at one time or another, playing tricks on people or bestowing unlikely favours. The tales were barely believable, yet Findmall told each one with a conviction that suggested he had personally witnessed each adventure.

"Do your own Gods not behave like this?" Findmall asked when Calgacus expressed some incredulity at one particularly outlandish tale about a God of Healing murdering his son out of jealousy at the younger God's greater skill.

"No, they do not," he admitted.

He could not find the words to explain it properly but his Gods simply *were;* they did not *do* anything except inflict mortals with hardship or bounty depending on their nature or, sometimes, on a whim.

He explained, "The Gods control the sky, the winds, the weather and the rivers. In our land, every rock or tree has its own spirit."

"Of course they do," Findmall agreed. "It is the same here."

"Yes, but our Gods have nothing to do with ordinary mortals. The Gods might send rain to make the crops grow or they might send storms, but they never arrive at a chieftain's door asking for shelter for the night."

"What a strange place your land must be," Findmall observed with a bemused shake of his head.

Calgacus wondered whether the druid was mocking him. It was hard to tell.

Towards evening, Findmall ceased his story-telling and announced that they were drawing near to Emain Macha. Calgacus called a halt.

"We don't want to give ourselves away," he warned. "Only a few of us should go on. The rest can stay here until we get back."

A few moments later, the two chariots bearing Calgacus, Findmall, Runt and Fiacha Cassan continued the journey, accompanied by Tuathal and Eudaf on horseback. They climbed a long, low hill, stopping just below the crest to dismount. The chariot drivers turned the vehicles so that they were ready to race away in case of danger while the six men walked to the top of the hill.

Calgacus stopped, taking in the view. Beyond the summit lay a wide, green valley dominated by a large, circular hillfort.

"Emain Macha," Findmall announced with a theatrical wave of his hand. "Built by the Goddess Macha herself. Home to warlords and kings. In times past it was the seat of the famous Conchobar mac Nessa. Once, it was the home of the mighty Cu Chulainn himself. Now it is held by Fergus mac Elim, a much lesser man than those great heroes."

Calgacus frowned. Findmall had warned him that Emain Macha housed only a chieftain's household but he had still expected to see a reasonably large settlement enclosed within the circumference of the ramparts. Instead, there seemed to be very little sign of life. The circular fort was at least three hundred paces in diameter, large enough to house a score or more roundhouses, but he could see the tops of only two or three thatched roofs. Instead of the usual tightly packed array of homes, the interior of the fort was dominated by a huge mound that lay off-centre to the north-west, an enormous grass-covered hill which looked too regular to be a natural feature.

"Where are all the houses?" he asked.

There was something else peculiar about the site, something that niggled at the edges of his consciousness, although he could not discern what it was that troubled him.

Findmall replied, "They're around and about. There's a village a little way to the west. Emain Macha is far too important a place for ordinary folk to make a home there. I told you, only Fergus and his family will be in there."

Calgacus stared at the hillfort again, noticing that the gates, although closed, were hardly substantial enough to keep out a determined assault. His eyes scanned the circular wall, looking for more weaknesses. As he studied the rampart, he realised what it was that was odd about the construction.

"Where is the ditch?" he asked.

"Ditch?" Findmall responded uncertainly.

Calgacus pointed to the walls.

"You build a protective wall by digging a ditch and throwing the earth up to form the actual rampart," he explained. "But that place has no ditch. So how did they build the wall?"

Findmall's face brightened. He said, "Oh, that. It is inside the wall, of course."

"Inside?"

"It was built in a single night by the Goddess Macha," Findmall related without any sense of irony.

"She doesn't know how to build a proper defensive wall, then," Calgacus derided. "The ditch should be on the outside so that men can stand on the wall and throw missiles down on their attackers."

In his mocking tone, as if the reasons for the unusual construction should be obvious, Fiacha Cassan explained, "This is

108

a ritual site, not a defensive one. Such places are often built with the ditch inside the wall."

Calgacus exchanged a look with Runt, who shook his head in bewilderment.

"All right," Calgacus sighed wearily. "Let's circle round and see if we can find the village. I want to know whether Elim has brought his army here."

Keeping below the skyline, they walked in a wide circuit, staying well away from the hillfort. On the far side of the low hill, nestled between small patches of woodland and spread across the lower land, they saw a collection of roundhouses. The homes were widely scattered, some with their own protective wooden stockades. Smoke rose in wispy columns from the thatched or turfed roofs. A few people were moving around or sitting at the doors of their homes, taking advantage of the summer sun, but most would be indoors, preparing their evening meal.

Sheep and cattle roamed around the foot of the fort's low hill, cropping the lush grass, while strips of land around the village had been sown with the barley, rye and oats that would provide the year's harvest.

"It's a nice place," observed Runt.

"It's a vulnerable place," Calgacus replied thoughtfully. "But I don't see any signs of an army."

He frowned as he added, "I wonder where Elim is. Have we missed him?"

"Perhaps he is not here yet," suggested Tuathal.

Runt laid a hand on Calgacus' arm to attract his attention.

"Look over there."

The little man pointed to the far distance where a group of riders were emerging from behind a woodland. They were too far away for Calgacus to make out any details but he instinctively dropped to a low crouch, gesturing for the others to make themselves less visible.

"It looks like a hunting party," Tuathal said, shading his eyes against the low sun.

They watched as the horsemen rode slowly towards the hillfort. Behind them came a gaggle of men on foot, some of them carrying long poles from which hung the carcasses of two boar.

"Fergus has been out hunting," Calgacus commented softly.

"There is nothing unusual about that," said Fiacha Cassan.

109

"There is if he knows that an invading war host is marching towards his home," Calgacus told him.

A broad smile crossed Tuathal's normally serious face.

"He does not know we are here," he grinned.

"Not yet, at any rate," Calgacus agreed. He rubbed his chin pensively as he added, "If only the rest of our army was here, we could take the place easily."

"Why wait?" Fiacha Cassan asked. "There are no more than half a dozen men in that hunting party. We have over a hundred. We should attack anyway."

Tuathal nodded eagerly, "We can take them by surprise."

"Then let's get on with it," Fiacha Cassan urged. "They'll be feasting tonight. It will be easy."

He gave Calgacus a withering look as he challenged, "Or are you too cautious to seize this opportunity?"

Calgacus glared back at the younger warrior. The barely disguised accusation of cowardice was one that needed to be answered. By tribal custom, he would be justified in drawing his sword to refute a taunt like that but another idea came to him.

He hesitated, knowing that it was a risk. It had come to him because he wanted to prove to Fiacha Cassan that he was the better man, that he was not afraid.

He knew that making plans based on pride was to invite failure but he could not help himself. The idea was there, a bold plan that a young Calgacus would have been proud of, but he was older, wiser now.

More cautious, a small voice inside his head whispered to him. *More afraid of failure. Fiacha Cassan is right. You are afraid.*

He knew it was foolish but there was only one way to silence that inner voice, only one way to quell Fiacha Cassan's provocations.

"Perhaps we can take the place without a fight," he suggested. "Unless you are afraid of taking a risk."

Chapter XIII

They waited until the sun had sunk below the horizon, abandoning the world to shades of black and grey. Two hours after sunset, Findmall led Calgacus, Runt and Fiacha Cassan, each of them now mounted on a horse, towards the fort, while Tuathal and the remaining warriors waited out of sight.

By the time they set off, the temperature had dropped rapidly, bringing a fine, grey mist that shrouded the evening, distorting shapes and playing tricks with sound. The mist was both a blessing and a curse, for it would help conceal their approach but it could also confuse them by masking the tell-tale flickers of light from the torches that burned at the gates of Emain Macha.

Calgacus was tempted to wait in the hope that the mist would disperse but he was not convinced that they could keep a force of one hundred men hidden, even at night, so he told Tuathal to give him enough time to reach the gates of the hillfort, then to bring the rest of the warriors as quickly as he could.

The mist dampened their hair and clothes with its clammy moisture as they rode towards the fort. Calgacus flicked a wet strand of hair back from his face, hoping that they were heading in the right direction. He had lost sight of the fort when the night and the mist closed in around them but Findmall, leading the way, seemed sure of the path. Then the ground began to rise slightly and Calgacus saw a faint orange glow, suffused by the damp, cloying murk. A second flame struggled to make itself seen but gradually flickered into sight, confirming the location of the gateway between the two sputtering torches.

Calgacus glanced to his left, where Runt rode alongside him. The little man's face was tense, his right hand hovering near the hilt of one of his swords while his left hand gripped the horse's reins. He returned Calgacus' look with an accusatory scowl.

While Fiacha Cassan had merely grinned and gone to sharpen his sword when he heard Calgacus' plan, Runt had not been at all happy. But then, Runt was never happy with Calgacus' plans.

"This is crazy even by your standards," the little man had complained. "Why don't we just send every man to rush the gates?"

"Because we may be able to take the place without any of our men being killed," Calgacus had explained. "With luck, nobody needs to die."

"Except Fergus," Runt had pointed out.

"I don't think we can avoid that," Calgacus had admitted.

He tried not to think about that aspect too much, telling himself to concentrate on the task in hand.

"You could at least send someone else," Runt had persisted. "We don't need to go."

Calgacus knew his friend was right but pride would not let him pull out.

"Findmall is the best person to do this," he had argued weakly, "but I don't want to let him out of my sight. He and his brother are too unpredictable."

"Look who's talking," Runt had muttered. "You are just being stubborn."

"Perhaps. But I want this done quickly and with as few killings as possible."

Runt knew when to stop pressing his case and had fallen into a grim silence. Despite his misgivings, they both knew he would go with Calgacus.

The path leading to the fort degenerated into a worn, rutted track. As they neared the gate, the sound of the horses' hooves seemed suddenly loud, amplified by the mist.

"Who's there?" a sullen voice called from beyond the gate which now loomed out of the night ahead of them.

Findmall called back, "Open up! We have a message for Lord Fergus."

They stopped at the gateway, the horses shaking their heads and stamping their feet in an attempt to throw off the damp air.

A pale face peered at them through a gap in the timber planks, eyes straining suspiciously.

"I don't recognise you," the man said gruffly. "Who is the message from?"

"From the High King," Findmall replied without hesitation. "Now open the gates and let us in. We've had a long journey and we're tired."

"You'd best give me your names," the guard requested.

"I am Cairbre of the Scotti," Findmall shot back, his voice now thick with impatience. He was giving a good impression of a man who was used to being obeyed without being subjected to questioning.

Calgacus had no idea whether Cairbre was a real person but either that name or the mention of the Scotti, the people led by the High King's witch, was sufficient to convince the sentry.

"Wait there while I go and tell the Lord," he instructed.

They waited anxiously in the damp night for what seemed an age until, at last, they heard the sounds of movement, then the grating of wood as the locking bar was lifted. With a slight creak, one of the tall gates swung inwards, revealing a solitary swordsman who wore a hooded cloak as protection against the damp night air. He waved them in, closing the gate behind them and heaving the locking bar back into place, sealing them inside.

"The Lord Fergus is feasting," the watchman told them in a surly tone. "He says you may join him. Leave your horses here and I will take you to the hall."

He sounded irritated, as if their arrival had disturbed him from some important task. Or perhaps he was simply annoyed at being on gate duty on such a miserable evening.

After they had dismounted, Fiacha Cassan asked the watchman, "Are you on your own out here?"

"Aye," the man grumbled. "Just me. Everyone else is getting drunk at the feast."

"That's a shame," said Fiacha Cassan sympathetically.

The gate warden nodded sourly. He moved past them, pointing into the mist-shrouded fort.

"Follow me," he told them.

Fiacha Cassan stepped behind the man. Without warning, he clamped his left hand over the guard's mouth and, with one brutal thrust, stabbed him in the back with a long dagger, forcing the blade deep between the man's ribs.

The guard stiffened, his eyes staring with shock and terror. A muffled grunt of pain escaped from him, then he slumped. Slowly, Fiacha Cassan lowered him to the ground before wiping his knife clean.

Calgacus nodded in grim approval of the quietly efficient killing.

"Get him out of sight," he ordered curtly. "And tether the horses over there, away from the gates."

Fiacha Cassan dragged the body of the gate warden into the shadows while Findmall led the horses in the opposite direction and Runt helped Calgacus lift the locking bar away from the gates.

"We've been lucky," Runt observed quietly. "I thought they would have more than one man on watch."

"So did I, but let's not complain. Fergus obviously isn't expecting trouble. Now all we need to do is wait for Tuathal to arrive with the rest of the lads."

Calgacus was still on edge. He strained all his senses, peering into the misty shadows, trying to detect signs of life but Emain Macha was unlike any hillfort he had ever visited. Findmall had told him it was a holy place, a place where the ancestors of the ruling families of the Ulaid, the men of Ulster, were buried, and where the people gathered at times of celebration. It may have been all of these things but it was not a home in the way that Calgacus understood. He caught a glimpse of cultivation in some small patches of earth but there was no light, no sounds of music or laughter, no smells of cooking, not even the stink of cesspits or middens. Like so much that he had experienced during the past day, it felt unfamiliar and wrong.

Findmall and Fiacha Cassan came to join them at the gate.

"We should go and deal with Fergus," Fiacha Cassan declared.

"Let's not push our luck," Calgacus told him.

"He is expecting a messenger," Findmall pointed out. "If we don't go to his hall, he will become suspicious."

"Let's wait a bit longer," Calgacus decided.

They stood in the mist, eyes and ears alert, for a long time, straining to hear the sounds of Tuathal's arrival but the night remained silent and empty until, eventually, they heard a distant voice calling for someone named Ban.

"They're coming to find out what has delayed us," Findmall said.

Before Calgacus could object, the young druid walked off into the mist, heading in the direction of the unseen speaker. His brother followed close on his heels.

Runt gave Calgacus a helpless look and sighed, "What do we do now?"

"We can't let them go alone. Come on."

114

"You are as crazy as they are," muttered Runt as he followed Calgacus deeper into the fort.

Some fifty paces into the compound, a large building loomed out of the fog. A man stood near a door, urinating against the wall. He gave them an apologetic smile as he finished and refastened his trews.

In a drunken voice, he explained, "I was sent to find you but I've had a drop too much ale."

"A nice problem to have," Findmall replied cheerfully. "Where's Ban? Why didn't he bring you?"

"He needed a piss too," Findmall explained. "But we found our own way."

The drunk man slurred, "You have a message for Fergus?"

"That's right. I am Cairbre of the Scotti. Fergus is inside?"

"Yes. He's at dinner. Come on, I'll show you."

He opened the door, allowing a pool of light to spill outside, and waved them in.

"Andraste preserve us!" breathed Runt. "Now we're really in trouble."

Findmall strode unhesitatingly towards the open doorway. Beside him, Fiacha Cassan glanced back over his shoulder at Calgacus, grinning broadly. Confidently, the two brothers marched into the large house.

"This is a bad idea," Runt warned in an urgent whisper.

"I know, but we don't have an excuse to stay out here," Calgacus replied with a shrug.

"What about the gates?"

"All Tuathal needs to do is push them open."

Runt shook his head as he looked at the open doorway through which Findmall and Fiacha Cassan had followed the drunken guide into the building.

"These two are even more crazy than you are," he muttered.

"We can't abandon them," Calgacus decided.

He hurried forwards, with Runt, still cursing softly, close behind.

As they reached the house, Calgacus saw that it was enormous, its bulk vague and indistinct as it stretched away into the mist. It lay close to the wall, as if it had been built to leave most of the wide interior of the fort clear of human dwellings. He could see enough to make out that the house was not round as he

115

had first thought, but had a more oval shape, its long side facing towards them. Its thatched roof vanished high into the opaque gloom above their heads. From inside, he heard the animated chatter of voices, the sounds of people laughing and talking loudly.

"There's a lot more than half a dozen people in there," Runt warned. "This is stupid."

Determinedly, Calgacus replied, "All we need to do is keep them talking until Tuathal gets here. Come on."

"You're all mad," Runt muttered under his breath as he followed Calgacus through the doorway.

Inside, Runt's fears were realised. The wave of heat and light that greeted them revealed a large cooking fire over which hung the remains of a roasted boar impaled on an iron spit. Surrounding the fire were several long, wooden tables where at least forty people were sitting, enjoying the food and drink that was spread along the tables. Half of them were unmistakeably warriors.

Calgacus muttered a soft curse. Findmall had assured them that Fergus would not have many warriors in his home but that assertion had clearly been wrong. Not only were there far more men seated around the tables than he had expected, one look at them was enough to tell him that these men would not be easily intimidated. They were tough characters, inured to violence, and the looks they gave the newcomers were hard and hostile.

But this was not a war gathering. Many of the men were more than slightly drunk. The strong aromas of roasted meat, beer and whiskey filled the large house, competing with the damp, earthy aroma of the peat that crackled and spat on the hearth fire.

There were women present too, some of them serving food and drink, others sitting at the tables among the men, joining in the meal, the laughter and the conversation.

Conversation that died away as the four strangers walked in through the doorway.

Findmall had paused just inside the door. Apparently unconcerned at the odds facing them, he repeated his story.

"I am Cairbre of the Scotti. I bring a message from the High King."

A young man, his hair a shade of flaming ginger that Calgacus had never seen before, sat at the head of the furthest table, a pretty young woman sitting on either side of him. He

116

looked to be in his mid-twenties, perhaps even younger. He had been laughing happily but now his eyes held a speculative look.

"A message from my father?"

Puzzled, he beckoned Findmall to him.

Findmall stepped forwards confidently, with Fiacha Cassan close beside him. Calgacus signalled to Runt to follow. They were committed now and their best hope lay in staying together. They moved between two tables, skirting the crackling, smoking fire.

Calgacus tapped Findmall's arm, trying to attract the druid's attention.

"Let me speak to him," he hissed under his breath.

Findmall did not appear to hear him, continuing to smile as he approached the table with Fiacha Cassan humming quietly to himself as he strode alongside his brother.

All eyes were on them, some men fidgeting nervously, others gripping their knives tightly. Calgacus noticed that most of the warriors had laid their swords on the ground behind them, or propped them against the side walls of the house. But each man had a knife that he used for eating his food, a knife that could cut human flesh as easily as it could carve roasted meat. Calgacus had no doubt that these men would know how to use the knives even if they could not reach their swords. The very fact that they possessed swords marked them as men of high standing, men who practised the art of war.

Calgacus knew they must stall for time, must distract Fergus long enough for Tuathal to arrive. Then they might be able to persuade Fergus to surrender without a fight.

What was more likely, he thought bitterly, was that Fergus and his men would kill them as soon as they realised they were under attack.

Then they were standing in front of Fergus. He still held a piece of dark meat in one hand. His left arm had been draped around the shoulders of the young woman who sat beside him, a pretty, dark-eyed brunette who gazed haughtily at the visitors. Now, Fergus waved that hand at Findmall.

"So tell me, what is this message?"

He sounded slightly drunk, as if he had been drinking for some time. Calgacus guessed that the hunters had probably broken out the ale as soon as they had returned from their successful trip.

117

Calgacus took a step forwards but Findmall immediately spoke in a loud voice, saying, "The message is from the High King, not from your father. The High King is Tuathal mac Fiacha who has returned to reclaim his birthright. He has declared your life forfeit."

Fergus blinked in astonishment but before he or any of his warriors could react, Fiacha Cassan moved. Like a cat pouncing on its prey, he leaped forwards, springing up onto the wooden table, drawing his sword in an easy, fluid movement as he did so.

The table wobbled alarmingly, platters and goblets were scattered and the women beside Fergus shrieked in terror as Fiacha Cassan's sword swung down, smashing into Fergus' skull, spraying the air with blood, fragments of bone and pieces of oozing brain.

Still moving, Fiacha Cassan jumped down behind the dead man, gripped Fergus' blood-soaked hair with his left hand and began hacking at the neck with his sword.

"Hold!" Calgacus bellowed, drawing his own sword from his back and sweeping round to his right. "You are surrounded! Nobody else needs to die."

It was too late. Women were already screaming, warriors were rising to their feet or twisting round to reach for their swords. One man threw his knife at Calgacus' head but Calgacus ducked just in time. The dagger vanished into the chaos behind him.

Instincts that had been honed by a lifetime of warfare took over. Calgacus had been willing to let these men live but Fiacha Cassan's reckless slaying of Fergus had changed everything. Now his only choices were to fight or to die.

He leaped towards the table to his right. Ignoring the people who yelled or screamed at him, he crouched, grabbed at the edge of the long wood and heaved. His grip was hampered by his sword but the table was not sturdy and he was able to lift it easily enough. He tipped it, then pushed with all his might, sending everyone behind it falling to the floor or reeling backwards. The plates and goblets fell with a prolonged smash or thudded onto the bodies of the men and women who had fallen beneath the long table.

He spun round, knowing that they must take advantage of the brief respite he had gained. Half of the warriors were temporarily out of the fight but it would not be long before they recovered. The other half were already scrabbling to the attack.

He saw Runt take down a swordsman with an almost casual thrust of his left hand while holding another at bay with his right. Calgacus dashed to his friend's side, smashed his sword down on the head of a third warrior who was trying to get behind Runt, then kicked out at the next table, trying to knock it over.

Fiacha Cassan bellowed a cry of savage triumph as he held Fergus' severed head aloft. Then, almost without looking, he swung his sword to knock aside an attack from an enraged warrior before spinning round to slash a second man across the throat. He spun again, facing his first attacker, let the man sweep a blow towards his head, then swayed back to let the blade pass him. He hacked back with a vicious blow that smashed his opponent's ribs, felling him instantly.

The young brunette who had been sitting beside Fergus lunged at Fiacha Cassan with a knife but the warrior laughed contemptuously as he used Fergus' severed head to knock the blow aside. A casual sweep of his sword sent the woman scurrying away in terror.

Calgacus slashed at another warrior, driving the man back. He reckoned that they had downed half a dozen but they were still horribly outnumbered. Only the confusion and the drink-induced dulling of their opponents' reactions were keeping them alive. Desperately, he swiped his sword at a warrior's face, forcing the man to jump back.

"Lay down your swords!" Calgacus bellowed. "The fort is surrounded."

The reply was a sword that arced towards his left side. He parried the blow, feeling the impact jar his arm, then swept his own blade up, twisting so that his opponent's sword was flung aside, leaving the man disarmed. Calgacus kicked at him before turning to block another attack.

Behind him, Findmall, whose only weapon was the dagger he wore at his belt, moved calmly towards the hearth as if he believed he was invulnerable. Calgacus had no time to see what the young druid was doing because he was forced to fend off an attack from two more warriors who had scrambled over the teetering table. He sent one reeling back with a half-severed arm and kicked the second man in the groin, sending him staggering away, doubled over and gasping in pain.

Risking a quick glance behind him, he saw Findmall scooping up a bundle of straw from the floor covering. Twisting

119

the strands together, the druid then held the crude torch to the flames. Casually, Findmall stood up, ignoring the fighting that raged all around him. He grabbed a small pitcher from one of the tables then hurled it against the nearest wall, sending his burning bundle of straw after it.

The pitcher spilled out a dark liquid which ignited as soon as the first tiny flame reached it, sending a curtain of bright flames up to the roof and filling the house with a roaring crackle.

The screams of the women redoubled while the men's yells of anger turned to shouts of alarm.

"'Tis a shame to spoil good whiskey like that," observed Findmall.

"Get outside!" Calgacus yelled.

Already people were streaming for the door, shoving frantically as they tried to escape the spreading flames.

Runt killed a warrior who was distracted by the uproar, then turned, holding his twin swords ready, but there was nobody left to fight. Fergus' men were crowding round the doorway, pushing and shoving desperately as they fought to get away from the rapidly spreading fire. In the panic, a woman fell, bringing down half a dozen more people in a horrible tangle of bodies and limbs. Men and women were crawling, scrambling, screaming as they tried to claw their way out before the flames could engulf them.

"We'll not get out that way," Runt said grimly.

Calgacus whirled, looking for another door but there was none. He looked up at the roof. The thatch on the outside would be damp but the inner layers were dry, allowing the flames to spread quickly. Tentacles of fire were already climbing up to the apex, licking like snakes' tongues around the huge beams that supported the roof. Small wisps of burning thatch were falling from the ceiling, setting light to the trampled straw and rushes that covered the earth floor. Smoke whirled and billowed over their heads, darkening the house despite the lurid light of the bright flames.

Calgacus felt his face break into a sweat, not only from the raging heat but also from fear. There was no way out except through the solitary door which was still jammed by a morass of fallen and struggling bodies.

Frantically, Calgacus looked around, hoping to see some way of escape, but there was nothing except smoke and raging flames filling one side of the room. With the only exit blocked by a mass of people, they were trapped.

Chapter XIV

Calgacus knew that they had only one chance. He doubted whether they would be able to force their way through the maddened, panic-stricken mob that was still clawing madly around the doorway, and even if they could escape, they would be in the midst of more than a dozen armed enemies. But there was no choice. Deciding that a warrior's death was preferable to being burned alive, Calgacus made for the doorway, prepared to hack a path through the panic-stricken mob.

"The wall!"

At first he could not work out who had called. Then he saw that it was Fiacha Cassan. The tall man was beckoning to him, summoning him to the wall furthest from the flames. It took a moment before he realised what Fiacha Cassan wanted him to do.

"Come on!" Findmall shouted eagerly as he dashed across the house to join his brother.

From somewhere among the debris, Fiacha Cassan had found a small axe. He had sheathed his sword but still held Fergus' severed head in his left hand, his fingers gripping the long, red hair tightly. With a shout of manic delight, he began attacking the wall with his axe.

"Bloody good idea!" exclaimed Runt as he ran to help. He used one of his short, Roman swords to cut at the wall, jabbing with the sharp point, then twisting the blade to dislodge the wattle and daub.

Calgacus could not use his long sword to hack at the wall but he copied Runt, thrusting the tip into the dried daub that covered the interior of the wall, then twisting and pulling so that it fell away in chunks.

"May the Dagda preserve us," Findmall breathed as he watched them. "A little faster would be good, my friends."

Calgacus swore at him.

It was hard, slow work but they were making a significant impression on the wall. Between the supporting upright timbers, the walls had been constructed of intertwined rods of hazel and willow, caked on both sides by a mixture of mud, straw and dung which had dried out to leave a strong, waterproof barrier. The mud cracked and broke away under the furious assault of their weapons but the wattle, woven tightly together, was much more difficult.

The heat was scorching their backs as they worked, the smoke now filling the house, making them cough and stinging their eyes. The raging heat clawed at their throats, making every breath an agony.

A flutter of searing heat brushed Calgacus' long hair as blazing straw tumbled down from the roof above him. Frantically, he drove his sword into the wall, jerking it left and right with all the strength he could muster. Fiacha Cassan smashed his small axe at the same point, then a rush of cold air told them they had cut through the wattle and dislodged some of the outer layer of daub. The hole was small but it seemed to feed the flames which roared and crackled above their heads.

Findmall beat out small sparks of fire from Calgacus' back, Runt stabbed and stabbed at the wall, while Fiacha Cassan frantically pounded his axe to make the gap larger. Then Calgacus waved the others aside, leaned down to put his shoulder to the hole and heaved.

He strained every muscle in his body as he pushed against the tiny opening. He felt the dried, caked mud crumble, felt the hazel and wicker wall resisting, but he kept pushing, scrabbling at the edges of the hole with his fingers as he tried to claw a way through. He was almost at the end of his massive strength when he mustered one final heave and the wall collapsed. Without warning, he tumbled through, lying with his upper body in the cold night air while his legs could still feel the heat of the flames.

He tried to move but a weight forced him down as someone stepped on him to escape the building.

Then he heard Findmall say, "Thank you, brother," as he was hauled outside over Calgacus' head.

Runt was next, crawling, coughing, and cursing furiously at a splinter of hazel which had snagged his cloak. He wriggled free, then Fiacha Cassan's strong hands were under Calgacus' armpits and pulling him away from the blazing building.

Calgacus could hardly believe they were still alive, nor that they had managed to wriggle through the jagged, splintered hole in the wall which seemed scarcely large enough for a child.

Angrily, he rounded on Findmall.

"What in Andraste's holy name were you thinking of?" he barked.

He was furious but his question lost most of its impact because the words left his scorched throat as a hoarse, rasping cough.

"I was thinking we were in trouble if I didn't do something drastic," Findmall replied calmly.

"Drastic?" Calgacus spluttered, still coughing. "You nearly killed us all!"

Runt waved a hand, urging him to calm down.

"We need to get out of here," the little man warned. "They'll see us easily in the light of the fire. We can argue later."

Fiacha Cassan laughed, "What is there to argue about? It worked, didn't it?"

He held up Fergus' head, showing them his trophy.

Grinning wildly at Calgacus, he said, "You did all right for a couple of old men."

"We'll be dead old men if we don't get away from the light," Runt insisted. "Come on. Follow me."

He set off, hurrying into the misty gloom.

"Let's go!" Calgacus hissed at the brothers. Still gripping his sword, he hurried after Runt.

"Watch out for the ditch!" Findmall called in a loud whisper.

"Shit!" Runt's voice echoed back from the murk. They heard him scrabbling. Calgacus almost fell over him in the darkness as Runt hauled himself up from the rim of the deep earthwork.

"Bloody stupid place to put a ditch," Runt complained.

Calgacus grabbed his friend's arm, hauling him upright.

"Anything broken?" he asked.

"No. Just my pride."

"We should circle round. We need to get back to the gates to meet Tuathal."

Crouching low, Calgacus led them in a wide circuit. He found a low hump of grass where they lay down to look back at the fire and get their bearings.

Fergus' hall was well ablaze. Flames had engulfed it now, writhing into the night sky, burning away the mist around the blaze. While they watched, the roof collapsed with a loud roar, throwing up gouts of flame and a searing crackle of bright sparks.

"That's the end of that, then," chuckled Findmall. "I heard they only finished building it last year."

Calgacus was still breathing heavily, trying to fill his lungs with fresh, smoke-free air. Now that they were relatively safe, his anger at Findmall was abating, gradually being supplanted by a sense of relief. They may have been lucky to escape but they had made their own luck. Others had probably not been so fortunate.

"I wonder how many of them are still inside?" he mused thoughtfully.

"I think most of them got out," Runt told him.

Calgacus stared at the raging fire. Anyone who had not forced a way out was beyond help now. He could see the dim outlines of small figures gathered round the inferno, the men and women who had escaped through the doorway. They stood or sat as close to the flames as they dared, watching helplessly while the fire consumed the great hall. Some of them were sobbing, others staring blankly at the hungry flames. From somewhere beyond the blaze came the sound of horses whinnying in panic.

After a short rest, Calgacus recovered his breath and his wits.

He whispered, "Right. We should go now, before they get themselves organised."

He pointed to the gloom beyond the burning house and said, "The gates are that way. We need to make sure they remain unbarred so that Tuathal can get in."

"He should be here by now," Findmall said in a matter-of-fact tone that suggested he had entirely forgotten Calgacus' earlier anger.

"Maybe he's lost his way in the mist," Calgacus suggested.

"I think we've lit rather a large beacon to guide him," Runt commented drily.

Calgacus declared, "Whatever has happened, we need to keep the gates open, so let's get moving. Stick together. We go straight for the gates. Don't stop for anything."

He looked at each of them, their faces smeared black by ash, their eyes red-rimmed from the effects of the smoke. Runt's expression was tense but he nodded his readiness. Fiacha Cassan grinned as if he was enjoying himself immensely.

Calgacus said, "Come on, then!"

Pushing himself to his feet, he ran into the misty darkness, hoping that he was heading in the right direction.

125

Moving like wraiths in the night, they passed the small crowd of survivors without being seen. The refugees seemed entranced by the sight of the burning hall and were oblivious to anything else. Offering up a silent prayer that their luck would hold, Calgacus forced his tired legs to run faster. As the dim outline of the perimeter ramparts appeared vaguely out of the mist, he saw that a handful of men were already at the fort's entrance.

"Faster!" he urged. "Don't let them bar the gates!"

But the men of Emain Macha were not trying to bar the gates. Instead, they pulled them open, swinging the doors wide.

"They're trying to get out!" Runt gasped breathlessly.

He was right. But there was no escape because Tuathal had arrived at last. He and a score of armed men reached the entrance just as the gates were swung open. They charged inside with a ferocious yell, mercilessly cutting down the helpless defenders.

Calgacus skidded to a halt, his companions gathering around him. For a moment he thought that Tuathal's warriors would charge at them, mistaking them for Fergus' men but Fiacha Cassan stepped forwards, holding the severed head high.

"Tuathal!" he called out. "Fergus is dead!"

With Eudaf close on his heels, Tuathal ran towards them, his face flushed with excitement.

"You did it!" he exclaimed. "By all the Gods, you did it."

Eudaf, eyeing Fiacha Cassan's grisly trophy with a mixture of awe and revulsion, said, "I thought you only intended to hold the gates for us."

"So did I," muttered Runt.

"We were lucky," Calgacus sighed wearily. "It was almost a disaster."

"But it was not. It was a great success. Emain Macha is ours."

Tuathal's men were streaming through the fort, hunting down the few remaining survivors of Fergus' war band. The sounds of fighting filtered through the mist, accompanied by screams and yells. The sounds did not last long. The resistance, such as it was, was quickly crushed.

Smiling broadly, Tuathal walked towards the still blazing hall. His men cheered him, raising their swords high. Some of them were especially happy because they had managed to capture one of the women who had escaped the fire.

126

Calgacus saw the brunette who had been sitting next to Fergus. Her hair was dishevelled, her dress torn, her face streaked with dark blotches. A big warrior had wrapped his left arm around her shoulders, clutching her tightly against his burly body. She looked small, helpless and terrified. Such was the price of defeat, Calgacus thought to himself as he looked at her. Whatever her background, whatever her hopes and dreams might have been, now she was simply a captive slave.

Calgacus felt another pang of conscience that he had been party to the young woman's fate. He had wanted to capture this fort with as little death as possible but this scene of fiery devastation and human misery was like a beacon illuminating his failure. He had made too many mistakes that evening. They should have brought more men with them at the outset; they should not have left the gates to venture into Fergus' hall. Looking back, he recognised those errors now and, worse, he knew it had been his stubborn pride that had driven him to make those mistakes, just as Runt had warned.

He felt tired and dismayed, sick at what circumstances had led him to do and at the misjudgements he had made.

Tuathal, though, was exultant. Findmall stood beside him.

The druid raised Tuathal's arm high, shouting, "Tuathal Techtmar has reclaimed the home of his ancestors! Tuathal the Legitimate has returned! Emain Macha is ours. Soon, Tara will also fall before us! Death to Elim mac Conrach!"

"Death to Elim!" the men echoed, cheering wildly.

Eudaf, his eyes bright, began chanting Tuathal's name, encouraging the warriors to join in. The sound of their acclamation soon filled the bowl of the hillfort. For the young prince, the fire that had engulfed Fergus' home was a blaze that would spread across the whole of Eriu.

Chapter XV

"We need to secure the village," Calgacus said to Tuathal once the cheering had subsided.

"I sent the rest of the men there as you suggested," Tuathal told him. "The village will be ours before midnight."

"I'd like to make sure it is," Calgacus replied. "I'll go and have a look. You'd better stay here, though."

He told Eudaf, "Stay close to him and keep your guards nearby. There may be some of Fergus' men who are still free and out for revenge."

Eudaf held up his sword in a gesture of readiness.

"I will protect him," he promised.

Calgacus nodded his approval then turned back to Tuathal and ordered, "Set a guard on the gates. In the morning, send a messenger back to the main force. Tell them to get here as quickly as they can."

Tuathal acknowledged, "I can do those things. But you should rest. You look exhausted."

"I'll rest when I know we have taken control of the village," Calgacus replied.

The truth was that he was dreadfully tired but it was a tiredness of the spirit as much as a tiredness of the body. Already he could see warriors stripping the captive women and forcing them to the ground. He knew he could not stop what would happen but he had no wish to watch the results of victory.

Fiacha Cassan offered, "I'll come with you."

He handed Fergus' bloody head to Eudaf and grinned, "Look after this for me."

Eudaf took the gory trophy with some reluctance. He asked, "Would it not be better for you to remain here? You should help us keep Tuathal safe."

"He has thirty men to watch over him," Fiacha Cassan replied. "I'll be of more use down in the village."

The wild smile of anticipation was back on his face as he added, "You never know, there might be some more fighting to be

128

done and these old men could probably do with someone to look after them."

Calgacus was too weary to take offence. Sheathing his sword, he said to Runt, "Come on. Let's see what is happening."

Giving Tuathal the slightest of bows, he turned away and headed for the gates.

Fiacha Cassan called, "I'll catch up with you in a moment. I'm going to get some whiskey before these bastards drink it all."

Calgacus replied with a tired wave of his hand. He had no real desire for the tall warrior's company so he did not wait for him. Without a backward glance, he made for the open gates.

Runt quickly fell into step beside him. As they passed through the gateway, avoiding the bodies of the fallen defenders, the little swordsman said softly, "I don't know how we got away with that, but we did."

"We were lucky. Those madmen nearly killed us. You were right. I'm sorry, Liscus."

"Everyone is allowed a mistake now and then, Cal. Even you. Stop fretting over it."

"It's not just that," Calgacus confessed. "I knew the plan was a bad one but I wanted to prove something. That was careless. I should know better. But more than that, I can't shake off the feeling that we are getting caught up in something that is not our affair. Other people are suffering because of what we are doing."

An image of the young brunette flashed across his mind as he continued, "People who have done nothing to harm us are suffering."

"You're getting soft in your old age," Runt chided. "Innocent people always get hurt in war. You can't be responsible for everything that happens."

"I just don't like fighting against people who have done me no harm," Calgacus said gloomily.

"You want things to be black and white," Runt gibed. "As if it was us against the Romans. But nothing is ever that simple, Cal. You know that. There are shades of grey everywhere."

He shot Calgacus a sideways look as he added, "You need to stop feeling sorry for yourself and start getting angry. As for these people not having done us any harm, Elim mac Conrach has sent men to kill you. Think about that."

129

Calgacus sighed, "You're right, Liscus. Whatever else we do, we need to kill the Usurper. That's the only way we'll get out of this mess."

"That's more like it," Runt smiled happily.

"And the next time anyone has a stupid, dangerous idea, remind me not to go along with it."

"You're just as bad as Fiacha Cassan," Runt laughed. "All your ideas are stupid and dangerous. I tell you that every time. The problem is, you never listen."

"I will next time," Calgacus promised.

"No you won't."

This time it was Calgacus' turn to laugh.

"Maybe not. But tell me anyway."

Runt remarked, "Since you mention it, walking into a strange village at night when you know there may be fighting going on and you can't see what's ahead because of the mist isn't the smartest thing you've ever done."

"I know. But I needed to get away from that place. Anyway, if Fergus had all his warriors in his home, there shouldn't be much resistance in the village. But we'll be careful."

Runt did not bother to reply. He knew Calgacus well enough to tell that the big warrior was beginning to shake off his despondent mood. For Runt, his task was quite simple; all he needed to do was keep Calgacus concentrating on what was important. If he could do that, everything else should take care of itself.

They were at the foot of the hill now, heading into the wide valley. At least, they thought they were. The night and the mist had combined to distort their surroundings, confusing them. Shapes appeared suddenly in the mist, strange and frightening, only to transform into trees or bushes. Sounds were either muffled or startlingly loud.

At one point, Calgacus thought he heard footsteps behind them. He turned, expecting to see Fiacha Cassan coming after them as he had promised but there was nobody in sight.

As they walked carefully on, he became aware of the dark bulk of looming trees to their left. From somewhere up ahead he could hear the distant but familiar sounds of raucous celebration. Whatever was happening in the village, there seemed to be no fighting.

130

Then the sound of slow, plodding hoofbeats drifted out of the mist. A man on horseback materialised out of the night, a dark shape on a dark horse. He swore when he realised there were men in front of him, raising his sword in alarm.

Calgacus shouted at him to hold his attack.

"I am Calgacus!" he barked.

The horseman swerved, pulling his mount to a halt.

"You startled me," he apologised as he patted the horse's neck to calm it.

"The same goes for us," Calgacus told him. "What's happening in the village?"

"We caught them sleeping," the man informed them. "It was a bit of a shambles because we couldn't see much but we reckon most of the men are dead or taken prisoner."

He gave an apologetic shrug as he added, "A few got away. You'd best be careful in case they are still hanging around."

"Thanks for the warning," Calgacus nodded. "So what is happening there now?"

"The women and children are our captives," the rider explained. "Our lads are having some fun now. I was sent to tell Tuathal we have taken control."

"Then you'd better go and deliver your message."

The horseman nodded a farewell, jabbed his mount's flanks, and soon disappeared into the night.

"Is there any point in going on?" Runt asked.

Calgacus frowned. The faint sounds from the village were not those of war but of celebration and he had no real desire to witness the aftermath of conquest. A sense of duty told him he had a responsibility to see for himself that the village had been properly secured yet he knew he had already made too many mistakes that evening and what he really wanted to do was find somewhere to rest and sleep.

Before he could reach a decision, Runt cocked his head, his expression suddenly puzzled.

"What is it?" Calgacus asked him.

Runt looked back over his shoulder, peering into the trees. He held up his left hand, signalling to Calgacus to be quiet. When nothing happened, he shrugged.

"I thought I heard something," he said sheepishly. "It must have been my imagination."

"It was probably just a fox," Calgacus told him.

131

"Probably," Runt agreed. Then he dropped his voice to a whisper and said, "There is someone there."

Calgacus nodded. Runt knew a fox when he heard one.

Deciding that reversing their direction might flush out whoever was lurking in the trees, he said, "Come on. Let's head back to the fort. We're not achieving anything out here."

"Best decision you've made all night," Runt agreed as they began retracing their steps.

The whisper of sound, when it came, was barely audible, so soft that they would have missed it if they had not been expecting it. Calgacus heard the rustle of footsteps as someone moved through long grass. He half turned to look back. As he did so, two shadowy figures emerged from the trees, each holding a long spear.

The men had been trying to step out quietly but as soon as Calgacus saw them, one of them let out an angry snarl and broke into a run, charging towards him. The second man was only a heartbeat behind.

Although he had been expecting some sort of attack, Calgacus had no time to draw his sword. The ambushers had been close and the first spearman was almost on him. Desperately trying to avoid the wickedly sharp spear, Calgacus jumped to the side but lost his footing on the damp grass, slipping wildly. He almost fell, flailing his arms as he tried to maintain his balance. The tip of the spear point followed, propelled by the charging attacker. Somehow, at the last moment, Calgacus swiped his left arm at the deadly shaft. His wrist slapped into the wood just behind the leaf-shaped metal blade, knocking it aside, but he could not stop the charging spearman who crashed into him with a bone-jarring thump that drove all the air from Calgacus' lungs. Already off-balance, he fell to the ground, landing on his back so heavily that he cracked the back of his head on the long hilt of his sword.

The spearman staggered but managed to stay on his feet. He raised his spear, standing over Calgacus like the shadowy figure of Elim's witch who had haunted Calgacus' dream; like the knifeman who had tried to kill him on the beach.

Except that, this time, he could not move. He had no breath and he had no time. All he could do was raise his arms in a futile attempt to protect himself from sharp, stabbing, imminent death.

The blow did not come. Before the spearman could plunge his weapon down, there was another sound, the sound of a foot stamping, immediately followed by a dull, sickening thud as a sword hacked against a man's body. To Calgacus, the scream of pain seemed to take an age to leave the spearman's throat but it came as the man staggered away from him. Then it died as another blow hacked the life from him.

"Are you all right, old man?"

It was Fiacha Cassan, holding out his left hand to help Calgacus to his feet.

"Liscus?" Calgacus gasped in alarm as Fiacha Cassan hauled him upright.

"I'm here," Runt assured him. "Thanks to our friend."

"I told you that you needed looking after," Fiacha Cassan grinned cheerfully.

"It was neat work," Runt acknowledged gratefully. "I couldn't have done it better myself."

"The first man was easy enough," Fiacha Cassan said immodestly. "But I should have killed the second with one blow. That was a bit sloppy. Then again, I thought speed was more important than finesse."

"You are not wrong there," Calgacus said with feeling. "He almost had me."

He arched his back and rubbed his head, wincing at the pain from the points where he had landed on his sword. He was sure he could already feel the bruises forming.

Looking down at the two crumpled bodies at his feet, he said, "We owe you our lives."

"Yes, you do," Fiacha Cassan agreed cheerfully.

Gesturing towards the two corpses, Calgacus sighed, "I suppose they are a couple of Fergus' men who escaped from the attack on the village."

Fiacha Cassan frowned as he said, "No. Their names are Gwrgi and Fechertne. I noticed them following you when you left the fort. I thought they were acting a bit suspiciously, so I decided to tag along after them to see what they were up to."

"They are your men?" Calgacus asked.

Fiacha Cassan shrugged, "They joined our war band. We knew them, although I can't say I knew anyone who had a good word to say about them. They were not much more than spears for hire."

133

"Why would they try to kill us?" Runt wondered. "Could Elim have hired them?"

"Who knows? Perhaps they just wanted to rob you. It wouldn't be the first time they've done something like that."

Calgacus knelt down beside the body of the man who had attacked him. He did not know whether this was Gwrgi or Fechertne and he did not much care, but Fiacha Cassan had said they were men who could be hired and that had set him thinking.

Rummaging around the dead man's belt, he ripped loose the small, leather pouch he knew would be there. Tearing the ties open, he tipped a handful of silver coins into his palm. He looked at Fiacha Cassan.

"It certainly looks as if someone paid them to do it," he mused. "Where would they get Roman coins from?"

Fiacha Cassan picked one of the coins from Calgacus' open hand. Holding it up, he studied it carefully, running his thumb over the small images and writing it bore on either side.

"I've never seen one of these before," he admitted. "Is it silver?"

"Mostly."

"There are no Romans here," Fiacha Cassan observed with a puzzled frown. "When their traders come, which is not very often, they bring wine and dyed cloth. Not coins."

Pensively, Calgacus said, "There may be no Romans here but a lot of wealthy men among the Pritani use Roman coins these days. They are a convenient way to carry silver around."

"So I see. Do the Romans give them to you? Or do you steal them?"

"Both. Raiding parties often bring them back. But sometimes the Romans give them to chieftains as a bribe to become friends of Rome."

Fiacha Cassan was still frowning uncertainly.

"I don't understand," he confessed. "What does this mean?"

"I think it means that whoever paid these two thugs to kill us came across the sea with us. Elim's killer is one of the Caledones. And he's still after me."

Chapter XVI

Scota rose before cock crow each day. She liked the early morning, the sound of the dawn chorus in the still air and the gradual lightening of the world, as if some celestial deity were drawing away a curtain to reveal the wonder of nature's creation. Even on a morning such as this, when the residual pockets of the unseasonal mist that had descended during the night were still stubbornly clinging to the lower parts of the land, Scota enjoyed the quiet peace of the pre-dawn. Soon, all too soon, the people would rouse themselves to begin the labour of another day but, for this short time, she felt that the world belonged to her alone.

She was not alone, of course. She never was. When she stepped outside, she immediately saw the two warriors who watched over her small roundhouse. They greeted her with polite, deferential words, although their faces bore the expressions of half-respect, half-fear that she had come to recognise. They were men of her own tribe, the Scotti, yet still they were uncomfortable around her. That was partly her own fault, she knew; it was the price she paid for the path she had chosen or, rather, for the path that had chosen her. It meant that, although she might never be alone, she was always lonely.

She nodded her head to acknowledge the men's presence but she did not smile. She rarely smiled. She had learned long ago that a sorceress was expected to be stern, unsmiling, diffident, so she always tried to maintain her aura of aloofness. It had been difficult at first, when she had been young and learning the craft of magic under old Dana's guidance, but the mark on her face, the pink-red blemish that marred the entire left side of her features, had marked her as someone apart. People had always feared her because of that mark and they had never trusted her smiles. So she had learned to be hard, to be tough, to be stern. She had learned to show people what they expected.

Clutching her cloak tightly around her slim body, she strolled slowly through the High King's hilltop settlement until she reached the gateway. The watchmen wordlessly opened the huge gates for her. They were not her men, not warriors of the Scotti, but they, too, feared her. They knew that she often left the hillfort before dawn, so they pulled the wide gates inwards without her needing to say anything. She walked through, made her way down the hill, and turned to face the east. Then she stood to greet the new day.

What would this day bring, she wondered? It was her task to foresee the future, to advise the High King so that he could outwit anyone who dared oppose him. It had taken her years to consolidate her position yet she knew that she could not afford to make any errors of judgement. A single mistake would be enough to rouse Elim's temper and could prove fatal. The failed revolt by Eochaid of Leinster had amply demonstrated the price of failure. Scota had not made any misjudgements so far but the High King was a harsh master and she dared not display any fallibility or doubt.

Her role was a difficult one but she had developed her arts over several years and had become adept at dealing in secrets. Her network of spies and informants had allowed her to predict where the next potential problem would arise. Yet she felt uneasy because she had been expecting word of another uprising in the North and she had, as yet, heard nothing. This worried her but she forced herself to push her concerns aside. There was little more she could do until someone brought her news. Knowledge was power, yet she had no information and that left her vulnerable.

She sighed, offering a silent prayer that she would hear word of trouble before the news reached Elim mac Conrach. Being forewarned, Scota could again demonstrate her value to the High King.

Yet she had waited for days and still there was no news, only vague rumours of unrest in Ulster and, although she had her suspicions, she had still not been able to positively identify the ringleaders.

She cast all such thoughts aside as the sun slowly cleared the horizon, its warmth slight but bearing the promise of a fine day to come. Soon, the last remnants of the mist would burn away and the sun would shine down on the fertile land of Eriu.

Scota gave a satisfied nod, as if the weather gods had done as she wished, then she returned to the hillfort, picking her way through the huddle of buildings to her own, small home that nestled close against the western edge of the settlement.

Her door, like most doors, faced eastwards in honour of the sunrise. This traditional arrangement also ensured that nobody could approach her home without being seen by the guards who stood at her doorway. One can never be too careful, Scota thought as she walked back to her house.

Other people were up and about now. The familiar sounds of movement and voices were clearly audible from the houses she passed. This was the homestead of the High King, so most of the inhabitants were either warriors, craftsmen or servants. They did not need to tend the sheep or cattle, nor did they work in the fields or forests. The people who lived outside the fort attended to all those menial tasks, supplying whatever the High King's household required for its daily needs.

Compared to the lives that most people led, those who lived inside the small fort inhabited a different world. The warriors had a relatively easy life, practising their weapon skills, or hunting deer and boar. They were privileged men, companions of the High King whose main duty was to protect their overlord and, if necessary, to die for him. The High King rewarded them well for this duty, feeding them and their families, distributing swords, rings and brooches, or awarding them the best cuts of meat.

The women, including the wives of the warriors, prepared the food for the entire household, sewed the clothes, spun the wool and generally ensured that the small society functioned smoothly.

Scota knew that some of the women resented their lot, that they felt the men did very little that was of practical use. Scota herself viewed things differently. She, of course, was one of the privileged. She never needed to cook for herself, never needed to spin wool or make her own clothes. She simply asked for whatever she wanted and somebody provided it for her. For Scota, this was perfectly proper. Like the warriors, she was one of those who protected the people. The women of Elim's household may have felt that they bore a heavy burden but they and their children were fed, clothed and, above all, kept safe.

That safety seemed assured now. After what had happened to Eochaid of Leinster, there were few people who would dare threaten the High King. The recent brief, bloody conflict had seen the deaths of some of Elim's warriors, yet the settlement had been unharmed, the women and children kept safe. Scota knew that the women who had been widowed had been able to find other warriors to protect them. The daily drudgery they were obliged to undertake was, in Scota's opinion, the price that they paid for their security.

Yet that security relied on one man and one man alone. Scota wondered what would happen if anyone did succeed in overthrowing Elim mac Conrach. He had overcome every previous attempt to oust him but every man was mortal and Elim was no longer young. There would, though, be no smooth transition if he died. For all his many faults, Elim mac Conrach was a clever man and skilful in war. He understood tactics and strategy better than any man Scota knew and she had grown up among warriors. Most of those men saw war as a glorious game in which the only tactic was to gather an army and charge at the enemy. Elim, however, had a talent for warfare which had allowed him to crush all opposition to his rule.

His two surviving sons, though, were not of the same mettle. They had inherited his cruelty but not his cunning or skill in battle. Which meant that Elim's passing would soon result in disaster for the whole of Eriu if a lesser man were to inherit his position.

That thought bothered Scota, as did the role of Elim's only daughter.

She saw Braine now, overseeing a group of serving girls who had been sent to collect eggs from the chicken roost. Carrying wicker baskets which they held like badges of office, the girls were chattering loudly about inconsequential things, just as they always did.

The girls noticed Scota and most of them fell into an awkward silence as they studiously ignored her but Braine gave a friendly wave.

"It looks like being another fine day," smiled Braine as she passed.

She was one of the few people who was not afraid of Scota. Even at the age of fifteen, she had a determined air about her, a sense of purpose, of knowing what she wanted and how to get it. That came from her father, of course, although Braine had none of Elim's delight in cruelty.

Scota wondered whether Braine's more considerate nature came from the girl's mother. Perhaps it did, but Braine's mother had died when the girl was very young. That was another thing she had in common with Scota, although Braine's mother had died giving birth to a stillborn son, not at all the fate that had claimed Scota's mother.

Scota pushed aside her memories and replied, "Yes, the Gods are smiling on us again today."

There was no time to say any more because Braine was gone, her long, brown hair neatly combed, her walk beginning to ape the older girls in the way she swung her hips. She would be married before long, Scota knew. She would have been married already if Elim had been able to find a suitable match for her. The problem, as always, was the ever-shifting politics of Eriu. Elim had only one daughter, so her marriage would have consequences for his relationships with the other kings. He needed to make the right choice of husband for her because any children she produced might also have a claim to the position of High King.

Things were, Scota reflected grimly, becoming complicated. Part of her felt sorry for Braine, who would be used as a pawn in the convoluted and often treacherous arena of Eriu's political power play. She hoped she might be able to do something to help the girl but her own plans and desires allowed little room for compassion so she hardened her heart towards Braine and tried to concentrate on the day ahead.

By the time Scota reached her home, a stool had been set in the open doorway and the two guards had been relieved. The replacement sentries stood a little distance away from her to give the illusion of privacy.

A young girl had arrived, bearing a bowl of steaming gruel, a hunk of the previous day's bread and a pitcher of small beer. Scota sat, accepting the food with a nod of thanks, being sure to maintain a stern expression on her face.

The girl was new to the settlement and plainly terrified at being given this duty. Scota's sharp eyes noticed the tiny sprig of rowan that the girl had stuffed under the collar of her dress as a protection against witchcraft. Many people wore such charms around Scota, although most concealed them rather better than this girl.

Scota did not speak to her. A normal woman would have asked her name, enquired as to whether she had been born nearby and who her family were. Scota did not ask because to do so would have gone against the aura of omniscience she needed to portray.

The girl, plainly relieved to escape without incident, scurried away as soon as she could.

Scota took her time, watching the tiny community begin its daily routine. She silently surveyed the people, knowing that they were aware of her and noting which ones studiously avoided her gaze.

She was momentarily distracted by the arrival of a cat, an old creature with mottled brown hair and a ragged notch torn in one ear. It came towards her without any trace of fear and began rubbing itself against her legs, twisting in and out between her feet, almost tangling itself in the folds of her long dress. She did not acknowledge the creature but neither did she chase it away. Scota did not show it outwardly but she rather liked cats. They were essential for keeping mice and rats away from stored food, of course, but she found them restful creatures who were content to laze around, biding their time until the right moment came to pounce on their prey. She admired that quality. She briefly considered bending down to pet the cat but decided against it. People would see.

When she finished her breakfast and the cat realised that its attempts to persuade her to share the food had been wasted, it sidled away in search of someone more welcoming.

After breakfast, the people began to arrive. Scota would have liked to sit in the warmth of the morning sun but she went back inside her house because the people who came to visit her demanded a degree of privacy. The fire was smoking, having been fed with fresh peat during Scota's early morning absence. It was not needed for warmth but a hearth fire should not be allowed to burn itself out. People expected to see a fire when they came to Scota's home and she always showed people what they expected to see.

Overhead, bundles of herbs and flowers hung from the roof beams. A wooden table to one side held jars of powders and potions. Scota had learned herb lore from old Dana and she liked the pleasant aroma the plants brought to her home, although she found the work of preparing potions more of a chore than an enjoyment. But people expected a witch to provide such things, so Scota did not disappoint them.

There were three visitors that morning. The first two, a thin woman with pinched features, and a beardless youth with eyes that squinted badly, were the usual sort of people who came to Scota. They offered trinkets or food in exchange for her attempts to invoke the Gods to cure their ills or to curse someone who had

140

wronged them. She accepted their gifts, then sent them away with potions and vague words that did not commit her to having provided what they wanted. She did not enjoy dealing with such foolish, superstitious people but, like so many things in her life, it was part of the price.

Then the third visitor came in and Scota's spirits rose as soon as she saw him.

He was middle-aged; a plain, almost nondescript man, with an ordinary, instantly forgettable face and wearing clothes that were equally plain and unremarkable. He was the sort of man who would almost vanish in a crowd, being so lacking in distinguishing features or habits that most people would never notice him.

He entered the house with the slightly anxious air that all of Scota's visitors betrayed but as soon as he was inside, he dropped the pretence, becoming instantly more confident.

Scota felt a rush of anticipation when she saw him because he was the one person she had been waiting for. She knew him as Feargal although she was not convinced that was his true name. That did not matter to her. What mattered was what he had come to tell her.

At a signal from Scota, he sat on a stool beside the hearth. He faced her, leaning forwards with his arms resting on his knees.

"Well?" Scota enquired.

"Tuathal is here," the man replied, his voice kept low so that there was no possibility of anyone outside overhearing.

Scota felt her heart beat faster. This was the news she had been waiting for.

"Where?" she asked.

"They landed in Ulster the day before yesterday. The brothers, Findmall and Fiacha Cassan, have raised an army and gone to join them."

"Those two? I should have known. But I am surprised they managed to keep their plotting so secret. From what little I know of them, they have few brains in their head but they do have rather loud tongues."

The spy shrugged, "It all seems to have been arranged in a very short time. I tagged along with their war band and asked as many questions as I dared but all I could learn was that the brothers had received a request to aid their cousin and they had raised their rebellion in only a few days."

"Which suggests to me," Scota reflected, "that they cannot have gathered a very large force. How many men does Tuathal have now that the brothers have joined him?"

"Around a thousand all told. Perhaps a few more."

"Is that all?" she frowned. "The High King can gather three times that in only a few days."

Feargal gave another shrug as he replied, "The men who crossed the sea with Tuathal are all hardened warriors, not recruited levies. They will be tough to beat despite their few numbers."

Scota nodded pensively before shooting her spy a sharp look.

"Who else came with Tuathal?"

The spy informed her, "Only a handful of advisors but one of them is the Warlord, Calgacus."

Scota smiled to herself. So Tuathal and Calgacus had taken the bait like fish caught on a hook. Now she needed to land them.

"Do you know their plans?" she asked.

Feargal shook his head.

"I waited only long enough to see the two war bands join together, then I rode to tell you."

"You have done well," she told him.

Rising, she moved to the rear of the house and opened a small chest from which she took a few silver rings and a brooch with a ruby embedded in its centre. She returned to the fire and handed the gift to her spy.

"I need no reward," he told her.

"You have risked your life to bring me this news," she said as she dismissed his protest and forced the trinkets into his hand. "You deserve this. Now I think it would be best if you disappeared for a while. It would be too dangerous for you to return to Tuathal's army in case someone recognises you."

"I shall return home," he told her. "I am no warrior in any case. There is little more I can do to help you."

"You have done enough," she assured him.

Feargal rose to his feet and turned to leave but then he stopped and turned back to face her, a question furrowing his brow.

"What will the High King do when he learns of this?" he asked her.

Scota's lips twitched in a crooked half-smile as she said, "I expect he will do what he always does when somebody stands up to him. But this is no time to be too hasty. I will think on what you have said before I inform the High King."

Her spy regarded her with surprise.

"You know best," he said. "But it strikes me that you are playing a dangerous game."

Scota shrugged, "All life is dangerous. But to react too soon might be just as big a mistake as waiting a little while. Who knows? Tuathal's arrival may smoke other rebels out from concealment. Then we shall know the full extent of the opposition to the High King. So, say nothing of this to anyone. I shall inform him when the time is right."

Scota spent most of the morning contemplating what to do next. She wondered what Tuathal could possibly achieve with only a thousand warriors but she also knew that having Calgacus with him gave him a considerable advantage. Calgacus was even more renowned as a war leader than Elim mac Conrach and would be capable of matching the High King's cunning in battle.

Yet she also knew that the situation facing the rebels was very different to the wars Calgacus had fought against the Romans. Trying to anticipate what he would do and how the High King would respond exercised her thoughts for the rest of the morning.

It was not until the afternoon, when the High King held his audience and when Scota's presence was required, that she had decided how she should act.

She donned her cloak and left her home, walking through the village to Elim's imposing roundhouse which was set at the very centre of the fortified hilltop settlement.

Elim was busy, as he always was. Half a dozen minor chieftains were in attendance, having brought gifts to the High King. Elim was interrogating them, demanding details of how their farms were faring, whether the harvest would be good, how many head of cattle they had, and what they were doing about keeping the livestock safe from raiders. As usual, he would pounce on the slightest hesitation or vague response, mercilessly deriding any man who dared to have any opinion that differed even slightly from his own.

Elim never shouted but he spoke loudly, forcefully, overwhelming any dissent with the power of his will and the pugnacious thrust of his chin. He was a hard man, as hard as solid rock and equally unmoving in his absolute conviction that his way was the right way; the only way.

Most of the chieftains knew better than to do anything except agree with whatever the High King said but when Scota entered the roundhouse, Elim was berating one of the more senior men, a man named Finn who was older than the High King, an experienced chieftain in his own right and well-liked by everyone.

That popularity counted for nothing with Elim mac Conrach.

The High King barked, "You let the men of Connacht take fifteen head of cattle? What were you doing? What were your men doing?"

The old chieftain held his head high under the onslaught as he explained, "They attacked at night. They distracted our dogs with chunks of meat."

"Meat?" Elim growled. "You are supposed to train your dogs to attack strangers, not to accept food from them. So you and your men were sleeping while your dogs were getting fat and your cattle were being led away? By the Gods, you are pathetic!"

Unable to withstand the High King's scorn, Finn bowed his head.

His cheeks flushed red as he pleaded, "I ask that you seek recompense from King Sanb of Connacht. Without recovering what has been stolen, I cannot pay you my tribute this year. My men are eager to recover the cattle but I fear things may develop into a feud."

"There will be no fighting," Elim commanded decisively. "Cattle raids are all very well, but I want no blood spilled between Ulster and Connacht."

He saw Scota over the heads of the men but did not acknowledge her, although his performance became even more intense when he saw that she had joined his audience.

Fixing his gleaming eyes on the old chieftain, he continued, "I will speak to Sanb about his raids when I see him. In the meantime, you will recover your cattle. Take them back but make sure that nobody dies. Is that clear?"

Finn mumbled his agreement, having more sense than to ask how he was supposed to accomplish this near-impossible task.

Elim added, "And you will still pay me your tribute. If you cannot do so in cattle, you will provide slaves from among your sons and daughters."

The old chieftain stiffened when he heard this pronouncement but his protest died under Elim's baleful glare and Finn meekly nodded his head in acceptance.

The other men stood quietly, relieved that the High King's anger had not been directed at them.

Elim waved his hand impatiently.

"Now go. I wish to speak to Scota."

The chieftains hurried away, some of them glancing nervously at Scota but most of them simply grateful to escape the High King's malevolent presence.

Scota saw old Finn's angry face as he made to pass her. She understood his fury. Not only had he been humiliated in front of his peers but the instructions he had been given were, as usual with Elim, explicit in what should be done but gave no direction as to how they should be accomplished. That, Scota knew, was Elim's way. If the cattle were recovered, the High King would claim the credit for his clear and decisive leadership. If the raid failed, the chieftain would bear the responsibility and his humiliation would be compounded by the need to sell his family into slavery.

Yet seeing Finn's barely suppressed rage gave her what she needed. There was always at least one man who left the High King bearing a grudge of some sort but Finn was ideal for the next stage in her plan.

As he passed her, she reached out a hand and touched him lightly on the arm.

Startled, Finn stopped abruptly, his eyes betraying his anger and a sudden dread which he struggled to conceal. He said nothing but looked at her with mute appeal, obviously suspecting that she was about to add to his misery.

"I wish to speak with you," she whispered softly. "I think I can help you with your problem. Go to my house and I will meet you there shortly."

Finn swallowed, his eyes seeking some sign of danger in her expression but she kept her marred face impassive and merely gestured for him to leave.

"Wait at my home," she told him as he made for the door.

When he had gone, she approached the High King.

145

Elim sat on a wooden chair that was carefully positioned opposite the door. There were other chairs and stools nearby but he did not invite her to sit. His hard, cold eyes studied her.

"Did you hear that?" he asked, his voice thick with contempt. "Those men are supposed to be leaders, men who command war bands. Sheep, the whole lot of them. Worse than sheep. Frightened, witless and useless."

You would not have it any other way, Scota thought. *You want them to be afraid of you. You want them to fail so that you can humiliate them. It is all a game to you.*

Unbidden, the thought continued, *Yet what you will face soon will be no game.*

Despite her strong temptation, she stuck to her decision not to inform him of the news she had heard. It was too soon to divulge everything although that did not mean she could not plant some seeds which should enhance her reputation for sorcery.

Her thoughts were interrupted when Elim demanded, "What did you say to Finn?"

She had known he would see her speaking to the old chieftain. Elim missed nothing.

She replied, "I merely told him that I wish to speak to him."

"Why?" Elim snapped.

Maintaining her stony mask, she replied, "I have seen things in my visions. I believe there may be trouble brewing in Ulster. Yet visions and scrying are difficult to interpret and I have no definite information. Finn is a man who has many contacts and I wish to interrogate him in case he has heard anything."

"If he had heard anything, he should have told me," Elim rasped.

"But he may not realise the significance of what he has heard," Scota replied smoothly. "Or perhaps I have misread my attempts to penetrate the veils of the future. As I have told you before, it is not a precise art. Finn may be able to clarify certain things for me."

"What things?" Elim challenged.

"Small things. Like which lords are speaking to which other lords. Or whether traders from across the sea have brought any news."

Elim sat back, clearly bored by the minutiae of her thinking, just as she had known he would be.

146

Elim stated, "You will tell me if he knows anything of importance."

"Of course."

"And what trouble do you think is brewing in Ulster? That is my own realm and my son, Fergus, rules it for me. He has sent no word of unrest."

"That is why I suspect I may be wrong," Scota said with a slight shrug. "The trouble I foresee may be little more than a natural storm which might cause damage, or perhaps an outbreak of plague. As yet, things are unclear."

"Then make them clearer," Elim told her sharply.

"I will, High King."

"Very well. Is there anything else you have to tell me?"

"Only one thing," she answered. "Your son, Niall, is in Leinster but I would advise calling him home."

Elim sat up, alert and aggressive as always.

"Why?" he demanded suspiciously.

"Whatever faces you in Ulster, I have seen clearly that Niall is important in combating it. At the moment, I cannot say more than that."

"You speak in riddles, as always," he grumbled.

"Not always, Lord," she reminded him. "You know I have often been able to give you precise information. But sorcery is a difficult art to control."

He nodded, then asked, "Why is Niall important? He has only just arrived in Leinster."

"As to why, I cannot say," she replied. "But Leinster will still be there when we have resolved whatever faces us. Besides, its men are cowed and demoralised. Perhaps you could have Niall bring some of the levies here. It would test their loyalty and provide extra manpower for whatever comes."

As Elim mulled her suggestion, she went on, "And if I am wrong and there is no trouble, we lose nothing by having Niall here. He can return easily enough."

Elim stared at her for a long, silent moment before giving a grudging nod.

"Very well. I shall send a messenger to Niall and order him to return. But if this trouble you see is in Ulster, I shall also warn Fergus. He may have heard something too."

"If he had, he would have told you by now," Scota pointed out. "Warn him, by all means, but I have not seen him in my scrying. I do not know the reason, but it is Niall who is important at this time."

"I shall warn Fergus anyway," Elim decided.

"Then I shall leave you to send your messages," Scota said. "And I shall interrogate Finn to see whether he knows anything that might help."

Elim dismissed her with a wave of one hand and she left his house with a feeling of satisfaction. She had laid the groundwork by hinting at trouble. Soon she would reveal more, thus demonstrating her skill and mysterious powers and showing the High King why he needed her. The more often she was proved correct, the stronger her influence over him would become.

She still had time, she told herself. Tuathal and Calgacus may have crossed the sea but, with only a thousand men, their choices were limited. If Calgacus adopted the strategy he had so often employed against the Romans, he would attempt to lure Elim into a trap. She suspected he might attempt to besiege Emain Macha, then retire when Elim arrived with a relief force and so lay a trap when the High King pursued him.

That did not suit Scota at all. This war needed to be concluded quickly and decisively, which meant that Tuathal and Calgacus must come to Tara as soon as possible. But Calgacus was, she knew, unpredictable and she needed to influence his thinking so that he would indeed bring Tuathal's war host to Tara without delay.

And Finn had given her the means to exert the influence she needed.

"You have taken the bait, Calgacus," she whispered. "Now come to me."

Chapter XVII

By the time Finn left Scota's roundhouse, he was a beaten man with only one real option facing him.

He had begun by regarding her with nervous apprehension, then had listened in open astonishment as she revealed what she knew about the rebel uprising. Finally, his brow furrowed in deep suspicion when she told him what part she required him to play.

She could understand his anxiety and she was prepared for it. When he maintained his protests, she supplied the threat that she knew would force his hand.

"You are a dead man, Finn," she told him. "The High King distrusts you. Why do you think he has given you an almost impossible task by ordering you to recover your cattle from Sanb of Connacht without starting a war? One way or another, you are doomed to fail. And when you do, the High King will exact his revenge. Your life and your lands will be forfeit. There is only one way you can prevent this."

He had thought long and hard, had made half-hearted objections but, in the end, he had sullenly agreed to do as she asked. Whether he actually would summon the courage to do her bidding was something about which Scota could not be entirely confident but she believed the combination of dire warnings and the prospect of salvation would be sufficient to prompt him to take the step she required of him. Finn had reached his advanced years by knowing which side to support in any crisis. He was not overly intelligent but he had a knack for survival and that, she hoped, would bring him to the conclusion that he should obey her instructions.

Now, all Scota could do was wait to see what happened next.

There was always a degree of uncertainty no matter how detailed her plans but what actually occurred took even her by surprise.

It was two days after she had sent Finn on his way. She had still not revealed any more of her knowledge to the High King, telling him that her attempts to see further into the future had

149

produced ambiguous results. Her delay was deliberate but it almost cost her life.

Towards evening, as she was eating a bowl of vegetable stew and mulling over her plans, she heard an uproar in the village outside. Curious, she laid down her nearly empty bowl and went to the door.

Outside, the sun was low in the sky, its warm light bathing the settlement with an amber tinge and casting long shadows. It was the time of day when people began to relax, to return to their homes and eat their main meal before spending time telling stories or singing songs before retiring to sleep.

But this evening was different. A crowd was making its way through the village, a noisy, anxious mob of men, women and children surrounding a man who was being protected by two of the High King's guards.

The man was near exhaustion, his tunic and trousers stained with mud, his hair dishevelled and his face a pale mask of weariness and shock.

"What is going on?" Scota asked her two sentries.

They did not know but one of them hurried over to the crowd as it made its way to the centre of the settlement. When he returned, his expression was one of shocked disbelief.

"The man has come from Emain Macha," he informed Scota. "The fortress has been captured by rebels."

It took all of Scota's long years of practice to prevent her betraying her own astonishment.

Emain Macha had been captured? That could only mean one thing, but how had Tuathal and Calgacus accomplished that feat so quickly?

More importantly, she thought to herself, how was she going to explain herself to Elim mac Conrach?

The High King was in a blazing mood by the time Scota forced her way through the milling crowd into his house. Inside, dozens of warriors and other important members of the High King's entourage were gathered in the gloom of firelight to witness what the exhausted messenger had to say. Scota eased her way through them until she was standing near the High King's chair where he sat like a brooding bear, his eyes glaring at the man from Emain Macha.

"The fort has fallen?" Elim rasped in disbelief. "How?"

The exhausted messenger shrugged, "I do not know, Lord. I was in the village. We were attacked at night by overwhelming numbers of raiders. I and a few other men managed to escape and we made our way to the fort, thinking to find safety there but the place was ablaze and the gates held by strangers."

"And my son, Fergus?" Elim growled menacingly. "What of him?"

"I cannot say, Lord," the man confessed despairingly. "We were being hunted, so we left and I came here as soon as I could in order to bring you the news."

"Who are these rebels who have defied me?" the High King demanded, pushing himself to his feet and stalking towards the terrified messenger.

"I do not know, Lord," the man repeated.

"You do not know very much, do you?"

"I am sorry, Lord."

"I am surrounded by fools and incompetents!" the High King roared.

His shout was enough to make most of the spectators flinch but the words were accompanied by a more deadly response as Elim drew his dagger and plunged it into the chest of the messenger.

The man gasped, staggering backwards as he gaped down at the knife in his chest. Then he fell, his heart having been ruptured by the fatal wound.

Nobody spoke. There was no sound in the house except the crackling of peat on the fire, the ghostly light adding to the horror of the scene as the High King stared down at the corpse at his feet.

He gave the body a kick as if to ensure that his victim really was dead, then his head came up and he whirled, his eyes locking onto Scota.

"Why did you not warn me?" he shouted furiously, his finger quivering with rage as he pointed at her.

Keeping her tone neutral and her voice at a normal level, Scota replied, "I did warn you of trouble in the north, Lord. What I did not foresee was the form this would take."

"Do you think that is good enough?" he roared, taking a step towards her and jabbing a ferocious finger at her face.

151

Scota was glad that Elim's dagger was still embedded in the messenger's chest because she could not be entirely sure that he might not use it on her if she failed to placate him.

Standing tall, she said, "Let me take the dagger while that man's blood is still on it. Give me a little time and I will know the truth of what has happened."

"How much time?" Elim challenged.

"An hour or so," she assured him.

"I want to know now!" he yelled, his mouth frothing with spittle. "Cast your spell here! Tell me what has happened at Emain Macha! Tell me what has happened to my son!"

Scota inclined her head in a swift bow of acknowledgement. Then she said, "I will need a small cauldron of heated water, some special ingredients from my house and, as I said, your dagger with that man's blood still on it, along with a lock of his hair."

"Bring what she needs!" Elim roared to his slaves.

"I will fetch the ingredients I need," Scota said.

"Be quick!" the High King ordered.

Scota walked hurriedly from the house, refusing to demean herself by running. She returned to her home, selected a few of the items she had collected in clay jars, placed them in a small pouch and left her house within a few moments.

As she closed the door, she said to one of her guards, "Go and fetch Aedan. Tell him to wait for me here."

The man nodded and hurried away, understanding the urgency.

Aedan, Scota reflected with grim humour, would be annoyed at being summoned to her home at any time but especially so late in the evening. Yet the news from Emain Macha meant that she needed to be prepared and Aedan, the War Leader of the Scotti, must be told what was at stake.

By the time she had returned to Elim's home, she had decided how much she should reveal and what advice she should provide. Her brief absence had also allowed Elim's slaves to remove the corpse and to set up a small, iron cauldron on a tripod over the hearth fire. The water was already steaming and bubbling.

"I require a small table," she demanded, taking immediate control.

A slave hurriedly brought a small table which he placed beside the boiling cauldron.

"The dagger is here," Elim rasped, handing the blood-stained weapon to the slave and signalling that it should be passed to Scota. "And a lock of the man's hair."

Scota nodded as she opened her pouch and began to sort through the items she had brought, spreading them on the table.

"You must understand," she told Elim, "that doing this quickly means I may not be able to discover everything you might wish to know. But the fact that your dagger has the man's life blood and that he was present when Emain Macha fell means that I should be able to discover the most important things."

"I will decide what is most important," he rumbled, reminding her that, despite her privileged position, she still served him.

Scota turned to her work, picking up individual items and dropping them into the steaming water. There were one or two foul-smelling plants, a dried frog, small pieces of worm, some scraps of wool which she knew would add pungency to the aroma, and, of course, the lock of hair from the dead messenger.

When she had cast all these into the pot, she picked up the blood-stained knife and used it to stir the contents of the cauldron. As she did so, she mumbled some words which sounded arcane and mystic but which were little more than invented sounds. Like the ingredients she had placed in the pot, they were meaningless and served no purpose except to impress the audience.

That audience was watching her intently, most of them nervous at being in the presence of sorcery yet fascinated to watch a witch at work.

Part of Scota despised them for their foolish gullibility yet she maintained her concentration because she knew that this small deception was less important than what she must say to the High King. She hoped that his killing of the messenger had assuaged some of his bloodlust but there was always a risk when dealing with his violent moods.

She had, at least, positioned herself so that the fire and the cauldron sat between them, making it more difficult for him to reach her if he should take it into his head to vent his temper on her.

Now, though, she decided, she would show him her worth. When he heard what she had to say, his anger would be directed elsewhere.

153

The heat from the fire brought beads of sweat to her face but she ignored the discomfort and carried on with her performance. She closed her eyes, continuing to mumble meaningless sounds. Then, when she felt enough time had passed, she stopped stirring the water, opened her eyes and leaned over to peer into the sticky mess of the cauldron's simmering contents, waving one hand to dispel the fingers of steam which rose from the pot.

"What do you see?" Elim demanded almost immediately.

"Fire," she replied, hoping that some of the spectators might have forgotten the messenger's comment about the fort being ablaze.

"Fire and death."

"Fergus?" Elim snapped.

"I cannot see for certain," she replied. "But he was there."

That was safe enough. Where else would Elim's son be? But whether he was dead or a prisoner was something she dared not express an opinion on in case she were proved wrong.

Before the High King could interrupt, she continued, "But I see who is behind this. It is Tuathal, son of Fiacha Finnolach. He has crossed the sea, raised a rebellion and seeks to reclaim his father's position as High King."

That news brought a loud stir of murmuring from the crowd but Elim simply snorted.

"Tuathal? He is a boy! Has he weaned himself away from his mother's tits to confront me?"

"His mother died many years ago," Scota replied automatically. "It is his grandfather, Coel of the Caledones, who has supplied him with men and boats."

"Then he is as much a fool as the puppy!" Elim declared.

Scota continued to peer into the cauldron, making a show of waving her hands over the surface of the water and occasionally stirring it with the dagger.

"There is more," she continued. "Some of the men of Ulster have already joined him. I see two brothers."

She hesitated, frowning in apparent concentration before explaining, "Findmall the druid and the swordmaster, Fiacha Cassan."

"Those two!" barked Elim. "I would have removed their heads years ago if they had not sworn loyalty and paid handsome tribute. Yet see how they repay me for my leniency?"

154

Scota had decided to keep Calgacus' presence to herself for the time being. The man's name was famous in song and even here in Eriu, everyone knew who he was. If Elim's warriors learned they were up against such a famous War Leader, some might become apprehensive while others might decide to challenge Calgacus in order to prove their bravery. Neither of those reactions suited Scota.

"What else do you see?" Elim asked her.

"They are coming to Tara," she replied. "Yet they have barely a thousand men."

"Is that all?" Elim scoffed. His scowl was replaced by a grim smile as he said, "It hardly seems worth worrying over."

"Yet they have taken Emain Macha," Scota reminded him. "The strongest fortress in Ulster has fallen to them."

Elim's expression darkened again but Scota stood up and faced him across the cauldron.

"It is as well that you summoned Niall from Leinster," she told him. "He will be here in a few days. With his forces and the Scotti, together with your own war band, you will have more than enough men to deal with this rebellion."

Elim nodded pensively, rubbing his chin with one hand.

"I will summon Sanb of Connacht as well," he decided. "The man has been troublesome of late and it would do him good to be reminded that he serves me."

Scota nodded, "Indeed it would, Lord. Yet his presence is hardly required. In any event, I believe Tuathal will get here before Sanb can reach us."

She could tell that Elim had calmed down. His mind was racing now, planning and calculating as he worked out distances and speed of march.

"You are sure they are coming directly here?" he asked her pointedly.

"I believe so, Lord. Of course, they may change their minds but that is their current intention."

She felt safe making that prediction. What other choice did Tuathal have? The longer he waited, the more men Elim could summon to help him crush the rebellion. Waiting was only an option if the High King decided to take the war to the rebels. Yet if he did that, Scota foresaw a problem. Both sides required an absolute victory, with the death of their enemy's leader. Anything less would leave the matter unresolved, with the prospect of years of further warfare.

She peered into the cauldron again, giving it another stir with the dagger.

"I see a hill," she murmured. "It is important."

"We have no shortage of hills," Elim remarked caustically.

"It is the Hill of Achall," Scota informed him. "That is where the decisive battle will be fought."

She heard another murmur from the audience. The Hill of Achall lay only a short distance from Tara and everyone in the house knew it well.

Elim's mouth twitched but he rubbed his hand over his mouth and cheeks before nodding his agreement.

"If he has only a thousand men and is coming to challenge me anyway, I see no need to tire our men out with long marches. Besides, gathering our war host here will take a few days. So, let the puppy come. He will walk into our trap like a fly into a spider's web and we shall crush him."

That brought a muted cheer from the warriors which, when Elim nodded his approval, grew to a rousing acclamation of his plan.

"You have done well," Elim told Scota. "Now go and tell your people I have need of them again."

"Of course, High King. I shall do so immediately."

Aedan, War Leader of the Scotti, was waiting for Scota when she returned to her home but his wrinkled, aged face showed the resentment which always simmered in his heart whenever she exercised her power over him.

He was over sixty years old now, a man used to command but who had been compelled to obey Scota because it was she who had saved their tribe from slavery and death.

The price she had paid for that was a burden she had learned to bear but it weighed more heavily on Aedan and he made little effort to conceal his bitterness.

Despite his advancing years and the silvery grey of his hair, he was still a powerful figure, deep-chested and broad-shouldered, with arms and legs twice the thickness of Scota's. He was a warrior born and bred but Scota regarded him as too unimaginative to be a truly effective War Leader. He was

156

undeniably brave but he lacked the genuine talent of someone like Elim mac Conrach or Calgacus.

His eyes regarded Scota with sullen indignation at being summoned to her house so late in the day but he gave his grudging understanding when she told him of the news from Emain Macha.

"The High King is gathering his war host," she informed him. "You will send word to all the fighting men of the Scotti. We are to muster on the Hill of Achall in three days' time."

"It shall be as you command," Aedan said grudgingly, his eyes betraying his lack of enthusiasm for yet another war at the behest of Elim mac Conrach.

"This rebellion presents a great threat to the High King," Scota warned. "Of all the men who have tried to oust him, Tuathal has the strongest claim to the Kingship."

"Yet he has only a thousand men," Aedan sniffed. "Why do we not march out and hunt him down? The High King can gather three thousand spears easily enough."

"Because Tuathal may decide to flee when he sees our power," Scota replied. "If he runs, the High King may never catch him and that means the threat will continue. The best strategy is to wait and let him come to us. He knows he must challenge the High King directly. He also knows that one of them must die if the rule of Eriu is to be decided."

"If he has any sense, he will run anyway," Aedan offered sourly.

"But the prize he seeks is a great one," Scota said. "He must fight if he is to gain that prize."

Aedan remained unconvinced.

"With a thousand men, he cannot defeat the High King if we gather on the Hill of Achall. That would be folly. His men will probably desert him as soon as they see the strength of our position."

"Which is why," Scota smiled, "I have a suggestion which I will persuade the High King to follow. There must be a battle and the issue must be settled."

Aedan did not offer any further arguments. He knew when Scota had made up her mind, just as he knew that the Scotti were pledged to the High King.

"I will gather our war band," he agreed. "Is there anything else I need to know?"

Scota shook her head. In truth, there was a great deal she wished to tell him but Aedan was too simple a man to harbour secrets and could easily give something away. She would keep her plans to herself until the day came when Tuathal faced Elim on the battlefield. Then, if the High King could be persuaded to adopt her plan, Tuathal would be the one who received the greatest surprise.

Aedan simply nodded and left, his feet stomping on the rush-strewn floor of the house to show his inner fury.

Scota listened to him depart, smiling to herself. Aedan was predictable and dull but he was perhaps the best man for her needs. He might grumble at what she asked of him but he would obey her because he had sworn to do so. That was what Scota required because the culmination of two years of planning lay just ahead of her.

That thought sent a shiver of anticipation, excitement and dread through her bones, a tremor which she struggled to quell.

"Remain calm," she told herself. "You cannot falter now."

But everything rested on Tuathal coming to the Hill of Achall. Which meant that Finn must play his part well.

Chapter XVIII

The bulk of Tuathal's army had at last reached Emain Macha, trudging in footsore and weary, with a long train of stragglers still slowly arriving piecemeal. All of these new arrivals needed to be fed and Tuathal's cavalry were kept busy foraging for supplies. But this was the lean time of year, when the previous year's stored harvest was almost depleted and the new crops had not had time to grow. Summer was always a hungry time of year and war bands were continually short of food. This made men resentful and tempers often flared so Calgacus insisted that all food must be shared out equally whenever possible.

Shelter was the other great problem. The village was not nearly large enough to house all the warriors and there were no other buildings inside the fortress other than the razed ashes of Fergus' hall. Some of the men constructed temporary shelters for themselves while others were too tired to do anything except spend the night sleeping on the ground with their cloaks as blankets.

"We need to allow them some rest," Tuathal declared.

Calgacus was feeling tired as well. Organising a large army was not easy. Quite apart from the logistical issues of food and shelter, there were scouts and sentries to be organised and the constant problem of preventing fights breaking out between the various rival war bands. In particular, those who had taken part in the stunning capture of Emain Macha had plunder and slaves to show off while the foot soldiers had nothing to show except the blisters they had earned on their long march.

"We cannot stay too long," Calgacus told Tuathal. "For one thing, an idle army creates its own problems. For another, we need a quick victory over Elim. Whether he comes to us or we go to him, we cannot afford to sit around doing nothing."

"We will rest for one day," Tuathal decided. "We cannot win if our men are exhausted."

Calgacus nodded his agreement. The more he saw of Tuathal, the more impressed he became with the young man. Coel's grandson might have some idealistic views on life but he was an inspiration to his warriors. He spent much of his time walking or riding through the widespread camp that was burgeoning out around the fortress of Emain Macha, talking to the men, praising them and providing encouragement. Calgacus could see the reaction Tuathal received and he knew that the young man had a talent for inspiring others. He was grateful for this because it meant he could concentrate on the main problem that now faced them.

"We have captured one of Elim's strongholds and we have the head of his son," he told Tuathal's war council. "If that does not bring him against us soon, I don't know what will."

"Your strategy is working so far," Tuathal remarked.

"Yes, but there is a problem. The best way to defeat a larger army is to set an ambush and catch them on the march. The trouble is, you need the right terrain for that. Steep hills, narrow valleys or trackways which run through dense forests are the best places for such traps. So far, this land doesn't present many opportunities."

"There is no need for that," declared Fiacha Cassan. "We should march on Tara and attack the Usurper before he has time to gather his full strength."

"How long will it take for our army to march there?" Calgacus asked.

"A few days," the tall warrior admitted.

"Which is more than enough time for Elim to summon a large war band. Remember, he has spies in our camp and he must know we are here."

"We could attack at night," Fiacha Cassan suggested. "Catch them by surprise."

"That is an option," Calgacus agreed reluctantly. "But night attacks are difficult to carry out effectively. Men can become lost or disoriented in the darkness."

"I know the truth of that," Tuathal agreed. "We almost got lost trying to find the gates of Emain Macha last night." Looking at Calgacus, he asked, "So what do you propose?"

"I think we should keep our options open," Calgacus replied. "An ambush is still the best plan and perhaps we will find a suitable site between here and Tara."

He gave the two brothers a searching look as he asked, "Do you know of any such places?"

Findmall and Fiacha Cassan exchanged a look before the druid confessed, "In truth, we do not know this area well. But Eriu

160

has a wonderful variety of landscape. There are marshes, rocky outcrops, and more hills and forests than you can count."

"Which doesn't really help me," Calgacus sighed.

"Then what do you suggest?" Tuathal asked.

"Liscus and I will ride out in the morning and scout the land. We'll try to find a suitable site for an ambush. You give your men the day's rest they need, then come after us. Head straight for Tara as quickly as you can. If we can't find a suitable place, we will have no alternative but to make a night attack on Tara in the hope of catching Elim unprepared."

He looked at their faces and saw their agreement but Runt objected, "That's not much of a plan, Cal."

"It's all I've got at the moment," Calgacus sighed. "We need a quick victory or we have no chance."

"What about Fergus' head?" Fiacha Cassan asked. "Do we send it to the Usurper? It is beginning to stink."

"There is no point in sending it unless we have found a place where we can beat him," Calgacus replied. "Keep it and hold your nose against the smell."

Fiacha Cassan pulled a face but did not argue.

"What about Emain Macha?" Tuathal asked. "How many men should we leave to hold it?"

"None," Calgacus told him. "We need every man we have. Emain Macha no longer matters. It seems unlikely Elim will be able to get past us to recapture it but even if he does, it won't make any real difference. If we win, you rule the entire country. If we lose, then Emain Macha is no refuge. We'll be doing well to reach the sea and escape."

"We will not lose," Tuathal asserted. "But I would not like to allow Emain Macha to fall into anyone else's hands. Why don't we occupy it and let the Usurper come to us? If we keep the bulk of our war host hidden some distance away, we could launch a surprise attack once his army has settled in for a siege."

"That's not a bad idea if we had more men and more time," Calgacus agreed. "The problem arises if he does not come straight away. What do we do if he raises a force of several thousand men before coming here? If he knows the place has fallen, he might not react the way we want him to."

"But you said taking Emain Macha would provoke him," Eudaf protested.

161

"I said it might provoke him. I hope it does but I have learned not to rely on the enemy doing what I want."

Tuathal frowned, "I understand what you are saying but I would not like to leave Emain Macha empty."

"Then leave behind any men who are sick or too tired to march any further. Put a good commander in charge if you must but don't garrison the place with fit men we need for the coming fight."

Tuathal nodded, "I hear you, Calgacus. I will follow your advice."

Calgacus gave the young man a nod of encouragement but he struggled to force a smile to his lips. No matter how he considered their options, he could see no way of defeating Elim mac Conrach without a huge amount of luck. Yet, apart from Runt, who understood the magnitude of what they faced, none of the others appeared to have any real concerns. Tuathal was determined that it was his destiny to rule Eriu, Eudaf smiled and nodded at everything his cousin said and the two brothers, Findmall and Fiacha Cassan, seemed to live in a world of absolute certainty.

The six of them were sharing one of the roundhouses in the village below Emain Macha. The fortress itself had little to offer now that the main building had been burned to the ground but Tuathal wished to be close to his warriors in any case.

"We should get some sleep," Calgacus suggested, although he knew he would find sleep difficult. The problem of how to defeat the High King would torment him until he was able to scout out the land and find a suitable site for an ambush.

And then his plans were cast into confusion because one of Tuathal's guards came in and announced that a local chieftain had come to join them and had insisted on speaking to Calgacus.

"Be careful, Cal," warned Runt. "He might be here to kill you. Elim has tried to get you three times already."

"I'll be careful. But let's keep him well away from Tuathal in case he has come with murder in mind."

They placed their stools in a semi-circle around the hearth fire which now blazed up again as Findmall placed another block of peat on the glowing embers. A seventh stool was set facing them, with Tuathal and Calgacus directly across the fire and Runt and Fiacha Cassan nearest the visitor's seat.

The man who entered was tall and proud, his hair greying but his shoulders set straight. He was a lean man, dressed in well

162

made clothing and wearing rings and brooches that marked him as a nobleman. He had only a dagger with him, the guards having insisted that he surrender his sword before he would be allowed to see Tuathal or Calgacus.

"I am Finn mac Finnbar," he announced proudly. "I am a chieftain of Ulster and lord of several villages."

"I know you, Finn," smiled Findmall. "You serve the Usurper, Elim mac Conrach."

"I did," Finn admitted. "Now I wish to serve Tuathal Techtmar. That is what they are calling you, is it not, Lord?"

Tuathal gave a smile and a nod, gesturing towards the empty stool.

"Sit and be welcome, Finn," he invited. "Let us drink some ale together while we talk."

Eudaf and Findmall dipped mugs into a small cask of ale they had taken from Fergus' fortress and passed the cups around. Tuathal poured a small libation to the Gods, then they drank.

"So you wish to join my army," Tuathal said. "How many men do you bring?"

"Forty seven," Finn replied. "All good men. But I bring more than that."

His eyes fixed on Calgacus as he added, "I bring a message from Scota."

Fiacha Cassan hissed a low curse and Findmall made a protective sign at the mention of the sorceress's name.

Calgacus managed to conceal his dismay at this confirmation that the High King knew of their arrival in Eriu.

Smiling, he asked Finn, "What message has she given you?"

Finn took a deep breath before answering, "She told me to tell you that you must march to Tara quickly. The High King will be gathering his army on the Hill of Achall to await you. There, she says, you will be victorious and Elim mac Conrach will die."

Eudaf blurted, "That is good news!"

Calgacus waved the young man to silence as he kept his eyes on Finn.

"You are telling us that the High King's witch wants us to win?"

Finn shrugged, "She claimed she had seen the future and that, while nothing is absolutely certain, she had foreseen your triumph as the most likely outcome. But only if you reach Tara quickly. Elim has summoned Sanb of Connacht to join him and will soon have so many warriors it will be impossible to defeat him."

"It's a trap!" muttered Runt.

"Very possibly," Calgacus agreed before asking Finn, "Do you believe her?"

"Who can believe a witch?" Finn retorted bitterly. "I was more than surprised when she told me to come to you and offer my sword. I thought she might be testing my loyalty to the High King and I expected her to denounce me if I agreed to do her bidding. But she told me Elim desires my death and that I had no choice but to join with you if I wish to survive."

He turned his attention to Tuathal as he went on, "I served your father loyally until his death."

"His murder," Findmall put in softly.

Finn ignored the interruption and continued, "I knelt to Elim mac Conrach because the only other choice was to die. He was too powerful for me to oppose."

"Others stood against him," Findmall remarked.

"And died," Finn shot back sharply. "And I note that you were not among them."

Fiacha Cassan was about to make a vociferous defence of his family's honour but Calgacus silenced him with a peremptory wave of his hand and a curt command to remain seated.

Calmly, Tuathal said, "Let the past be forgotten. It is the future we must face. Together."

Calgacus asked Finn, "Tell me about this hill you mentioned where Elim is supposed to be waiting for us."

"It lies near Tara," Finn said. "It blocks your path to the sacred site."

Findmall interjected, "Achall was a princess of the elder days. She is said to have gone to the hill to mourn her brother who was slain in battle. She died of grief and the hill is named for her."

"I am less interested in stories than in the lie of the land," Calgacus told him. "What are the approaches like? Is the hill steep and high?"

A man can stroll up it easily in less time than it takes a pot to boil," Finn replied. "It is not high but it stands at one side of a wide valley which is mostly meadow and farmland, so it overlooks all the approaches."

"Any rivers or forests nearby?" Calgacus probed.

"A small stream or two," Finn told him. "There are some small patches of woodland but nothing to speak of. The ground is relatively open."

Runt snorted, "A frontal attack on a hill where he can see us coming."

"The Romans have beaten tribes who defend hilltops," Calgacus reminded him.

"Yes," agreed Runt. "But we don't have a Roman Legion under our command."

Calgacus tried not to show his anxiety. What Finn had told him had only confirmed his worst fears.

"So why does Scota think we can win? Apart from her visions, of course."

"I do not know," Finn admitted. "All I can say is that, if Scota is prepared to turn against Elim, the Scotti will follow her lead. They are ferocious fighters and there are several hundred of them in the High King's war host."

"That could tip the scales in our favour," Tuathal murmured.

"Only if she really has decided to switch sides," Calgacus cautioned. "This could be nothing but a ploy to make us walk into a trap."

"Do we have a choice?" Tuathal countered. "If Scota knows we are here, we need to act before the Usurper gathers too strong a force."

"He might be planning exactly what I was thinking about," Calgacus said thoughtfully. "He could catch us on the march."

"He had not yet summoned his war host when I left Tara," Finn put in.

Fiacha Cassan muttered, "So you say."

Finn shot the swordsman a dark look but bit back his retort and said, "Anyone who knows me can tell you that I am a man of honour. I cannot speak for Scota. She is close-mouthed and secretive, as well as being a witch. I would not trust her unless I had no choice. It may be that she has duped me into coming here but I do know that Elim mac Conrach is a tyrant and I would gladly see him overthrown. By coming here, I have made myself his enemy and he does not treat his enemies well."

Tuathal said, "Then we need to win for all our sakes."

Calgacus continued to question the old chieftain for a long time, asking him to sketch a map of the area around the Hill of

165

Achall and demanding as much information as he could glean about the High King's war band. Finn's knowledge of the terrain was vague but he was helpful when it came to describing the High King's warriors, their weapons and tactics. Most of what he told Calgacus was little more than confirmation of what Calgacus had already surmised but even that was helpful.

Eventually, long after the others had grown bored, Calgacus thanked Finn and allowed him to leave, with Tuathal promising the chieftain a place of honour in his war host.

When the old man had left, Calgacus looked at the others with a worried frown on his face.

"This changes very little," he told them. "Except that now they definitely know we are coming, so there is no hope of making a surprise attack."

"Do you believe him?" Tuathal asked. "He seems an honest fellow."

"If I didn't have to stake all our lives on it, I'd say he is as honest as anyone," Calgacus agreed. "Whether what he has told us is true, though, is another matter. Why would the High King's witch turn against him? And why does she want us to march straight to Tara?"

"Never do what your enemy wants," Runt reminded him.

"You are right, Liscus," Calgacus nodded. "But I don't think we have a great deal of choice. The longer we wait, the stronger Elim grows."

"You cannot trust the words of the sorceress!" Findmall objected.

"I don't. But we have little option other than to go with the plan I outlined earlier. Liscus and I will scout ahead and Tuathal will bring the army as quickly as possible."

Then he gave Fiacha Cassan a hard smile as he added, "But I have a special job for you."

Chapter XIX

A warm sun bathed the gentle slopes of the Hill of Achall where the lush grass grew thick and wild flowers decorated the meadows with splashes of bright colour. This was normally a peaceful place, occupied by sheep and cattle but the beasts had been driven away and now the grass and flowers were being trampled as the High King's army assembled.

Scota watched as the warriors trudged up from Tara and gathered in their war bands on the crown of the hill that overlooked the wide plain. They came carrying spears, shields and swords, proclaiming their prowess and boasting of the slaughter they would accomplish.

"If the puppy dares show his face," Elim mac Conrach constantly cautioned. "He is likely to piss himself and run back to his grandfather when he sees our strength."

The High King's war host numbered nearly three thousand, most of them veterans of his long campaigns to subdue the other Kings of Eriu. Even without the additional strength of the men of Connacht whose King, the wily Sanb, had sent word of his approach but who had not yet arrived, Elim was confident that he had more than enough proven warriors to defeat Tuathal. His son, Niall, had hurried north from Leinster, bringing a cadre of his own fighting men along with the levies from Leinster who had so recently fought against the High King. These men were now placed in the front ranks where they would be able to demonstrate their renewed loyalty to Elim.

The war bands gathered throughout the morning and Elim's greatest worry was that Tuathal would refuse to fight him.

"I want this finished quickly," he growled. "I want his head on a spike and I want his army crushed."

Elim's disdain for Tuathal was evident as the High King organised his war host, directing the various tribal groups to where he wanted them positioned.

"Our scouts say he has only a few hundred men," Elim scoffed. "It won't take us long to beat them. If they attack us at all."

167

His son, Niall, offered, "If they refuse to fight, we can hunt them down. Most of them are on foot and we have chariots and horsemen who can chase them back to the sea."

"I do not want to chase them," Elim growled. "I want them dead."

Scota, seeing an opportunity to ensure the battle was a decisive one, said, "Perhaps it would help if we did not appear quite as strong as we are."

Niall regarded her with a puzzled frown but Elim, always quick when it came to matters of war, nodded, "You are right, Scota. If our position appears unassailable, they might turn and run. I want to draw them onto our spears, then crush them."

"How can we do that?" Niall asked, perplexed.

"By hiding some of our warriors," Elim told him with a scathing glance. "If we conceal part of our army on the rear slope of the hill, they will think we are weaker than we are. Then, when they march up to join battle, our hidden reserves will sweep round behind them and surround them."

Niall grinned, beaming his approval of his father's cunning.

"I would be honoured if the Scotti could perform this task for you, High King," Scota ventured.

Elim nodded, "Very well. Tell your people to remain out of sight on our right flank. I shall place some of my own warriors from Ulster on the left."

"I shall inform my people immediately," Scota promised.

She turned and walked to where her chariot was waiting for her a short distance away. Amhairgin, her driver, offered a hand to help her climb onto the platform before nimbly leaping aboard and taking up the reins. Amhairgin, like all charioteers, was slightly built and wiry. He was, though, older than most drivers, being over fifty years of age. He had been Scota's driver for fifteen years, ever since she had risen to her position as ruler of the Scotti and in all that time she had rarely exchanged more than a few words with the man. As far as Scota was concerned, Amhairgin was the ideal driver for her; he was loyal, obedient and completely indifferent to anything except the care of his ponies and chariot.

That chariot gleamed, the wood polished to a bright sheen, ribbons and tassels of red, yellow and blue decorating the side loops, and the iron rims of the wheels glistening in the bright sun. The ponies' manes were braided and also decorated by ribbons of cloth, and their tails were docked so as to prevent them flicking into Amhairgin's face when he stood at the front of the chariot.

Scota smiled to herself when she studied the immaculate condition of the vehicle. Only the central platform, suspended on its web of ropes to provide an element of comfort for the passengers, was unpolished, the rougher surface providing more grip for her feet.

Standing tall, she placed one hand on the curved rim of a side loop and told Amhairgin, "Take me to Aedan."

Amhairgin flicked the reins and called to his ponies who hauled the chariot into motion.

The hilltop was a mass of warriors, together with clusters of women and even a few children who had come to witness the battle and who had brought provisions of meat, cheese and bread which they were sharing with their menfolk. Amhairgin picked a slow, cautious route through the crowd, heading to where the Scotti waited in the place of honour on the right flank.

As they rode, Scota noticed a familiar figure among the women and tapped Amhairgin's shoulder as a signal to stop.

"Braine?" she called.

The other women glanced at Scota before averting their eyes in case she cast a spell on them but Elim's daughter stood and walked slowly over to the chariot.

"Does your father know you are here?" Scota asked the girl.

Braine shrugged, "I just wanted to see what happens. I've never seen a battle before."

"It is too dangerous for you here," Scota told her.

"Other women are here," Braine retorted. "You are here."

"That is different," Scota replied. "I am not the High King's daughter. You should return to Tara."

"I will be safe," Braine argued. "My father and brother both say this fight will be over quickly. The rebels cannot beat us."

"That is not the point," Scota said firmly. "There will be spears thrown, slingstones hurled and possibly arrows shot. Horses might lose their riders and run in panic. Even if you stay well back, you might be hurt or even killed."

"I will take good care to stay away from the fighting," Braine insisted.

"Then why don't you come with me to the Scotti? I can have some men appointed to protect you."

169

"There is no need," Braine declared with all the finality of a teenage girl who had made up her mind what she wanted.

Scota decided that arguing would serve no purpose, so she sighed, nodded and told Amhairgin to continue. The best way to keep Braine safe would be to inform the High King of the girl's presence. Elim would no doubt send some men to escort Braine back to Tara.

First, though, Scota needed to give her instructions to Aedan and the warriors of the Scotti.

Aedan came to meet her as she dismounted from her chariot. The burly War Leader, dressed in a thick leather tunic that was dotted with iron studs and wearing an iron helmet, listened gravely to the High King's commands before grunting his understanding.

"This is an important day," Scota told him. "The fate of Eriu rests on victory."

"I understand," Aedan replied dourly.

Scota could read the impatience and irritation in Aedan's eyes but she did not release him until she had given very specific instructions on what she needed the Scotti to do when the battle began.

"Everything rests on you," she insisted.

Aedan's reply was cut short by the sudden blaring of war horns from the hilltop.

"They are coming!" was the cry that echoed through the ranks of the High King's war host.

"Go!" Scota ordered Aedan. "Take your position and watch for my signal."

Aedan hurried away, barking orders to the warriors of the Scotti and Scota turned to mount her chariot. As she climbed aboard, she found her heart was thumping in her chest.

Remain calm, she told herself. Yet it was not easy because she knew how uncertain battle could be. She had done all she could to arrange things so that victory could be achieved but there was always an element of doubt, especially when the combatants were led by men like Elim and Calgacus.

"What have you got planned, Calgacus?" she wondered aloud.

Chapter XX

Calgacus sat astride his war pony as he gazed across the wide valley, taking his first look at the Hill of Achall and the High King's war host.

Behind him, he could hear the druid, Findmall, chivvying the warriors into position and calling for the horns to blow and the men to sing while they thrust their spears high into the air and proclaimed their loyal support for Tuathal Techtmar.

The druid was doing a decent job, Calgacus thought. He had insisted that the warriors should sing on their march in order to bolster their morale yet he had known they would falter when they first saw the enemy forces awaiting them and had told Findmall to keep their passions aroused.

He pushed Findmall to the back of his mind. The army was slowly extending from a ragged column into a long line which would face the hill opposite. Yet it was a pitifully small army and Calgacus could feel his own dismay that he had been unable to think of a strategy which would give them a genuine chance to defeat the High King.

His efforts to find a suitable place for an ambush had been hampered by the gently rolling terrain and by Elim's scouts who had been out in force and had driven him and Runt back to the security of the advancing war host. Their own scouts had been few in number since Fiacha Cassan had ridden away with the bulk of their mounted men, promising to follow Calgacus' instructions. Fiacha Cassan was Calgacus' only real hope of giving the High King a surprise. He was the right man for the task because he was brave and fearless but Calgacus knew the swordsman was also impetuous. That meant he might not follow his orders properly and any slim chance they had of victory might be lost as a result.

Calgacus, normally so confident when it came to war, was assailed by doubt. He kept wondering whether he should have followed Tuathal's suggestion of remaining at Emain Macha but he told himself that would have been folly. Inviting Elim to attack them when the High King could afford to wait would have achieved nothing except to increase their chances of being utterly defeated.

On the other hand, he reflected bitterly, he was doing precisely what the enemy wanted him to do and now faced the prospect of launching an assault against superior numbers who held a stronger position.

To add to his worries, Finn, the elderly chieftain who had brought Scota's message, had deserted them, taking his men away during the night and presumably returning to his home to await the outcome of the battle.

"He has deceived us!" Findmall complained. "He has tricked us into coming here and now he has gone back to his master."

Calgacus could not deny that possibility but he made an effort to appear unconcerned.

"We always knew we had to come here," he shrugged. "Losing fifty men will not affect the outcome of the battle."

"We have had more than that join us since we began the march," Tuathal insisted. "Finn is a frightened old man who simply wants to avoid danger. I will not forget that he has deserted us but he is a problem for another day. We can win without him."

Calgacus hoped the young Prince was correct. For his own part, he felt trapped and angry with himself for being dragged into fighting for a cause he did not believe in, especially when their chances of success were so slim.

But they were here and he had run out of options. Now they faced the prospect of Tuathal's dream being shattered on the slopes of the Hill of Achall.

That hill was crowned by Elim's war host, a strong phalanx of spears and swords, with horns and drums of their own and totems held aloft to taunt their enemies. Fox skulls, horse manes, boar's heads and a myriad other emblems adorned the poles that were waved above the heads of the warriors who held the high ground.

"There don't seem to be as many as we thought," Runt observed.

Calgacus nodded, "I'd say around two thousand at most."

"Their numbers are not important," Tuathal declared from where his pony sat next to Calgacus. "We can beat them."

172

"They still outnumber us two to one," Calgacus pointed out. And they hold the high ground. If we attack, our men will be tired by the time they reach them."

Tuathal gave a dismissive shrug.

"Would you have me run away?" he asked. "Your plan is a good one."

Calgacus shook his head. He knew his battle plan was little more than desperation. During his long life of war, he had specialised in ambush, in tricking his enemy into situations where he held the advantages. Yet now he was directing the aggressors, not the defenders, and he was all too aware of how inadequate their army was.

Eudaf, whose normal good humour had been replaced by a nervous anxiety, sat pale-faced and wide-eyed beside Tuathal.

He ventured, "It is good that they do not have as many men as we feared, though, isn't it?"

Calgacus grunted, "Unless he has more men hidden out of sight behind the hill. That's what I'd do if I were him."

"Best keep that to ourselves," Tuathal suggested.

Calgacus nodded his agreement. Tuathal, he thought, had genuine potential as an effective ruler. The aspiring High King appeared calm and relaxed, exuding an air of confidence which would, Calgacus knew, inspire the men who were about to follow him into battle. Tuathal was dressed in a coat of chainmail and wearing a gleaming helmet of polished iron, with a sword on his back and an iron-rimmed shield on his left arm. There was no doubt he looked the part of a warrior king and now it was time for him to act like one.

"They have chariots," Runt warned, nodding his head to indicate around forty of the nimble war vehicles which were already riding to and fro across the plain at the foot of the hill.

Calgacus shrugged, "They won't do us much harm. There aren't enough of them. If they deliver their riders into battle on foot, we'll swamp them, so all they can do is ride across our front and throw spears. It will be a nuisance but it won't affect the outcome of the battle."

He looked again at the force confronting them and clucked his tongue thoughtfully.

"I'm more worried about their cavalry," he admitted. "They could make life difficult for us if they get round our flanks but he doesn't seem to have more than a few dozen."

173

"He's fighting the old-fashioned way," Runt put in. "Stand on a hill and dare your enemy to come up to face you."

Calgacus nodded, "Then it's time we tried to provoke him into coming down onto the plain."

That was his main hope. Tuathal's war host was in an extended line, its left flank partly protected by a patch of boggy ground which would slow down any enemy who attempted to encircle them on that side. On the right was a small patch of woodland which would block any cavalry attack. It also contained a hundred warriors who had been instructed to remain hidden in the hope they could spring a surprise attack of their own if the High King's war host could be tempted to come down to fight.

It was the best stratagem Calgacus could devise but he was not confident it would succeed because he doubted whether Elim would abandon his strong position. Even if he did, his superior numbers might still sweep away Tuathal's thin battle line. But it was the only hope Calgacus had and he had no further excuses for delay.

He took a piece of cord from a belt pouch and tied back his long, dark hair. Then he reached out and took his shield from Runt, looping it over his left arm. It was made of wicker and covered with tough leather, with an iron rim and central boss.

Eudaf, still looking nervous, asked, "What about the witch? She might cast a spell on us."

Calgacus snorted to show what he thought of that. He had spent years watching druids perform magical rites which they insisted would halt the advance of the Roman Legions. Yet the soldiers of Rome had smashed through ghost fences and trampled sacred ground with seeming impunity from the curses that were supposed to strike them dead. He doubted whether Elim's sorceress would be any more successful in using magic against them. Yet he knew that was not what Tuathal's warriors needed to hear, so he replied, "Don't worry about her. I have my magic sword, remember?"

He could almost feel Runt chuckling softly. The little man knew how much Calgacus despised the stories about his magical sword but he also understood the necessity of using those stories.

Calgacus looked back over his shoulder and saw that Findmall had nearly completed the manoeuvre of ordering the war host into some sort of line along the face of the low ridge. He signalled to the druid that they were about to begin and saw the man's wave of acknowledgement.

"Let's go!" he declared, lifting his feet to prod his pony into motion. The beast set off at a trot, its stocky body somehow supporting Calgacus' enormous frame. His feet dangled so low that they almost brushed the ground but he had ridden such horses all his life and he knew that, while the pony might not be able to gallop very quickly under his weight, it had enough stamina to keep going for a long time.

He led Runt, Tuathal, Eudaf and the four Caledones who had been selected to protect Tuathal, out onto the open field.

This valley was lush and green, obviously grazing land for herds of cattle and flocks of sheep which had been led away at the news of the war host's approach. As Calgacus had feared, there was no cover at all, nowhere to conceal men in ambush and nowhere to hide if the enemy's horsemen rode around their flanks.

The chariots ahead of them ceased their display of manoeuvre and turned to face them. One of the vehicles lumbered into motion and came to meet them.

"There's always one," Calgacus muttered.

His small band of riders reined in two hundred paces from where the land began to rise, sitting patiently on their ponies as the chariot swung round and the long-haired warrior it bore leaped to the ground, spear in hand. He was a young man, barely in his twenties, his muscular arms bare and his body protected by a tunic of stiff leather. He wore rings and arm bands of silver and bronze and he carried a slender sword, the mark of a nobleman, at his left hip.

"I am Podraig mac Donnchad," he declared proudly as he thumped a fist against his chest. "I challenge your champion to single combat!"

It was not entirely clear who he had directed the challenge to but Calgacus slowly eased his pony forwards and forced the young warrior to look at him.

He said, "We are not here to waste time with young peacocks who should know better than to oppose their rightful High King. Go and tell Elim mac Conrach that Tuathal mac Finnolach wishes to speak to him."

"You are afraid to fight me!" the young warrior mocked.

"Terrified," Calgacus agreed caustically. "Go and tell Elim that as well if you wish, but go and fetch him."

175

Podraig mac Donnchad returned a contemptuous snort.

"You are a big fellow, Tuathal," he sneered. "That is good. It will add to my renown when I sing of how I bested you."

"I am not Tuathal," Calgacus shot back. "He is here to speak to Elim mac Conrach, not with you."

Podraig was not at all put out by his error. He demanded, "Then give me your name so that I can remember your death when I celebrate our victory."

Calgacus was not a boastful man but he knew the value of his reputation and he also understood that a braggart like Podraig would not respond to pleading, so he replied, "I am Calgacus, son of Cunobelinos, son of Tasciovanus, son of the great Cassivellaunos who defeated Julius Caesar. I was War Leader of the Silures when they destroyed a Roman Legion and I led the Iceni when they annihilated another. I have defeated the Brigantes, killing their champion in single combat and, as War Leader of the Boresti, I have slaughtered their foes so that none dare come against us."

He could see the young warrior's eyes widening as he continued, "You may have heard of me. I am the only living man who has beaten the Romans. I opposed the druids and won. And I have a magical sword which means no man can beat me in single combat. No doubt you have heard about that, too."

He could see Podraig was about to bluster, so he hurriedly added, "Listen to me, boy. I have no wish to kill you. There is no disgrace in refusing to fight me here and now. There will be plenty of time for killing once the battle starts. Now, if you want to retire without losing face, go and tell your comrades that I refused to fight you. But, by all the Gods, go and tell Elim mac Conrach that I want to talk to him. Do you understand me?"

Podraig mac Donnchad lifted his chin and stood tall as he retorted, "Even if you are who you say you are, old man, you are a proven coward. I see that you are too frightened to face me."

Calgacus ignored the taunt, merely sitting on his pony and staring, stony-faced, at the young warrior. Eventually, after a few more jibes and insults, Podraig spat on the ground and contemptuously turned his back, striding over to his waiting chariot and leaping nimbly onto the fighting platform.

As his driver flicked the two ponies into motion, Podraig turned back and called, "Be sure your name will be forever tainted by the tale of your cowardice!"

176

Calgacus shook his head sadly as he turned his pony and rejoined his companions.

"As I said, there is always one," he sighed.

"Will he fetch Elim, do you think?" Tuathal asked.

"I think so," Calgacus nodded. "He won't want to give up the chance to boast about how he scared me into refusing to fight him. If he can tell his King a story like that, he'll do it."

"Then let us hope Elim heeds him," Tuathal said.

Calgacus shared the young man's concern. It was normal for opposing sides to send heralds to one another to formally demand surrender or the swearing of allegiance before battle was joined. Such demands were rarely heeded but still the heralds were sent to invite the enemy to concede defeat before blood was spilled. What was less common was for the leaders of the opposing sides to meet face to face in the centre of the battlefield.

"He'll come," Calgacus declared. "He'll be curious and want to see us."

Runt put in, "Either that or he'll send his chariots to kill us."

"We can outrun them," Calgacus assured him.

"The rest of us can," Runt agreed. "You can't. That poor pony can barely manage a trot under your weight. Still, at least the rest of us will get away since the enemy will concentrate on you when you lag behind us."

"Not if I grab you and throw you off your horse," Calgacus responded.

"They won't bother with me," Runt grinned. "I'm too small for them to trouble themselves over."

Eudaf gave a nervous laugh and Tuathal smiled at the banter between the two friends.

"I don't like the idea of running away from anything," Tuathal declared.

"There are times when it is necessary," Calgacus told him. "There is a big difference between being brave and being foolhardy. If anything happens here, you make sure you get away. If you are killed, the entire war is over. There will be plenty of time for heroics once you are High King but, until then, stay out of danger."

They had held this conversation several times and Eudaf was under strict instructions to make sure that Tuathal was kept well away from any trouble. Tuathal himself was not entirely comfortable with the thought of remaining out of danger but he had grudgingly accepted Calgacus' instructions.

Now he studied the crest of the crowded hill, seeking signs of Elim's response to their demand for a parley. It seemed to take an age but, eventually, there were indications that Elim had decided to accept their challenge.

"Someone is coming," Runt remarked. "There are at least three chariots heading down here."

One of the chariots was that of Podraig mac Donnchad. His vehicle rejoined the other war chariots at the foot of the hill but the other two, escorted by half a dozen men on horseback, came on and approached Tuathal's waiting group.

"That will be Elim," Tuathal declared when he saw the man in the lead chariot who was wearing a coat of mail, a helmet and a golden torc at his throat.

"But who's that in the other one?" Calgacus wondered.

"It's a woman," Runt replied. "I'd guess it is Scota, the witch."

Calgacus turned his attention to the famous sorceress. He could see that she was tall for a woman, with a mane of long, red hair. She also appeared to be wearing a mask of some sort which covered half of her face. It was only when the chariots came within speaking range that he realised the mark was part of her, a vivid blemish on her skin. Despite his determination not to believe she could perform genuine feats of magic, the sight made him shudder.

Scota seemed to notice his gaze and fixed a speculative look on him, her eyes locking with his. He had the impression she was attempting to communicate with him in some way but he could not read her intentions. Had her message been genuine, he wondered, or had she truly lured them into a trap? Despite the intentness of her gaze, he could tell nothing from the hard expression on her blighted face.

Disturbed by Scota's enigmatic stare, he turned his attention to Elim mac Conrach, High King of Eriu.

Elim's face was harsh and scornful as he cast his baleful gaze over the riders facing him. He quickly dismissed Runt and Eudaf, his concentration first fixing on Tuathal.

"So you are the puppy who thinks he can take my kingdom from me with a rag-tag bunch of vagabonds?" he sneered. "You've got more guts than sense, boy, I'll say that for you."

178

Tuathal simply patted his horse's neck as he replied, "I am the rightful High King, as you know well enough since you murdered my father when you usurped the High Kingship. I have come to reclaim what is mine and I offer you a simple choice."

"Oh, I've already made up my mind what I am going to do," Elim growled menacingly.

The High King had a powerful personality and all of his aggression was centred on Tuathal but the young man did not show any sign of being intimidated.

He said, "You have not yet heard my terms."

"I don't give a shit what your terms are, boy. I will see your head, and those of all your band of rebels, on spikes in front of my hall tonight. That is all that matters. I only came down here to tell you that."

"I see you are as stubborn as you are stupid," Tuathal shot back. "There is no need for so many deaths. Only two are required. Those of you and your son. The rest of your men may go free as long as they swear allegiance to me."

A dark shadow crossed Elim's face as he shot a searching look at Tuathal.

"Two lives?" he snarled. "I have two sons."

"Had," Tuathal corrected. "Show him, Eudaf."

Eudaf, whose face was still pale and nervous, fumbled behind his saddle and tugged a leather sack free from its bindings. Yanking it open, he reached inside and pulled out the now half-rotten head of Fergus mac Elim. With a grimace of distaste, he tossed it so that it bounced along the ground beside Elim's chariot, making the ponies skitter.

One of the riders uttered a yell of dismay and outrage but Elim snapped, "Be silent, Niall!"

Then the High King regarded Tuathal with a look of such venom it might have shaken a lesser man.

"If I could kill you twice for that, I would," he hissed. "As it is, I will need to be content with killing you slowly."

Elim's anger was a palpable force but he managed to keep it under control and, having failed to rattle Tuathal, he turned his attention to Calgacus.

"Are you really who you claim to be?" he demanded.

"I am," Calgacus confirmed.

179

"Then you are a bigger fool than the songs make you out to be," Elim rasped. "What madness brought you to Eriu to die alongside this whelp?"

Calgacus' first thought was of his family who were being held hostage to force him into this venture but he would not admit that to Elim. Instead, he answered, "I am here because you have sent men to kill me. You have declared yourself my enemy and I know only one way to deal with enemies."

For the first time, Elim looked surprised.

"Me?" he scowled. "I have no interest in you. Why should I? You are plainly as deluded as this puppy. But, since you are here, your head will join his."

Calgacus was puzzled by the High King's response but he had no time to react to the strange denial of complicity because Scota had tapped her driver on the shoulder and he had eased her chariot forwards so that the ponies were scarcely three paces from Calgacus' own mount.

Calgacus was almost mesmerised by Scota. She had a striking appearance which was only enhanced by the blemish on her skin. She exuded an air of calm conviction and authority, and her green eyes seemed to read the very souls of the men she faced. Now, those eyes fixed on Calgacus with an intensity he could almost feel.

"Did Finn come to you?" she demanded.

Calgacus nodded, "He did."

"That traitor!" Elim barked. "He, too, will suffer a slow death. I will cut his eyes out before I kill him."

Scota ignored the High King, keeping her attention on Calgacus.

She said, "Then you know where I stand."

"I know where you claim to stand," he corrected.

A faint, half-smile touched her lips but Elim was not one to stand aside and let others dominate the discussion.

He barked, "Scota! What are you talking about? You stand with me! You are sworn to my service!"

Scota turned to face the High King and Calgacus thought she looked almost regal, her tall, slender body proud and erect as she faced her master from the platform of her chariot.

"I have seen the future," she told Elim. "You will not survive this day, Elim mac Conrach."

She raised her right arm and pointed at him as she went on, "I have seen the future and I speak the day of your death. Your rule is over and I forswear my oaths to you. Tuathal Techtmar is the rightful High King and will rule in your stead."

Calgacus could see the stir of confusion and fear ripple through Elim's escort. The rider he had named as Niall, his son, gaped open-mouthed and even Elim himself seemed momentarily stunned by Scota's revelation.

Scota turned away from him, giving a bow of her head to Tuathal.

"I have been waiting for you for many years," she told him. "Now it is time for me to join you."

"No!" shouted Elim. "Come back! I command it!"

Scota's chariot driver was already edging her ponies forwards, easing them around the side of Tuathal's group where Runt sat guard on the left of the line. Scota herself turned back to Elim once more, bracing herself with one hand on a side loop of the chariot while she pointed back up the Hill of Achall with her other hand.

"It is too late for you, Elim mac Conrach," she called. "Behold! The Scotti have renounced their service to you and your rule is over!"

All eyes turned to the top of the hill. Even Elim spun round on his chariot and gazed upwards with mounting horror as a phalanx of spears and shields appeared over the low crest of the hill from where they had been hidden from view. With determined inexorability, they began advancing on the rear of Elim's main battle line.

Calgacus felt a surge of excitement. Scota, it seemed, had been genuine and her people had turned against Elim. The Battle of the Hill of Achall had begun and, suddenly and unexpectedly, Tuathal had a genuine chance to win.

Then Elim broke all the rules and turned the tables again.

Calgacus had wanted to cloud Elim's judgement by angering him in an effort to entice him to abandon the hill and launch an attack across the plain. But the High King, already enraged at seeing his dead son's head cast on the ground at his feet, was almost apoplectic with fury at Scota's betrayal. He drew his sword, jabbed it furiously at Tuathal and screamed to his riders, "Kill them all!"

Chapter XXI

Calgacus reacted first. He reached back over his shoulder and hauled out his sword, at the same time kicking his heels into his pony's flanks and urging it forwards, using his thighs to guide it.

While everyone else was momentarily stunned by Elim's breaking of the parley truce, Calgacus charged into the open space where Scota's chariot had stood beside the High King.

It was only a matter of moments before everyone else responded and the meeting dissolved into a deafening chaos of shouts as men and animals attacked one another.

Calgacus hoped Eudaf was following his orders and making sure that Tuathal was being led to safety, but he had no time to check because three of Elim's riders were kicking their mounts into action and coming to intercept him.

He had time, though. Not much, but enough. As his pony reached the rear of Elim's chariot, he leaned to one side, planting his right foot on the ground and hurriedly lifting his left leg over the high pommels of the saddle. It was an awkward move but, for once, he was grateful that his size gave him an advantage because his foot was already so close to the ground. He swung off the pony just as a spear was thrust at him but he batted it away with his shield and turned to leap onto the rear of the High King's chariot, knowing that his pony was blocking the spearman's path.

The chariot driver was attempting to take Elim out of danger but a chariot needed room to turn and the only space was directly ahead because mounted warriors were battling one another on either side.

Calgacus was aware of the men and horses fighting, screaming and yelling all around him as Tuathal's escort hurled themselves at Elim's riders so that Tuathal could make his escape. Runt was also there, blocking a spear thrust with one of his two short swords and plunging his second blade into the chest of his opponent.

Calgacus almost lost his balance as the chariot lurched and began to turn but he managed to stay upright and use his shield to block a clumsy attack from Elim.

The High King was cursing him loudly, screaming at his warriors to kill Calgacus but his driver was taking them further away from any help.

Both men were unbalanced by the bouncing motion of the chariot but Calgacus had spent a lifetime fighting while Elim was clearly no swordsman. He slashed wildly with his short sword while extending his left arm in an attempt to maintain his balance.

Calgacus blocked the attack with his shield, the blade ringing off the iron rim and bouncing harmlessly away. Then he shoved forwards, driving Elim back with his shield while bringing his own enormous blade down in a savage blow which caught the High King on the top of his shoulder. Elim was wearing a tunic of chainmail but Calgacus' massive longsword smashed down with such ferocity that it snapped metal ringlets along with Elim's collar bone.

Elim staggered, crying out in pain, but he still made a feeble attempt to stab Calgacus with his own sword. Calgacus swore at him as he knocked the blade away then hacked at Elim's neck.

Elim wore a golden torc around his throat but there was still unprotected flesh between his helmet and this mark of his kingship. Even though Calgacus was unable to put his full weight behind the attack because of the lurching movement of the chariot, the blade bit deeply into Elim's flesh, gouging a wicked wound that cut so deep it reached bone.

Elim's eyes widened in shock as blood spurted from the awful wound. He dropped his sword and jerked both hands up as if to stem the flow but Calgacus yanked him sideways as he pulled his sword free and Elim toppled across the front of the chariot.

In the confined space, Elim crashed against the legs of his driver, while Calgacus' swinging blade also caught the man a glancing blow on the top of his head. The driver had been twisting round in an effort to see what was happening while still attempting to steer the ponies away from the melee that surrounded them. Caught off balance by the impact of the sword and Elim's fall, the driver fell off the open front of the chariot and hit the ground hard. For a moment, he maintained his hold on the reins which panicked the ponies as he tugged frantically but then he lost his grip and the chariot bounced high as one of the iron-rimmed wheels struck him.

Calgacus heard the man scream as the chariot bounced wildly and he, too, fell, landing face down on top of Elim's twitching, gasping body.

The fall saved him from a spear thrust which one of Elim's riders, galloping alongside the careering chariot, had aimed at him. Struggling to roll over, Calgacus saw the man draw back his arm for another thrust over the top of the chariot's side but then the warrior arched his back, uttering a cry of pain and one of Tuathal's Caledones appeared behind him, sword in hand. Calgacus' assailant fell from his galloping horse and Tuathal's man took up position beside the chariot which was now racing across the grass in an uncontrolled charge.

Calgacus groggily pushed himself to his knees but the chariot was out of control and bouncing ferociously so he dared not attempt to stand. For an instant, his eyes locked onto Elim's face and he saw the light of life vanish from the High King's eyes as the body went limp

He crouched on hands and knees, weapons still grasped tightly, trying to feel some emotion over what he had done but Elim's death left him feeling empty. He had always known it would be necessary for Elim to die but Calgacus took no pleasure in seeing the man lying in a pool of blood with his head half-severed.

Another jolt from a violent bounce forced him to pay attention to his next problem. He needed to bring the chariot under control but the reins were trailing on the ground and he could not reach them.

Then Runt appeared on his right, urging his own horse alongside the panicked ponies who were hauling the chariot across the valley floor.

At last, Calgacus had a chance to take in what was happening around him. With no guidance from their driver, Elim's ponies had followed their herd instinct and were chasing Scota's chariot which was racing beside Tuathal and Eudaf as they galloped for the safety of their own army.

That army was now surging across the field, the men running as they sought to protect their leader from what they believed was a treacherous attack.

Calgacus risked a look behind and saw that only two of Tuathal's four guards were still with him.

There were also two of Elim's riders galloping in pursuit. Their High King might be dead but for them to outlive him was a disgrace they could never live down and they were out for revenge, their faces grim and determined.

Calgacus took all this in while the chariot continued to pound across the valley, the thud of hooves all around him and the loud yelling of Tuathal's army adding to the cacophony.

Some of Elim's charioteers were also chasing them but they were a long way behind and would not catch them before they reached the onrushing war host. Others among the charioteers were still milling in confusion, unsure of what was happening on the Hill of Achall behind them but knowing that something had gone wrong with the High King's plan.

Calgacus' own plan had also collapsed into chaos but, against all expectation, he had already achieved his main objective which had been to kill Elim mac Conrach. Whether that would be enough to ensure Tuathal's victory remained to be seen but it had certainly created confusion among the High King's war host.

Some of Elim's cavalry had hurried forwards but had come to an uncertain halt when they saw Tuathal's army rushing towards them. Outnumbered, the horsemen decided not to press the issue but clearly were not sure what they should do.

Calgacus took only a moment to understand all this before he turned his attention back to what Runt was doing. The little man leaned over from his saddle and caught hold of the bridle of the nearest of the racing ponies. Gradually, he slowed its wild pace, allowing Calgacus to rise to his feet.

He turned, sword in hand and saw Elim's two riders coming for him, swords held high.

"Deal with those two!" Runt called and Tuathal's two surviving guards wheeled their ponies round and tried to intercept their pursuers. One of them managed to barge his pony into his opponent and knock him to the ground in a screaming tangle of arms and legs but the second man was not so fortunate and Elim's rider slashed him across the face, killing him instantly.

Elim's man yelled as he charged at the chariot, aiming to run alongside and hack at Calgacus as he passed.

Calgacus turned, facing the left side of the chariot so that his shield could block the attack. As the yelling horseman struck at him, he felt the impact as the sword gouged into his wicker shield but his sword arm was already moving and he caught the rider as he passed, the end of his long blade smashing into the man's ribs and tumbling him from his horse.

The impact of the blow almost toppled Calgacus again but the chariot was slowing now and he spread his feet to keep his balance.

"That was neatly done!" Runt called approvingly.

Then the chariot was down to walking pace, eventually coming to a halt amidst a milling crowd of warriors who were surrounding Tuathal and demanding to know that he was safe.

Calgacus was breathing heavily, sweat making his tunic stick to his back but he had no time to do anything other than check that Tuathal was unharmed before he heard Scota's voice shouting to him.

"Calgacus! My people are dying up there! You must help them!"

He saw her pointing to the summit of the hill where everything was in confusion but where he could make out the Scotti battling against Elim's main force, driving them down from the hilltop. Elim's men were startled and confused but they outnumbered the Scotti and might soon be able to surround them if they possessed a leader who could exert some control on the chaos. For the moment, though, it seemed the Scotti would drive Elim's war host off the hill in confusion and Calgacus could not understand Scota's urgent plea for help.

"He has more men hidden further along the hill!" Scota yelled. "My people cannot defeat them alone!"

Now Calgacus understood. He jumped down from the chariot and raced to where Tuathal was assuring his men that he was unharmed. The young princeling saw Calgacus and grinned hugely.

"You killed him!" he beamed.

"Yes, but the battle is not over. Get this lot up there. We need to finish this. And tell them to walk, not run or they'll be exhausted by the time they climb the hill."

Tuathal took a moment to study the hilltop, then began shouting commands, urging his men to the attack. The warriors, their bloodlust up, yelled their enthusiasm and, with all shape and order abandoned, set off to join the fight. The men who had been concealed in the woodland emerged in response to Tuathal's urgent signals and joined the assault.

Elim's cavalry, seeing the advance, turned tail and rode away but a handful of the dead High King's chariots skidded across the face of the advancing army, allowing their warriors to hurl spears at the mass of men. Calgacus recognised Podraig mac Donnchad as one of the chariot riders and gave a soft shake of his head when he saw the young braggart flee, his driver turning the chariot away rather than be swamped under a tide of vengeful Caledones and Ulstermen.

"There are times when it is better to run," he whispered to himself as he watched the chariot race away.

Calgacus took a deep breath, wondering what he should do next. He had lost his pony and had no real desire to mount Elim's chariot again. Then Scota appeared, with Runt escorting her. In her hand, she held Elim's head which had been hacked from his corpse. She thrust it towards Tuathal.

"Take this!" she commanded. "Let Elim's men see it and most of them will lose the will to fight. And ride in Elim's chariot. Let everyone see that you have bested him."

Tuathal dismounted from his horse and accepted the gory trophy from Scota.

"We must talk later," he told her. "But, for now, I thank you for your help."

"The battle is not won yet," she replied. "What happened to Elim's son, Niall?"

"He's dead," Runt informed her. "I killed him. Snotty little bugger scratched me, though."

Calgacus noticed for the first time that Runt's left arm was bleeding, his sleeve dark with blood.

"It's not serious," Runt assured him when he saw Calgacus' concerned look.

"I will tend it," Scota offered.

Runt hesitated for only a moment before nodding his thanks.

"Come!" Tuathal called to Findmall and Eudaf. "We have a battle and a kingdom to win!"

Several men of the Caledones had appointed themselves as Tuathal's new guardians. They quickly heaved Elim's headless corpse from the chariot and one of them claimed the right to serve as Tuathal's driver. Holding Elim's dripping head aloft, Tuathal climbed aboard and set off in pursuit of his advancing war host which was now spreading out as it neared the foot of the hill.

Calgacus watched, knowing there was little more he could do.

He turned to Scota and asked, "You said there are more men hidden behind the hill?"

"On Elim's left flank. His best men."

"Let's hope we can deal with them," he sighed. "But this is more like a brawl than a battle."

The entire field was a scene of bedlam. Most of Elim's chariots had fled, the few who had dared confront Tuathal's army being swept aside by the superior numbers. Some of Elim's cavalry had plucked up enough courage to make a tentative attack on the flanks of the advancing warriors but the sight of Elim's head held in Tuathal's hand had discouraged them and most of them had ridden away.

On the hilltop, the men of Leinster who had been placed in the front rank now found themselves pressed from behind by the Scotti and faced with Tuathal's warriors climbing up the slope in front of them. Most of them threw down their weapons and pleaded for mercy.

Others of Elim's warriors were less inclined to give up the fight and Calgacus saw a phalanx of spears top the crest of the hill and advance on the Scotti.

"Elim's veteran war band," Scota said, her voice aching with dread. "They could still turn the battle."

Calgacus knew she was right. There might be chaos and confusion in front of them but Elim's men could still defeat the Scotti and then hold the high ground against Tuathal's main force. There were only five hundred of them but they were Elim's best men, his hardened, battle-trained veterans who would not be easy to overcome.

And then Fiacha Cassan arrived.

Calgacus' original plan had been to provoke Elim into bringing his army down from the high ground. Tuathal's smaller force would confront them and then, when battle had been joined, Fiacha Cassan, who had led nearly two hundred and fifty riders in a wide circuit of Tara to arrive at a spot behind the Hill of Achall, would charge in at the rear of Elim's army, hopefully killing the High King himself.

As with most battle plans, though, it had not survived the first contact with the enemy. Elim had been provoked but his reaction had been unexpected. Now he was dead but his veterans fought on, their honour preventing them from surrendering.

Fiacha Cassan could not have known what was happening but he must have seen the Scotti attack the rear of Elim's army and then seen Elim's hidden reserves counter that attack. Using his initiative, or perhaps simply charging at the nearest enemy, Fiacha Cassan led his riders into a charge against the unsuspecting men of Elim's elite warriors.

There were fewer than two hundred and fifty horsemen with Fiacha Cassan but numbers were not the decisive factor. Surprise and shock, with the riders having greater speed and reach, created havoc in the ranks of Elim's phalanx as soon as the assault struck their unprotected rear. Men fell and died by the score and panic quickly shattered the veterans' resolve. They broke and fled, streaming down the reverse slope of the hill in a desperate attempt to escape the slaughter.

And slaughter it was. Tuathal's men did not bother with the warriors who had laid down their arms but they hacked and battered at any who offered resistance. With the collapse of the reserve, though, most resistance crumbled and the fight became a rout as men fled in panic, with Fiacha Cassan's horsemen chasing them and cutting down anyone they overtook.

"So you did have a surprise in store," Scota remarked. "I thought you would."

Calgacus shrugged. Sending Fiacha Cassan to attack from the rear had been a gamble. In fact, everything he had done since arriving in Eriu had been a gamble. Now, as he stared up at the hill where Tuathal's triumphant war host was sweeping the remnants of Elim's army before them, he could scarcely believe what they had accomplished. He had expected defeat but, thanks to Scota, they had achieved an unlikely and relatively bloodless victory and he wondered whether Tuathal had not been correct after all; that it was the young man's destiny to become High King.

Yet that no longer mattered to Calgacus. He felt as if a great weight had been lifted from his shoulders because nothing mattered now except the knowledge that he and Runt could return home to their families.

Part II – Kings And Consorts

Chapter XXII

Beatha's heart sank when she watched Calgacus sail away in the flotilla of small boats. She kept her eyes fixed on him as the fleet slowly made its way down the loch towards the sea, until she could no longer make him out. When his boat disappeared from her sight, she felt a tight knot in her stomach, like a stone weighing her down, and she shivered as the sea breeze touched her suddenly cold and clammy skin.

"He'll be back," Emmelia whispered as she squeezed Beatha's hand.

Beatha could not answer. She was afraid that if she tried to speak, she would break down in tears. She could not allow herself to show such weakness, not when Fallar and young Tegan were watching. She needed to be strong, like Emmelia. But Emmelia's husband was still with her, so it was easy for her to be strong. Caedmon was no warrior. There was never any chance that he would go to war.

Beatha felt a stab of jealousy that Emmelia, who was always so self-assured and confident, should have no cause to fear losing her husband. The feeling died away almost immediately because Beatha hated herself for even contemplating jealousy. Besides, Caedmon was in as much danger as any of them. They were all hostages for Calgacus' compliance with Coel's wishes.

Fallar gave Beatha a concerned look.

"Mother? Are you all right? You look very pale."

Beatha forced a weak smile. Fallar was a grown woman now but she was still Beatha's child. Like all mothers, Beatha's first instinct was to protect her daughter by concealing her own fears.

"I'm fine," she managed to whisper.

"He will come back," Emmelia repeated. Then, seeing Tegan's worried expression, she added, "They will both come back. They always do. I have never known two more capable men."

Beatha hardly dared to look at Tegan. The young girl was a mother herself now. Her baby was clutched to her chest, wriggling furiously in her arms as Tegan stared at the receding shapes of the last boats.

Beatha's heart lurched again, this time in sympathy for what she knew Tegan must be feeling. Tegan had only been with Runt for a short time and now she was standing on this sun-dappled shore watching her new-found husband sail away with Calgacus. Tegan looked absurdly young and vulnerable, yet Beatha knew the girl had an inner strength, a resolve that would not let her surrender to despair.

Beatha felt her own vulnerability like a tangible force which threatened to crush her. She fought her fear by telling herself that what Emmelia had said was true. Calgacus was more capable than any man she knew. He had been away before. He was a warrior, a chieftain, a war leader. He had often left her to go to war and he had always returned. She must believe that he would return again.

But this time was different. This time, Beatha was not at home. This time she was a prisoner. She understood that the threat to Calgacus and Fallar from the mysteriously malevolent High King of Eriu was very real. She understood that Calgacus knew only one way to deal with such threats, and yet she knew that he had been forced into leaving her. Coel had been insistent that Calgacus' family remain in his home until they learned the outcome of Tuathal's attempt to depose the usurper. That insistence, Beatha knew, was a knife held to Calgacus' throat.

She looked along the shore to where Coel was standing alongside the druid, Broichan. The old man was berating his son, Crixus, for some perceived fault. Crixus, a grown man with sons of his own, stood like a young child, meekly accepting his old father's chastisement.

Beatha turned away. She did not care what they were arguing about. At that moment, all she knew was that she hated them. It was an emotion she was not accustomed to but, with sudden realisation, she understood what was causing her so much distress. She had felt the same helpless anger and despair before, many years ago.

The memories flooded back, stark and vivid in her mind. They were memories of her childhood and adolescence, most of which she had spent as a prisoner of one sort or another. She had almost forgotten the anguish that captivity imposed but now it had gripped her once again and she did not know whether she possessed the strength to fight it.

She had been a hostage at the age of eight, a terrified young girl who had not understood why her brother, King of the Regni, had given her away to another tribe. Later, when the Romans came, she had returned to her former home but had discovered that her brother wanted her to become a Roman, in the same way that he was adopting a new way of life, copying Roman customs, speaking Latin and wearing Roman clothes. He had wanted her to be the same and he had beaten obedience into her. She had been a prisoner in her own home and when she had eventually been married off to a Roman Centurion, she had remained a captive, subject to Roman law; a law that allowed married women few rights. Her husband, Gnaeus, had beaten her too.

Then Calgacus had come. He had rescued her from her life of continual fear and she had been able to stand proud in the knowledge that she was no longer a prisoner. In the years that had passed since then, she had tried hard to forget the perpetual fear. Now, when she had least expected it, when she had thought she was coming to celebrate her daughter's wedding, she was a captive once more.

She realised that the boats and curraghs had vanished from sight. She could not prevent a deep sigh escaping her lips but then, with Emmelia clasping her hand to comfort her and with Fallar and Tegan looking to her for guidance, Beatha found her strength.

She had survived the long years as a hostage and as an imprisoned Roman wife. She had never been outgoing, never one to stand up and confront her enemies. But, like Tegan, she had endured. She had taken the physical and mental blows that had been cast at her and she had survived. She had done it before; she could do it again.

She straightened her shoulders, standing tall and proud.

"Yes," she decided, "they will come back. All we need to do is wait."

The days passed slowly. News came from Tuathal, brought by small boats that crossed the sea bearing messengers. Beatha and the others gathered in Coel's great chamber, eager yet also fearful to hear what the messengers had to say.

Each day there was a new report. They heard that the army had landed safely and had met with the brothers, Findmall and Fiacha Cassan; then that Tuathal had captured the fortress of Emain Macha and killed Elim's son.

"That was quick work," Coel grinned happily. "I knew sending Calgacus was a good idea but even I did not expect him to achieve so much so soon."

The news lifted everyone's spirits and Beatha began to hope that Calgacus might return in a few days if he could repeat his initial success.

"The army is marching to Tara," the next messenger reported.

"Things are going well," Broichan commented that evening as they sat in the great, circular hall in Coel's tower.

Coel nodded but his earlier joy had been tempered by other news the messengers had brought and he frowned as he pondered the unexpected problem.

"There is an assassin in their camp," he mused darkly.

Beatha's heart had pounded when she heard that an unknown assailant had tried to kill Calgacus. The messenger had said only that Calgacus had suffered a flesh wound and was well but that the attacker had escaped. It was both too much and too little information to comfort her. When news arrived that a second attempt had been made on his life, she felt her fear mounting once again.

As soon as the evening meal was finished, she made her excuses and climbed the stairs to the tiny, stone-lined chamber she shared with Fallar and Tegan.

Emmelia joined them, saying, "I have no wish to sit with the men. I expect they will be drinking themselves senseless and watching Coel's dancing girls."

"They usually do," Beatha agreed. "What about your children?"

"Caedmon is with them," Emmelia replied as she squeezed into the cramped room and took a seat on one of the straw-filled mattresses. "They will be asleep soon. But what about the rest of you? How are you doing?"

194

Tegan was holding baby Sorcha to her breast. The child's eyes were closed as she suckled, almost asleep.

Tegan said, "I am glad to be away from them. I never feel comfortable with Coel and his family."

"I know what you mean," Beatha agreed. "There is a lot of hostility there. Coel favours Drust, so he and Crixus are always arguing."

"Drust is a disgusting drunk," Fallar said with unusual venom. "He makes my skin crawl when he looks at me."

"Crixus is not much better," Beatha commented. She shivered as she added, "He has a lecher's eyes."

"It is more than that," Emmelia remarked. "I think something else is going on."

"What do you mean?" Beatha asked anxiously.

"I don't know. But I have a feeling that there are secrets being kept from us."

"Coel is an old fox," Beatha said scathingly. "He would keep secrets from himself if he could."

"It is not only Coel," Emmelia mused thoughtfully. "They all have secrets. Especially Crixus. I can see it in his face."

Beatha clasped her hands in her lap as she stated, "I am not interested in their secrets. The best thing we can do is avoid them as much as possible."

"That won't be easy," Emmelia pointed out.

"Coel's men follow us everywhere," Fallar agreed. "Tegan and I went to see Adelligus and the other men today. Two of Coel's warriors followed us all the way there and back."

She shivered as she explained, "It was very scary."

Emmelia nodded, "Caedmon said they followed him, too." She gave a soft smile as she added, "He was scared, too."

"How is Adelligus?" Beatha asked.

Fallar hesitated slightly but Tegan answered, "Frustrated and angry. But he promised not to do anything to annoy Coel."

"He's a clever young man," Beatha commented approvingly.

Tegan and Fallar exchanged a look. Beatha noticed but said nothing. Adelligus, Runt's son, was older than his new step-mother, an arrangement that had led to a coolness in their relationship. Beatha decided to let that pass without comment and changed the subject.

She turned to Emmelia.

"So what do you think is going on? With Coel, I mean. What is it you suspect?"

Emmelia shook her head, frowning.

"I wish it was more than suspicion. The trouble is, I can't work out what is going on. Broichan and Coel are almost impossible to read."

"They have had years of practice at concealing their true thoughts," Beatha told her.

"I know," Emmelia agreed before giving Fallar a reassuring smile and saying, "I don't think you need worry about Drust, though. He will look at you but he won't try anything without Coel's permission, and Coel knows he needs to keep us safe until Calgacus and Liscus return."

Beatha put in, "Maybe so, but none of us should go anywhere alone."

"As for Crixus," Emmelia continued, "he has a cruel edge to him. They say he hunted down those brigands and slaughtered them."

"They deserved it," Tegan spat harshly.

"Most men would have done the same," Beatha agreed.

"Yes, but Crixus enjoyed it," said Emmelia. "I could see it in his eyes when he told the story. Coel was not happy that he did not question them about the druid who hired them but Crixus didn't care. He accepted Coel's tirade but I don't believe it had any lasting effect on him."

"He has probably been on the receiving end of too many of Coel's rants for it to make much difference," Beatha remarked.

"Possibly. But I gained the impression that he was simply enduring it as a necessary inconvenience. It was ..." she shrugged, "as if he has his own plans."

Tegan put in, "I think he's just waiting for the old man to die. He'll be able to do as he pleases once Coel is gone."

Emmelia nodded, "Yes, perhaps that is it."

Fallar murmured, "I am not sure which of them is the worst."

"The sooner Calgacus and Liscus return, the better," Beatha declared. "Then we can go home."

Emmelia looked at Fallar and raised an eyebrow in question.

"There will be no wedding, then?"

196

"After the way they have treated us?" Fallar replied indignantly. "I have no wish to join a family like theirs."

"I can't say I blame you but I suggest you keep your decision quiet until your father returns. Coel likes to get his own way and it would be sensible not to annoy him."

Once again, the two younger women exchanged a secretive smile. Emmelia guessed they had been discussing Fallar's future but she decided not to enquire too closely. Let them keep their secrets for the moment. She wondered whether she should remind Fallar that her marriage had been arranged to secure the alliance that Calgacus needed, but she decided against raising that subject now. They had enough problems to worry about without that.

She stood up, saying, "It is getting late. I will see you in the morning."

Emmelia left the room quietly. In the passageway outside, the shadows were dark, with only feeble illumination coming from tiny, tallow candles that were set in small recesses in the walls. She reached out to feel the stone wall, gently brushing her fingertips against its cold, rough, hardness to guide her.

As she slowly traced her way back to her own chamber, she frowned thoughtfully. She hated unsolved puzzles and her curiosity regarding Coel and his sons had not diminished. She was still puzzling over how to discover the truth of what was going on when her thoughts were interrupted by the sounds of raised, angry voices from the floor below.

Crixus drained another mug of beer, then slammed the clay beaker onto the table.

"You are an old fool!" he shouted, jabbing a finger at his father.

The room fell silent. Only a handful of Coel's warriors remained at the table, along with half a dozen of the girls who had danced for them earlier. Drust's head was slumped on the table and he was snoring loudly. Everyone else had long since left and those who remained were more than half drunk.

All except Crixus, who had consumed very little ale and was feigning drunkenness. This was the moment he had been waiting for. He had been especially pleased when old Broichan had made his excuses and retired for the night. Without the druid's restraining influence, Crixus knew how Coel would react to any show of defiance. With others, Coel was cool and calculating but when it came to dealing with his sons, his temper was always on a short rein. Now he slammed his own fist down on the table, rattling the plates and beakers.

"You are the fool, boy!" he shouted back. "You always have been."

"Not like Drust, I suppose," Crixus sneered.

He waved his empty mug to where Drust sat slumped, oblivious to the argument raging over his head.

Sitting around the unconscious Drust, the other warriors, the trusted men of Coel's household, fidgeted in discomfort as their chieftain and his eldest son gave voice to their long-simmering antagonism.

"Drust is a loyal and obedient son!" Coel snapped.

Scornfully, Crixus snorted, "He never had an original thought in his life. He does exactly what you tell him. No more, no less."

"At least he does not always defy me," Coel growled menacingly.

"That is because he is usually drunk," retorted Crixus. "And even when he is sober, he is too dull-witted to think for himself. Believe me, Father, Drust will reveal your secrets. That witch-woman who came with Calgacus suspects you already."

"I have no secrets!" Coel declared angrily.

"No?" Crixus sneered. "You tricked Calgacus into going to Eriu."

Coel thumped his fist on the table again, striking the wood so hard that his bronze mug toppled, spilling a puddle of dark beer across the table and onto the rush-strewn floor.

"I did no such thing!" he shouted.

"Of course you did. You told us to keep quiet about the reward the Romans have offered for him and his wife. The attempt on his life may have been someone seeking to claim that reward. Elim mac Conrach probably had nothing to do with it. But you didn't tell him about that, did you? You wanted him to help Tuathal, so you kept that information from him."

Coel's face was taut with icy fury. He stabbed a finger towards his son.

"I said you are a fool and I was right," he snarled. "I make decisions that are in the best interests of my people. That is what it means to be a King. The story you heard was a distraction that

198

Calgacus did not need to know about. Think about it. The Romans have no interest in Tuathal, yet someone tried to kill him. It must have been Elim."

He gave his son a contemptuous look, adding, "If you want to follow me as a King of the Caledones, you had better start learning how to use your mind properly instead of constantly arguing with me."

"Has it ever occurred to you that I disagree with you because you are wrong?" Crixus challenged. "What do you think Calgacus' niece would do to you if she ever discovered the truth? You have seen she has magical powers. What if she learns of your secret and places a curse on you?"

Instinctively, Coel crossed his fingers to ward off witchcraft.

"Then we had better make sure she does not hear of it," he snapped.

"That should be easy enough," Crixus snorted. "You surround yourself with men who dare not say a word against you. But I have had enough of obeying you."

Coel's eyes were bright with reflected firelight and inner rage as he threatened, "Do not defy me, boy."

Crixus laughed. He had never dared do such a thing to his father's face before but it felt good. The old man had no power over him now.

"What will you do to stop me?" he asked scathingly. "Set your guards on me?"

His eyes scanned the watching faces. Many of them were appalled at the scene they were witnessing.

Crixus bared his teeth in a fierce grin as he went on, "These men are not fools. They know you cannot live much longer. They will not dare lay hands on me because they know I will soon be King in your place."

Coel pushed himself to his feet, his hand fumbling drunkenly for his dagger.

"You will be King of nothing!" he yelled, his voice almost cracking with fury.

Crixus leaped up, reaching for his own knife. Other men jumped to their feet and voices shouted, urging calm.

Eurgain, who had been sitting beside his father, also stood. He put his arms around Crixus, pulling him back.

"Stop, Father!" he shouted as he barred Crixus' path.

Crixus tried to shake off his son but Eurgain held him tightly. Then the young man spun him round, pushing him back and stepping between Crixus and Coel. He raised his hands appealingly.

"Please," he implored. "There is no need for this. We are family."

"I will take such abuse from no man," Coel declared. "Not even from my son."

"Then my father will apologise," Eurgain said reasonably.

"For being called a fool?" Crixus snapped angrily. "Why should I apologise?"

Eurgain looked from one to the other, anxious appeal etched on his face.

"You should both apologise," he told them.

Coel spat in derision.

"King's do not apologise," he growled.

"But fathers should," Eurgain pleaded. "Please, Grandfather. For my sake, if for nothing else."

While Coel hesitated, Crixus grumbled, "Very well. I will apologise if he does."

"Grandfather?" Eurgain prompted.

Coel's lips twitched. Then he nodded curtly.

Eurgain smiled as if Coel had made the most gracious apology he had ever heard. "Come, then!" he urged them. "Clasp hands and I will pour fresh drinks to seal the matter."

Taking a deep breath, Crixus took a few steps towards his father, his right arm extended. Coel's expression was hard but he grudgingly took the offered hand. The two men grasped each other's forearm. They stared into each other's eyes for a long moment, neither giving way. Then Eurgain gently eased them apart by offering two fresh mugs of beer.

"Drink!" he encouraged. "To family!"

"To family," Crixus responded dully, raising his goblet.

"Family," Coel muttered, the word barely audible.

They both drank deeply, though neither of them took his eyes from the other's face.

Crixus placed his goblet on the table.

"Since we are now friends again, I will take my leave," he said coldly. "I am tired."

He nodded to where Drust still lay snoring softly and drawled, "I will leave you to speak to my brother. It will be a dull conversation but at least you will get no arguments from him."

"Father!" Eurgain hissed sharply. "That is enough."

Crixus gave an abrupt nod to Coel, then turned away, marching for the door. With a helpless shrug to his grandfather, Eurgain hurried after him.

Coel watched them go. Once they had left the chamber, he sat down again, drained his goblet and barked at one of the serving girls to re-fill it.

Emmelia heard the sound of heavy footsteps climbing the stone stairs. She had reached the small room where her family were sleeping but she stopped in the dark doorway, listening to the sound of voices echoing up the winding stair.

"What is it?" Caedmon asked sleepily from behind her.

Emmelia waved a hand at him.

"Sshh!" she commanded.

Caedmon lay down again. Emmelia felt a pang of sympathy for her husband. He was clever and he was a loving father to their children, but he was no warrior. In this place of dangerous secrets, he was out of his depth. Here, she would need to be the strong one, the decisive one.

There was a decision to be made now. She could step into her room, draw the heavy curtain and ignore whatever was going on. But that was not Emmelia's way. She had heard raised voices and her curiosity was aroused.

She waited, standing silently in the darkness, scarcely daring to breathe.

There were two men on the stairs, she was certain of that, and they were climbing towards her. She leaned out slightly, looking towards the faint glimmer of light that marked the stairwell. Between the top step and where she stood were two more rooms. Two dark shapes came into view, heading for the doorway furthest from her.

"Are you sure nobody saw you?" one asked.

That was Crixus. She recognised his voice instantly.

"I am sure," the second man replied. "They were all too busy watching you."

That is Eurgain, Emmelia thought. *Father and son together.*

201

The two dark shapes vanished into their chamber.

Emmelia slipped her feet out of her shoes. Barefoot, she crept silently along the cold, wooden floorboards of the passageway until she was outside their door. They had pulled the heavy curtain across the entrance but she could hear their voices. They were speaking softly but she could tell that they were excited about something.

"How long?" Crixus wondered.

"Not long."

Eurgain hesitated before adding, "Perhaps not long enough. Some people may suspect."

"I thought you said it left no traces. His death should appear natural."

"It should. That is what I was told. But still ..."

"Don't worry," Crixus stated. "The old fool had too much to drink and it killed him. Anyway, if need be, we will simply blame Calgacus' niece. Everyone knows she is a witch. Now, lie down and pretend to be asleep. No doubt they will come to wake us shortly."

Standing in the chilly corridor, Emmelia felt her blood run cold. She closed her eyes, trying to decide what to do. Crixus had said, "Old fool". He could only have been talking about Coel or Broichan. One of them was in danger.

She made up her mind. Slowly, silently, she padded down the stairs, feeling her way until she reached the central chamber. Inside, light blazed from the fire and dozens of candles. She stepped through the low doorway, her bare feet rustling the rush-strewn floor.

Men sat at the long tables, still drinking, talking in desultory, nervous tones. Something had happened here, she knew. The atmosphere of tension still hung in the air.

She looked for Coel. He was sitting at the head of the table, downing another mug of beer. At his side, cuddling into him, was one of the dancing girls. She was the first to notice Emmelia. She nudged Coel gently.

The King stared at Emmelia. His face grew suddenly pale, as if he had been caught in the act of stealing something.

"What do you want?" he demanded roughly.

"I need to speak to you," Emmelia told him urgently.

She walked across the wooden floor, aware that all eyes were on her as she approached the King. That was natural, she knew, for people always study a new arrival, but she sensed an unease grip the chamber.

"I have no wish to speak to you," Coel said harshly.

"But you must," Emmelia insisted. "I have heard something that is vitally important."

The look of guilt that flashed across Coel's features was unlike any expression she had ever witnessed on his face. It was so out of character that she studied him more closely.

He was afraid of her! Tiny beads of sweat were visible on his lined face and his breathing was slightly laboured. It was as if he feared what she was about to say.

Perplexed, Emmelia hesitated.

"Are you well?" she asked.

"Never better," Coel assured her gruffly.

He squeezed an arm round the girl beside him as he leered, "As this young filly will shortly discover."

"Then perhaps it is Broichan who is in danger," Emmelia said quietly.

"What are you talking about?"

Emmelia leaned towards him. She saw him edge back but she did not let him escape. Whispering so that only he and the girl could hear, she said, "I overheard two men talking. One said that the old man would be dead by morning."

"Which men?"

"They are upstairs."

The anxiety she had seen in his eyes vanished, to be replaced by a harsh fury, but the young girl's face was alarmed now, her painted lips crimson against the sudden paleness of her skin.

"Lord?" she asked plaintively.

Coel pushed her aside. Gripping the edge of the table, he hauled himself unsteadily to his feet.

Emmelia reached out to help him.

"You are unwell," she said, her alarm growing.

Then fear clawed at her heart when she saw him stagger.

"Too much beer," he mumbled drunkenly, shrugging off her offer of assistance. "Come on. I wish to talk to these men. If what you say is true, I will have a lot to say to them."

Emmelia turned towards the door while Coel signalled to his men to follow him. Unsteady on their feet, several of them heaved themselves upright.

203

"Crixus?" Coel asked softly.

Emmelia nodded.

Coel made a soft, wheezing sound of anger. He pushed past her, leading the way out of the chamber. As he reached the door, he staggered slightly, bumping his shoulder against the hard stonework.

"Careful," Emmelia warned.

She reached for him but, as he half-turned towards her, she saw that it was too late. Coel's hands clutched at his heart. He moaned in pain, his face contorted with shock and terror.

"No!" he gasped.

Then his eyes rolled upwards in his head and he was falling, toppling through the narrow doorway and tumbling down the curving stairs, evading her desperate lunge to catch him. His head struck the stone steps with a loud crack but Coel of the Caledones did not feel the blow because he was already dead.

Chapter XXIII

Publius Cornelius Tacitus, resplendent in his polished breastplate and leg greaves, red cloak and plumed helmet, stepped from the gently rocking galley onto a narrow wooden jetty at the foot of a steep cliff. The planking was wet and slippery underfoot but a soldier was waiting and dutifully held out a hand to steady the Tribune as he stepped ashore.

"Thank you," Tacitus said, attempting to show that he had not really required any assistance.

The truth was that his legs felt strangely frail and unsteady after several hours at sea but he did not want to show any weakness in front of the soldiers. He straightened his shoulders and looked at the man who had helped him.

"Where is Julius Macrinus?"

"Up there, Sir," the soldier replied, pointing to a narrow path of rough-hewn steps which had been carved into the side of the rocky cliff.

Tacitus eyed the perilous path with some trepidation but he was aware that men were waiting for him to move so that they could disembark. Not only that, there were other boats waiting. His was the fifth ship to have berthed here and there were seven more still moored out in the small bay, waiting their turn. It would take the rest of the day for all of the men to get ashore.

He looked over his shoulder to see his secretaries and servants watching him expectantly.

"Come, then," he said. "Let us see what this place has to offer."

The narrow path was every bit as treacherous as he had feared but he went up slowly and steadily, taking care to tread cautiously. To his right, the steep drop grew ever higher as he climbed. Far below, he could hear the waves lapping on the rocks that awaited anyone who lost their footing. Concentrating on the solid stone of the path, he trudged up to the settlement.

More soldiers waited at the top of the path, commanded by a Centurion of Auxiliaries.

"Welcome to Hibernia, Sir," the officer greeted cheerily.

"Thank you."

Tacitus recognised the Centurion's face but could not recall his name. The expedition had been formed so quickly that there had been little time to get to know any of the junior officers.

"Julius Macrinus is at the gate, Sir," the Centurion reported. "He has commandeered the chieftain's house for you and the other senior officers. I'll get one of the lads to show you the way."

"I'd prefer to speak to Macrinus first," Tacitus replied. "But you can have my scribes and slaves taken to the house. They will attend to my luggage."

"Very good, Sir."

The Centurion quickly detailed one of the soldiers to escort Tacitus and another to show the Tribune's staff to the house that had been claimed for them.

Tacitus made his way through the crowded settlement. Frightened faces peered at him from doorways or from small clusters of barbarians who had gathered in sullen groups to watch these strange foreigners. They were, Tacitus noticed, mostly women, old men or children. He recalled that young Domnan had told him that many of the young men of Leinster had not survived their recent rebellion.

Scattered throughout the settlement were Roman soldiers. They stood in twos and threes, watching the barbarians in the same way that the locals watched them. Tacitus could feel the nervousness that hung over the clifftop village, a quiet that was broken only by the shouted commands of officers and the tramp of a growing number of military feet as more and more troops climbed up from the tiny dock.

Tacitus heard some of the soldiers speaking in their own, unfamiliar language. These men were not Roman citizens but were Auxiliaries, recruited from tribes whose lands bordered the empire. Most of them were, he knew, from various Germanic tribes whose homeland lay in the forests beyond the two great rivers that marked the edge of the civilised world, the Rhenus and the Ister.

These men were a long way from home but they had joined the army because Rome offered them the chance to become full citizens if they served loyally for twenty-five years. Like most Auxiliary troops, they understood Latin well enough but amongst themselves they reverted to speaking in their own tongue, a language which sounded harsh and guttural to Tacitus' refined ear.

206

Still, they looked efficient enough and when they saw him coming they saluted him and assured him they were keen to fight. They did not seem too concerned about who their opponents might be. Smiling his acknowledgement, Tacitus moved through the village to the main gates.

He found Julius Macrinus standing on the earth rampart beside the gateway. The commander of the Auxiliary Cohorts was organising a small detachment of men who had been detailed to guard the gate and patrol the wall but he greeted Tacitus with a smart salute and a cheerful smile.

"Good afternoon, Tribune. What do you think of our new camp?"

"It's everything I expected," Tacitus replied with a faint smile.

"Aye, it's squalid, dirty and it stinks. It reminds me of home."

"Home? Where is that? Originally, I mean."

Macrinus grinned, "It's been so long since I left, I can hardly remember."

Tacitus smiled, "I'm serious. I am interested to know where the men who serve under me come from."

"You want to write about me in your journal?" Macrinus enquired cheerfully.

"Perhaps."

"Well, I was born among the Marcomanni," Macrinus related. "But I joined the Roman Army when I was eighteen years old. Too many older brothers at home, you see. I wouldn't have inherited much from my father."

"Your father was a chieftain, though?"

"He was a King, of sorts. That's why I was appointed as an officer as soon as I joined up."

"You have done well for yourself," Tacitus observed.

"For a barbarian, you mean?"

Tacitus gave an apologetic smile.

"I didn't mean it that way."

Macrinus laughed, "Don't worry, Tribune. I got used to Roman ways a long time ago. Besides, I'm a citizen now myself. I've done my twenty-five years."

"But you are still with the army? You could have returned home."

207

"I like the life," Macrinus smiled. "I have a certain talent for fighting and Rome is good enough to pay me to do it. That's more than I would get if I went back home."

Tacitus nodded his understanding. He liked Macrinus although he was still slightly in awe of the man's easy confidence. Tacitus had asked Agricola about the Auxiliary commander and had learned that Macrinus had demonstrated his ability as a soldier at a young age and had risen to command two Cohorts of his fellow Germans.

"He's a good man," Agricola had told him. "You can trust him."

Which, from a general as demanding as Agricola, was high praise.

And now they were here, in the strange and unexplored land of Hibernia, where Tacitus would need to rely on all of Macrinus' skill and experience. Yet Tacitus was determined that this would be his expedition, his command, not Macrinus'. The German could advise him but, ultimately, the decisions would be Tacitus'.

He looked around the drab settlement, deciding it was time he took an interest in the expedition's progress.

"How are things going?"

"Slowly," Macrinus answered. "That path up from the dock is a real bugger. I expect we'll lose a few men before the day is out."

"It is rather dangerous," Tacitus agreed. "We should do something to make it safer."

"I've told some of the lads to rig up a rope so that the men have something to hang onto. That should help. Getting the horses up will be a problem but I'm sure we'll manage, although I expect we might need to blindfold them."

"It will take a long time to get everyone ashore," Tacitus observed.

"Can't be helped," Macrinus shrugged. "We could land some men further up the coast and let them walk here but we don't know the lie of the land and I'd rather keep everyone together if we can."

"Yes," Tacitus agreed uncertainly.

He felt rather superfluous. The more he saw of the Auxiliary commander, the more he understood why Agricola had chosen the German for this mission. Feeling that he should make

208

some contribution, Tacitus turned to look back over the crowded rooftops of the village.

"Do you think we will have enough room for everyone?" he asked.

Macrinus also looked down from the high rampart to study their new home. There was an open space between the wall and the houses but Tacitus doubted whether it was large enough to accommodate their entire force. The settlement was perched on a peninsula that jutted into the sea, with a protective ditch and rampart across the landward side. They had been assured by the young prince, Domnan, that this place was the home of the King of Leinster but to Tacitus' eyes it looked a shabby place.

"We'll be all right for a day or two," Macrinus declared after a moment's thought. "Once the legionary troops arrive, it will be a squeeze, but there is a large island a little way offshore. The villagers keep their sheep there at lambing time because there are no predators. I suggest we tell the bulk of the people to go there for a few days. We probably don't want too many of the local women around anyway. That would just cause trouble."

"I agree. That will give us a bit more space."

"And once we get all our troops here, I presume we'll be marching out and leaving only a small garrison. The locals can come back then if they want."

"That sounds sensible," Tacitus agreed. "Can you take care of all that?"

"Of course, Sir," was Macrinus' confident reply.

"Thank you."

"Don't worry," Macrinus assured him. "Things are going well so far."

"It's the lack of transport that still bothers me," Tacitus complained with a grimace.

"There's nothing we can do to change that, Sir. But we'll be fine. You made the proper sacrifices and the omens were good."

Tacitus gave the Centurion a sharp look, suspecting that Macrinus was mocking the ritual of sacrifice, but the German's face was a mask of sincerity. Tacitus nodded distractedly. The omens had been propitious but that did not prevent him worrying about the lack of transport ships.

Most of the Imperial Navy was supplying the Governor's northern base in preparation for the next year's campaign, so there had been few ships available for this expedition. Much to his annoyance, Tacitus had been obliged to plan a two-stage landing. They had been able to gather together enough vessels to carry the Auxiliary Cohorts across the narrow sea from Britannia but there had been no room for the two legionary Cohorts. Once Macrinus' men were ashore, the galleys would need to sail back to Deva to collect the legionaries. It would be at least three more days before Tacitus' entire force would be assembled in Hibernia.

He would not have contemplated such a disjointed arrangement had it not been for Domnan's assurances that their landing would be unopposed.

That thought reminded him of his other duties.

"Where is Domnan?" he asked. "I suppose I had better go and meet his father."

Macrinus scratched his cheek pensively.

"Ah," he said. "There's a slight problem with that."

"A problem?"

"Well, not so much a problem as a change of circumstance."

Macrinus tugged off his plumed helmet and ran a hand through his close-cropped, wolf-grey hair as he explained, "It seems that Domnan's father is dead. He went to pay tribute to the High King but he was murdered as soon as he got there."

Tacitus clucked his tongue. He almost made a deprecating comment about barbarians but stopped himself just in time.

"I take it Domnan knows?" he asked.

"Yes. He's a bit upset, as you can imagine, but it has made him more determined than ever to help us. He's speaking to the senior tribesmen just now."

"So he is King by right of birth?" Tacitus ventured.

"That depends on your point of view, I suppose," Macrinus replied with a wry laugh. "Apparently, the High King sent his own son here to take over."

He waved a hand when he saw Tacitus' surprise and explained, "Don't worry, Sir. He rode out again a few days ago, taking most of his men with him. It appears that there is some sort of power struggle going on. From what the prisoners told me, there is someone else claiming to be High King, so it looks as if there will be a battle soon."

Tacitus' mind raced on hearing this new information. He had only just arrived, yet already the situation had altered

210

dramatically. To gain time to think about the inferences, he asked a more mundane question.

"Prisoners? What prisoners?"

"The High King's son left a few men here to keep the place secure," Macrinus informed him with a wry chuckle. "Most of them ran when they saw our ships arriving but a handful decided to try to stop us getting in. We killed three, captured four and had only one of our men slightly wounded."

Tacitus again felt less than capable when he heard Macrinus give the details so laconically. A fight that left three men dead must have been brutal and bloody, however little time it had taken. Yet Macrinus reported it as being almost of no consequence.

Tacitus decided that he should take some sort of decision. After all, he was supposed to be in command of this expedition.

He said, "Send the prisoners back on one of the ships. They can be delivered to the slave market."

"I'll see to it," Macrinus acknowledged briskly.

"And have the bodies burned or buried as soon as you can."

"No need," Macrinus replied casually. "We tossed them into the sea."

Tacitus nodded. Having gained some time to think, he turned his attention to the main issue.

"So there are two men claiming to be High King now?" he enquired.

"So it seems," Macrinus confirmed. "That should be good for us."

"Because we can let them fight it out, then walk in and take over?"

"Precisely," Macrinus agreed cheerfully. "Tomorrow I'll send out some mounted scouts to see if they can get any more information. Then, as soon as the legionary Cohorts arrive, I suggest we head straight for Tara. According to Domnan, it is little more than a day's march from here. With luck, we'll be able to strike at them before they even know we are here."

Tacitus stared out across the wooden rampart, looking inland to the gently rolling green countryside of this unfamiliar land.

"It will be a few days before we have our full force here," he commented, half to himself. "If the barbarians resolve their dispute, the High King may well send men back here before we are ready."

"Possibly," Macrinus conceded. "But I'll set men digging a perimeter ditch all around this place. We should be able to turn it into a proper Roman camp. That will keep the lads busy and impress the locals. It will also make this place impregnable. If we are discovered, all we need to do is hold on until the legionary troops get here, then we can march out and smash anyone who opposes us."

"You make it sound very simple," Tacitus remarked.

"War is simple," stated Macrinus. "Find the enemy. Destroy him."

"There may be another way," Tacitus mused.

He tried to sound confident in the face of Macrinus' certainty as he continued, "The Governor wants this mission completed quickly, through a combination of diplomacy and military force. Even when we have all of our troops here, we will still not have enough to conquer the entire island."

"We'll have enough to win one battle," Macrinus objected. "Especially if we catch them unprepared."

"I agree," Tacitus said smoothly. "But we do not know who will win this contest to become High King. If we decide to attack whichever contender is victorious, we may well be attacking a potential ally."

"I thought the plan was to install Domnan as High King," Macrinus queried.

Tacitus shrugged, "It makes no difference who rules here, as long as they submit to Rome."

"I understand that, Sir. But, with respect, these barbarians will only respond to force. It does not matter who we are dealing with, we need to show them that we are stronger than they are. That is how we will ensure their submission."

Tacitus drew on all his reserves to face the veteran soldier. He said, "I appreciate your advice, Macrinus. That is why you are here; to advise me. But I am in command of this expedition. It is up to me to decide how we proceed."

Macrinus responded with a curt nod which made Tacitus wonder whether he had gone too far in asserting his authority. No, he decided. He could not afford to allow Macrinus to take control of the expedition. When it came to military dispositions Tacitus would have no hesitation in heeding the veteran Centurion's advice

212

but, in dealing with the barbarians, Tacitus had his own ideas about the best way to proceed.

"We cannot afford a protracted war," he insisted firmly. "We must either bring the rulers of this place to our side and obtain their allegiance, or we must destroy them. Is that not so?"

"Of course," Macrinus agreed a little grudgingly, as if he knew he had lost the argument already.

"If we can win their allegiance without a battle, we will save Roman blood being spilled. The Governor needs our troops back before the end of summer. His instructions were quite explicit. We are not to risk losing our soldiers."

"Which is why a quick strike to the heart of the enemy is essential," Macrinus blurted. "Nobody ever won a war without shedding some blood."

Tacitus held up his hand, palm towards the Centurion.

"No, it is why a diplomatic victory would be preferable. If that does not work, then you will have your battle, but I want to try talking to the High King first. Whoever he might be."

Macrinus' scowl deepened.

"Sir," he said testily, "if you warn the enemy that we are here, we lose a significant advantage."

"If we attack without giving the enemy an opportunity to submit, we could lose much more," Tacitus countered. "You said you would send out scouts. They may give away our presence without learning anything of great value. We already know where the High King will be."

"Then may I ask what it is you are proposing?" Macrinus asked stiffly.

Tacitus felt a surge of confidence. He was in command. He had won this argument not only by virtue of his rank but by his reasoning.

He explained, "Tomorrow, you and I will ride out with a troop of mounted men as escort. We will go to Tara and meet the High King."

Macrinus could not conceal his frustration.

"Sir! The last man who went to the High King was murdered for his trouble. It is too dangerous. We only have around thirty horses. It is foolish to go with such a small force."

"The last man who went to the High King was not a Roman," Tacitus replied haughtily. "And thirty men is more than sufficient when backed by the majesty and power of Rome."

Macrinus understood Roman aristocrats well enough to know that he could not argue with such stubborn logic but he made one final plea.

"Then let me go. I can speak their language well enough. You should remain here. You are the commander. We cannot risk your life on such a dangerous gamble."

Tacitus shook his head.

"No, Macrinus. I appreciate your concern but if we are to deal with a man who claims to rule the whole of Hibernia, I must go. We need to show him that we feel he is important enough to merit a visit from a Roman Tribune, but, equally, that we do not fear him. Besides, until the legionary Cohorts arrive, there is nothing to do here except build some turf walls and supervise the distribution of rations. Your Centurions can handle that easily enough. No, I have made my decision. You, I, and as many troopers as you can gather, will go to Tara tomorrow."

Chapter XXIV

Calgacus rode in Scota's chariot, with Runt's pony trotting alongside as Amhairgin steered the vehicle up the slope of the Hill of Achall, doing his best to avoid the debris of the battle.

It was a sight that always left Calgacus feeling depressed. Swords, spears, shields, horns and drums were scattered all across the hill, with the bloodstained and horribly mutilated bodies of the dead and wounded sprawled amongst them.

"Not many have died," Scota remarked coldly. "It looks as if most of Elim's war host has fled or surrendered."

Calgacus nodded. There were some men being held captive who turned out to be Elim's less than willing levies from Leinster but the majority of the High King's force had fled when they had seen Tuathal riding forwards with Elim's head held high in his hand. This spectacle, allied to the unexpected attack by Fiacha Cassan's horsemen and the even more unexpected defection of the Scotti, had persuaded most of Elim's men to flee rather than fight for a cause that was already lost. Now Tuathal's men were pursuing them, not to kill them but to drive them back to the hill where they could save their lives by swearing loyalty to their new High King. Hundreds had already bowed to the inevitable and given their oaths of allegiance to Tuathal and more were being shepherded back by Fiacha Cassan's horsemen.

Calgacus, his sword once again on his back and his shield fastened to Runt's saddle, gripped one of the curved sides of the chariot's rails with his left hand as he braced himself against the bouncing motion of the wooden platform beneath his feet. He glanced at the tall, elegant figure of Scota who stood beside him, her pose mirroring his own.

She fascinated him. The mark on her face aside, she was, he thought, a fine looking woman and she carried herself with a poise he had rarely seen, but it was her motivation and thinking he wanted to understand. She projected an image of aloofness and detachment yet she also appeared to be struggling to keep her emotions in check as she surveyed the aftermath of the brief battle. Calgacus wanted to understand the contradictions in both her demeanour and her actions. In fact, he had a great many questions he wanted her to answer but she had refused to discuss anything at all.

"We can talk later," she had insisted as she ordered him to climb aboard her chariot. "There are more important things we need to do now."

"Such as?"

"We must find Braine," she informed him as she instructed her driver, Amhairgin, to return to the Hill of Achall.

"Who is Braine?" Calgacus asked.

"Elim's daughter. With both his sons dead, she is his only surviving descendant. If she lives, we must find her."

"I do not kill women or children," Calgacus told her sternly, thinking she wanted to ensure the destruction of Elim's entire family.

Scota shot him a quick look, her lips twisting in a faint, crooked half-smile.

"I do not want to kill her," she assured him.

"Then why do we need to find her?"

"Because she must marry Tuathal," Scota told him in a matter of fact voice.

Calgacus could not conceal his surprise.

"Tuathal is betrothed to my daughter," he said, even though the thought of that marriage left him with conflicting emotions. The marriage had been arranged in order to secure Coel's alliance against Rome but Fallar, he knew, did not view being held hostage as a promising prelude to a wedding. She might change her mind once she learned she would be High Queen of Eriu but he knew she could be strong-willed and stubborn and he suspected she would refuse to marry Tuathal no matter what position he held.

Scota, however, was not interested in his dilemma.

"That does not matter," she stated calmly. "Tuathal must marry Braine if she is still alive. That way, he ensures there can be no rival claimants to his position. Why do you think I arranged things so that the battle took place close to Tara?"

"I am not at all sure why you have done anything," Calgacus replied sourly.

"Because," Scota sighed patiently, "he can now march into Tara unopposed and, more importantly, immediately. He will be declared High King tomorrow and, if he marries Braine at the same time, nobody will dispute his rule."

They were nearing the top of the hill now and the Scotti had seen Scota returning. They hurried to meet her, crowding in front of her chariot, forcing Amhairgin to come to a halt.

They were a warlike lot, armed with spears and wicker shields, wearing their hair long and many of them bearing tattoos on their faces and arms. Calgacus could see the splashes of blood on clothing and skin but he was puzzled by the grim expressions of these men who had ensured Tuathal's victory and should have been exultant at their triumph. Instead, an air of despondency hung over them and their faces were set and hard.

Scota asked them, "Where is Aedan?"

One of the warriors replied, "He is wounded. He is dying."

Scota turned and jumped down from the chariot as she demanded, "Take me to him."

"He killed three men but he took a spear to the belly," a tribesman informed her.

Calgacus followed Scota as the warriors stood back, clearing a path for her until she reached a spot where a huddle of fallen bodies and discarded weapons showed there had been some fierce fighting. She knelt beside one of the fallen, a powerfully built man with grey hair who held his hands clamped to his belly where his metal-studded leather tunic had been slashed by a blade. Blood oozed between his fingers and his face was grey and etched with pain but he was still alert enough to raise his head when he saw Scota.

"They tell me the day is won," he gasped through gritted teeth.

"Yes. Elim and his sons are dead. Tuathal will be High King and the Scotti are free again."

"You planned this all along," he said, his tone turning the statement into an accusation.

"Yes."

"But you did not tell me."

"I did not tell anyone, Aedan. I could not risk Elim discovering my plots."

Aedan gave a resigned sigh as he slumped back and laid his head on the trampled grass.

"At least I lived to see the end of Elim's reign," he sighed. "That is something."

217

"You will see more than that," Scota assured him. "You will see Tuathal as High King."

Aedan coughed a grunt of denial and wheezed, "It is too late for me, Scota. Not even you can save me from this. I may be old and slow but I've seen enough belly wounds in my time to know this is the end for me."

Scota did not attempt to argue. She merely placed her hand over his and leaned close so that she could whisper into his ear. Calgacus could not hear what she said to him but he saw the old warrior smile and say something in return.

Scota looked around, located Aedan's sword and picked it up from where he had dropped it. She placed it in his hands, his blood quickly smearing the hilt as he clumsily wrapped his fingers around it.

Then Scota stood and told the watching warriors, "Stand over him. He wishes to end knowing his men are around him."

The Scotti dutifully formed a guard around their fallen leader and Scota turned back towards her chariot, wiping a tear from her eye with the back of her hand.

"He was a close friend?" Calgacus asked her as he accompanied her.

"No. He was a cantankerous old man who disliked me and resented the fact that I held power over him. But he was a man of honour and he died because I asked him to trust me."

She sniffed, then he saw her compose herself and her cool demeanour returned. A slight frown crossed her face and she stopped in her tracks, signalling to a group of half a dozen warriors who stood on the fringes of the Scotti's war band.

"I have a task for you," she told them. "The body of Elim's son, Niall, is down there in the valley. Find him and bring back his head, along with that of Fergus, which has already been detached from its owner's shoulders and is lying near the spot where Tuathal met with the Usurper."

"Others are already collecting Macha's Acorns," one of the men pointed out.

"Then be quick. If someone has taken the heads, reclaim them. I need them."

The men nodded and set off down the hill.

"Macha's Acorns?" Calgacus asked, not understanding the reference.

218

Scota explained, "Macha, the Goddess, and her sister, The Morrigan, roam the battlefield, taking the souls of the dead. When we collect their heads, the warriors refer to them as Macha's Acorns."

"Why do you want those heads?" Calgacus asked.

"As proof," she replied as if her reason should have been obvious. "And now we must find Braine."

"Perhaps we should go to Tara," Calgacus suggested. "If that was her home, she might have gone back there."

Scota frowned, pursing her lips.

"Braine is too clever to return home," she reflected. "She will know Tuathal will head there first."

Calgacus could see her pondering how best to locate the girl but they were interrupted by the arrival of a chariot and several horsemen who came galloping across the hill towards them.

The Scotti parted, clearing a way for the new arrivals, some of them bowing their heads in respect when they realised that it was Tuathal himself who was riding in the gaudily painted chariot. Behind him, Eudaf now held Elim's severed head while Findmall and Fiacha Cassan rode close beside him.

"High King!" called Scota in greeting, "The men of the Scotti salute you!"

The warriors dutifully raised their weapons in salute but Tuathal's response was curt.

"I thank you for your assistance," he told them. "But the day is not over yet and we face another problem."

"What is that?" Scota asked.

In response, Tuathal turned to Fiacha Cassan, who looked uneasy at the thought of addressing the sorceress. Hesitantly, the swordsman explained, "When I was leading my men around behind the enemy, we caught sight of other riders in the distance, away to the west. They are closer now and there are a lot of them. Several hundred horsemen and chariots, all coming this way."

"Who in the name of all the Gods can that be?" Calgacus wondered.

It was Scota who answered, "I would guess it is Sanb of Connacht. Elim summoned him to join the battle. He must have ridden hard to get here so soon."

Calgacus felt his heart sink. He had believed they had accomplished everything they had set out to do but now, it seemed, they must win another fight.

219

Tuathal declared that Sanb would not fight once he knew Elim was dead, and Scota backed him up.

"He has no reason to begin a war," she announced.

"Unless he sees a chance to become High King himself," Calgacus warned.

"I shall persuade him of the folly of that," Tuathal declared. "But it would be best to be prepared. Let us form up our war host on the hill where he can see us."

It took some time to arrange things. Tuathal's army was widely scattered, with many of the men roaming the countryside in search of plunder or rounding up Elim's fleeing warriors. The approach of Sanb's horsemen drove most of these men back but it still took some time to organise them into a semblance of battle order.

"The Scotti should be on the right, nearest the enemy," Calgacus advised. "And Elim's men who have agreed to swear loyalty should be on the left."

Tuathal understood Calgacus' reasoning. Elim's men had already run from one battle and their loyalty to him was questionable at best. If they decided to turn tail again, it would be best to have them furthest from the approaching men of Connacht. The problem was that the Scotti were on the wrong flank of the war host, so there was considerable confusion as men hurried to and fro, exchanging positions under the shouted commands of Tuathal and Fiacha Cassan. The Scotti, in particular, were reluctant to abandon their dying War Leader but Scota spoke to Aedan and he ordered the warriors to obey their new High King. Four of them remained with him but the rest gathered up their weapons and marched along the hilltop to take up their new position.

Calgacus and Runt had nothing to do except watch the confusion and hurried realignment but, after passing Elim's head into the care of another of her warriors, with instructions to take it and the heads of his two sons to her roundhouse, Scota dismounted and began searching through the bodies of the fallen. After some time, she returned with a grim expression on her face.

"I cannot find Braine," she sighed.

"Then there is a good chance she is alive," Calgacus told her.

"But where is she?"

Calgacus had no answer and pushed the matter aside because, out to the west, approaching from the mouth of a glen that lay between two low hills, the army of Connacht was drawing closer.

Sanb of Connacht's army was much smaller than Tuathal's force but they were well-formed and reasonably fresh, while Tuathal's men were scattered all across the hill and the valley of Tara. The sun was past its zenith but the day was far from over and there was plenty of time for more killing.

The men of Connacht approached steadily, fanning out across the green meadows to lengthen their line.

"Let us go and speak to Sanb," Tuathal declared.

Leaving his chieftains to harry their war bands into some sort of battle order, Tuathal rode down the hill. With him went Eudaf, Findmall and Fiacha Cassan, with Calgacus and Runt riding just behind them. Calgacus was now mounted on a horse Runt had found wandering without a rider, meaning Scota now had her chariot to herself. She stood tall and imperious as Amhairgin guided the vehicle alongside Tuathal's chariot.

Calgacus watched the approaching horsemen carefully, trying to anticipate their reaction. They appeared to be adopting a cautious approach and he was not surprised when the army of Connacht drew to a halt some three hundred paces from the foot of the hill.

"It looks as if they are happy to talk," he murmured thankfully. "If he was going to attack us, he's already missed his best chance."

Behind them, many of Tuathal's warriors were still scattered and in confusion but the five hundred men of the Scotti had gathered to form a bristling hedge of spears, ready to fend off any attack. Alongside them, the rest of the war bands were slowly sorting themselves into a solid phalanx which would be impervious to mounted warriors because no horse would charge a solid line of well-formed foot soldiers.

Fiacha Cassan cursed as a solitary chariot detached itself from Sanb's war host. "Nobody wants to fight today," he muttered morosely.

The lone chariot was accompanied by four mounted warriors who rode behind it.

221

"That is Sanb," Calgacus heard Scota call to Tuathal over the noise of horses and chariots. "He knows me, so he will realise that you are now High King when he sees that I support you."

"Modesty isn't her strong point, is it?" Runt commented quietly.

"She seems to be very sure of herself," Calgacus agreed.

"Not bad looking either, if you ignore that mark on her face."

"I hadn't noticed," Calgacus replied casually.

Runt laughed, "Yeah, I noticed you hadn't noticed. It must have been coincidence when your tongue fell out of your mouth."

"Shut up, Liscus," Calgacus told him.

Runt's response was another chuckle but he resumed a more serious expression when the two groups of riders met in the open space between the armies.

The King of Connacht was a lean, middle-aged man with brown hair and blue eyes which sparkled with a lively intelligence. He wore a coat of chainmail and had a sword at his hip which glittered with jewels but he held his iron helmet in the crook of his left arm to show that he had not come to fight.

His long, thin face wore a sardonic smile as his eyes darted from one person to the next and his eyebrows lifted slightly when he saw Scota was with them.

Tuathal spoke first, in a loud, confident voice. He may have been the youngest man there but he had been raised to be a King and his victory over Elim had clearly reinforced his belief in his destiny.

"I am Tuathal Techtmar," he declared, adopting the name that Findmall had bestowed on him. "I am the legitimate High King of Eriu."

Sanb did not waste time with useless questions. In a soft, slightly amused voice, he replied, "I am Sanb, son of Cet, King of Connacht. Elim mac Conrach sent for me to fight against you."

He bared his teeth in a humourless grin as he went on, "It seems I have arrived too late."

"Elim is dead," Tuathal confirmed.

"I did not think he would lend you his chariot out of generosity," Sanb observed drily. "Generosity was not one of his finer points."

"His sons are also dead," Tuathal informed him.

Sanb gave a slow nod, as if he had expected that news.

222

"So," he drawled slowly, "what happens now?"

"That is up to you," Tuathal told him. "But I will make you the offer that I made to Elim's warriors, an offer that most of them have gladly accepted. If you swear loyalty to me as High King, then we shall be friends."

"Friends?" Sanb asked in mock surprise. "But the High King normally demands tribute. That is not friendly."

"Tribute is given in exchange for protection," Tuathal replied smoothly.

"I don't need protection," Sanb rasped sharply.

"Not if you are my friend, you won't," Tuathal shot back equally promptly.

Sanb gave a throaty laugh, his eyes sparkling.

"In that case," he suggested, "perhaps you would consider reviewing the amount that Connacht sends to Tara each year. Perhaps half of the current tribute would be appropriate."

"Or perhaps double," Tuathal countered. "I have not yet had time to review such details so I cannot make a decision just now. When I do decide, I will take the nature of our relationship into account."

Sanb's air of genial forcefulness shifted to one of careful appraisal as he eyed Tuathal coolly. The young man had countered every challenge with supreme confidence. If Sanb had hoped to intimidate him, he had failed.

With grudging respect, Sanb said, "Elim told me you were a puppy. I think he misjudged you."

"To his cost," Tuathal agreed. "He mistook youth for foolishness."

Sanb nodded. Then his eyes turned to Scota.

"What do you say, Scota? Have you thrown in your lot with this wolf cub?"

"Tuathal Techtmar is the High King," Scota replied evenly. "The Dagda came to me in a dream and foretold his triumph. The Ulaid and the Scotti follow him. I recommend that you do likewise."

Sanb smiled at the thinly veiled threat in her words. After a moment's thought, he spat on the ground to avert bad luck, then declared, "It is a foolish man who opposes the Gods. Elim is dead and it seems that his army has joined you. In those circumstances, I can do no less."

Tuathal inclined his head in acknowledgement.

"Then I would like to invite you to come to Tara tomorrow to witness my formal acclamation as High King."

"I will be there," Sanb promised. "I will even present you with a gift right now."

Turning to one of his warriors, he commanded, "Fetch the girl!"

"I am grateful for your offer," said Tuathal. "But I have no need of a girl at the moment."

"You have need of this one," Sanb assured him.

The rider galloped back to the war band, quickly returning with a smaller figure sitting behind him, her bare legs visible behind his, and her arms looped awkwardly around his neck. As he drew closer, they could see that whoever his passenger was, her wrists were bound together.

The warrior hauled his horse to a halt in front of Tuathal's chariot, then swung round to sweep a naked girl to the ground.

The girl staggered, almost fell, but managed to retain her balance. As the rider retreated, she slowly stood to face Tuathal, looking at him over the heads of his war ponies. Her face was streaked with dust and dirt, her hair dishevelled, but Scota recognised her instantly.

"Braine!"

"My scouts caught her trying to run away from the battle," Sanb explained. "I managed to prevent them doing any real damage to her but, as you can see, she lost her clothing in the struggle."

He grinned as he waved his arm to present her to Tuathal.

"I give her to you as a gesture of my goodwill. Do with her as you please. Now, I had better go and find somewhere for my lads to camp for the night. Until tomorrow."

He placed his helmet on his head, nodded a farewell and tapped his driver on the arm. The chariot swung away, the escorting riders falling into place behind it, leaving Braine standing alone and naked in front of Tuathal and his advisors.

She did not try to hide her nakedness. She stood there, arms bound in front of her, with dark bruises on her face and a livid scratch on her left breast, but she held her head high. She may have been young but she was the daughter of a King and she would not beg for mercy.

She glared at Scota.

224

"You betrayed my father," she said coldly. Then her gaze flicked to Calgacus. "And you killed him," she accused. "I saw you."

Calgacus struggled to find a suitable response. He did not know this young girl who stood defiantly in front of him but seeing her reminded him of the pretty brunette who had been captured at Emain Macha. Like her, Braine was an innocent victim of his success.

Braine, using anger as a weapon, blazed a challenge at Tuathal.

"You must be Tuathal," she said. "I suppose you are going to kill me now."

Tuathal had retained his composure throughout his meeting with Sanb but he wore an expression of uncertainty in the face of Braine's accusation.

"Well?" the girl demanded, as if she were in a hurry to learn her fate. "My father would not have hesitated. Ask Scota. She saw what he did to Eochaid's family. Isn't that right, Scota? The family of a defeated King must die?"

"It is the custom," Scota agreed flatly, her expression grim.

Still Tuathal did not speak. In the doom-laden silence, Fiacha Cassan edged his horse forwards.

"Give the command and I will do it," he told the young High King.

Braine closed her eyes, waiting for Tuathal's decision. She was bravely trying to remain defiant but Fiacha Cassan had clearly frightened her. Confronted by his callous confirmation that he would gladly kill her, her anger had ebbed away to be replaced by dread and she was visibly trembling.

"There is another way," Scota interjected, her voice full of command.

"What is that?" Tuathal asked, his expression puzzled.

In response, Scota turned to look at Calgacus and he realised that, although she had appeared to dismiss his comment about Tuathal's betrothal to Fallar, she had clearly appreciated the implications and was passing the burden of the decision to him.

He frowned as he considered the great alliance he had wanted to build and how Fallar's marriage to Tuathal would have sealed the bargain with old Coel. Without that marriage, would the alliance hold? Without that alliance, could he resist the Roman tide when the Legions marched north?

He knew the answer to that final question. Even with all the tribes joining together, defeating Rome would be a momentous task. Without the Caledones, it would be virtually impossible.

Then he looked at Braine, naked and defenceless, her wrists lashed together as if she were a slave, her brown hair tangled around her bowed head, and he imagined how he would feel if his own daughter had been placed in a similar position.

Slowly, he dismounted and walked towards the terrified girl, unfastening his cloak as he did so. When he reached her, he wrapped it around her, covering her bruised body. She flinched slightly as he wrapped the cloak around her shoulders and he realised that, although she was the daughter of a King, she was a young, frightened girl. He grasped her hands then, taking his dagger from his belt, sliced through the ropes that bound her wrists.

"What are you doing, old man?" Fiacha Cassan protested. "She must die."

"I don't kill women or children," Calgacus growled back at him.

"Then what will you do with her?" Fiacha Cassan asked scornfully. "As long as she lives, she presents a threat to the High King. Through her, others may dispute his right to rule."

Calgacus had made up his mind. In the end, it had been an easy decision.

"Not if he marries her," he stated, locking eyes with Tuathal.

Tuathal stared at him in astonishment but Fiacha Cassan blurted, "She cannot be trusted! She is the daughter of the Usurper."

Tuathal turned to Scota, raising an eyebrow in question as he sought reassurance.

The sorceress nodded, "Calgacus is right. Braine is not her father. If you marry her, then the two claims to the High Kingship are united. Nobody can threaten either of you."

Tuathal nodded but he remained uncertain.

Turning to Calgacus, he pointed out, "It was my grandfather's wish that I marry your daughter."

"Your grandfather is not the High King of Eriu," Calgacus countered. "You are. You must do what is best for your new kingdom."

Tuathal frowned thoughtfully. Calgacus could see Runt nodding in approval and Scota's half-smile of relief.

He gave Braine a gentle shake, still with his arm around her shoulders.

"What do you say?" he asked her as gently as he could.

Braine's eyelids fluttered open and she regarded him with a strange, lost look. He could still feel the tension in her body and he saw a tear slowly trickle down her cheek.

"Do I have a choice?" she whispered hoarsely.

"Not much of one," he admitted gently. "But it is a chance of life."

She tried to speak but no words came, so she weakly nodded her head.

Calgacus looked questioningly at Tuathal.

"You have done all the right things so far. Do the right thing now. Send a message to the people of Eriu that you have not come to conquer them but to join them."

Tuathal still wavered. He looked around, seeking the opinions of his companions.

Scota nodded her approval and Findmall, who instinctively distrusted the sorceress, nevertheless agreed with her. Fiacha Cassan scowled but shrugged indifferently.

Eudaf gave a smile of encouragement and remarked, "She's pretty enough."

Tuathal looked down at Braine.

"If you agree, I will go along with this idea. It will protect both of us from those who would seek our deaths."

If Braine had any opinions on the fact that it was Tuathal's own followers who might seek her death, she wisely kept them to herself. Still unable to summon any words, she meekly nodded her assent.

Tuathal stepped down from the chariot and walked around it to reach her. Calgacus gently nudged her forwards and Tuathal put his arms out to catch her as if she were in danger of falling. Her head was bowed and she was crying now although Calgacus could not tell whether her tears stemmed from sorrow or relief.

Putting an arm around her shoulder, Tuathal led her back to the chariot. Wordlessly, he signalled to his driver to take them back to the army.

Calgacus watched as the two chariots wheeled away. Then he sighed and walked to where Runt was holding the reins of his pony.

As he mounted, Runt said, "You made the right choice."

"I know, but Coel might not think so."

"Bugger Coel. We can beat the Romans without him."

"He still has our families held hostage," Calgacus reminded his friend.

"But the High King of Eriu owes us a big favour," Runt countered. "He'll help us make sure they are released unharmed."

Calgacus nodded but he could not help thinking that he might have ruined any chances of creating an alliance of tribes. Yet he did not regret his decision.

Fiacha Cassan clearly disagreed. He hung back from the others and brought his pony alongside Calgacus as they trotted back up the slope.

"You're a bloody fool," the warrior told him, although there was more amusement than animosity in his voice. "She'll probably knife him to death on their wedding night."

"Then you can do whatever you like to her," Calgacus replied. "But if she doesn't, and if things turn out right, remember that you were the one who offered to kill her. I don't expect she'll ever forget that."

Fiacha Cassan laughed, "And I won't forget that it was all your fault. If she ever tries to do anything to me, I'll hunt you down and cut your throat."

Calgacus briefly considered pointing out that the marriage had actually been Scota's idea but he knew that passing the blame to a woman, even a sorceress, would appear cowardly, so he simply responded to the tall warrior's threat with a wry smile.

He said, "Then I hope for both our sakes that the marriage turns out well."

He eased his horse into a canter, following the chariots back to the Hill of Achall. Whether or not he had made the right decision, he could not alter it now. Besides which, he had other things on his mind. He had done everything he had been sent to do. Elim was dead and tomorrow Tuathal would be High King. After that, he could return home.

Chapter XXV

Tuathal's war host swarmed into the valley around Tara and he quickly sent men to secure the sacred site while he headed for Elim's former homestead. He hurried because he was concerned that some of the more fleet-footed of his warriors might have already begun ransacking the settlement in search of plunder but Scota had foreseen this possibility and a group of Scotti, sent by Aedan as soon as the victory had been achieved, stood guard at the gates, preventing anyone from entering the hillfort. Their presence also meant that many of the village's inhabitants had been prevented from abandoning the settlement.

Tuathal rode his chariot right up to the gates, then sent the Scotti into the fort to round up the townspeople. He waited patiently until they had been assembled, then, standing on the platform of his chariot, he addressed both them and his warriors at the same time, promising there would be no plundering, killing or rape.

"This is my home now," he warned his warriors. "And these are my people, just as you are. Any man who abuses my people will find himself hanged as a common criminal."

He then dismounted and, accompanied by his advisors and a horde of Caledones and Scotti, took control of the fortress unopposed.

His first act on claiming Elim's former residence as his own was to free all of Elim's slaves and to inform the newly liberated men and women, along with those who had served the Usurper as freeborn servants, that he was happy for them to continue in their roles and serve him. His only concession to Findmall's objections was that he appointed one of his own trusted men to act as his food taster.

"These people are used to serving a High King," he explained, "even if their former ruler was a Usurper. And I have no quarrel with the people of Eriu. My fight was with Elim and I have won that struggle."

His second proclamation was that he and Braine would be married the following day, immediately after he had been formally declared High King. Findmall would arrange the two ceremonies and Tuathal ordered that a feast be prepared to celebrate the events.

"Most of the lads are celebrating already," Fiacha Cassan grinned, jerking his head to indicate the sounds of laughter and revelry from outside the roundhouse Tuathal had inherited from Elim.

"They deserve it," was Tuathal's happy response.

Braine, her face stained with dirt and tears and her hair bedraggled, was escorted to her former home and two warriors were posted outside her door.

With sullen, downcast eyes, she asked, "Am I a prisoner?"

"No," Tuathal assured her. "You will be my Queen. These men are here to ensure your safety. You should rest now. Wash and dress. We will speak later."

It was a clumsy beginning to their betrothal but Braine was too tired and miserable to protest. She meekly entered the small house which, along with a clutch of other buildings set aside for the royal household, lay at the rear of the High King's much larger residence.

Tuathal and his advisors now occupied that large house where they sat around the freshly lit hearth fire.

"We have a great deal to discuss," Tuathal announced, looking directly at Scota.

The sorceress nodded but demurred, "I think I should go and speak to Braine first. She has suffered several shocks today and she is without friends or family to support her."

Findmall, who had done his best to avoid speaking to Scota until that moment, protested, "She knows you betrayed her father. Do you really think she will trust you?"

Scota replied to the druid's accusation calmly, saying, "Braine is a young girl but she is intelligent enough to understand the choice she faces. She always knew she would be married off to someone to seal some sort of pact. She would have had no say in the matter. Her current situation is no different except that the importance of the marriage is more significant than if she had been married off to some minor Lord. In fact, it is so important that I think it would be better if Tuathal married her tonight."

"You think the girl will change her mind by morning?" Findmall scoffed. "She knows the consequences."

230

He drew a finger across his throat as a reminder of Braine's potential fate.

Scota shot back, "And how would that look to the other Kings of Eriu? Even as things stand, tongues will wag and accusations be murmured. Killing the Usurper and marrying his daughter on the same day could be seen as the act of an unscrupulous man. But to murder the girl in cold blood because she refuses to marry Tuathal would be unwise. It would mark the beginning of Tuathal's reign as that of a ruthless murderer who is little better than Elim."

"The Kings of Eriu are not stupid," Findmall countered. "They will understand the necessity of either action. Sanb said as much when he handed the girl over."

"What the Kings know and what whispers they send abroad to rouse the populace are two different things," Scota shot back. "Far better if Braine is seen to be a willing partner, or even to announce that she secretly supported Tuathal from the start. Perhaps it was she who sent a secret message, urging him to overthrow her father."

"Why would she say such a thing?" Eudaf interjected.

"Because I will persuade her that it is the best course of action for all of us," Scota told him. "If both Tuathal and Braine are seen to be willing partners, there is much less chance of anyone contesting Tuathal's rule."

"You have a devious mind, Witch," Findmall muttered darkly.

"So it has been said," Scota acknowledged without any sign of rancour.

Findmall regarded her with a look which revealed his distrust of her.

"Have no fears about my motives, Druid," she assured him. "I did not help you simply in order to throw everything away once Tuathal had won his victory."

"But you served the Usurper for many years," Findmall said accusingly.

"I did. It was out of necessity."

"And you are a witch who performs dark rituals," Findmall persisted.

"So people say," Scota confirmed with little apparent concern for what others might say of her.

"Is it true?"

"Would you believe me if I denied it?"

"I am not sure I would believe anything you say," Findmall rasped.

Calgacus fired an impatient look at Tuathal who intervened, "That is enough, Cousin. Scota has helped us more than we could have asked for. I will not question her motives now."

Findmall fell silent but his brother, Fiacha Cassan, protested, "Perhaps it would be wise to question her. All we know of her is what we have heard for the past score of years while she served the Usurper."

Calgacus put in, "I do not distrust Scota but I do have many questions I would like answered."

All eyes were on Scota and she gave a reluctant sigh.

"I did it for the good of Eriu," she stated. "Elim mac Conrach was a cruel man, perhaps worthy of being called evil. But he was a strong ruler. Without him, war would have raged all across the land as the sub-Kings fought one another to claim the High Kingship. And none of them would have been as capable as he."

She looked at Tuathal as she added, "I knew only one man could take Elim's place and keep the peace. But you were too young, so I needed to bide my time."

Turning to Findmall, she went on, "As for my motives in serving Elim, I once faced the same choice that Braine faces now. I chose life, for myself and for all my people."

"Perhaps you should explain the whole story," Calgacus suggested.

Tuathal agreed, "I, too, would like to hear why you helped us. But let us have some food and drink brought so that we can eat while we listen."

That was a welcome suggestion because none of them had eaten since early morning. Tuathal summoned his new servants who quickly brought platters of meat, cheese and bread, accompanied by mugs of dark beer.

Once the servants had departed, Scota began her story.

"The Scotti are a small tribe," she recounted. "We have been wanderers ever since our ancestors came to Eriu countless generations ago. But our men are among the finest warriors in the land and that has been both a blessing and a curse."

She took a mouthful of bread, chewed, swallowed, then resumed, "Our skill in battle was such that many lords and sub-kings would pay us to join them when they were in dispute with a neighbour. When that happened, they always won their battles. But once the victory was won, they soon wanted rid of us because they could not afford to feed our entire tribe and they feared we might turn against them, so they would drive us away and we would resume our wandering."

She slowly chewed another mouthful of bread and cheese before continuing, "I learned these things as a child and by the time I was grown I understood the truth of the matter. We were never a numerous people and, for all our prowess in battle, we could not carve a kingdom for ourselves. If truth be told, our menfolk took some pride in being mercenaries.

"Then," she sighed, "Elim mac Conrach seized the rule of Eriu. I was young then, sixteen years of age but unmarried because of ..."

She gestured towards the mottled side of her face as she went on, "Because of this mark and because I already had a reputation as a user of magic. But I was something of an outsider even then and I was not privy to the talking and arguing that always seemed to occupy our elders. But I know something of what happened.

"Elim was supported by many of Eriu's chieftains and sub-kings but opposed by others. With wars on several fronts, he sent word to the Scotti that he wished to hire us."

Scota shrugged as she recalled, "Some among his foes had also asked for our help and our elders were divided as to what to do. Elim was a powerful man, with many warriors at his back but he was known to be cruel and quick to punish anyone who disagreed with him."

"The Scotti refused to help him?" Calgacus guessed.

Scota shook her head.

"We had not reached a decision but the delay convinced Elim that he must deal with us in case we joined one of his enemies. So he attacked us before we even knew he was nearby."

Nodding thoughtfully, Fiacha Cassan murmured, "The Usurper was always quick to act in war."

Scota agreed, "He struck at night, when it was raining heavily. I still cannot fathom exactly how he found us but his men attacked while our sentries were sheltering from the rain and they slaughtered many of our people on that dreadful night.

"Some of us managed to escape and we fled to the forests where, over the next few days, others straggled in to join us."

Her eyes held a distant look as she explained, "By my reckoning, we lost around half our men of fighting age, along with many women and children. All of our leaders were dead and the Usurper's men were still hunting us."

"So you surrendered?" Calgacus asked.

Scota's mouth curled in her crooked half-smile as she admitted, "None of the people knew what to do. There were arguments and strong words spoken, with some advocating surrender and others insisting we should fight on. That was a hopeless cause, I knew, because there was nobody strong enough to bind the remnants of our people together. So I stood up and offered to go to speak to Elim and arrange a peace."

She paused, gathering her thoughts before admitting, "I think most people agreed to let me go because they thought it would be a way to get rid of me once and for all."

She shot Calgacus a meaningful look as she added, "It will not surprise you to know that Aedan was one of those people."

Calgacus shifted uncomfortably. Aedan had passed away while they had been speaking to Sanb, his life ebbing out of his ravaged body. Yet Calgacus remembered the tears Scota had wiped from her eyes and he wondered at her apparent ability to separate her personal feelings from her duties as a leader.

Resuming her tale, she went on, "I managed to gain an audience with Elim and I showed him some of my magical powers. He was so impressed that he allowed me to speak on behalf of my tribe and I arranged an end to the fighting."

"That must have been quite a display of magic," Calgacus ventured.

Scota's half-smile played around her lips as she shrugged, "I cut the head off a dove, then brought it back to life and let it fly free."

"You can do that?" Eudaf exclaimed while Findmall hissed in disapproval and made a warding sign against evil.

Scota ignored both of them as she recalled, "So we had peace but the price was high. The Scotti were bonded to Elim and I was appointed as their leader and as his sorceress."

234

"And you served him well!" Fiacha Cassan muttered darkly.

"Indeed I did," Scota admitted. "But I saved my people and Elim brought peace to the land thanks to our help in his wars."

"He brought peace by crushing all opposition," Findmall argued.

"Is that not what all Kings do?" Scota countered, her hard stare silencing the young druid.

She went on, "But, as I said, the price was high. I never forgot the people who died when he attacked us. I wanted my revenge but simply killing him would have solved nothing unless I could be sure that someone could replace him."

She looked at Tuathal as she added, "Someone who had a legitimate claim to be High King."

Calgacus still had questions he wanted answered but Scota stood up and inclined her head in a bow to Tuathal.

"With your permission," she said, "I really must go and speak to Braine. It is important that she understands what is at stake."

"I will join you later," Tuathal nodded. "But now I ought to visit my men to see that they are being properly fed and to make sure they are not too drunk to attend tomorrow's ceremony."

Calgacus and Runt tagged along at the rear of Tuathal's procession. It was dark outside, clouds obscuring the moon and stars, with a threat of imminent rain but the prospect had not dampened the spirits of the warriors. With the exception of the sentries who had been posted to guard the doors of Tuathal's roundhouse, most men they encountered had been celebrating the discovery of Elim's stores of ale. Some were still singing songs or laughing at bawdy jokes while others had already designated themselves as protectors of the women whose husbands had been killed or had fled after the battle.

Outside the fort, camp fires sparkled across the valley floor and here the celebrations were just as noisy. When Tuathal put in an appearance, he was mobbed by hordes of drunken warriors who all wanted to clasp his hand or clap him on the back and tell him what part they had played in his victory.

Calgacus watched as a disinterested spectator, unable to feel part of the festivities. Frowning, he murmured to Runt, "I hope Sanb of Connacht doesn't take it into his head to make a bid for the High Kingship by eliminating Tuathal tonight. This lot are in no condition to put up a fight."

"You worry too much," Runt told him. "If Sanb wanted to make that sort of play, he'd have kept hold of Braine. Besides, Tuathal will be safe enough once he gets back inside the fort."

Calgacus was not completely reassured.

"Are you forgetting there's a killer on the loose somewhere in this army? If one of them has a knife, he could stab Tuathal easily enough and there's nothing anyone could do to stop him."

Runt let out a soft curse and joined Calgacus in fretting until, around midnight, Tuathal announced that he needed to return to his house and get some sleep.

"It has been a momentous day," he told his admiring warriors, "and tomorrow will be another one. Try not to drink all the beer tonight."

The men laughed and assured him they would save some drink for the following day as a grinning Tuathal slowly made his return to the fortified homestead that was now his home.

"Do you think Scota will have persuaded Braine?" Runt wondered.

"I expect so," Calgacus replied. "She has a forceful way about her. And the girl doesn't have much of a choice, does she?"

"Do you believe her? Scota, I mean."

Calgacus shrugged, "I think so. I can't see what she has to gain by betraying Tuathal after helping him depose Elim. But I'm not convinced she told us everything. There are still some questions I'd like to ask her."

"Now's your chance," Runt told him, gesturing to where Scota had emerged from the darkness between two buildings to meet Tuathal.

The sorceress exchanged a few words with Tuathal, assuring him that Braine would play her part as required.

"I should talk to her," Tuathal said. "The rest of you can bed down in my house. I'll join you soon."

"I'll come with you," Eudaf declared, insisting on maintaining his role as Tuathal's protector.

With one of Tuathal's bodyguards holding aloft a blazing torch to light their way, the new High King went to speak to his bride-to-be. Calgacus watched them vanish into the night then turned to follow Fiacha Cassan and Findmall back to Tuathal's great house but Scota moved towards him and reached out to touch his arm.

"I wish to speak to you in private," she said softly. "Will you come with me to my own home?"

"Now?" Calgacus asked.

"Why not? We may not have time to talk tomorrow and I can tell that you have questions for me. Come with me and I will do my best to answer them."

Calgacus glanced at Runt. The little man grinned and told him, "Go on. I'll bed down with the others."

"Don't you want to hear what Scota has to say?" Calgacus asked.

"I'm sure you can tell me all about it tomorrow," Runt smirked. "I don't want to intrude. You two go and enjoy yourselves."

He pressed his thumb against his forefinger and mimed stitching his lips together in a pledge of silence. If Scota saw the gesture, she did not deign to comment on it.

"Come," she said to Calgacus. "It is not far."

So, as his friend hurried off in pursuit of Fiacha Cassan and Findmall, Calgacus followed the witch to her lair.

Chapter XXVI

The hilltop village was gradually settling down for the night, only the hardiest souls still managing to stay awake, but Calgacus was pleasantly surprised to see that two stern, if rather unhappy, guards stood outside Scota's door. The Scotti, it appeared, had not forgotten their duties.

The two men wordlessly stepped aside to allow Scota and Calgacus to pass, only their furtive glances at him betraying their curiosity.

Calgacus soon forgot them as he followed Scota into her small roundhouse. The interior was unlike most homes, he quickly realised. The hearth fire, glowing red and sparking with fresh peat having recently been added, and the bracken-filled mattress covered by blankets which lay huddled at the far side were familiar but nearly everything else was unusual.

A long, wooden table sat to his right, its surface covered by a clutter of pots, clay jars, bowls, platters, spoons, knives and other implements he did not recognise. Bundles of herbs hung from beams above his head, just below the layer of hearth smoke which gathered beneath the thatched roof. The herbs sent an unfamiliar, although not unpleasant, tang to his nostrils. Apart from four wooden stools, there was little else in the house and it was the absence of such things as a quern stone for grinding grain or the clutter of children's toys or large storage chests that struck him as most peculiar.

Scota, though, seemed to match her surroundings perfectly.

"Please sit," she invited, gesturing to the stools that circled the stone-lined hearth pit.

Calgacus took his sword belt off over his head and laid the weapon on the floor beside a stool before sitting. He expected Scota to join him but she moved over to the long table and bent down to retrieve a linen sack.

"I need to get rid of these," she told him as she lifted the bag.

Calgacus could see the dark stain on the sack and noticed the lumpy, misshapen bulk of its contents.

Scota returned to the door and handed the sack to one of her guards.

"Have these buried somewhere secret," she ordered. "I want nobody digging them up or finding them by accident."

Calgacus heard the warrior promise to follow her instructions and then she closed the door and came to sit opposite him, facing him across the smoky fire.

"That was the heads of Elim and his sons," she explained. "I had them brought here to prevent anyone placing them on spikes at the gates."

"So that Braine would not see them?" he ventured.

"Yes. If we had been unable to find her or if she had been killed, it might have been necessary to proclaim Tuathal's victory by displaying the heads of his enemies but it is better now that they disappear."

"You think of everything," Calgacus told her with a smile.

"I try," she shrugged. "It is not always possible to anticipate every eventuality."

"You seem to have done remarkably well so far," he assured her.

She rose again, moving to the table.

"Forgive me. I am not used to guests. I can only offer you small beer to drink."

"That will do," he assured her.

She picked up two clay mugs and poured from a large jug, bringing him the thrice-brewed drink that was normally offered only to women and children.

"I could send for something stronger if you wish," she told him as she passed him the mug.

"I think I perhaps need my wits about me," he replied. "It is not every day I converse with a sorceress."

Scota gave a faint smile as she replied, "It is not every day I converse with a legendary War Leader."

She sat down again, very deliberately putting her mug to her lips and drinking.

"It is perfectly safe to drink," she told him, noticing that he was still holding his mug. "It contains no secret potions or poison."

Feeling slightly embarrassed, Calgacus took a sip of the dark liquid and found it surprisingly refreshing.

239

"I know you have questions," Scota continued. "I, too, have questions for you. But first I should tell you my story. I did not want to reveal all the details in the presence of your companions."

"Findmall and Fiacha Cassan, you mean?"

She nodded, "They do not trust me and I have my doubts about them. I would prefer that they know as little as possible about my past."

"What about Tuathal? Shouldn't he know?"

She shrugged, "My life is not a secret, but I am a private person. All he needs to know is that I will serve him as best I can."

"So what is it you did not tell us earlier?" he asked.

She sat silently for a moment, staring into the flickering flames of the hearth fire before looking at him and touching her index finger to the left side of her face where the skin was a shade of reddish pink.

"You see this, of course," she said. "You could not fail to. And, like all men, it fascinates and horrifies you."

She held up a hand to stifle his protest.

"You do not need to deny it," she said. "You do your best to disguise your fascination but I can see it in your eyes."

"I mean no offence," he told her.

"And I take none," she assured him. "I have grown accustomed to seeing fear and loathing in the eyes of those who look upon me."

"I am merely curious about you," he told her.

"I can see that," she nodded. "Yet you cannot deny that my face repels you. You hide it better than most people but I know the sight of such disfigurement produces a natural reaction."

Calgacus made no reply. In his youth, he had learned the secret of how druids could read people's gestures and facial expressions and he had tried to adopt a calm, neutral exterior so as to conceal his true thoughts. It occurred to him that either Scota's disfigurement was so noticeable that he had given away too much or that she was very skilled at reading people.

"That mark is the cause of how my life has turned out," Scota explained.

"Does it hurt?" he asked.

"No. It is merely a birthmark. Just a very prominent one."

He nodded, tapping his right hand against his thigh.

"I, too, have a birthmark. It is in the shape of a sword."

240

"The mark of a warrior," she observed.

He told her, "When I was born, an old druid said it was a star, not a sword. He announced that I would become a druid. He was wrong about that, as he was wrong about many things."

"I have heard of your conflicts with the greybeards," Scota said. "Few men would dare such open defiance. The penalty for disobeying the druids were severe, were they not?"

"Yes. But I had some help. And now the druids are mostly gone while I am still here."

"I know your story, Calgacus," she informed him. "Now you must learn mine. I owe you that much."

She again tapped a finger to her cheek as she went on, "I was born with this and it marked out my life. My parents did not know whether it was a sign that I had been blessed by the Gods or cursed by some demon. My father wanted to take me out into the woods and abandon me to fate but my mother, so I am told, insisted on keeping me. She had already lost two infants and did not wish to lose a third, even though I was clearly not a normal child."

She took a sip of her small beer before going on, "Unfortunately, she died when I was only a year old and people said it was because I had drained the life from her while she suckled me."

Calgacus could hear the hurt in her voice, the bitterness against opinions and judgements passed on a small child.

She went on, "I might have died then but an old woman, whom some called wise and others named a witch, said that she would adopt me. My father was only too glad to be rid of me, so I went to live with old Dana."

Scota's voice softened as she recalled, "Dana brought me up and taught me many things. She was an expert in herbs and potions and I learned a great deal. She was also a midwife and helped deliver many babies. She had been at my birth which was why she was not afraid of me."

Another pang of regret tinged her voice as she added, "I was never permitted to aid her in delivering children. No mother would let me near her when her time came."

Calgacus thought Scota must have had a lonely childhood, shunned by all and hated by everyone except one old woman. Perhaps that explained why she appeared aloof from other people.

241

Like Calgacus, she had learned to present a face to the world that would protect her.

"What about your father? Did he not have any interest in you?"

"He was killed in one of our many battles," Scota informed him. "I have no real memory of him. Dana was the only family I had. She brought me up but she also taught me some magic; tricks to make things appear and disappear."

As she spoke, she transferred her mug to her left hand and held up her right. Suddenly, with no transition other than a flick of her fingers, a small, sharp knife appeared in her fist.

"Like that," she smiled.

Calgacus blinked as Scota moved her hand and the knife vanished again.

"You are very good," he told her. "My niece, Emmelia, has some skill at such sleight of hand but even she is not as good as that."

"So you have some understanding of magic?" Scota asked keenly.

"Emmelia says there is no such thing as true magic," he replied. "There is only a learned skill and the knowledge of how the world works."

"She sounds like a clever woman," Scota remarked.

"So Findmall's concerns about your dark rituals are unfounded?" Calgacus probed.

Scota's half-smile flashed briefly across her lips.

"People have seen me perform many rituals," she admitted. "Afterwards, I have usually made some prediction or performed some feat which has amazed my audience."

"Which does not prove that magic is real," he said. "Only that you are very skilful and very clever."

She flashed her crooked smile again and he realised that this awkward response was probably because, as a child, she had known few opportunities to smile.

She said, "I see I was right about you, Calgacus. You can think for yourself. That is a rare thing in a warrior. As is your lack of boastfulness."

"I can brag when necessary," he assured her. "But I learned a long time ago that deeds are more important than words."

Scota nodded, "Indeed they are. Yet few men seem to understand that. I grew up among warriors and have seen how they

242

strut around, bragging and boasting, taking what they want because they are strong. And when it comes to battle, most of them believe the only way to fight is to gather your war band and charge at the enemy."

"I know the type of man you mean," Calgacus smiled. "Yet we cannot live without them. Given proper leadership, they can achieve great things."

"Leadership," she agreed. "That is the essential ingredient that so many lack. You have it, and so did Elim. For all his faults, he was cunning and he understood how wars can be won. His warriors were always fed and well equipped, his marches made with purpose, and he knew when to strike at his opponents."

"As he struck at the Scotti?"

"Exactly."

Scota paused, her face sombre as she recalled, "That was a dark, evil night. They came among our tents and shelters and they killed everyone they found. They had surprised our sentries and we had no warning until the shouting and screaming began."

With a visible shudder, she continued, "Dana and I tried to run but it was difficult for her. We stumbled in the darkness, lost our way and then one of Elim's men found us. He drove his spear into Dana's back with such force that the point burst out through her chest."

Calgacus had seen such massacres before and could imagine the terror of the women and children as they ran through driving rain and near total darkness in panic.

Scota recounted, "I was still young then but I had already mastered many skills. As the warrior struggled to withdraw his spear from Dana's body, I found my knife and I slashed him across the throat."

She sighed at the memories as she added, "It was too late for Dana. She was already near death and she urged me to run. So I did, finding my way into the woods and eventually meeting up with other survivors."

"Which was when you took charge?"

She nodded, "I understood what our remaining warriors did not; that any man who could lead a surprise attack on the Scotti at night was a man to be reckoned with. So I offered to go to him and arrange a treaty."

"You said you sacrificed a dove and brought it back to life?"

243

Scota smiled, "I cut its head off, then replaced it and let it fly away."

"That sounds ... improbable," he ventured.

"Many things are possible when you know how they can be accomplished," she smiled. "Elim and his warriors believed what they saw. Your niece might have another explanation."

"It was a trick?"

"It is a talent," Scota told him. "But that is not important. What mattered was that I pledged the Scotti to Elim mac Conrach in exchange for our lives."

"And you waited twenty years to take your revenge?"

"Do not misunderstand me, Calgacus. I had thoughts of getting close to Elim and killing him myself but I realised that would achieve little. His men would turn on us again and then the other Kings would rend Eriu apart as they battled for supremacy. So I bided my time and made myself invaluable to the High King until I could arrange things so that his fall was inevitable."

"You planned it for twenty years?"

"I made many plans during those years. But events can alter any plan. For example, I knew that Eochaid of Leinster was unhappy with Elim's rule. I had hoped to send him to join Tuathal when you landed but the old fool began his own rebellion which ended in disaster for him. Even then, I believed I had persuaded Elim to let him live so that I could bring him into my confidence when the right time came. But Elim was always unpredictable. He murdered Eochaid and his family, so my plans were set back and Tuathal's task made more difficult. That is why I was glad you were with him. He needed help if he was to confront Elim."

"You also helped him," Calgacus reminded her. "My own part was a small one."

"Not so small," she countered. "You seized Emain Macha much more quickly than even I had dared to hope. That proves your worth."

Calgacus could not reveal that he had devised a plan to take Emain Macha solely because he had been angered by Fiacha Cassan's accusations of cowardice. Instead, he said, "We would still have lost if you had not turned against Elim."

Scota shrugged, "But you did not lose. Has it occurred to you that many of the men who followed Tuathal did so because they knew you were with him? Your reputation counts for a great deal, you know. That is one of the reasons I wanted you to accompany him. Elim was a master of war and I knew Tuathal would need someone who could match him."

"So you chose me?" he scowled.

"You were the obvious choice," she told him. "I first heard your name not long after Elim came to power. I had realised that, even if I arranged things so that Elim remained on the defensive and lost the initiative in a war, it would take a great tactician to defeat him. The problem was that I had no idea who that might be. But, as you know, boats cross the sea between Eriu and the western lands of the Pritani all the time. Among the many trade goods they bring back, they also return with tales and songs. That was when I first heard your name. The songs said you had a magical sword and that you were the only man who could defeat the Legions of Rome."

"You should not believe everything you hear in songs," he cautioned her with his customary response.

"Oh, I know how bards do their work," she smiled. "Yet, although the songs may embellish the facts, there is often a kernel of truth behind them."

She went on, "It was the time of the great rebellion of Boudica. We heard about that after it was over. Yet you were named as the man who had destroyed a Legion."

Calgacus grunted, "I am surprised you heard that. Others took the credit at the time. Not that it matters, for we lost that war because my sister followed the advice of men who did not understand how to fight the Romans."

"The war may have been lost but your reputation was not," Scota told him. "But, of course, my situation was unchanged. I needed to wait until Tuathal was old enough to reclaim his birthright."

She paused to gather her thoughts before explaining, "Then, when my spies were among Coel's people, they heard about Tuathal's betrothal to the daughter of a mighty War Leader named Calgacus. I remembered those songs from twenty years earlier and I soon learned that you were indeed the same man. When I discovered that, I knew you were the right person to help me overthrow Elim. Tuathal may be the legitimate heir but he is young and inexperienced. I knew he would need a real War Leader to aid him. That is why I sent for you."

Calgacus cocked his head on one side as he regarded her intently.

245

"You sent for me?"

"As I sent for Tuathal."

"We came," Calgacus informed her slowly, "because Elim had sent men to kill us."

Again, Scota's lips formed her crooked smile.

"Elim did no such thing," she told him. "He dismissed Tuathal as an inexperienced youth and all he knew of you was what he had heard when the bards sang those tales of your deeds during the long, winter nights."

Calgacus frowned, realising he had been duped but not sure who had been responsible.

"If Elim did not send the killers," he asked her, "who did?"

Scota regarded him frankly as she admitted, "I did."

Calgacus' muscles tensed and he readied himself to reach for his sword at the first sign of treachery, but Scota sat facing him across the smoky fire and calmly took a sip from her mug.

"Do not be alarmed," she told him reassuringly. "I did not actually send men to kill either of you. I merely sent rumours that assassins were seeking your deaths."

"They were more than rumours," Calgacus retorted heatedly. "I have been attacked three times and been lucky to survive."

Scota seemed genuinely surprised. Frowning, she said, "That was none of my doing. Tell me what happened."

"First, you tell me exactly what you did," he shot back.

Scota considered his demand for a moment, then explained, "I sent rumours to Coel's home that Elim was seeking Tuathal's death. I knew the old man had dreamed of installing his grandson as High King and, of course, that was my goal also. However, I could not trust to sending direct messages. There was far too much danger in that. So I tried to encourage him to take action by painting Elim as a threat."

"Someone tried to kill Tuathal," Calgacus growled.

"One of my men did shoot an arrow at him," Scota admitted. "But he missed on purpose. It was merely done to encourage Coel to speed up his preparations."

"What about the attempts to poison him?" Calgacus challenged.

"That was not my doing," Scota responded firmly. "Poison is a dangerous tool. It can strike at the wrong person or sometimes

246

not have the desired effect. Besides, I wanted Tuathal to cross the sea and overthrow Elim. I did not want him dead."

"Somebody wants him dead," Calgacus grunted.

"He is a Prince," Scota said. "Such men always have enemies. But I can assure you that I am not among them. Tell me, has anyone made an attempt on his life since you left Coel's home?"

Calgacus cast his mind back over the days since they had landed in Eriu before shaking his head.

"No. The attacks have been aimed at me."

Scota frowned, "I do not understand that. Tell me what happened."

Quickly, Calgacus told her about the raiders led by Greumaich who had attacked his party while they were travelling to Coel's home, then about the assassin on the beach and the two men who had tried to kill him on the night of the attack on Emain Macha.

"I can understand why you believed it was an agent of Elim who was behind those attempts on your life," Scota frowned. "But I can assure you it was not his doing. He would not have been able to keep such a secret from me because he always liked to boast of his cleverness."

"If not him, then who?" Calgacus asked. "Somebody paid Roman coins to those two thugs."

"Another reason to discount Elim," Scota insisted. "Roman coins are rare things in Eriu."

"But not among the Pritani," Calgacus reflected. "But neither Coel nor Broichan have any reason to want me dead. They need me to help Tuathal."

Scota regarded him with a look akin to sympathy as she said, "Or perhaps they merely wanted you to think they needed your help."

Calgacus felt a sharp pang of fear when he heard that. Coel and Broichan had both shown that they were as devious as Scota. Could they have sent him on this mission with the intention of having him killed?

"No," he decided. "They have nothing to gain from my death. And if they did want to get rid of me, all they needed to do was tell Tuathal to have me killed as soon as we landed in Eriu. He could send back a story about me falling in battle and nobody would be able to challenge his account."

"Perhaps you are right," Scota agreed. "Then that leaves only one conclusion."

"What is that?"

"That the Romans are behind the attacks on you. They know you remain their enemy and will oppose them. With you dead, the alliance you seek to build will crumble and their conquest will be that much easier."

Calgacus was not entirely convinced by this explanation but something else in Scota's words dismayed him far more than the thought that the Empire might be sending assassins after him.

"How do you know about my plans for an alliance?" he demanded.

"Why else would you marry your daughter to Coel's grandson?" she answered smoothly.

Calgacus felt a flash of irritation that she had guessed his intentions so easily.

He said, "Yet you wanted Tuathal to marry Braine, knowing that I desired an alliance with his family?"

"My concerns are with Eriu," she shrugged. "Tuathal will be accepted here because of his lineage. A foreign Queen might not be so welcome. Besides, as I told you earlier, marrying Braine strengthens his position enormously."

Calgacus felt himself growing angry. He had been used and manipulated by Coel, by Broichan and by Scota. Each of them, for their own reasons, had forced him into situations he would have preferred to avoid and he had played his part like a gaming piece on a board of King's Stone.

Yet this was no game and he felt a surge of resentment at the way he had been duped.

"You play with people's lives," he muttered darkly.

"As do you when you lead men into battle," she shot back instantly. "It is part of being a leader."

Calgacus could not argue with her on that point but his resentment did not lessen.

"I am done with your games," he told her. "As soon as Tuathal has been proclaimed High King, I intend to return home."

Scota's mood relaxed slightly and she said, "I am sorry I have angered you, Calgacus. That was not my intention. I admit I misled you in order to bring you here but I had no other way to achieve that without endangering my plans."

248

Calgacus stared into the red glow of the fire, still resentful but knowing that his anger stemmed from being outwitted as much as anything. He had prided himself that, when it came to battle strategy, he could trick his opponents and spring a surprise which would give him an advantage but this expedition to Eriu had shown him that there were other minds that were cunning in ways he would never be capable of matching.

As he stared into the dancing flames, he heard the patter of raindrops on the thatched roof, a gentle sound which slowly increased in volume as the shower became a downpour.

Scota also glanced up, then treated him to her crooked smile once again.

"You may as well stay here for the night," she said softly, her eyes sparking with invitation.

Calgacus shot her a sharp look, recognising the desire in her expression but noting, too, the stiffness of her posture which revealed an uncharacteristic anxiety.

He returned her smile with one of his own.

"I think I should go back to Tuathal's home," he replied.

"You will get very wet. And it is dark. Why not stay here? Am I so ugly?"

He shook his head.

"You are far from ugly," he told her. "But you and I are not what I would term friends."

"What has that to do with anything?" she challenged. Then her mood softened again and she sighed, "I am sorry. I told you I am not used to having guests. Nor am I accustomed to dealing with men in this sort of situation."

She fluttered an arm as she sought for the right words.

"I know this may sound foolish, Calgacus, but those songs about you gave me inspiration when I needed it. My resolve to defeat Elim was founded on your example. That was another reason I wanted you to come here. I wanted to meet the man behind the tales."

Calgacus could find no answer but, speaking with a frankness which astonished him, Scota continued, "I am thirty-five years old but I have never been with a man. At my age, most women have had a dozen children but I have never even known what it is to lie with a man."

She sighed as she admitted, "They are all too afraid of this mark on my face and of the dark powers they believe I possess. It

249

is part of the price I pay but it is a heavy burden. Can you understand that?"

"I think so," he said softly.

"You are the first man I have met who is not afraid of me," she told him. "Is it so wrong that I should want you?"

"It is not wrong," he replied. "But I have a wife."

"She is not here," Scota countered. "She need never know."

"I would know," he told her.

"Then tell her you were bewitched," she said. "I am a sorceress, after all. You could tell her I cast a spell on you."

Calgacus began to wonder whether Scota had indeed cast a spell on him. The warmth of the fire, the thrumming of the rain on the roof and the intensity of her desire was undoubtedly having an effect on him.

"You will be leaving the day after tomorrow," she reminded him. "What harm would it do to show me what it is to be loved by a man?"

She rose to her feet, unclasping her brooch and letting her cloak fall to the floor, revealing her bare arms and her slender figure beneath the green wool of her dress.

"Do not tell me you do not find me attractive," she whispered hoarsely. "I can see desire in your eyes."

"I do not deny that," Calgacus managed to say through the thickening of his throat. "But I have a wife and I do not wish to betray her trust in me."

The rain hammered more heavily on the roof and a crash of distant thunder rumbled from the sky.

"You should not go out in that," Scota persisted. "The gods are playing and it is dangerous for men to venture outside when that happens."

Taranis, God of thunder and storms, was a special deity to Calgacus and had often aided him in the past. Now he began to wonder whether the Storm God was giving him a sign.

"I will stay," he told her. "But I will sleep here, beside the fire."

Scota regarded him thoughtfully for a moment.

"Are you sure?" she asked as she reached for the horn fastenings at the shoulders of her dress.

"Yes," he stated, cursing himself as he gestured for her to stop.

She hesitated and he saw what his refusal had cost her. It had taken a great deal of resolve for her to declare her feelings and she was obviously used to men obeying her. By declining her invitation, he had clearly hurt her.

But Scota was strong. Despite his rejection, she quickly assumed the stern, aloof expression she normally showed in public.

"You are a remarkable man, Calgacus," she observed with more than a tinge of regret. "If that is truly your wish, I will make up a bed for you."

Then she smiled as she gestured towards her own mattress and blankets at the rear of the house.

"But I will be over there if you change your mind."

Chapter XXVII

It was still dark when Calgacus was woken by someone calling his name and shaking his shoulder. He wiped sleep from his eyes and blinked at the brightness of a flame that bobbed in front of his face.

As he surfaced from his deep slumber, he recognised that it was Scota standing over him, a tallow candle held in one hand.

"What is wrong?" he mumbled.

"Wake up!" she hissed urgently. "Somebody has tried to kill Tuathal."

He came alert, pushing himself up from the mattress and casting the blankets aside.

"Braine?" he asked, thinking that Fiacha Cassan's warning might have come true.

"She is unharmed as far as I know," Scota replied, misunderstanding his concern. "But Tuathal has been wounded."

"How bad is it?" Calgacus asked as he scrabbled to find his clothes and get dressed.

"Not serious as far as I can tell," she replied although the anxiety in her voice told him that she was worried.

"What time is it?" he asked as he fastened his tunic.

"A couple of hours before dawn, I think," Scota replied.

He saw that she was already dressed, her cloak fastened over her green dress.

"Where are my bloody boots?" he growled as he fumbled in the dim light.

"Here."

He hurriedly rammed his feet into the boots and tied the laces before throwing his cloak around his shoulders and fastening the brooch.

"Your friend is waiting outside," Scota informed him as he finished dressing.

Calgacus felt a stab of guilt when he heard that but Scota seemed unconcerned by what Runt might say. Wordlessly, she handed him his sword which he slung over his back before nodding that he was ready.

Scota moved to the door, blowing out the candle and carefully placing it on the table before pulling the door open and admitting a whisper of cool, night air.

By the fading light of the hearth fire and the blazing beacons of burning torches outside the door, Calgacus could see Runt standing impatiently with Scota's two guards.

The rain had stopped, the thunderstorm leaving the air cool and crisp, but the ground was sodden and churning to mud where the sentries stood watch. Huddled in their hooded cloaks, the men looked as if they had spent a miserable night even though the overhang of the house's roof provided a low shelter.

"Sleep well?" Runt asked as Calgacus and Scota emerged from the house.

"Never mind that," Calgacus growled. "What happened to Tuathal?"

"All I know is that somebody sneaked into the house and attacked him. He got a nasty cut on his side but the assassin ran off."

"Has he been caught?"

"Not as far as I know."

"How in Andraste's holy name did an assassin get past the guards?" Calgacus demanded as Runt led the way back to Tuathal's house, holding a burning torch to light their way.

"The two men at the rear door are dead," Runt explained. "Findmall reckons they were poisoned. He found an empty aleskin beside their bodies."

"So the killer walked in the back way?"

"That's right. But he made a noise and Tuathal woke up. The assassin had time for one swing with a knife but then Eudaf, who was sleeping near Tuathal's bedchamber, went for him and he ran off. The rest of us chased him but he had vanished by the time we got outside."

"Holy Dis!" breathed Calgacus.

News of the attack had obviously spread. Warriors were prowling the settlement, anxiously peering into shadows as they searched for Tuathal's assailant. They were knocking on doors and barging into homes, shouting their anger that someone had tried to kill their High King.

Tuathal's roundhouse was ringed by warriors and a crowd of worried people was gathering nearby but Fiacha Cassan, standing at the door like an angry bear, was making sure nobody came too close. He wordlessly stood aside when Scota and Calgacus arrived. Runt handed his torch to one of the warriors and followed them inside.

The great roundhouse was so large that additional pillars had been set in the floor to support the high vault of the roof. At the rear of the house, behind where the High King normally sat to receive his visitors, wooden walls had been built between two of these pillars and the outer wall to create a private space where the High King slept.

Eudaf was at the entrance to this chamber, pacing to and fro with an expression of grave concern on his young face but he stood to one side as Calgacus and his companions crossed the house and approached the bedchamber.

Inside this inner chamber, by the light of several candles, Findmall was attending to Tuathal who sat on a chair, naked to the waist, while the druid stitched a wound in his side.

Tuathal managed to smile through gritted teeth as he looked up at his new visitors.

"It is not too serious," he assured them.

"A flesh wound," Findmall confirmed. "But any wound can turn bad. I will apply a poultice and say the appropriate prayers."

"Why not ask the Gods to locate the killer while you are at it?" Calgacus muttered.

Findmall shot him a frown before returning his attention to his patient but Tuathal said, "I think the Gods have done enough in preserving my life. I was fortunate that the killer tripped over a stool as he entered my chamber. The sound woke me just in time."

"It is a sign that you are favoured by the Gods," Findmall clucked.

"Not everyone was so fortunate," Calgacus pointed out. "Liscus tells me the guards are dead."

Eudaf, his voice trembling with outrage and fear, confirmed, "We think they were poisoned. There was an empty skin beside them."

"Where did they get that from?" Scota asked sharply.

Eudaf shrugged, "I don't know. I went out a couple of times to check on them. The last time was just before the thunderstorm. They had it then but I don't know where they got it from. I couldn't blame them because everyone was celebrating, so I just told them not to get too drunk and to stay alert."

The young man looked embarrassed as he continued, "Then, what with the thunder keeping me awake and the long day we had, I fell asleep once the storm passed and didn't make any more rounds. I only woke up when I heard Tuathal shout for help."

"You were sleeping nearby?" Scota enquired, her question probing.

"Over there," Eudaf said, pointing to a spot on the floor opposite the entrance to Tuathal's sleeping chamber.

Calgacus looked from that location to the rear door of the roundhouse which was normally used by the slaves and servants when bringing food for the High King. It was a distance of little more than three paces.

"It was very dark," Eudaf explained. "All I saw was a dark shadow but I heard him move and I tried to grab him."

He grimaced as he confessed, "I was too slow and he got to the door. When I ran out after him, I tripped over one of the guards and fell flat on my face. By the time I got up, he had vanished."

Runt confirmed, "Fiacha Cassan and I came running as soon as we could but, as Eudaf says, it was very dark. We found him and the two dead guards on the ground outside."

"Fiacha Cassan has men searching the village now," Eudaf assured them.

"Somehow, I doubt whether they will find the man," sighed Calgacus.

He went to the rear door and pulled it open but the two dead guards had been removed and replaced by four grim-looking spearmen who regarded him curiously for a moment before turning back to watch the night for any signs of another attack.

Calgacus closed the door and turned to Scota.

"Do you have any suggestions?" he asked her.

She shook her head and he added, "You do realise this means you were wrong."

"Wrong?" she queried, cocking her head to one side.

"About the threat to Tuathal having ended."

"So it seems," she nodded, obviously concerned. "But we should announce that it was one of Elim's men who made the attack. It would not do for anyone to suspect we have a traitor in our midst."

"Yes," Tuathal nodded, silencing Findmall's mutter of protest. "That is a good idea."

255

"And you should go out and let everyone see that you are unharmed," the sorceress added.

"I will do that in a moment," Tuathal agreed. "I doubt that the assassin will try again. There are plenty of warriors around me now."

"Make sure it stays that way," Calgacus told him.

Fiacha Cassan came in to report that his search of the village had found no trace of any assassin, news which elicited dark mutterings from Findmall.

"I do not understand it," Fiacha Cassan grumbled. "He cannot simply have vanished."

"He may be hiding in plain sight," Scota commented. "There are scores of warriors from various tribes in the homestead."

"Aye," growled Findmall. "Who knows who we can trust?"

His gaze was directed towards Scota but the sorceress ignored the implicit accusation and stated, "Nevertheless, the ceremony must proceed. We must rely on our trusted men to ensure that the killer does not have an opportunity to strike again."

"Yes," agreed Tuathal. "I will not allow this to change our plans. The trouble is, I am not sure I could walk all the way from here to Tara as Findmall tells me is the custom."

"Ride in your chariot," Scota suggested. "With Braine alongside you. Create a new custom."

"That is a good idea," Tuathal smiled.

"I shall go and arrange it," Scota offered.

Tuathal nodded his approval and the sorceress turned and left, giving none of them so much as a second glance.

"There is still a great deal to be done," Findmall reminded them. "There are several thousand people to be fed at the feast."

"Then go and make sure all is in hand," Tuathal commanded.

Findmall hurried off, leaving Eudaf and Fiacha Cassan to stay close to Tuathal. He went to the main door, stepped outside and addressed the assembled villagers and warriors, assuring them that he was perfectly well and had suffered no more than a scratch. Then he came back inside and slumped wearily on his chair, his face pale and his breath coming in gasps.

256

"I think riding the chariot is an excellent idea," he said, forcing a smile.

Dawn had lightened the sky and with it the homestead came properly to life. Half a dozen servants soon arrived, bringing hot food and fresh clothing for Tuathal. The men ate hungrily then Calgacus grabbed a stool and went to sit outside where he could shave. Guards still surrounded the house but most of the spectators had left once they were satisfied Tuathal was alive and well.

Calgacus sat down, unfolded his old, iron razor and wetted his chin with some cold water. Runt joined him, setting down another stool and slurping at some hot tisane.

"So how was your night?" the little man enquired cheerfully.

Pretending to concentrate on scraping dark stubble from his cheeks and chin, Calgacus gave a non-committal grunt in response.

"That good?" Runt grinned. "I know she's all frost and ice on the outside but I thought she'd be all fire underneath."

"I wouldn't know," Calgacus replied as he shaved. "We just talked."

"All night?" Runt scoffed.

"It was late when we finished. She made up a bed for me because of the storm."

"Uh-huh," Runt smirked. "Is that what you are going to tell Beatha?"

"I am not going to tell her anything," Calgacus answered sharply. "Because nothing happened."

"If you say so," grinned Runt.

"I do say so."

"If that's what really happened," Runt mused, "you're a bigger fool than I thought you were. Underneath all that icy demeanour, she's not a bad looking woman. And women are in short supply around here just now."

"Drop it, Liscus," Calgacus warned.

"Righto," Runt smiled. "So you won't be spending the night with her again tonight?"

"No. And tomorrow we are going home."

"Sounds good to me," Runt nodded. "Coel should be happy with what we've done, although I'm not sure how he'll take the news that Fallar won't be marrying Tuathal."

257

Calgacus shrugged, "That doesn't matter. He owes me now. He can't refuse to join the alliance."

Runt did not argue but his expression suggested he had some reservations about Coel's commitment. He also had another concern.

"Tuathal may be guarded," he observed, "but you are still a target. You should be careful today."

"I've got you to watch my back," Calgacus told him.

"I know," Runt sighed. "But you make a large target. And there will be a big crowd. Just be careful, Cal."

Chapter XXVIII

Runt was right about the large crowd. In addition to the warriors from Ulster, from the Caledones and the Scotti, Sanb and his men from Connacht joined the spectacle. There were also men, women and children from the outlying districts who had overcome their fear of war and come to Tara because Tuathal had promised a feast. Such a treat was one that few people would spurn.

By mid-day, Findmall returned to announce that, despite the short time he had been allowed, the ceremony could now take place. Escorted by a score of warriors and followed by dozens more, Tuathal and Braine walked down to the gates where their chariot, decked in bright ribbons and with the ponies' harness jingling, waited for them.

Tuathal was dressed in patterned trousers topped by a yellow tunic, with a cloak of the deepest blue fastened by a golden brooch. His hair had been washed and combed and hung loose about his shoulders while a golden torc sat around his neck. Long boots of doeskin completed his outfit which had been liberated from the possessions of Elim's son, Niall.

"Elim's stuff was all too large for me," he had explained. "I shall give it away to my warriors."

Braine also wore yellow, her outfit being a long dress which flared about her young hips and had a tight bodice to show off her small breasts. A golden pendant bearing a bright garnet stone hung around her neck and she wore a garland of flowers in her long, brown hair. She smiled as she walked at Tuathal's side but Calgacus thought the smile seemed a little forced and there was a tenseness in her eyes. Still, she performed her part and dutifully waved to the crowd when she reached the gates of the hillfort.

A fanfare of horns greeted the couple, drums boomed and the spectators cheered at the sight of their new High King and his young bride.

Calgacus and Runt watched as the royal couple climbed aboard their chariot.

Calgacus noticed Scota standing to one side, her own chariot ready to carry her to the site of the ceremony. He made his way over to her, with Runt in close attendance.

Scota regarded him with her habitual stern expression, all signs of the woman he had encountered the previous night banished beneath a detached exterior. Even so, he detected an air of apprehension about the way she was watching Tuathal and Braine.

"Is something wrong?" he asked her.

She shot him a swift glance before returning her attention to the High King's chariot.

"Not really," she replied. "I am merely concerned that Braine plays her part well."

"She looks happy enough," Calgacus remarked.

"Oh, she understands the necessity of appearing to be happy," Scota nodded. "But you should not forget that Tuathal is responsible for the deaths of her father and brothers. She may have agreed to marry him but that does not mean she might not harbour some resentment."

"I'm sure you will offer her suitable advice and guidance," Calgacus said with rather more sarcasm than he had intended.

Scota did not react to his jibe, merely nodding and saying, "Naturally."

Then Findmall called out that the procession was to begin and Scota turned away to climb aboard her own chariot, leaving Calgacus perplexed at her aloofness which Runt had also noticed.

"Had a tiff with the girlfriend, have you?" he chuckled.

Calgacus grunted something unintelligible as he watched Scota depart.

Runt suggested, "Maybe you were a disappointment. She doesn't seem all that interested in you now."

"Shut up, Liscus."

"Right you are. Anyway, it's time to enjoy ourselves."

The parade was led by Findmall who walked on foot ahead of Tuathal's chariot. Fiacha Cassan and Eudaf, along with the warriors who had been tasked with protecting Tuathal, followed close behind.

Next in line came Scota, riding on her own chariot. She stood tall and proud, looking straight ahead, her presence a reminder to the spectators that she supported the High King.

There were thousands of people watching the procession. They formed a path that led to the entrance to the sacred hill of Tara, cheering and clapping as the High King and his new bride passed. Some threw flowers, others called blessings or offered prayers to the Gods for a long and peaceful reign, while Tuathal and Braine returned their good wishes with smiles and waves of their hands.

Even the weather seemed to look on the occasion with favour. The thunderstorm was little more than a memory and the sky was clear and blue, the sun bathing the parade in early summer warmth.

Everyone appeared to be enjoying the special occasion. Even Sanb of Connacht, riding in his chariot with a score of his warriors marching proudly in his wake, attracted cheers and applause which pleased him immensely.

Next came Calgacus and Runt, on foot, with an honour guard of the Scotti tramping along behind them.

Calgacus disliked such public displays and had not wanted to take part in the formal parade but Tuathal had insisted, so he trudged along, looking grim and sombre, while Runt smiled and waved at any pretty girls he saw in the crowd.

"Relax and enjoy yourself," he told Calgacus.

"I'll enjoy myself when this is over," Calgacus muttered.

He remained watchful and apprehensive, still concerned that there was an assassin lurking somewhere.

Yet the crowd was in good humour, the sun was shining and no danger reared its head on the occasion, although none of that improved Calgacus' mood.

"You are no fun," Runt chided as he stooped to pick up a flower thrown by a pretty young woman in the crowd. He raised it to his lips, then threw the woman a kiss which made her smile broadly.

"I wonder if she's married?" he mused.

"Almost certainly," Calgacus told him dourly.

"Ah well, never mind," sighed Runt.

The procession walked on. They passed into the long avenue, the route marked on either side by tall, wooden pillars. Once the last of the chieftains had made their way into this path, the spectators jostled after them. With the crowd now following in its wake, the cavalcade reached the Hill of Tara and, as Calgacus stepped through the towering gateway of the ceremonial entrance, he was able to take his first look at the holy site he had heard so much about.

Like Emain Macha, the ditch at Tara was inside the ramparts of the long, oval perimeter wall and, like Emain Macha, the hill was reserved for rituals, containing only a few small houses for the families who watched over and tended the sacred site.

Beyond these houses, more ditches and walls surrounded low mounds, ancient earthworks that had stood here from the beginnings of time, from the days of the long-forgotten ancestors.

As they walked on, with the milling crowd spreading out to fill the wide enclosure and children gleefully scampering to keep up with the leading chariots, Calgacus saw another timeworn mound on the north side of the hilltop. He recognised it as a tomb of the Old People. A stone-lined passageway ran into the heart of the mound where the bones of long-dead people could still be found. Findmall had approached this chamber but stopped at the entrance because, standing just outside the mouth of the ancient passage was a solitary, cylindrical stone.

It was an insignificant thing compared to many standing stones, less than the height of an averagely tall man. It bore no carvings or decoration yet it caught the eye because of its isolation and because it was unusually smooth and rounded.

"That must be the *Lia Fail*," Runt whispered.

"The what?"

"The Stone of Destiny, they call it."

With a chuckle Runt added, "It looks like it is pleased to see us."

Despite his surliness at being compelled to take part in the formalities, Calgacus smiled at Runt's remark. He had seen many standing stones but none that were quite so phallic in shape.

"Findmall said Tuathal is supposed to embrace it as a symbol of his union with the land," Runt explained. "But now that I've seen it, I am not quite sure about the symbolism."

Seeing Calgacus' smile, Runt confided, "Findmall also told me that the stone is supposed to roar if the true King touches it."

"That would be a good trick," nodded Calgacus.

Findmall stood in front of the stone. He turned, waiting patiently until the others had reached him. Tuathal and Braine climbed down from their chariot and stood before him. Then

Findmall took a flagon of ale from one of the men designated to assist him and poured a libation to the Gods.

Next, he gestured to a man who brought forward a magnificent black ram. The beast was nervous at the presence of so many people but the handler kept it still while Findmall produced a curved knife and deftly cut the animal's throat, allowing the blood to stain the grass at his feet while he called on the Gods to accept this sacrifice and bless the reign of a new High King.

The animal bucked and kicked but soon became still as its life blood drained away. When it was dead, the handler, with the assistance of two teenage boys, dragged the carcass away to the cooking fires which had been blazing for most of the morning. The animal would be skinned, butchered and cooked to add to the meat for the feast.

Findmall turned his attention to the next part of the ceremony. He held up his arms, calling on everyone to bear witness that Tuathal Techtmar had come to claim the High Kingship by right of birth and conquest.

As Tuathal approached the stone, Findmall called out in a loud voice, asking, "Have you come to claim the position of High King?"

"I have," Tuathal replied confidently.

As usual with such ceremonies, there was a great deal of formality. Calgacus barely paid attention while Findmall asked Tuathal whether he understood the various duties of a High King, his responsibilities to the land and the people.

Speaking in a clear voice, Tuathal gave a decisive, affirmative answer to each question.

Calgacus supposed that Elim had given the same responses to the same questions twenty years earlier. He felt rather old and cynical as the thought came to him that this was all a meaningless ritual, designed to impress people and to formalise the fact that Tuathal was already the effective overlord of Eriu. But he knew that people liked, even craved, ritual. Most members of the huge crowd certainly seemed to be enjoying the spectacle. Calgacus wanted nothing more than for the day to be over.

Bored, he glanced towards Scota who stood like a statue watching the proceedings, seemingly oblivious to everything else. She almost appeared to be alone in the crowd, with nobody wishing to stand close to her. Then Calgacus noticed that, for all

263

her apparent stillness, her eyes were darting around, studying the people who stood watching Tuathal make his promises. Briefly, her eyes met his and she regarded him coolly for a moment before turning her attention back to the new High King in whom she had invested so many of her hopes.

Calgacus was confused by her attitude. For all his feelings of guilt, he had thought she might be a little more friendly towards him but, in public at least, she had once again become a distant figure.

He scolded himself and decided to forget her. In the morning, he would be going home. All he had to do was see this day through.

At last, Findmall indicated that Tuathal should touch the monolith. Tuathal stepped forwards, stretched out his arms and embraced the stone. At once, a great cheer went up from the crowd, the warriors shouting to the accompaniment of blasts on war-horns and the thunder of drums. Unheard amidst the cacophony, Findmall called on all the gods to witness this acclamation of a new High King.

Tuathal held the stone for several heartbeats before releasing his grip and turning to acknowledge the crowd.

The cheering died away, leaving a sense of anticipation hanging over the scene. Findmall beamed happily.

"Once again, the Stone has brought forth a shout that will be heard all across Eriu!" he proclaimed.

Another wild roar of approval erupted. When the noise eventually subsided, Braine was called forward and took her place beside Tuathal who took her hand and raised it to his lips, a gesture which elicited yet more enthusiastic cheering.

To Calgacus' eyes, Braine appeared young, small and vulnerable, but she smiled for the crowd and did her best to appear happy.

The couple faced Findmall who draped cords over their wrists as a token of them being bound together. They made their vows, their words barely audible, but Findmall smiled broadly and announced to the watching crowd that the hand-fasting ceremony was complete and that the High King had a new wife, an announcement which was greeted by yet another roar of approval.

Findmall then declared that it was time for the formal submissions. One by one, the chieftains came forwards to bow their heads to the new High King.

Sanb of Connacht was first. It was normal for gifts to be exchanged but the ceremony had been arranged so quickly that few of the chieftains had anything to offer. Sanb, though, presented Tuathal with a fine dagger in a hand-crafted, decorated scabbard which Tuathal accepted graciously.

Scota offered her submission on behalf of the Scotti, then the other chieftains took their turn. At last, Findmall signalled to Calgacus that he should also present himself. Frowning and self-conscious under the eyes of the crowd, Calgacus walked to stand in front of Tuathal and his new bride.

Towering over them, he gave them a perfunctory nod that told them he acknowledged their position but that he would not submit to anyone.

"We both owe you our thanks," Tuathal said.

Calgacus hated such formal presentations. He never knew what to say, especially when there were thousands of people watching and listening.

"You owe me nothing," he managed.

"Tuathal smiled, "It was you who took Emain Macha. It was you who helped me to victory. It was you who suggested our marriage. I think we owe you a great deal."

It did not escape Calgacus' notice that Tuathal omitted to mention it was he who had killed Elim. Nor, from the brief frown he saw on Braine's young face, had she forgotten that deed. The memory made him feel uncomfortable but he knew he needed to say something to direct their attention to the future, not the past.

He said to both of them, "Then make it all worthwhile. Rule wisely. Whatever you do, your decisions should be for the benefit of your people, not for yourselves."

"Philosophy from a warrior," Tuathal smiled. "We will do our best to live up to those words."

Braine gave a thoughtful nod of tentative agreement. Calgacus held her gaze for a moment and gave what he hoped was a reassuring smile.

With the submissions completed, Findmall announced that it was time for the feast to begin. Cooking fires had been lit hours earlier and the carcasses of cows, pigs and sheep were already roasting. Beer and whiskey were distributed, fish and wildfowl were cooked, along with freshly baked bread, sweetened bannocks and baskets of newly-picked berries.

Several large awnings had been erected to provide some shade but there were so many people on the hill that most simply spread their cloaks on the grass and sat to eat and drink as much as they could.

By late afternoon, most of the people were well-fed and more than slightly drunk.

Calgacus restricted himself to a few mugs of beer, sitting with his back to the side of the ancient stone mound.

"It's a damned good feast," Runt declared as he devoured a chunk of beef. "This is much better than the horsemeat we had to eat on the march."

Calgacus nodded his agreement as he gnawed on a chicken bone. He almost felt relaxed now, sitting in the warm sun, eating and drinking while he let the celebrations go on around him. Music was playing, people were laughing, talking and even singing or dancing. Tuathal and Braine, with Eudaf, Findmall and Fiacha Cassan in close attendance, were walking among the crowd, chatting pleasantly to everyone they met and clearly making a good impression.

"Here comes your girlfriend," Runt warned in a low whisper, dragging Calgacus' attention away from the young couple's progress.

He looked up to see Scota walking towards them. He made to rise but she signalled for him to remain seated.

"May I join you?" she asked.

"Of course."

She sat down beside him, spreading the edges of her cloak as she did so but maintaining a polite distance between them. Her stiff manner and serious expression made it plain that she had not come to engage in small talk.

"I'll fetch you some food," Runt offered.

"No need," Scota replied. "I have eaten enough. Besides, I seek your advice as much as anyone's."

Runt returned a puzzled look but Scota went on, "I need to identify the assassin who tried to kill Tuathal."

"I don't think we can help you much with that," Calgacus informed her. "There are too many potential suspects."

"Yes," agreed Runt. "And they are all capable of murder. Most of them are hardened warriors who would kill their own grandmothers if you paid them well enough."

Scota nodded absently, her gaze still scanning the crowd around Tuathal.

She said, "I know. But that must not stop me seeking the killer."

After a short pause, she went on, "The poison worries me. I told you it is an imprecise weapon and not always effective. The fact that only the two guards at Tuathal's rear door were poisoned suggests it was given to them by somebody who knew precisely where Tuathal would be sleeping and who protected him."

"That wouldn't have been too difficult to work out," Calgacus pointed out.

"I suppose not. But it suggests to me that this assassin is a cunning man who prefers stealth and wishes to avoid being caught once he has killed Tuathal."

Calgacus nodded, "I can't argue with that. If someone really wanted Tuathal dead, they could attack him any time he is out in the open but the killer would certainly not escape."

"It is not the sort of behaviour one would expect from a simple warrior," Scota observed.

Runt put in, "Now that I think about it, the killer doesn't seem all that competent. I know he poisoned those guards but the few times he has tried to attack someone with his dagger, he has failed to kill anyone."

"More through luck than anything else," Calgacus countered, recalling how close he had come to death on the beach. That memory still gave him a cold shiver.

Scota pursed her lips as she nodded pensively, "It is not the mark of a warrior, though, is it?"

"What are you suggesting?" Calgacus asked her.

"I am not sure," she admitted with a soft sigh. "But I was watching the faces of those who stood nearest to Tuathal during the ceremony."

"You were reading their emotions?" Calgacus guessed.

"It is a skill I have," Scota confirmed.

"And what did you see?"

"I concentrated on those who came with you," she explained. "I cannot completely ignore the possibility that it was one of Elim's supporters who attacked Tuathal last night but I think that is unlikely. And, for the present, I am hoping that there is only one assassin."

267

"It's still like looking for a needle in a haystack," Runt reflected.

Perhaps not," Scota replied. "For example, I do not like Findmall but I trust his loyalty to Tuathal so I do not count him as a suspect. I can also discount any of Sanb's men. They arrived late and could not possibly have had anything to do with the attacks on Calgacus. The same goes for the Scotti. I can also discount Fiacha Cassan. He is easy to read and I see his devotion to Tuathal. Besides which, he saved your lives when you were attacked by assassins."

She frowned as she continued, "But I am less sure of his brother. It is difficult to read him because of his training."

"He has helped us at every step," Calgacus pointed out.

"Which does not preclude the possibility of him desiring Tuathal's death. Especially since, as Liscus said, the assassin does not seem all that competent at wielding weapons."

"Findmall knows how to use a knife," Calgacus argued. "You saw him slit the throat of that ram. Besides, he was sleeping in the house along with Liscus and Fiacha Cassan."

"He was right next to me," Runt confirmed.

Scota nodded, "I did not say he was an assassin, only that I could not completely discount him. Remember that the man we seek may not wield the weapons himself. You know he has hired others to attack you on one occasion already."

"What would Findmall have to gain from Tuathal's death?" Calgacus challenged. "He will be as influential as any man in Eriu if he stays close to Tuathal."

"That is a good point," Scota agreed. "I cannot see that he has a motive but I will watch him closely nonetheless."

"Who else do you have on your list of suspects?"

"Every other man who crossed the sea with Tuathal," she replied. "But I noticed that his other cousin, Eudaf, is nervous about something."

"Eudaf?" Calgacus frowned. "He's nervous because he is a young man who has found himself out of his depth in war."

"He harbours a secret," Scota insisted. "I think I should keep a close eye on him."

Runt put in, "He may have a secret but he can't be the assassin. He was wounded by the killer that night on the beach."

Scota sighed, "Then it seems I have a long and difficult search ahead of me. But I will find this killer soon."

"How can you be so confident of that?" Calgacus asked her.

"I am a witch and a sorceress," she replied, treating him to her crooked smile for the first time that day. "I will let it be known that I am looking for a traitor and I will speak to every man of the Caledones. Unless he is very skilled at concealing his thoughts, the killer will betray himself to me."

Runt gave a soft laugh as he said, "I believe you. Nobody can keep a secret from Emmelia when she starts questioning them. I expect you'll be even more successful."

Scota gave a nod, acknowledging his compliment but Calgacus had suddenly turned his attention elsewhere.

"By Camulos!" he hissed under his breath, his eyes widening in shocked amazement as he looked down the hill towards the gates of the enclosure.

People were turning their heads, moving aside as a group of riders trotted slowly up to the wide hilltop. There were around thirty of them, each one wearing a helmet and coat of mail, and carrying a long lance. They were led by two men who wore bronze breastplates, red cloaks and plumed helmets. One of these men held the branch of a yew tree as a sign that they came to parley but their unexpected arrival caused men to reach for their own swords and spears.

Runt clambered to his feet to watch.

"Oh, shit," he muttered. "Where did they come from?"

Calgacus could only shake his head. The yew branch announced the riders' peaceful intentions but he knew from bitter experience that these men had come to deliver an ultimatum of some sort and would have no qualms about resorting to war if their demands were not met.

Because, on this day of peace and celebration, the Romans had come to Tara.

Chapter XXIX

"I know him," Calgacus remarked, frowning as he sought to identify the lead rider. "The older one, carrying the branch. I've seen him somewhere before."

Runt stared at the approaching Romans through drink-clouded eyes.

"I'm not sure," he murmured uncertainly. "He looks vaguely familiar."

The riders came to a halt near the *Lia Fail* where Tuathal had gone to meet them. Fiacha Cassan and Eudaf were standing in close attendance, their hands hovering near their swords, while a dozen, half-drunk warriors hurried to form a protective bodyguard. Behind them, Findmall was ushering Braine away from any potential danger.

Calgacus, Runt and Scota strode purposefully to join Tuathal and confront the Romans. Scota took up a position beside Tuathal but Calgacus stepped forwards and placed himself in front of the High King. The soldier holding the yew branch glanced at him then stared in amazement.

"Calgacus? Is that you?"

Calgacus stood a few paces in front of the horses, his bunched hands planted on his hips. He looked up at the mounted man, surprised that the question had been put to him in Brythonic rather than Latin.

"Do I know you?" he queried.

The man pulled a face, pretending to be aggrieved.

"You mean you don't remember me?"

"I suppose I should," Calgacus responded. "You are still alive, which makes you special. I kill most Romans I meet."

The man laughed at the boast. He turned, casually tossing the yew branch to the soldier behind him, then he removed his helmet as he faced Calgacus once again.

"I am Julius Macrinus," he announced. "We met nearly ten years ago, when I rescued Cartimandua of the Brigantes."

Recognition dawned on Calgacus. He could place the man now. They had met briefly when Calgacus had aided the former

Queen of Brigantia to escape a revolt among her tribe. With nowhere else to go, she had fled to the Romans. It had been Macrinus who had commanded the soldiers sent to escort her.

Keeping his expression grim, Calgacus observed, "As I recall, *I* rescued her, and you as well."

"And as I remember it, you were going under a different name at the time," Macrinus countered. "But perhaps we can argue about who rescued whom over a drink? We have ridden a long way to meet the High King."

A look of mock horror crossed Macrinus' face as he asked, "By the Gods, they haven't made you High King, have they?"

Macrinus' irreverent good humour forced a reluctant smile to Calgacus' lips.

"No. I'm only here to help out."

Indicating Tuathal, he explained, "That is the new High King. Tuathal Techtmar, they call him."

Macrinus studied Tuathal curiously.

"Then the old High King, Elim mac Conrach, is dead?"

"Yes."

"In that case, we have arrived at the perfect time," Macrinus smiled affably.

He gestured to the young officer beside him as he informed them, "This is my commander, Publius Cornelius Tacitus, a Tribune and representative of the Governor. He has come to speak to the High King. May we dismount?"

Calgacus glanced back at Tuathal who took a few paces forwards, saying, "Welcome to Tara. I would be glad to speak to your commander but, as you can see, we are in the middle of a celebration."

He gave an apologetic smile as he added, "We may be too drunk to make any proper decisions."

Macrinus grinned, "Then we should have a Persian negotiation."

Tuathal gave him a puzzled look.

"What is that?"

Smiling broadly, Macrinus explained, "In Persia, whenever there was something important to discuss, the King and all his advisors would sit down and get drunk while they talked about what should be done. They would make a decision, then go to sleep. When they woke up in the morning, they would review their decision and, if it still made sense, they would abide by it."

271

Tuathal gave a wry smile as he shrugged, "Well, perhaps we can do the same, although I have never heard of Persia. Where is it?"

Macrinus waved an arm vaguely.

"Far away to the south and east. It is a hot place. Persia was once the mightiest empire in the world, until the Greeks defeated them and took over."

"I have heard of the Greeks," Tuathal commented. "But I did not think they ruled an empire."

"They don't any longer," Macrinus grinned wolfishly. "These days, they are subject to Rome. That's something for you to think about while we talk."

Calgacus interjected, "Perhaps you should think about it yourself. Empires fall. Rome will do the same."

"Perhaps one day," Macrinus agreed amiably. "But not today."

Turning his attention back to Tuathal, he asked, "May we join you?"

Tuathal nodded, "You are welcome."

Switching to Latin, Macrinus quickly spoke to Tacitus who had been waiting with growing impatience. The two men dismounted, then ordered their soldiers to take the horses to one side of the enclosure where Tuathal promised they would be brought food and drink.

Tuathal invited Tacitus and Macrinus to join him and his advisers under one of the large awnings that had been erected near the *Lia Fail*. Food and drink were brought for the guests although Tacitus grimaced when he tasted the beer.

"We don't have any Roman wine," Calgacus informed him in Latin.

Tacitus looked momentarily surprised at hearing his own language spoken, however barbaric the accent, but he quickly recovered, saying, "That can change. That is why I am here."

"I know why you are here," Calgacus rasped, making no attempt to disguise his animosity. "You are here because Rome always wants more land and more subjects."

Tacitus retained his poise in the face of Calgacus' hostility. He explained, "We came at the invitation of the King of Leinster, to help him overthrow the High King. It seems that you have done that for us."

272

Calgacus frowned. He briefly switched to his native tongue to confer with Scota before telling the Roman, "The King of Leinster is dead."

"Not so," Tacitus countered easily. "The old King was, I understand, executed by the former High King but his son escaped and came to seek our assistance."

"But, as you say, the old High King has been overthrown, so you may as well leave," Calgacus replied sharply.

Runt was hurriedly translating the exchange for the benefit of Tuathal and the others. To Calgacus' surprise, it was Braine who spoke when she heard his objections.

"Our guests have come a long way," she reminded him. "The rules of hospitality require that we hear what they have to say."

Tuathal nodded his agreement.

"Let us listen first, then we can make a decision."

Calgacus snorted, "Rome only offers one thing. They will say they can give you silver and gold, that they will bring wine and exotic foods, that they will build houses of stone for you. In exchange, all they will want is everything you have. They will take your grain to feed their army and take your young men to join that army. If they can, they will take your women from you. And if you complain, or try to stand up for yourselves, their army will turn on you."

He turned his head to spit on the ground before continuing, "Rome offers nothing we could ever want."

Tacitus was shocked by the obvious vehemence of Calgacus' speech but he had been taught rhetoric from a young age and he knew better than to respond with anything other than reason.

With Macrinus translating for him, he addressed his words to Tuathal and Braine, speaking calmly but firmly.

"Rome offers peace," he assured them. "An ally of Rome may call on the Emperor for aid against any enemy."

"Rome is only at peace when her enemies are all dead," interjected Calgacus. "You kill everyone, destroy everything and when there is nothing left, you survey the wilderness you have created and say that you have established peace."

Tacitus ignored him.

"Your friend is not helping," he told Tuathal. "He exaggerates everything to suit himself. Rome does not demand

273

anything except your friendship and loyalty. We ask that you allow our traders and merchants to travel freely through your land. They will bring goods the likes of which you have never seen. Rome offers soldiers to aid you against any enemy who threatens you, but we will not send an army unless you ask us to. Rome offers education for your children, proper housing and fresh water for everyone."

He ended by saying, "Friends of Rome prosper. We want you to be our friend."

Tuathal considered his reply carefully before saying, "What does Rome ask in return? Only our friendship? No tribute?"

"Perhaps some small tokens," Tacitus shrugged. "Nothing more than you can afford. Cattle or hunting dogs perhaps."

"How many?" Tuathal asked.

Tacitus' face showed no hint of concern as he answered, "We can discuss the details later. I do not know what your land holds, so I can hardly tell you what gifts we would like to receive from you in exchange for what we offer. But I can assure you that it will not be onerous. We seek friendship above all else."

"And if we refuse?" Tuathal enquired. "The people of Eriu are content as they are. What will you do if I tell you to leave our land?"

"Why would you do that?" Tacitus asked smoothly. "The Empire is just across the sea. We are neighbours. Neighbours should be friends."

"Not everyone wants to be a friend of Rome," Calgacus muttered darkly.

"Some people do not know what is good for them," Tacitus replied.

Tuathal persisted, "You have not answered my question. I would be happy to see Eochaid's son as King of Leinster but I see no need for him to have a Roman army at his back. If I tell you to sail away, will you simply go? Being neighbours is not the same as having your neighbour stay in your own home."

"The Governor of Britannia has no wish to base troops in your land," Tacitus told him. "Perhaps he will wish to establish a small garrison to protect a trading outpost but he told me to assure you that his soldiers are needed elsewhere."

Calgacus gave another wry snort and demanded, "Are you telling me you brought Eochaid's son here to overthrow Elim mac Conrach without bringing several cohorts to back him up?"

274

"That is not the point," Tacitus countered. "Whatever troops we have can easily sail back across the sea if the High King agrees to become our ally."

"And if I do not agree?" Tuathal asked pointedly.

"Why would you not? Everyone will benefit. To prove what I say, I will send you enough gold and silver to make you the wealthiest King this island has ever seen."

Tuathal's face was impassive as he said, "Then I think we understand one another. You and your men may sleep here in safety. I will give you my answer in the morning."

Tacitus nodded, deciding that there was nothing to be gained by pressing his case any further. Tuathal returned the gesture with a polite bow of his own.

The audience was over but as the two Romans rose to their feet, Macrinus whispered to Calgacus, "May I speak to you in private?"

Calgacus stood. He waited while Tacitus said his formal farewell and made his way to the side of the enclosure where his escort of troopers was waiting. Macrinus followed a few paces behind, walking slowly with his helmet tucked under his left arm. Calgacus joined him, waiting for the Centurion to speak.

"Can we trust this young High King?" Macrinus asked at last. "I know it is growing late in the day but I'd prefer to risk a ride in the dark than have my throat slit during the night."

"You will be safe," Calgacus assured him. "The rules of hospitality mean that you are under his protection until you leave. Even I am bound by those rules."

Macrinus smiled. Then, after a short pause, he said, "I never expected to see you here. I know you will never agree to join the Empire but this is not your home. Why are you here?"

"It's a long story," Calgacus shrugged. "I was asked to come as a favour to a friend."

Macrinus nodded. Personal service as a favour was a gift and he knew that gifts were important among the Britons.

"Your young High King seems a capable lad," he observed. "I hope he makes the right decision."

"So do I."

Macrinus gave a soft chuckle.

"I know what your advice will be but what about his other advisors? That woman with the scarred face did not say anything but I could see that she was paying close attention."

"She's a witch," Calgacus informed him.

"Truly?"

"On my life."

Macrinus shivered as he sighed, "Well, perhaps the High King will make up his own mind."

"You won't leave if he says no, will you?"

"That is not my decision," Macrinus replied with an evasive shrug. "If it had been up to me, we would have come here with our full force instead of just a small escort. I'd have preferred to settle things quickly without all this talking."

Calgacus recognised the threat and the capable professionalism beneath the Centurion's bluff good humour. For all his apparent friendliness, Macrinus was a tough, seasoned soldier. Calgacus knew that the Centurion was not joking about what he would have done if he had been in command. If the Romans had killed Tuathal and destroyed his army, they would have virtually conquered Eriu in a single afternoon.

"So, how many men have you brought across the sea?" Calgacus asked.

"Enough."

It was Calgacus' turn to laugh.

"I doubt that," he grinned.

Macrinus stopped, his face suddenly serious.

"Look," he said insistently, "I owe you my life, Calgacus. I haven't forgotten how you got me and my men out of that hole we were in when the Brigantes caught us. Let me make you an offer to repay that debt. Go home now. Leave these people to choose their own path before Tacitus decides that part of the deal is for you to be handed over as an enemy of Rome. I don't know whether he has recognised your name or not, but if he has, he will want you dead. Did you know there is a reward being offered for your head?"

"Nobody has collected it yet," Calgacus shot back.

"Somebody will try before long," Macrinus asserted. "The Governor wants your head and King Cogidubnus of the Regni has promised to reward anyone who can bring your wife back to him."

"Then he's a fool," Calgacus rasped, doing his best to conceal his concern at this unexpected news. "Beatha hasn't seen Cogidubnus in years. Why would he want her back?"

Macrinus shrugged, "He's a powerful King. She is his sister and you stole her away. Kings are proud people and I

276

suppose it was a slap in the face for his attempts to become a proper Roman. His sister should have been a dutiful, obedient wife to whoever he picked out for her. Instead, she ran off with a notorious barbarian."

"That was more than twenty years ago, Calgacus snorted.

"Kings have long memories," Macrinus remarked.

Calgacus replied, "He's going to be disappointed. And so is your young Tribune if he thinks he can collect the price on my head."

"Be sensible," Macrinus urged. "Go home while you still can."

Calgacus was tempted to say that he could not go home because his home, the place he had known as Camulodunon, the settlement where he had grown up, had been a Roman town for almost forty years. He had been forced to leave as a boy, travelling to the far west with his brother, Caratacus. Since then, he had returned only once, to witness the Roman colony being razed by Bonduca's raging army during the Great Revolt. He wanted to say that his home had been destroyed many years before but the retort died on his tongue because he rather liked Macrinus. The Centurion did not deserve such an accusation.

Instead of flinging harsh words, Calgacus said, "I'll think about it. If Tuathal decides not to fight, I will need to go home anyway."

"And if he decides to oppose us?" Macrinus asked.

"You mean you are not just going to sail away?" Calgacus retorted.

"Don't put words in my mouth," Macrinus scowled. "You know what I mean."

He jerked his head, using his chin to point at Tacitus as he explained, "He's a good man but these young Roman aristocrats can be stubborn, especially when they are dealing with barbarians."

Calgacus asked, "And if he decides to be stubborn? Will you do his fighting for him?"

The Centurion shrugged, "I am a soldier. I will do as I am commanded."

"It would not be a good idea for you to become involved here," Calgacus warned. "This would be one fight you could not win."

"Then let's hope it does not come to that," Macrinus replied. "But you should know better than to try to bluff me, Calgacus. I know how to win. I've been a soldier most of my life. I'm good at it."

"I remember," Calgacus acknowledged. "Just don't go and get yourself into another hole like you did before because this time I won't pull you out. I'm more likely to shovel the earth back on top of you."

Macrinus' face was stern as he replied, "Don't be foolish, Calgacus. Even if you did somehow manage to beat us, you know you must lose in the end. Rome is far too powerful for you. The best you can ever do is postpone the inevitable. And I warn you, the Governor wants your head."

"You think you can collect the reward?" Calgacus growled.

"I'd rather not," Macrinus said in a more conciliatory tone. "Like I told you, I still owe you a life. Go home, Calgacus. If you stay and this thing turns nasty, I won't be able to save you."

Chapter XXX

As dusk fell, the people slowly filed out of the enclosure, leaving the hill of Tara to the Romans. There was some grumbling about this until Tuathal pointed out that it would be easier to keep an eye on the visitors by posting guards at the gateway.

"There is only one way for them to leave," he said as he instructed his warriors to maintain a watch throughout the night.

He then summoned his advisors to meet with him in his roundhouse where they could discuss the situation in privacy.

"It is supposed to be your wedding night," Eudaf reminded him.

"I have not forgotten," Tuathal smiled as he clasped Braine's hand. "There is still time for that but we must discuss the question of the Romans first."

So Braine, her face tense and fearful, was escorted back to her small roundhouse while Tuathal and his advisors gathered in his own hall.

"You should include her in the discussion," Scota chided. "She is your Queen and has as much right as anyone to be involved."

"I think she has enough things to worry about at the moment," Tuathal shrugged, attempting to justify his decision as an act of kindness, but he saw Scota's frown and hastily added, "I will discuss it with her in private later."

"How romantic," Runt murmured under his breath.

Scota clearly disapproved of Tuathal's decision but did not press Braine's case. As Tuathal had pointed out, it was more important to decide how he should respond to Tacitus' proposal.

Pressing a hand gingerly to his wounded side as he took his seat, the High King said, "I would like to hear what each of you has to say. Please speak openly. This is no time to keep silent about your true feelings."

He looked first to Sanb who sat on his right in the position of honour.

"I will abide by whatever decision you make," the King of Connacht stated. "But if you are asking for my advice, I would say

279

that the men of Eriu would prefer to be their own masters. We of Connacht are not afraid to fight and I have more men on the way."

When Sanb fell silent, obviously having said all that he felt necessary, it was Calgacus' turn to speak.

"The Romans are my enemies," he declared. "They are the enemies of all who want to remain free. Whatever they say, they desire only to rule you. You should order them to leave."

Runt quickly added his agreement.

"Rome does not have friends," he averred. "Rome only has subjects."

Findmall, sitting to Runt's right, clasped his hands together as he gathered his thoughts. Giving Calgacus an apologetic look, he said, "With all due respect to Calgacus and Liscus, they will not have to live with the consequences of what we decide. Whatever happens, they will soon return to their own home while we will remain here. Rome's power is well known. Can we be sure that we can defeat them in war? For all his valour, Calgacus has failed to stem their advance through the lands of the Pritani. But if we agree to become an ally of Rome, we will avoid conflict while remaining outside the empire. We might benefit from what Rome can offer without becoming their subjects."

Scota shot Calgacus a look to silence his protest at Findmall's opinion before she quickly added her own advice.

"I know what it is to be ruled by someone with a greater power," she recounted. "It is difficult to bear, but we must remember the consequences of opposing Rome. What I know is that the man who calls himself Tacitus has no intention of leaving. I could read it in his face. If we refuse his offer, he intends to use force to crush us."

"If he has enough men," Sanb interjected. "We don't know how many he has brought."

"He will not have come without a sizeable force," Calgacus observed.

"Maybe so, but the Romans have never fought the men of Connacht," Sanb boasted. "We should not fear them."

"Neither should we underestimate them," Calgacus warned.

Predictably, Fiacha Cassan was for war. He said, "I am happy to fight. I agree with Sanb. We should not be afraid of their threats."

Eudaf, looking more serious than usual, added, "I agree. We should not give in to threats."

Tuathal sat silently for a moment before nodding slowly.

"Thank you. There is a great deal to think about. Although the majority of you are for rejecting the Romans, I understand the concerns Findmall and Scota have raised and they are not inconsiderable. It strikes me that we face problems whatever we do. What I need to know is that each of you will support me whatever I decide."

He looked around the circle at their faces. All nodded except Calgacus who said, "If you decide to surrender to them, I will return home tomorrow."

"And if I decide to reject them and they turn against us? Will you stay to help us? You and Liscus are the only ones who have any experience of fighting Romans."

There is always a choice, Calgacus told himself. Yet there was only one decision he could make because he knew he could not tell these people to fight and then abandon them.

"If it turns to war, I will stay," he promised.

"Thank you," said Tuathal. "I will make my decision in the morning. Now, as you know, it is my wedding night, so I have other, more pleasant duties to attend to."

He winced as he stood, clasping a hand to his injured side.

"I hope I am up to the task," he grinned through the pain.

"I am sure she will be gentle with you," Eudaf chuckled. "Would you like me to bring her here now?"

Tuathal nodded his thanks and Eudaf headed for the rear door while Findmall announced that he had appropriated another house for the rest of them in order to provide the married couple with some privacy. They said their farewells to Tuathal and made their way outside where Calgacus took Scota and Runt aside.

Quickly, he explained what Macrinus had told him about the Governor putting a price on his head.

"It means you were right," he told Scota. "The assassin who is after me has been sent by the Romans."

Scota immediately understood the implications of his words.

She said, "But the Romans have no interest in Tuathal. That means there must be two assassins."

"Just what we need," sighed Runt.

"It certainly makes my task more difficult," Scota agreed pensively.

"That depends on what Tuathal decides to do," Calgacus told her. "If he agrees to ally with Rome, we will be leaving in the morning."

"And now you are going to ask me what he intends to do?" Scota guessed.

"Well?"

She shrugged, "He is torn. I can understand that. Elim mac Conrach was a powerful King but even he feared Rome. Opposing the Empire is no small matter."

"Neither is giving in to them," Calgacus argued.

"It is for the High King to decide," Scota asserted. "We will know in the morning."

Calgacus sighed. He could understand Tuathal's indecision. He was torn between two conflicting desires himself. He had always opposed Rome and would do so again whenever he could but a part of him almost wished that Tuathal would give in to Tacitus' demands so that he and Runt could return home and take up the fight on their own ground.

"I think it will depend on what Braine tells him," said Runt. "Any man will do pretty much whatever his wife tells him to on their wedding night."

Braine sat in her roundhouse with only two serving maids for company and she had no desire to talk to either of them. This small dwelling had been her home for as long as she could remember but now it seemed alien and unwelcoming.

That, she realised, was because it was almost empty. She had shared the house with several older women, the slaves who had been her father's concubines. Those women were all gone now. Tuathal may have decreed that there should be no rape when his war host took control but slave women, even if Tuathal had freed them, were part of the plunder and had been carried off by the triumphant warriors, leaving the house empty and forlorn.

She sat, feeling abandoned and miserable, waiting to be summoned to Tuathal's bed and dreading the prospect of what that might entail. He seemed a decent enough man but he had been raised as a Prince and she knew how such men could behave. Being accustomed to getting their own way, they could become

282

aggressive if their desires were thwarted. Certainly her own brothers had been like that.

And Tuathal, for all his public displays of affection, had sent her away while he held a Council meeting with his advisors. Braine had little experience of such matters but she instinctively felt that, as Queen, she should have been involved in the discussion. Was she to be nothing more than a decorative part of Tuathal's entourage, she wondered? Would he exclude her from all important matters and treat her as little better than a concubine? She knew from listening to the gossip of the slave women who had once lived alongside her that they had held little influence over her father except when it came to asking for trinkets or personal favours. The thought that Tuathal might treat her the same way left her feeling more alone and desolate than ever.

She looked up in startled surprise when the door opened and Eudaf stepped into the house. He gave her a warm smile before signalling to the servant girls to leave.

"I wish to speak to the Queen," he told them.

The girls scurried out and Eudaf pulled over a stool so that he could sit facing Braine.

"Is it time?" she asked.

"In a moment. I just wanted to say that I thought you should have been included in the discussion. You are High Queen now and should have a say."

"What has he decided?" she asked.

"He has not reached a decision yet," Eudaf informed her. "He says he will make up his mind in the morning."

"What do you think he will do?"

"I fear he is minded to agree to the Romans' demands. But what I wanted to say to you is that you should not fear either choice of action."

Braine furrowed her brow as she looked at him in puzzlement.

"What do you mean?"

He leaned close, reaching out to take her small hands in his as he said softly, "Just this. You stand to gain whatever happens. If Tuathal agrees to become a Roman ally, you will live in peace as his Queen. You will have great power."

"Do you think so?"

"I am sure of it. I will ensure that he treats you as befits your rank."

283

Braine gave a cautious nod.

"That is all I ask," she said softly.

Eudaf leaned even closer and dropped his voice to little more than a whisper as he told her, "But if he decides to oppose them and there is a war, you could gain even more."

"I don't understand," she responded warily.

"It is like this," he told her. "If he fights and wins, you will be Queen to a mighty King. That is no small thing."

He paused, glancing around as if to check that nobody was lurking in the shadows of the house before resuming, "but if he were to lose, things could be even better for you."

"How could they be better?" she asked in increasing astonishment.

"Think about it," he urged. "If Tuathal were to die in battle, the Romans would wish to install someone else as High King to rule as their ally."

"They have Eochaid's son, Domnan," she pointed out.

"The son of a minor King?" Eudaf scoffed. "A better choice would be the High Queen."

"Me?"

She was amazed at the audacity of his idea.

"You would need to surrender to them, of course," he explained. "But you would be the legitimate ruler. You are daughter to one High King and wife of another. The warriors of Eriu would follow your lead, especially if they have suffered a defeat. And if you happen to be with child, your claim becomes even stronger. Nobody could dispute your right."

Braine instinctively glanced down at her belly, wondering what it would be like to bear a child. The thought left her flustered but Eudaf's words had caused her even greater confusion. Could she really become ruler of Eriu, even if she must bend the knee to the Romans?

Eudaf, sensing her uncertainty, squeezed her hands and gave her a reassuring smile.

"I did not mean to upset you," he assured her. "I only wanted to tell you that you will be safe whatever happens. You cannot lose."

Braine tried to relax and managed to nod her head.

"Thank you," she whispered.

"And now," Eudaf told her as he stood up and eased her to her feet, "it is time for you to go to Tuathal."

She offered no resistance as he led her to the High King's bedchamber but her mind was racing with possibilities. Eudaf may have intended to calm her fears but he had, instead, sparked a dream.

Chapter XXXI

The morning dawned bright and fine, with a brisk breeze chasing the clouds but the sun promising another warm day. On the broad summit of the hill, Cornelius Tacitus waited for word of the High King's decision.

He had spent a restless night, wondering whether he had blundered by coming on this diplomatic visit rather than waiting until his full force had arrived and then striking hard and fast as Macrinus had suggested. Having seen the unpreparedness of the barbarians, he could not ignore a gnawing concern that the big Centurion had been correct.

It was too late now but the knowledge that he might have made a mistake bothered Tacitus, especially since he was fairly certain what answer the High King would give him. In Tacitus' opinion, the unexpected presence of Calgacus made that almost inevitable.

He would never have given the barbarians the satisfaction of seeing his dismay but the presence of Calgacus had shocked him to the core.

He knew all about Calgacus, of course. When he had first arrived in Britannia as aide to his father-in-law, Agricola, their first task had been to quell a rebellion among a western tribe known as the Ordovices. The barbarian uprising had been led by a young hothead named Brennus who had drawn men to him through his strength and cunning but who had also claimed to be the son of the infamous Calgacus. For the tribes of the West, Calgacus' name still held power even though the fabled warrior had not been seen or heard of for many years.

Naturally, the Legions had crushed the Ordovices and Agricola had ordered that the survivors of the battle should be either killed or enslaved to make an example of them. But Brennus had escaped, aided by the unexpected and unlikely arrival of Calgacus who had, it transpired, travelled from the obscurity of his northern fastness to help the man who claimed to be his son. The two of them, accompanied by a small band of refugees, had fled

286

into the wilderness of Brigantia where they had been pursued by a cold-eyed Centurion named Casca.

Later, Tacitus had spoken to the survivors of Casca's mission and learned that the Centurion had allied himself with a Brigante leader named Venutius who had long held a grudge against Calgacus and who had been only too willing to help hunt down his nemesis.

The combined force of Romans and Brigantes had pursued the refugees and trapped them on a lonely hilltop escarpment. That should have been the end of both Brennus and Calgacus but Tacitus could still see the awe in the eyes of the three survivors of Casca's troop when they had recounted the story of that day.

"The big bastard charged straight at us," the Decurion had explained. "I mean, they were outnumbered five or six to one and he charged at us. I've never seen anything like it. He killed the Centurion and several others and the Brigantes ran away."

Tacitus could only imagine how dreadful the fight must have been. Several Romans had died along with a dozen Brigantes, and Venutius, in panic, had led the flight of his remaining men.

So Calgacus had escaped although his son, Brennus, had died in the fighting. That had been a small consolation for the Romans but the day had been an inglorious end to what should have been a simple mission, with only three of Casca's men living to tell the tale. One of them had been wounded but the three had somehow contrived to cross dozens of miles of hostile territory in the middle of winter and had eventually reached the safety of the Roman Legions. And yet, for all they had suffered, the main thing they spoke about was their encounter with Calgacus.

Tacitus had dismissed much of what they had told him as exaggeration but he was now having second thoughts. He had seen for himself that Calgacus' physical size was intimidating but far more worrying was his absolute antipathy towards Rome. If Calgacus held any sway over the young High King, Tacitus knew they would need to resort to force to bring Hibernia under Roman control. That prospect worried him more than he would ever admit but so, too, did the lengthy conversations Macrinus had held with Calgacus.

Tacitus had quizzed the Centurion about those discussions but what Macrinus told him had provided no reassurance at all.

"I've met him before," the Centurion explained. "It was when I was sent to rescue Cartimandua of the Brigantes when her tribe rebelled and threw her out. I found her all right. Or, rather, she found me. But so, too, did an army of the rebels who wanted her dead. We were entrenched in camp but faced thirty thousand of them and we had no way of marching back without risking being wiped out."

Macrinus had grinned as he recounted, "But Calgacus was with Cartimandua. I didn't know it was him at the time, of course. But he and that little man with him walked into the barbarian camp where he challenged the enemy champion to single combat. He won and the rebels went back home. Don't ask me how he managed it but I've never seen anything like it before or since. Two men advancing on an army of thirty thousand and expecting to win."

"It sounds unbelievable," Tacitus opined.

"I saw it," Macrinus shrugged.

This revelation, combined with his recollections of what he had been told about Casca's failed attempt to trap Calgacus, left Tacitus more than a little worried but he managed to compose himself so that nobody could guess at his fears.

Displaying a calm he did not feel, he asked Macrinus, "So what were the two of you talking about?"

"I was trying to persuade him to go home and forget this place."

"Will he do that?"

"I doubt it."

Tacitus nodded gravely, "Then let us hope the new High King does not listen to him."

Now the Tribune stood beside the Centurion as they waited in the coolness of the morning. Apart from the low murmur of chatter from their troopers and the snorting and stamping of horses, the only sounds were the singing of birds and the distant lowing of cattle. The hill of Tara, so crowded the day before, was like an empty tomb.

Or a prison," Tacitus reflected grimly, knowing that he and his small troop could not hope to escape if the barbarians turned on them.

He was still fretting when Macrinus let out a soft whistle of surprise and nodded towards the entrance to the processional way where a group of figures had appeared.

"It looks as if he's coming here in person," the Centurion observed.

288

Tacitus raised his eyebrows, wondering what this portended. He had expected to be summoned to the High King's home to be told the young man's decision but he could see Tuathal, accompanied by his usual gathering of advisors and a dozen armed warriors, slowly making his way up the hill.

"Should we go to meet him?" Macrinus enquired.

"No. We are Romans. Let him come to us."

Tacitus began to feel more confident. If Tuathal was prepared to come to him like a supplicant, it suggested he might have decided to acknowledge the power of Rome and accede to Tacitus' request to become a client King under Roman protection.

As the High King and his entourage drew nearer, Tacitus tried to read Tuathal's expression but the High King was giving nothing away. Even his followers seemed uncertain of what decision he had made because Tacitus could see a wary caution in the way they approached. Calgacus, in particular, looked stern and concerned, a fact which made Tacitus wonder whether he could allow himself to hope that he had succeeded; that Macrinus' gloomy warnings had been wrong and his own fears unfounded. Perhaps, he mused, he had conquered Hibernia already.

"Good morning," he said as Tuathal reached him. He did not offer his hand. "I hope you have decided to accept my offer."

Tuathal's face was pale with the exertion of his long walk but he fixed Tacitus with a firm gaze and the Tribune realised before the High King spoke that he had been wrong to hope.

Every word crushed him as Tuathal said, "No. I became High King only yesterday. I will not surrender that position to anyone. I will be delighted to trade with you but that is as far as I will go. I do not seek an alliance, nor do I have any wish to see Roman troops on my island. You and your men should leave Eriu. I will allow you three days. If you are still here after that time, I will regard you as my enemies."

Calgacus could not conceal his satisfaction as he watched the Romans depart. Macrinus had exchanged a look with him as he rode past but the big Centurion had not spoken, merely shaking his head as if to imply he would regret killing them all but would do it nonetheless.

"They will not leave," Scota sighed. "We now face a war we probably cannot win."

"You thought that when you pledged your tribe to Elim," Calgacus reminded her. "Yet you won in the end."

"But how long will this war last?" Scota scowled. "Eriu has been relatively peaceful for twenty years. Now many people will die because of this decision."

"Some things are worth fighting for," Calgacus told her.

"I would expect a warrior to say that," she frowned.

"Perhaps. But you promised to help Tuathal whatever he decided."

"I know. And I will. But I had thought my struggles were at an end."

"Life is a struggle," Calgacus shrugged. "Whether it be warriors fighting to protect their people or farmers battling nature to grow their crops, we all spend our lives in some sort of struggle."

Scota nodded, "I understand that. Just as I understand what we face now. I will help Tuathal in any way I can but I hope we do not live to regret his decision."

"I must admit I thought he was going to make terms with them," Calgacus said. "I wonder what made up his mind."

"It was Braine," Scota informed him.

"I told you," Runt chuckled softly.

Calgacus looked in surprise to where Braine stood beside Tuathal as they kept their eyes on the departing Roman horsemen. The young couple were holding hands but whether that signified any genuine affection, he could not tell.

"What did she say to him?" he asked Scota.

"She told him she had agreed to marry the High King of Eriu, not a weakling who would give away what others had worked so hard to help him achieve."

"Ouch!" muttered Runt. "That must have hit him where it hurts."

"So it seems," Scota agreed.

"The girl has courage," Calgacus remarked.

"Indeed she does," Scota nodded. "I suspect we will all need plenty of that soon."

Calgacus did not mind Scota's grumbling. He recalled how he had witnessed her tears when old Aedan had lain dying and he guessed that her stern mood resulted from her attempt to quell her fear of what lay ahead.

He could understand her concern but, for the first time since Coel had extorted his cooperation, things suddenly became very clear for him. He was no longer facing an enemy he had never met, no longer concerned with civil war among the people of Eriu. Now he faced his old enemy, the Empire of Rome.

He was almost happy as he watched the last of the departing riders disappear behind a stretch of woodland. Because the war that faced him now was one he understood. He had plans to make, battles to fight and Romans to kill.

Chapter XXXII

Tacitus and Macrinus returned to the peninsular fortress of Droim Meanach to discover that the galleys had made the second sea crossing from Deva and that the bulk of the legionary troops had already disembarked. Their arrival caused a logistical headache as the Centurions tried to find enough space for the men to pitch their tents. Most of the inhabitants of the village had been evacuated to the island that lay offshore but squeezing two thousand armed men and their equipment into the confined space between the houses was still a difficult task.

Tacitus spent an awkward evening overseeing the dispositions, eventually ordering the men to ignore the usual structured layout of a marching camp and to pitch their tents closer together than regulations stipulated. The small vegetable plots and patches of grazing land that surrounded each roundhouse were soon trampled into camping spots for the soldiers but tempers frayed and Tacitus was obliged to intervene in some squabbling between the new arrivals and Macrinus' Auxiliaries who had, quite naturally, taken the best spots for themselves.

"It's a bloody shambles," Macrinus observed dourly.

"At least we have our whole force here," Tacitus replied. "Find the two Legionary Commanders and bring them to my hut. I want to march tomorrow, so we must make our plans tonight."

When Tacitus entered the chieftain's house that had been set aside for him, he could not disguise his distaste. He had become accustomed to living in army tents during the campaigning season but he had never felt comfortable in one of these round, wooden homes. A peat fire crackled in the hearth, the smoke gathering in the circular cone of the thatched roof, giving the place a claustrophobic air. The smells of smoke, wood and the rushes scattered on the earthen floor were completely alien to Tacitus' life and he dreaded the thought of remaining here any longer than absolutely necessary. He suspected the place was infested by vermin and lice, a thought that made his skin crawl.

Nevertheless, he was a Roman soldier and he vowed to make the best of a bad situation. In fairness, his slaves had done their best to make the place comfortable, setting up a table laid with Roman crockery and pitchers of wine. The familiar folding stools used by army officers were set around the table and his sleeping mat and blankets now occupied the place where straw-filled mattresses had provided beds for the original inhabitants. His luggage chests had been placed around the walls and his writing tools had been neatly laid out on a small desk which had been placed to one side of the wide interior.

"Not exactly a palace, is it?" he remarked to Macrinus as his slaves helped him remove his armour.

"At least it is warm and dry," Macrinus shrugged. "I've stayed in worse places."

Young Domnan, looking more like a lost boy than ever, greeted them anxiously, asking Macrinus what had happened at Tara. When he heard the Centurion's explanation, his young face fell but he was prevented from asking any further questions by one of Tacitus' slaves who announced the arrival of the two Legionary Centurions and then stood aside to allow the men to enter through the low doorway.

Each of the soldiers wore a red cloak, a helmet with the stiff, cross-wise plume of a Centurion and had medals of honour hung on their armoured chests. They stood erect, thumping their fists to their chests in salute to Tacitus.

"Hail, Tribune!" they said in unison.

"Welcome, Gentlemen," Tacitus replied affably. "I am pleased to see that you got here safely. Please sit down. We can eat while we discuss what needs to be done."

Macrinus nodded a cautious greeting to the two Centurions as they took their seats at the table. He had met them briefly at Deva but he was always wary around legionary officers who tended to look down on Auxiliary troops.

The taller man responded to his greeting with a curt, barely polite nod. His name was Caecilius Macer, commander of the junior Cohort of the Ninth *Hispana*. Macrinus had taken a dislike to the man at their first meeting in Deva and the feeling appeared to be mutual. Macer was a competent soldier but harsh to the men under his command and, like many Roman officers, seemed unimaginative. Macrinus had little time for such men, especially because, as legionary Centurions, they outranked him.

The second man was shorter, stockily built and had a less than handsome face that was deeply tanned and weathered by

293

years of service. It was also scarred by ugly pock-marks. His skin was dark and his short hair had been bleached by the sun, legacies of many years spent in the heat of Africa and Asia. This was Gracchus Rufus, the Cohort commander of the Second *Adiutrix*. From what little Macrinus knew of him, Rufus appeared to be a no-nonsense man who could think for himself.

"Well, Macrinus?" Rufus asked in a gruff, throaty rasp of a voice. "Have your bandits left anything for our lads or have they eaten all the food and claimed all the women for themselves?"

"The women have all gone," Macrinus replied with a smile. "There are some sheep if your boys are desperate."

Rufus laughed but Macer frowned.

"There will be trouble with so many units jammed together like this," he complained in a nasal whine.

His voice grated on Macrinus' ears, as if Macer was trying to imitate the speech of upper class Romans but had not quite mastered the accent. His warped vowels annoyed Macrinus almost as much as the man's supercilious attitude.

Tacitus assured them, "There is no need to worry. We are leaving in the morning. I have ordered a red tunic to be displayed with the standards."

Rufus and Macer nodded approvingly. The standards of each Cohort had been planted in the earth outside the commander's hut. They were guarded by the *signifers* who would carry them when the Cohorts marched. The standards were the army's talismans, symbols which represented the history and the fortune of each Century and each Cohort. If a *signifer* should happen to drop his standard, the men would view it as a bad omen and might refuse to leave the camp, so great care was taken when handling the slim, painted poles with their decorated flags.

This evening, an additional standard was on display. It was a red tunic, a message to every soldier that they would be marching to war the following day.

"How many men do we have fit for duty?" Tacitus enquired.

Rufus responded promptly and confidently.

"Four hundred and twenty three, excluding Centurions."

Macer was less certain of his facts.

"At the last count we had three hundred and ninety seven, excluding Centurions. I suspect one or two may claim to have fallen sick after the voyage."

Tacitus clucked his tongue. A Cohort consisted of six Centuries, with each Century having a nominal strength of eighty legionaries. That was the ideal, of course, a figure that was rarely maintained in practice. A Cohort should have numbered four hundred and eighty men but illness, disease and casualties of war invariably meant that Centuries operated at well below their nominal strength.

Tacitus glanced at Macrinus.

"And your unit?" he asked.

"Eight hundred and forty two foot, thirty eight horse," Macrinus replied, taking a perverse satisfaction that his two Cohorts were nearer full strength than the two legionary units.

"It will suffice," Tacitus declared.

"So the savages are going to fight?" Rufus asked, his dark eyes flashing with anticipation.

"Indeed they are," Tacitus confirmed.

Wine was served, along with some bread, a few dried olives and slices of pork coated in garum, a pungent fish sauce that was an essential part of Roman diet. While they ate, Tacitus outlined what had happened at Tara.

Macer cast an uncertain look at Domnan.

"What about the barbarian boy? Can we trust him?"

"We may need him," Tacitus explained.

"As a puppet King?"

"Yes."

Macer frowned, clearly distrusting Domnan's presence.

"So he will be marching with us?"

"No," Tacitus replied. "He has no army and he speaks no Latin. We will leave him here under guard until we know whether we have need of him."

Domnan's eyes moved from one man to another. He clearly knew that they were talking about him but the perplexed expression on his youthful face showed that he could not understand what was being said. His presence was tolerated because he was King of Leinster and an ally of Rome, but he had little to offer in practical terms, so the officers excluded him from their discussion.

Rufus asked, "So you reckon the barbarians can muster around six thousand?"

"I think so," Macrinus answered. "It's a rough count but I had some of my men make independent estimates and we all came up with more or less the same figure."

"A bit more than three to one," Macer commented. "We can handle that."

He made a show of being unconcerned by the odds, although Macrinus thought the man's eyes suggested that he was not as confident as he tried to sound.

"There is a complication," Macrinus informed them. "Calgacus is here."

"The Calgacus?" Rufus asked. "The one who killed Casca?"

"The very same," Tacitus confirmed. "Although I do not think it necessarily changes our plans."

"He is formidable," Macrinus cautioned.

"You sound as if you are afraid of him," sneered Macer. "He killed one Centurion of Auxiliaries and everyone seems to think he is some sort of invincible demi-god."

Macrinus leaned forwards to stare at Macer. Speaking firmly, he said, "I am not afraid of him but I respect him. He is clever and he does not shrink from a fight."

"So he is brave," Macer shrugged, maintaining his scepticism. "Many barbarians profess bravery. They always run when faced by the legions."

Tacitus raised a hand to soothe the antagonism that was building.

"Gentlemen, you are both correct," he said calmly.

He nodded to Macrinus before addressing Macer.

"Calgacus is indeed a man to be wary of. I learned quite a lot about him when we sent Casca after him. From what I discovered, it seems that he has opposed Rome since the days of Ostorius Scapula's governorship, when he fought alongside the Silures. He defeated the Second *Augusta* in that war, and during the revolt of Boudica he destroyed half of the Ninth *Hispana,* as well as managing to keep the Second *Augusta* penned into their fort for fear of him."

Macer's thin lips twitched at the reference to the defeat of the Ninth Legion.

"That was before my time," he muttered sullenly.

Rufus rumbled, "Those events were a long time ago but the lads all know the stories of Calgacus. Even my boys have heard them."

Tacitus acknowledged the fact with a slight nod. In military terms, the Second *Adiutrix* was a relatively new Legion, having been raised by the Emperor Vespasian only eight years previously. Not only that, the men in Rufus' Cohort were the least experienced in the Legion, many of them new recruits. Yet they knew the tales about Calgacus because the old hands always relayed the horror stories of what new men could expect to find in Britannia. Tales of monsters abounded; stories of death-defying, blue-painted, head-hunting fanatics were told to frighten the new men. The accounts of what Calgacus had done to the legions were not broadcast to the citizens of the empire but they were well known among the soldiers in Britannia.

"The Governor has offered a reward to the man who kills or captures Calgacus," Tacitus reminded them.

"It would be well deserved," Macrinus commented softly.

"He is just one man," Macer insisted.

"Indeed he is," Tacitus agreed. "But we shall keep his presence to ourselves. There is no need to cause unnecessary alarm among the men. As far as they are concerned, the leader of the barbarians is named Tuathal. He is the man we need to capture or kill. What we must decide now is how to achieve that."

"We should stay here," Macrinus advised. "Let them come to us. We can be supplied by the fleet and we are protected by the sea and the walls. Let the Hibernians throw themselves against us, then, when they have exhausted themselves trying to storm the walls, we can march out and destroy them."

"You don't win a war by sitting behind walls," Macer objected. "We should march out to meet them. Attack. That is what the legions do best."

His final comment, a reminder that he led citizen legionaries, seemed designed to denigrate Macrinus' Auxiliary troops.

"We don't have enough cavalry," Macrinus pointed out. "We have fewer than forty fit horses. If we march out, we will be blind to what the enemy are doing. Believe me, Calgacus will not miss an opportunity like that."

"Cavalry won't win the war," Rufus interjected. "We need to close with the enemy and get them within reach of our swords."

"Which is why we should stay here," Macrinus insisted. "They will come to us, which means they will have no opportunity to ambush us on the march. We will be able to see exactly how many there are and we can attack them when it suits us."

"What was the point in crossing the sea to sit in a walled fort?" Macer asked scornfully.

Rufus rubbed his pock-marked chin as he said, "I agree that we should attack but there is the question of transport. We don't have many mules, so the lads will either need to march light or carry a lot of kit themselves."

All three men looked at Tacitus. For a long moment he sat thinking. He was the youngest, least experienced man there but he knew he must make the final decision. The Governor had told him to heed Macrinus' advice but there were other considerations.

Choosing his words carefully, he said, "It will not be good for morale if we stay here. The Governor wants a quick solution to the campaign and I believe that the best way to achieve that is to bring the barbarians to battle. If we wait here, they may gather more men. But their sacred site at Tara is only two days' march from here. If we threaten that place, they will have no option but to face us. When they do, we will destroy them."

Macrinus face was heavy with disapproval.

"Sir," he protested. "I must advise against this. It is too great a risk."

"You can stay here and guard the fort if you wish," Macer suggested acidly.

Macrinus tensed. For a moment it seemed he might challenge Macer to a fight but he restrained himself.

"I will follow orders," he replied coldly. "But I was charged by the Governor to give my advice. I have given it."

"And I appreciate it," Tacitus assured him. "But the Governor himself has shown many times that bold, decisive attack is the way to defeat the barbarians. I have made my decision. We will march to Tara."

The soldiers were roused at daybreak by the call of a *buccina*. The summons of the brass horn was greeted by groans and grumbles as the men crept from their tents to cook a hurried breakfast before packing their kit and dressing in their armour in preparation for the day's march.

Macrinus walked around his unit's section of the encampment, giving words of encouragement but prepared to bark at anyone who was even a fraction slow to carry out their duties. He need not have worried. His Centurions and Optios knew what was at stake. Impressing barbarians was one thing but there were legionary troops nearby and nobody wanted to be mocked by the citizen soldiery for being slow or incompetent. Spurred on by fear of failure, Macrinus' two Cohorts were on parade inside the fort's gates while the legionary Cohorts were still packing their tents away.

Macrinus patrolled the ranks, giving the men a cursory inspection. Although they wore no uniform, the soldiers' equipment was more or less standard as far as armour and weapons were concerned. Macrinus was not bothered about how the men looked as long as they kept their swords sharp, so he randomly picked out men and asked to see their blades. They were all perfect, as he had known they would be.

He exchanged some banter while he walked up and down the lines, sharing the men's undisguised pleasure at beating the legionaries to the makeshift parade ground.

"Well done, lads," he told them. "Extra wine ration tonight."

"How about some women as well?" a voice called from behind his back.

Macrinus turned. He was fairly sure he knew who had spoken. It had probably been Honorius, who was always ready with a quip or a complaint. Macrinus chose to join in the laughter and pretended not to know who had spoken.

He grinned, "If you can fit one in your pack, you can bring her along."

When he had completed the hurried inspection he walked to the front to see whether the other Cohorts were ready.

The legionaries were assembling to the left of Macrinus' men. He saw Rufus strolling over to meet him, carrying a vine stick in his left hand as a symbol of his rank. The wooden rod also served as a disciplinary weapon which Centurions could use to beat their soldiers into obedience. Macrinus prided himself that he had never needed to carry a vine rod.

Rufus wiped small pieces of crust away from his eyes, which were bloodshot and sunken, making his tanned and pock-marked face appear even more unwholesome than it had the night before. Still, his manner was cheerful enough as he walked up to Macrinus.

"Your lads are keen," Rufus observed amiably.

"Keen and efficient," Macrinus agreed.

Rufus laughed, a hoarse, throaty rumble from the back of his throat.

"You don't need to prove anything to me," he grinned. "I've heard all about you."

"The only person I am trying to prove anything to is myself," Macrinus replied, knowing that was only partly true.

"But I suppose it helps that you are ready before Macer's men, eh?"

Macrinus gave a faint smile as he admitted, "It doesn't hurt."

"He's a pompous sod," Rufus observed breezily. "He thinks he's seen it all but he spent most of his career patrolling the Limes on the borders of Germania. I doubt whether he's ever faced anything more than a few small raiding parties. But he's probably a good enough soldier. The Ninth is a good Legion."

"He wouldn't command a Cohort if he wasn't a competent soldier," shrugged Macrinus.

Rufus' throaty laugh gurgled again.

"Now you've managed to compliment us all, including yourself."

"Just stating facts," shrugged Macrinus.

That was true enough. His personal dislike of Macer did not alter the fact that any man who became a Centurion must be tougher than the men under his command. Centurions were expected to lead by example and usually fought in the front rank. Casualties among Centurions were horribly high but that did not prevent men from competing for the position because Centurions were very well paid and were held in high esteem by every citizen of the Empire.

Macrinus may have had a grudging respect for the regular army's Centurions but that did not mean he had to like them. Years of scorn from legionary officers like Macer had hardened his attitude towards them but, despite his inherent antipathy, he recognised a kindred spirit in Rufus, so he added, "The Army does not usually promote men without a good reason."

"That's bollocks!" Rufus laughed. "You know as well as I do that being a good soldier doesn't mean a man will make a good officer. If you ask me, Macer's been promoted beyond his ability. Don't look so shocked. It's true. That's why he falls back on harsh discipline and slavish obedience to regulations. He has no idea how to be a leader, so he resorts to being a bully."

"I've come across the type before," Macrinus commented.

"So have I. They are the Army's greatest weakness, yet at the same time they are its greatest strength."

"Because discipline and slavish obedience make the soldiers strong," observed Macrinus.

"Exactly."

Rufus' swarthy face broke into another mocking smile as he added, "Being stubborn is what we Romans are good at."

"Yes, I am aware of that," Macrinus replied cautiously.

Rufus gave him a sharp look and said, "For what it is worth, I've been thinking about what you said last night. On reflection, I think you may be right about marching inland with a force this small. But orders are orders. We'll see what happens. Nobody lives forever, especially not soldiers. Let's hope the youngster has made the right call."

Macrinus said, "I am sure the Tribune has thought about things carefully."

Rufus laughed again while ostentatiously scratching his backside.

"Thinking is easy," he observed. "Making the right decision is the tricky bit."

"It always is," agreed Macrinus. "In war, it is the side that makes the fewest mistakes which wins. We do not make many mistakes."

"That's true," nodded Rufus. "But this fellow, Calgacus, seems to have a habit of beating the Legions."

"Oh, he's cunning and unpredictable," Macrinus told him. "He's as good a leader as the Britons have but his troops are not as good as ours."

"Barbarian rabble," Rufus suggested. "Macer is right about that. They won't stand when they face the Legions."

Macrinus nodded. Rome had the only professional standing army in the world. The soldiers practised the art of war every day and they were accustomed to victory.

"The trouble is," he said softly, "Calgacus does not fight open battles. He uses ambush and stealth."

"Then maybe the youngster is right," Rufus declared. "If we march on their holy site, the barbarians will be forced to face us."

"Yes," Macrinus agreed. "That might work."

If Rufus heard the doubt in his voice, he did not show it. Instead, he grinned and announced, "Well, I'd best go and beat some sense into my lads."

With a friendly wave of his hand, he walked back to where his men were assembling in ranks. Macrinus heard him call a cheerful insult to Macer who was whining at his Cohort to form up in the cramped space between the wall and the roundhouses. Macer's response to Rufus was an angry glare.

Macrinus frowned to himself. The conversation with Rufus had unsettled him in some indefinable way. The man's fatalistic acceptance of whatever lay ahead was typical of a soldier's response but the fact that Rufus was having second thoughts about the proposed plan of action only served to make Macrinus more despondent.

He was momentarily distracted when the *buccina* sounded again. Tacitus appeared, wearing a flowing toga over his tunic and followed by his clerks and slaves. They made their way to the gates, turning to face the assembled soldiers.

Seeing that the formal proceedings were about to begin, Macrinus took up his position at the head of his Cohorts, standing beside the *signifer* who held the standard on its wooden pole. The flag fluttered noisily in the breeze above Macrinus' head. The familiar sound gave him some comfort. A unit's standard was a source of pride, a thing to be protected. It proclaimed the unit's identity. The *signifer* was a *duplicarius*, a man who received double the rate of pay of the ordinary soldiers but who was expected to act as a rallying point for the men in battle and to protect the embroidered flag with his life.

Macrinus, still feeling uneasy despite the comforting sounds of the gently flapping standard, looked towards the gates, which remained closed and barred.

Tacitus stood just inside the gateway, bathed in the morning sunshine with a fold of his toga draped over his head in imitation of a priest. His slaves hurried to set up a small, portable altar while one of them led a young, white goat on a short length of rope. When the slaves withdrew, Tacitus raised his arms. In his right hand he held a ceremonial sacrificial knife. He called on

Jupiter, Greatest and Best, to bless their noble enterprise, to give strength to their arms and to their hearts, and he called on Mars, God of War, to aid them in whatever struggles lay ahead. He asked the gods to accept the sacrifice he was about to offer.

The slave tugged the goat towards the altar. While he held it in place, a second slave produced an iron hammer which, at a nod from Tacitus, he used to club the goat on the head. The animal fell, stunned, but was held up by the first slave, who cupped a hand under its chin to lift its head.

Acting the part of the *haruspex*, Tacitus quickly slit the goat's throat, allowing the blood to soak the small altar stone. He performed the task efficiently, for the beast barely made a sound as it dropped to the ground, its legs thrashing. The slaves held it down while Tacitus used his knife to cut its belly open and let the entrails spill out.

He stooped, almost crouching because the altar was so low.

He poked at the goat's innards with his knife before standing up to proclaim, "The auspices are favourable! The Gods smile on us!"

The men cheered loudly. Good omens were essential for any military venture. If the auspices had been unfavourable, Tacitus would have been obliged to call off the march. No soldier would willingly go to war if the gods did not approve of the enterprise.

Macrinus saw gulls circling overhead, already attracted by the smell of the goat's sacrifice. He wondered what an *augur* would make of their flight but there were no *augurs* here. Roman priests rarely ventured into the wild lands with the army, which was why the senior officers usually performed the sacrifices themselves.

In contrast, Macrinus had seen the druids who often went to battle alongside the Britons. Their magic and screeching threats never seemed to do any good but Macrinus thought that at least the druids had the courage of their beliefs and often put themselves into positions of danger. Roman priests, *augurs* and *haruspices* preferred temples of stone or marble to battlefields.

The constant raucous cries of the gulls annoyed Macrinus. They added to his sense of foreboding as if they were mocking him, ridiculing the sacrifice and the favourable omens revealed by the goat's unblemished organs. He could not shake off the feeling

303

that something was wrong, as if some threat hung over this expedition.

Macrinus exhaled loudly, annoyed at himself for the feeling of gloom that shrouded his thoughts. Calgacus could not win, he told himself. His sense of disquiet probably stemmed from nothing more than the fact that Tacitus had ignored his advice, combined with the knowledge that Macer would undoubtedly gloat once Tuathal had been killed or captured. The haughty Centurion's barely disguised accusation of timidity had rankled Macrinus. He told himself to forget it. Now was the time to prove that his men were the equal of any legionary Cohort. He would take great delight in showing Macer just what his men were capable of.

Another cheer jerked him from his reverie. It was time. The goat's carcass had been carried away and the altar stone removed. A slave had brought a bowl of water so that Tacitus could wash the blood from his hands and the Tribune had removed his toga. A second slave was helping him fasten his armoured breastplate and short kilt of leather straps. As soon as these were in place, a red cloak was fastened around his shoulders and his sword strapped around his waist.

Tacitus took his helmet, then called for his horse.

Macrinus' own mount was brought to him, the trooper who led it clasping his hands to make a step for Macrinus to hoist himself into the saddle. Then the gates were swung open and the soldiers began the march that would lead them to the conquest of Hibernia.

Chapter XXXIII

Macrinus divided his small cavalry force into three sections, sending them scouting ahead and to either side of the marching column. He knew that, at best, they would only be able to bring warning when they located the enemy but it was better than marching blindly into hostile territory. The troopers rode off willingly enough although they knew that, in such small numbers, they might easily be attacked and killed before they had any chance of escaping.

Macrinus had an unwelcome thought that the Roman general, Crassus, had lost his life and his army when his cavalry had been ambushed by the Parthians. That disaster had occurred a hundred years earlier but was still large in the memory of most Romans. Macrinus knew that it was infantry who won battles but cavalry made the victories possible. Without horsemen, they would have no idea where the barbarians were and could easily blunder into a trap. The one good thing that Macrinus could see was that the gently rolling hills did not provide much opportunity to conceal a large force in ambush.

"What did you say?" Tacitus asked.

Macrinus inwardly cursed. He had not realised that he had spoken aloud.

"I was thinking there are few places where Calgacus can lure us into a trap," he explained.

"Indeed. I expect he will find a suitable hill and wait for us," Tacitus stated. "That is their usual tactic."

He caught the look on Macrinus' face and hurriedly added, "I am sorry. I have only ever seen a handful of actions, and only one of those was a major battle. You must think that I am very presumptuous."

Macrinus shook his head.

"No. You are probably correct. But I have learned that it is wise not to presume too much about what our enemies will do."

"Of course," Tacitus nodded. "I value your advice, Macrinus. I know you think this march is unwise but these savages have never seen the power of Rome. I am sure they will make a stand if we threaten Tara. Then we shall crush them."

"I hope you are right, Sir," Macrinus said as evenly as he could manage. "That would make things very simple."

He did not repeat his concern over the lack of cavalry. The barbarians may well stand but if Tuathal's army ran, the High King would run as well. The Roman cavalry would need to catch him if they wanted a quick end to the war. With fewer than forty horsemen available, Macrinus doubted whether that would be possible.

Tacitus waved an arm, taking in the long column of marching men.

"The sight of our brave soldiers will terrify them," he declared with a conviction that brooked no argument.

Macrinus surveyed the men. Ahead of him was one of his own Auxiliary Cohorts, marching six abreast, with their standards held high and the plumed helmets of the Centurions visible over the heads of the soldiers, the stiff, horsehair fans bobbing in time to the heavy tramp of the men's feet. He and Tacitus rode behind the leading Cohort, along with four mounted messengers, a scribe and three of Tacitus' slaves. Behind them marched Macer's Cohort of the Ninth *Hispana*, with Macer himself marching at the head. Then came Rufus and the men of the Second *Adiutrix*, followed by the baggage train of mules with Macrinus' second Cohort bringing up the rear. In all, the column stretched for nearly three thousand paces, three Roman miles. It would have been longer had they been able to bring all their mules but the baggage train had been cut to the minimum they could afford.

Macer had scoffed at the line of march, insisting that it was foolish to have an entire Cohort marching behind the baggage train.

"It will take them too long to deploy when we meet the enemy," he had complained.

"It will protect the baggage train if the enemy try to circle round us," Macrinus had replied. "We have few enough mules as it is. We need to safeguard the ones we have."

Tacitus had settled the argument by agreeing with Macrinus, although Macrinus suspected that was more because he wished to be seen to be following his advice than because he believed there was a chance of an attack from the rear.

Macer had given Macrinus a look that suggested he considered the decision to be overly cautious. Macrinus, though, was past caring what Macer thought. Taking some precautions was sensible. With that in mind, two of Macrinus' Centuries had been left at Droim Meanach to protect their supply base. That had been necessary but it meant that one hundred and twenty seven men were not available for the impending battle.

"It's a fine sight," Tacitus remarked proudly as he twisted in his saddle to look back at the marching column. "A very fine sight indeed."

They marched all morning without a halt, following the ancient trackway which they knew led all the way to Tara. It was little more than rutted lines of hard-packed earth crossing the grass of the valley but Macrinus knew from his earlier visit to the High King's home that this track, gouged by the wheels of countless carts and the steps of generations of people and horses, followed the most direct route. That was important because reaching Tara quickly was their prime objective. The Governor required a quick victory and seizing Hibernia's most sacred site was the best way to accomplish that aim.

The men carried waterskins and had lengths of sausage meat hung at their belts so that they could cut slices to eat while they marched. There was no need to stop, so they continued all through the afternoon, skirting round marshlands and woods, splashing across small streams and climbing low hills. Like all Roman armies, they marched in silence, the only sounds being the steady tramp of feet, the clinking of armour and equipment, the dull clop of hooves and the occasional braying of a pack mule.

Macrinus looked up at the overcast sky. The fine weather of the previous few days was giving way to cooler air and duller skies which the rational part of his brain told him was normal for this part of the world but which a small core of superstition warned him was a bad omen.

Telling himself to forget such nonsense, he tried to locate the position of the sun through the grey layer of clouds.

"We will need to make camp soon," he observed. "If I remember correctly, there is a small lake beyond that next hill. That will provide fresh water but it is also the most dangerous part of our journey."

"How so?" Tacitus asked.

"Because the track leads through a large patch of woodland. If Calgacus is going to spring a surprise, that's where he'll do it."

"Our scouts will surely detect them," Tacitus remarked.

Macrinus hoped the Tribune was correct. He trusted his scouts but he also knew that Calgacus was a formidable enemy and he could not shake off his inner fears.

He chewed his lower lip while he stared ahead. The leading Cohort was approaching a long escarpment which marked the head of the broad, open valley they were marching through. The ridge lay across their path like a giant's finger, a low but fairly steep slope leading up to a grass-covered summit a hundred paces above the plain. Apart from some scraps of gorse and brambles, the escarpment seemed bare but Macrinus could see the tops of trees denoting a patch of woodland covering the right section of the far side.

"I recall the terrain being fairly rough on the other side of that ridge," he frowned. "The next suitable place for a camp is beyond the lake and woods."

"Then we should press on quickly," Tacitus declared.

Macrinus hesitated, an uneasy feeling of foreboding coming over him.

"Perhaps we should make a detour," he suggested, gesturing to the more open ground to the right of their line of march. "If we go that way, we can circle round the ridge and the woods and rejoin the track beyond them."

"That would add several miles to our journey!" exclaimed Tacitus.

"Yes, but it would avoid the riskiest part of the march and, if Calgacus is waiting for us in the woods, it would put us between him and Tara."

Tacitus frowned uncertainly, his eyes following the line of the trackway which led up the slope in a series of zig-zag turns before disappearing beyond the summit of the escarpment.

"Our scouts have not brought any word of danger," he pointed out.

"I still think it would be wise to take precautions," Macrinus replied, silently hearing the mocking voice of Macer chiding him for cowardice.

Tacitus said, "We can send the first Cohort into the trees in battle order. That will flush out any ambush."

"But gives the enemy an advantage," Macrinus insisted. "Our men fight best on open ground. That's why the barbarians choose ambush in woods."

He was becoming increasingly convinced that Calgacus would have concealed his warriors in the woods. Macrinus had spotted the site on their earlier trip to Tara and had noted it as one of the few places that offered any real prospect of concealing a large number of men. He was about to insist that they alter their route when the decision was taken out of his hands.

A warning exclamation from one of Tacitus' messengers alerted them to the sight of their scouts galloping back from the right flank, the direction Macrinus had wanted to follow. The horsemen were bent low over their mounts' necks, urging the beasts on because, in their wake came at least a hundred barbarian riders mounted on their small war ponies and brandishing spears and long swords. The Roman cavalry, on bigger mounts, were outdistancing the pursuit but the presence of the enemy told Macrinus that Calgacus had anticipated the possibility that the Romans might choose a longer but safer route to Tara.

"Sound the halt!" Macrinus yelled to the *buccina* signaller.

Even as the brass horn called the column to a halt, Macrinus saw another rider appear but this man had come charging over the top of the ridge ahead of the column, crouched low in the saddle and lashing his horse furiously as he galloped back at breakneck speed.

Macrinus swore. A glance to his right told him that the scouts would soon reach the safety of the column and the barbarian horsemen had reined in, content to have chased the Romans away, but things were very different on the route in front of the column.

A second Roman rider came into sight, charging over the ridge with a swarm of barbarian horsemen in close pursuit.

"Drop packs!" Macrinus bellowed. "Prepare to ward off cavalry!"

He heard a series of thumps as the men dropped the heavy, wooden cross-pieces they held over one shoulder. These wooden frames were used to carry their packs, waterskins, entrenching tools and assorted equipment. They were an essential part of each soldier's kit but they were heavy and cumbersome and could not be carried when the men needed to fight.

They needed to fight now, Macrinus knew.

"Form maniples!" he ordered, the *buccina* relaying the signal. "Close order!"

Then he jabbed an urgent finger at one of Tacitus' messengers.

"Tell the other cohorts to close up and deploy for battle on our right, facing the ridge. Quickly, or we are all dead!"

Tacitus protested, "Facing the ridge? The enemy are to our right as well."

"That's a feint," Macrinus declared.

He did not explain himself but barked at the messenger to relay his orders. The rider raced away and Macrinus could do no more until the column was deployed from line of march into battle order.

"How do you know it's a feint?" Tacitus demanded peremptorily, waving an arm towards the barbarian horsemen who were lurking on their right flank.

"Because Calgacus isn't stupid enough to confront us on open ground. He wants us to follow the track through the woods, so he's sent a cavalry screen to our right to make us keep to the path."

He spoke with deliberate confidence, dispelling the tiny voice of doubt which told him Calgacus might have tricked him. But the horde of horsemen surging over the ridge told him he was correct.

Up ahead, the leading Roman rider had almost reached the safety of the column but his companion was not so fortunate. His horse stumbled on the steep slope, cartwheeling over in a flurry of legs and throwing the rider from his saddle. In an instant, the fallen man was surrounded by a dozen barbarians who wheeled around him, hacking down with their long, round-tipped swords, yelling in triumph as they chopped the Roman to a bloody mess.

Macrinus swore again. There was no sign of the scouting party he had sent to watch the left flank but he knew his lead group had been virtually annihilated, only one frightened man on an exhausted horse surviving to reach safety.

But there would be no safety unless the Romans deployed quickly. Macrinus grinned as he watched his men perform the manoeuvre with the speed and precision engendered by long years of practice.

Tacitus had his eyes on the barbarian horsemen and his face betrayed his horror at what he saw.

310

"There are hundreds of them!" he exclaimed as more and more riders swarmed over the crest of the ridge.

"They won't charge a wall of spears," Macrinus assured him. "I suggest we get inside one of the Maniples."

Tacitus hurried to follow the advice, leading his messengers and slaves forwards to take shelter in the midst of the leading Cohort.

The scouts who had been driven in from the right brought their tired mounts to rest as the Decurion in charge gasped a brief report to Macrinus.

"The enemy are out there in strength, Sir," he said breathlessly.

"You saw their main force?" Macrinus demanded.

"No, Sir. Just the cavalry. They chased us away before we could see anything."

Macrinus gave a grim nod. The scout's report convinced him more than ever that the barbarian cavalry screen was protecting nothing at all, merely giving the impression that the main enemy force was waiting somewhere out of sight on the Roman right.

Macrinus knew indecision was a fatal flaw, so he stuck to his conviction that the main threat lay beyond the ridge.

"Get out of here!" he told the scouts. "You can't do anything against that many mounted men. Go south and stay out of trouble. Rejoin us when you can."

The Decurion seemed about to protest but a harsh glare from Macrinus spurred him into obedience. He led his tired troop away, returning past the infantry to the far end of the valley, pushing their horses to run as fast as they dared.

Even as they rode away, the sole survivor of the leading scouting party reached the sanctuary of the Cohort. Men moved aside to let him pass, his horse snorting, steam rising from its flanks and its chest heaving with exertion.

The rider, too, looked exhausted and terrified as he blurted out his report.

"We were ambushed! There are thousands of them just ahead. They were hiding in the trees."

The man looked back, his face deathly pale when he realised he was the only survivor of the scouting party but Macrinus felt vindicated. Calgacus had laid an ambush but the trap had been sprung by the scouts, even if only one of them had escaped with his life. Calgacus' plan had failed and now Macrinus was ready for him.

"Stay here," Macrinus told the frightened young man. "You'll be safe enough. We are ready for them."

Looking left and right, he noted that his men had formed themselves into Maniples as quickly and efficiently as the legionaries. Each Maniple comprised two Centuries, the men formed up close together, almost shoulder to shoulder rather than in their usual spaced formation, so that they could present a solid wall of shields and spears to the enemy cavalry.

Many of Macrinus' German Auxiliaries were equipped with *hastas*, long, heavy spears with broad, leaf-shaped blades designed to ward off cavalry. These sharp points now jutted from between their shields, daring the enemy horsemen to come close.

Although the men in each Maniple were packed tightly together, the Maniples did not form a solid phalanx. Instead, the left and right Maniples left a gap between them while the centre Maniple formed behind them so that it could provide support to either of them. This arrangement also meant that any enemy foolish enough to charge into the gap between the front two Maniples would find himself hemmed in on three sides.

Behind Macrinus, the long marching column was pivoting. As they formed into their Maniples, Macer's and Rufus' Cohorts were wheeling round to form up on the right of Macrinus' leading Cohort which had anchored itself as the left of the line. It would take a few moments for the manoeuvre to be completed and the barbarian horsemen were already charging into the gaps between the Cohorts but the Roman infantry were disciplined and highly trained. Whenever the enemy cavalry came near, the riders were faced by a wall of shields and *hastas* or the sharp spikes of the legionary javelins. No horse would charge home against a solid block of men and the barbarians screamed in frustration as they wheeled away, uselessly slashing their swords at the spear points.

"Steady, lads!" Macrinus called to his grim-faced men as they gripped shields and spears tightly, remaining silent while the barbarians yelled incoherent challenges.

Unable to break the defence, the enemy rode uselessly across the front of the Roman line, turning, wheeling and slashing with their long swords but making no impression on the stolid, determined infantry.

One rider did venture too close and a *hasta* was rammed into the chest of his war pony, bringing the screaming animal to the ground and spilling the warrior from his saddle. In an instant, two more *hastas* plunged into him and left him bleeding to death on the grass.

The barbarians may have been thwarted but the Roman line was crooked, bent at an angle because Macer and Rufus had been unable to complete their wheeling turn. The barbarians were all around them, joined by the riders who had first appeared out on the right flank. These men, who had been content to do nothing more than drive in Macrinus' scouts now joined the frenzied attack on the Roman infantry.

But these infantrymen were soldiers of Rome, the best trained fighting men in the world and they slowly edged forwards, stopping to drive off the horsemen when necessary and gradually moving into position alongside Macrinus' leading Cohort. The three units now presented a staggered line of alternating Maniples, with the entire line facing the ridge but with the men on the edges of each Maniple facing outwards to ward off an attack from any direction.

It was the trailing Cohort which concerned Macrinus. Looking back, he could see that this Cohort had formed up and was advancing, passing the baggage train as it attempted to close up with the main column but the men had too far to cover and the barbarians whooped in delight as they charged at this smaller number of Romans, thinking to overwhelm it. Again, though, Macrinus' Auxiliaries demonstrated that they were as well drilled as the legionaries and they formed into tight-knit blocks, jabbing their long *hastas* between their shields and turning their formation into a hedgehog of sharp points to drive off the horses.

Macrinus watched, his face etched by a deep frown but he knew his men were safe as long as they held their formation. They were surrounded and unable to move but the barbarians could not harm them unless the Romans lost their nerve and broke ranks. The only other way the enemy could possibly break them was by dismounting and attacking on foot but Macrinus did not think there were enough of the enemy to do that. He guessed there must have been nearly four hundred mounted barbarians and that was not enough to defeat a similar number of his Auxiliaries. His Cohort might be stranded but it was not likely to be destroyed.

313

The barbarians must have come to the same conclusion. Frustrated again, they turned their attention to the baggage train and set off to capture the mules. The handful of soldiers who had been appointed to guard the mule train had been attempting to lead the animals away to safety but they were quickly overtaken and overwhelmed, cut down by the savage swords of the barbarians who then rounded up and captured the braying mules.

"We must stop them!" Tacitus blurted angrily as he pointed to where the mules were being led away.

"How?" Macrinus asked.

"So what do we do now?" the Tribune scowled.

Macrinus swivelled in his saddle, checking in all directions. His main line was secure and the barbarian horsemen, after making another impotent attack on the trailing Cohort, rode off to their left, yelling taunts and gesturing towards the mules they had captured but leaving the Roman infantry unmolested.

"We've lost all our tents and heavy equipment!" Tacitus complained.

"But we're still alive," Macrinus replied calmly.

"We must do something!" Tacitus insisted.

Macrinus made up his mind.

"We dig in here for the night," he told Tacitus.

The Tribune raised his eyebrows in surprise.

"Here? With no fresh water?"

"There is nowhere to build a camp beyond that ridge," Macrinus told him. "And the place is infested with savages."

"Then we should attack them," Tacitus declared.

"They'll just melt away into the woods," Macrinus insisted. "We'll spend the rest of the day chasing shadows and then there will be no time to dig in for the night. No, it's better to camp here. In the morning, we take the longer route and go around that forest."

"They might attack us here while we're making the camp," Tacitus frowned.

Macrinus checked the progress of the enemy cavalry. They were slowly climbing the ridge, their ponies exhausted by their long chase of the scouts and their fruitless charges against his infantry.

"Then we'd better hurry," he stated. "My lads can do the digging while the legionary Cohorts stand to arms."

314

"But we have no tents and we've lost most of our food," Tacitus reminded him.

"Then we'll be hungry and wet if it rains," Macrinus shrugged. "But we'll be safe behind a rampart. In the morning, we resume the march. Once we get to Tara, we'll find food and shelter, I'm sure."

"What about the barbarians? Won't they try to stop us?"

"Oh, I do hope so," grinned Macrinus.

Chapter XXXIV

Some of the barbarian cavalry harassed them while the camp was being dug but the legionaries held them off while Macrinus' men dug feverishly under the lashing tongues of their Centurions and Optios. Occasionally, when the enemy pressed hard, the Auxiliaries dropped their tools and picked up their weapons until the horsemen had been driven off, then they resumed their digging, flinging the earth up to form a rampart, covering the face with the turf they had cut, then placing a palisade of wooden stakes on the top. Each man carried three of these stakes as part of his equipment and they often grumbled about the weight but there were no complaints now as they hurriedly created the fortifications that would keep them safe.

With eight hundred men hacking at the soft turf, the ditch and rampart grew steadily. This was routine, for the Roman Army insisted on a marching camp being dug each night. Each soldier was equipped with a *dolabra*, a multi-purpose digging implement which could be used as both a pick and a shovel. With well-practised hard work, Macrinus' men could create a strong defensive position in around an hour. It took longer this time because of the ever-present threat of attack but soon the wall and ditch began to take shape.

As the marching camp progressed, the legionaries drew back within the new fortification and the barbarians gave up their pointless attacks.

"Well done, lads!" Macrinus told them encouragingly. "Tomorrow we will show them how to fight properly."

The men grinned but even Macrinus could not conceal the difficulties confronting them. With no tents and little food or water, they faced an uncomfortable night.

Rufus was philosophical about the prospect but Macer complained that they should have advanced instead of digging in.

"Where to?" Macrinus asked scathingly. "The terrain beyond that ridge suits the savages and offers no place for a marching camp. It is nearly dark already and we would have been stranded out there, with thousands of barbarians surrounding us."

"We could at least have taken the high ground," Macer grumbled, gesturing towards the ridge.

"And then what? We would have had to come back down again," Macrinus told him.

Tacitus silenced Macer's complaints by confirming his agreement with Macrinus' tactics.

"We will advance in the morning," he declared. "Now we know the site of their ambush, we can avoid it."

Macer remained unhappy but Macrinus had no time to argue with the surly Centurion. He needed to think; to try to anticipate what Calgacus would do now that his first attempt to snare them had failed.

The situation was not good, he knew. He had been in a similar position once before, when he had been sent to rescue Cartimandua of the Brigantes. On that occasion, he had been entrenched in camp beneath a ridge on which had sat thirty thousand Brigante warriors. Calgacus had saved him that day but this time the big Briton would be doing his best to destroy him.

Macrinus gave a mental shrug. They might be outnumbered and have little food or shelter but they were still Romans and he knew, just as Calgacus knew, that the barbarians would not stand against the Roman heavy infantry.

It was the lack of cavalry that bothered him. Once the barbarian horsemen had withdrawn, all of his remaining scouts had returned, riding into the camp on tired horses and receiving some barbed comments from the foot soldiers who accused them of having run away. Macrinus quickly squashed the rancour because he knew there was nothing two dozen men could have done to combat several hundred barbarians but there was always ill-feeling between the infantry and the cavalry who were often kept apart in separate camps to prevent trouble flaring up. This night, the few surviving horsemen would need to bed down in the fort like everyone else. With no tents, little food and no fuel for fires, they would suffer along with the infantry.

Macrinus had other problems to consider. He climbed to the rampart near the gap which had been left in the northern wall. There were four such gateways in the rectangular fort, each one barred by a barrier of stakes. Normally, these barriers would be made by felling saplings and resting the trunks on supports made by lashing stakes together. With no access to trees, the Romans had simply built more supports than normal and set these up in a

317

line, creating an artificial hedge of pointed stakes behind which stood a Century of armed men.

Macrinus eyed the surrounding countryside warily, attempting to put himself in Calgacus' place and work out what the Briton would do.

Tacitus clambered up to join him.

"Can you see anything?" the Tribune asked.

Macrinus pointed as he replied, "There are horsemen patrolling the slopes to the west and the open ground to the east. There's been some movement on the ridge but only a few men have shown themselves so far."

He shrugged as he added, "They are doing nothing more than watch us."

Tacitus pointed south, back down the route they had followed to reach this place. "They have no patrols back there?"

"They are inviting us to go back," Macrinus informed him. "Leaving us an escape route."

"Escape?"

Tacitus seemed offended by the notion.

"Don't worry, Tribune," Macrinus grinned. "I have no intention of retreating just yet. Calgacus has had his chance and he has lost it. He knows he must either stand and face us or withdraw and let us seize Tara. Either way, we will win."

Tacitus seemed to take comfort from Macrinus' confidence but gave a sudden start as he stared up at the ridge which blocked their route to the north.

"There are chariots up there," he remarked.

Macrinus looked to where Tacitus was pointing. Three chariots had appeared on the skyline, their silhouettes just visible against the darkening sky. Horsemen also came into sight and several figures dismounted, clustering together to look down on the Roman camp.

"That's Calgacus," Macrinus said, indicating the tallest figure. "I wonder what he's planning next?"

"What do we do now?" Tuathal asked.

Calgacus did not reply. He was still angry at the failure of his plan. He had hoped to trick the Romans into following the trackway by driving in their scouts on the right flank as if to suggest that his main force was concealed somewhere out there. It had been a double bluff because his warriors had lain in wait in the

318

forest where the Romans might have expected such a trap. Yet the plan might have worked had the Roman scouting party been annihilated. Everything had depended on that but the Romans had been wary, sending in a few of their number to scour the trees while a handful had hung back. The trap had been detected and the Romans had turned tail. Most of them had been caught by Fiacha Cassan's mounted warriors but two had crossed the ridge and alerted the Roman infantry.

Calgacus had warned Fiacha Cassan not to attack the column unless he could catch the Romans unprepared. The tall swordsman had ignored that advice and wasted his energy but at least he had the sense to capture the Roman baggage train. Yet even that success had been a double-edged sword because the warriors had found wine among the packs they had captured and already many of them were drinking themselves into insensibility. Calgacus had told Tuathal to confiscate or spill the wine but it was too late.

All in all, things had not gone well and Calgacus' mood was sour as he studied the Roman camp and considered his options.

"What are you thinking?" Tuathal asked him.

Calgacus exhaled a long breath as he considered his response.

"We have two chances," he said at last. "I'd prefer to frighten them into turning back but, if we can't do that, we will need to face them in open battle."

"You don't sound confident," Tuathal observed, giving the big warrior an anxious look.

"I am not. Romans don't frighten easily. They may have lost their baggage but I don't think that will stop them."

"So we must face them?"

Calgacus nodded pensively as he sighed, "And nobody can beat them in an open battle."

"So what do we do?" Tuathal persisted. "I will not submit to them without a fight."

Calgacus looked around at the faces of the people surrounding him. Even in the gathering gloom he could sense their disappointment. His well laid plan for an ambush had failed and now he needed to come up with a stratagem that would rescue success from potential disaster.

Fiacha Cassan and Sanb were already grumbling. Fiacha Cassan had wanted to launch their entire war host against the Romans while they were building their fort but Calgacus had refused to send in the foot soldiers, knowing there was too much open ground to cover. By the time the warriors reached the Romans, the soldiers would have dropped their tools and picked up their weapons. Even with superior numbers, Calgacus knew that facing the Romans on open ground was to invite disaster.

But what alternative did he have? Should he have followed Fiacha Cassan's advice? Had he missed his best chance because he was being overly cautious?

There was, he knew, only one way to intimidate the Romans and that was to put on a display of strength, to line this ridge with warriors and frighten the enemy into withdrawing.

Yet he knew that was a forlorn hope. In his mind's eye he could already see the Romans marching out of their camp, forming into their Maniples and advancing up the slope. His cavalry might delay them, might slow the advance by forcing the Romans to maintain an outward barrier of spears but, eventually, the heavily armoured legionaries would reach the top of the slope and then the killing would begin. He had seen it too often to believe the outcome could be different this time. No matter how bravely Tuathal's warriors fought, unarmoured men could not withstand the attack of the Roman heavy infantry. The legionaries would break the defensive line and Tuathal's men would scatter in panic.

And everyone expected him to find an alternative. If circumstances had been different, he would have advocated dispersing the war host, splitting into smaller groups and harassing the Romans on the march, picking them off one at a time. But those tactics would not work here, he knew. If the Romans reached Tara, Tuathal would be High King only in name. Not only that, the Romans could turn Tara or any of the neighbouring hilltop settlements into impregnable fortresses from where it would be impossible to dislodge them. If Tuathal lost control of Tara so soon after claiming the High Kingship, the other Kings might decide to make peace with Rome and Tuathal would become little more than a renegade and fugitive.

Everyone waited for Calgacus to speak. Tuathal and Runt, Sanb, Fiacha Cassan, Findmall and Eudaf. They waited, and the longer he said nothing, the more their concern would grow. Scota was there, as was young Braine, who had refused to remain behind

320

while Tuathal went to war. She caught his eye and he thought he detected a hint of hope in her expression.

But there was no hope. The Romans would advance, men would die and then the warriors would break and run.

He turned again, looking speculatively back across the ridge as an idea began to form.

The warriors would run. And if they ran ...

Without a word, he walked back across the broad ridge until he could see down the northern side of the escarpment. The reverse slope was less steep than the southern face but the ground was more broken here, rocky and uneven, a wilderness of ditches, hummocks, furrows, rocky outcrops and clumps of gorse bushes which eventually gave way to reed beds and pools of marshy bogland that fringed the small lake that glimmered darkly in the fading light several hundred paces from where he stood.

To his right was a dark patch of woodland that extended along the eastern end of the ridge and down to the fringes of the lake shore, while to the left was a steeper slope that fell away to another broad stretch of boggy, reed-infested ground.

"What are you thinking?" Runt asked as he moved alongside.

"I'm thinking that this side of the hill is not much use as a battlefield."

Runt studied the terrain.

"Chariots won't be much use here," he agreed.

"Even horses won't be able to move easily," Calgacus observed.

That, he knew, was why Fiacha Cassan's horsemen had been unable to catch the Roman scouts. The narrow, rutted trackway which meandered down the slope before vanishing into the murky depths of the forest was the only path by which horses could easily cross this rugged terrain. He had made a mistake by not allowing for that when planning his ambush but now he studied the land more closely, imagining how he might turn it to his advantage.

Again he visualised the scene of fleeing men. Thoughtfully, he rubbed at his chin. "It'll do," he whispered softly.

"You have an idea?"

Calgacus' response was a grim smile. He turned and walked back across the ridge to rejoin the others.

"Well?" Tuathal asked.

"There is only one thing we can do," Calgacus announced decisively. "We will make a stand here."

Tuathal frowned, "Isn't that what they want us to do?"

"Yes, so we will oblige them by being predictable."

Sanb objected, "I thought you said they were too strong."

"They are. But I intend to turn their strength against them."

They listened intently as he outlined what he proposed. It was bold and dangerous but Fiacha Cassan grinned expectantly and Sanb's face was alive with eager anticipation.

Eudaf was more anxious, his voice strained as he asked, "Do you really think it can work?"

"It will work if everyone plays their part," Calgacus assured him.

Findmall put in, "I will offer sacrifices to the Gods. That will ensure our victory."

Normally, Calgacus would have ignored such comments because he had seen druids offer all sorts of sacrifices which had failed to stop the Romans. This time, though, the memory of those failures gave him another idea.

He looked at Scota, noting that she was watching him intently.

"You told me you once impressed Elim with your magic. Can you do the same to the Romans?"

"What sort of magic do you have in mind?" she asked cautiously.

"Findmall is right," he told her. "We should offer sacrifices. In particular, we should offer a human sacrifice."

Chapter XXXV

Macrinus had spent an uncomfortable night and only managed to snatch a few hours' sleep but that made him no different to any of the men who were crowded inside the marching camp.

It had been a long, cold, miserable night. Those who did manage to sleep did so wrapped in their cloaks, lying on the hard earth with no tent and no fire to warm them. Periods of drizzly rain had made matters more miserable but the main problem had been the constant threat of attack from the barbarians.

The Britons had occupied the ridge, lighting fires, blowing horns, banging drums, shouting, singing and laughing for much of the night. The men in the camp had heard the shrill screams of horses which were suddenly cut off as the animals were slaughtered either as sacrifices to the savages' Gods or to provide meat for the warriors.

Figures could be glimpsed when they moved in front of the fires high on the escarpment and the dull glow of the flames reflected from the low clouds which obscured the moon and stars and made the darkness appear even more threatening.

The threat was very real. Macrinus had been surprised when the barbarians had settled on the hilltop. He had not thought Calgacus would be so desperate that he would resort to such a tactic. Tacitus had suggested that Calgacus, not being in command, might have been overruled by the High King who was desperate to prevent the Romans from reaching Tara. Macrinus, while conceding this might be true, had nevertheless suspected Calgacus might try something else.

His suspicion was correct. While the noise of drums, horns and voices did not cease, several hundred barbarians had crept down the slope and launched a silent attack on the north gate of the fort, an attack which was followed moments later by a similar assault on the eastern gate.

There had been some desperate, furious fighting but the discipline of the Romans had proved its worth. With the soldiers barring the gate and using their spears to drive off the savages who attempted to haul away the barricade of stakes, the dead had soon created an additional barrier.

It had, though, been brutal, terrifying and bloody work in the darkness. With little illumination, the fight had become a savage struggle of yelling, grunting, sweating men who stabbed blindly at their foes while attempting to keep their own bodies hidden behind their shields. It was the armour and large shields of the Romans as much as anything else which gave the defenders the advantage. The barbarians, most of whom fought semi-naked or with little more than leather tunics padded by wool to protect them, could not withstand the vicious thrusts of *hastas* and short swords. More than a dozen barbarians were killed and many others wounded while the defenders lost only three men dead.

Not that the disparity made life any easier because, in the darkness, it was virtually impossible for any of the men to grasp what was going on around them. All they could do was hold their line, stab and stab again while trusting to the men around them to do the same.

While the fighting continued at the two gates, other barbarians attempted to cross the ditch and scale the ramparts. Again, the defences proved their worth. The ditch, used by the soldiers as a latrine, had a narrow channel dug at its foot. When there were sufficient wooden stakes available, this smaller trench would be filled with a line of sharpened wood but the channel was effective even without this additional hazard because anyone who slithered down the far slope of the ditch was likely to break their ankle when their foot caught in the deep gully. As if this were not enough, the legionaries lined the rampart and hurled javelins down at the mob of warriors who were attempting to clamber up to them. Not a single man reached the top of the ramparts and, eventually, the barbarians gave up.

"They'll come again," Macrinus warned.

And they did. Twice more men came screaming out of the darkness to fling themselves at the Romans who lined the gateways. Twice more they were repulsed with heavy losses until, well past midnight, they withdrew to the top of the ridge, dragging their wounded but leaving their dead behind.

"Tough bastards," commented Rufus as he and Macrinus stood near the north gate, straining to hear signs that the savages might be preparing another assault.

"Tough and brave," Macrinus agreed. "But they can't beat us like this. They would need a lot more men before they could storm the camp."

"What about tomorrow?" Rufus enquired.

"Tomorrow we crush them," Macrinus declared.

Once the fighting had ceased, the four senior officers gathered in the centre of the camp to make their plans. It was an odd occasion. With no tents, everyone in the camp could see them and the nearest men could probably hear what they were discussing. Most of the soldiers were, though, too tired to eavesdrop and stretched out on the ground in an effort to sleep while those who stood guard at the gates concentrated their attention on the darkness beyond the barricades.

"Do you think they will still be up on the ridge in the morning?" Tacitus asked Macrinus.

"I'm not sure. Calgacus knows it would be futile but perhaps he has no alternative now. All his tricks have failed and he has no choice but to face us or abandon Tara to us."

Macer, his face drawn and tired, ventured, "If they are there, how can we reach them before their cavalry cut us off?"

"We can handle them," Macrinus asserted.

Macer stared at him in some disbelief but Macrinus laid out his plan with easy confidence.

"It's straightforward enough," he told them. The two Legionary Cohorts will form the centre, deployed in normal Maniples and extended order. Their job is to climb that slope and attack the enemy line. My lads will form the wings, in close order to keep the enemy cavalry away from the legionaries. I'll also place a detachment at the rear to protect our backsides. Our own cavalry won't be able to do much but I'll have them watch the rear as well. Their presence might be enough to prevent the barbarians surrounding us."

"What about the camp?" Tacitus asked. "How many men do we leave to guard our packs?"

"None," Macrinus told him.

"You're going to gamble on all or nothing?" Macer scowled.

"Yes. But there is another reason for leaving the packs unprotected."

"Plunder," Rufus grinned.

"Exactly. It might prove a tempting target for the enemy horsemen. They are always on the lookout for booty. If they see an unguarded camp, they might be distracted from attacking our rear."

"We could lose everything!" Tacitus exclaimed.

"I doubt they could carry off every pack," Macrinus replied calmly. "But protecting our baggage isn't as important as destroying the High King's army."

He waited for more objections but there were none. After a long pause, Tacitus nodded his head.

"We have a plan," he declared. "Let us make it work."

Macrinus was woken from a restless sleep by Rufus shaking his shoulder.

"Something is happening," Rufus hissed urgently.

"Another attack?" Macrinus asked groggily as he wiped sleep from his eyes.

"No. Something else. It's still too dark to make it out clearly."

Rufus paused, then added, "You'd better come and take a look."

Macrinus smiled to himself. Rufus, despite being a Legionary Centurion, was smart enough to recognise that Macrinus was the expert when it came to dealing with the barbarians. It made a pleasant change to be wanted, Macrinus thought. He adjusted his cloak, picked up his helmet and placed it carefully on his head.

"All right, let's see what they are up to this time."

They walked through the camp towards the northern rampart. Macrinus took his time, letting the men see that he was not anxious.

"It's been a long night," Rufus remarked casually. "But at least they haven't attacked us for a while. It got a bit hairy for a moment or two."

He chuckled softly as he added, "I don't think Macer's ever encountered anything quite like that. He's in a foul mood and he's looking for an excuse to flog someone."

"Macer's an idiot," was Macrinus' opinion.

"He is that," agreed Rufus. "All the lads need is a bit of sleep."

"Or a victory," said Macrinus.

"Aye, that will do the trick every time," Rufus agreed.

Macrinus smiled. He liked Rufus and admired the man for his phlegmatic calm. Both of them knew that, despite Macrinus' confident assertion that they could win easily, the battle they faced was a difficult one. Without cavalry, there was a very real chance of being surrounded before they could engage the main barbarian force. Rufus understood this but also understood that their best chance lay in attacking the enemy. Macer, though, could be a problem if he allowed his own nervousness to transmit itself to his men. There was little Macrinus could do about that except hope that the army's instilled discipline would override the Centurion's fears.

"Nearly dawn," Rufus commented as they approached the ramparts. "The barbarians are still at the top of the hill but their cavalry are already prowling around the lower ground to the east. It looks as if they are waiting for us to make the next move."

Macrinus nodded. All around them the camp was getting ready for the coming day. Centurions and Optios were chivvying the men, insisting that they prepare for battle. Tired or not, years of ingrained discipline would ensure that the soldiers were ready.

Tacitus and Macer were at the gate, looking northwards. All around, legionaries and Auxiliaries who had spent the night listening to the shouts and chants of the barbarians were staring anxiously towards the latest threat. Bodies still lay in crumpled heaps beyond the tangle of stakes that barricaded the gateway but nobody paid much heed to them. They would be dragged aside and tossed into the ditch before the Romans marched out for battle but, for now, they provided a useful addition to the defence by blocking the approach to the camp.

"What's happening?" Macrinus asked cheerfully as he came alongside Tacitus.

He noticed Macer's pale, tense expression and gave the man a broad smile. Macer's response was a surly scowl.

"Something strange is going on," Tacitus answered.

Macrinus looked out to see four figures walking slowly down the slope towards the camp, their dark, shadowy forms becoming clearer as the first hints of daylight lit the countryside. He recognised Calgacus immediately, although the big warrior was not wearing his usual tunic and trousers but was enveloped in a voluminous robe that fluttered around his legs as he walked.

One of the other figures was the small man, Liscus, who was Calgacus' constant companion, while the third man was older. He was leading a goat by a long halter rope.

Macrinus took in all of these things quickly but it was the fourth figure, walking alongside Calgacus, who drew his attention.

"Is that a woman?"

"Good looking one, too," Rufus said, "although she seems to be wearing a mask of some sort."

"It's the woman we saw at Tara," Tacitus observed. "The one with the marked face."

Macrinus nodded. He decided against mentioning that Calgacus had told him the woman was a witch. Macer was nervous enough as it was and he could sense a growing tension among the soldiers around him.

As if on cue, Macer asked in a voice that was clipped and urgent with suppressed anxiety, "Do they want to talk, do you think?"

"Perhaps," Macrinus replied thoughtfully. "I think Calgacus knows they can't beat us in a straight fight, so he may try to convince us to retreat."

"He underestimates us," Tacitus observed.

Macrinus pursed his lips as he gazed out into the early morning gloom.

"It doesn't look like a group of emissaries, though," he mused.

"So what is this all about?" Macer asked anxiously.

Tacitus said, "I would guess they are about to offer a sacrifice. That is what the goat is for."

He looked at Macrinus and asked, "Do they usually do this sort of thing?"

"I've not seen it before," Macrinus admitted cautiously. "But maybe they do things differently in Hibernia."

They watched as the four barbarians came to a halt around sixty paces from the fort where they were well out of range of any thrown javelins. Several hundred paces beyond them, spread across the slope of the low ridge, the barbarian army was standing in silence, every man watching the four figures intently. Thousands of warriors lined the hillside, stretching all along the low ridge that barred the route to Tara. Their stillness was so unusual that Macrinus found it unsettling. The shouts, chants, drums and horns of the previous night had fallen silent and, as the darkness slowly faded away, the damp, grey daylight revealed only an eerily mute audience for whatever was about to unfold.

Macer fidgeted nervously.

"We should do something," he said softly.

Nobody answered. They were all watching the four figures who stood outside the camp.

As Calgacus knelt on the ground, Macrinus breathed, "It's not the goat that's going to be sacrificed."

He spoke softly, as if he could scarcely believe his own words.

"What?" frowned Tacitus.

"Calgacus is giving up his life as an offering to their Gods," Macrinus said in wonder. "Look, his hair is tied back and his hands are behind his back. They must be bound, too."

"Why would he do that?" Macer asked in horrified disbelief.

"Perhaps he has angered the new High King in some way?" suggested Rufus.

"All his attempts to defeat us have failed," Macer agreed with obvious relief. "Perhaps this is the price of failure."

Tacitus offered, "It is more likely that he was chosen because he is an important man. It will be a powerful sacrifice. That is how these barbarians think."

Macrinus frowned, "I can't believe it. Not Calgacus."

Rufus let out a throaty chuckle.

"The stupid buggers are doing our work for us. Good riddance to him."

Macrinus persisted, "This makes no sense. Unless he's been forced into it."

He shook his head. Calgacus' arms may have been bound but there was no sign of anyone threatening him.

The woman, the hem of her long dress damp with dew from the wet grass, stepped in front of Calgacus but kept her back to him. Facing the watching Romans, she lifted her arms to the sky, then dropped them, made a rapid gesture, then raised her hands again. A knife glinted in her right hand, the watery sun reflecting dully on the blade.

"Immortal Gods!" Macer breathed. "Witchcraft!"

The woman turned to face Calgacus. She showed him the dagger, then circled him to stand behind him. Her left hand came round to hold his chin.

329

"By Jupiter, she's really going to kill him!" exclaimed Tacitus.

His tone was surprised but not shocked. Violent death was nothing out of the ordinary and most Romans had plenty of opportunity to witness such things in the amphitheatre, but to see someone voluntarily give themselves up as a sacrifice was unsettling. The four officers watched in fascination, unable to take their eyes from the scene.

It happened quickly. The woman tilted Calgacus' head back, then her right hand flashed across his throat. The knife cut, blood sprayed and, after a few, awful moments, Calgacus slumped sideways, falling limply to the ground. He lay on his side, his face towards the Roman fort. His mouth was open, as if in pain, but they were too far away to hear any sound. The bright smear of red across the front of his throat showed that he was, if not already dead, mortally wounded.

A great cheer resounded from the barbarian army on the hilltop, startlingly loud after their earlier silence. War-horns trumpeted as if in victory. Arms were raised skywards, swords and spears held high. They were greeted by the first, gentle spots of rain that began to fall from the overcast sky.

Macrinus stared at Calgacus. The body hardly had time to stop twitching before the woman knelt, plunging the knife down into his belly, ripping the blade up towards his heart. Blood and guts spilled out from the dark, baggy robe, soaking the damp grass. The woman thrust her hands into the bloody mass, as if searching for something. She cut and sawed, tossing the innards to the grass. Then she stood, holding something in her fist. She raised it high, turning to display her gory trophy to the army above her. Another roar of approval greeted the sight.

"She's cut his heart out," Macer croaked in disgust.

He spat on the ground as if to clear an unpleasant taste from his mouth before muttering, "Bloody savages!"

Macrinus stared in disbelief. He had liked Calgacus, had respected him. He had thought he understood him but he had never expected that the big Briton would sacrifice himself to no apparent purpose.

Yet there could be no doubt about it. Calgacus was dead.

Chapter XXXVI

Several thousand people gathered to say farewell to Coel. He had been the foremost King of the Caledones for longer than most of the tribe could remember, had been the only King that many of them had ever known, so they came to pay their respects and to witness his burial. Farmers, fishermen and herders brought their wives and children; chieftains brought their warriors. Other kings also came, bringing their war bands with them. There were minor kings of the Caledones who had grudgingly acknowledged Coel as their overlord, and there were leaders from the neighbouring tribes of the Damnonii, the Epidii and the Creones.

Emmelia, who watched them all with her usual thoughtfulness, suspected that these kings had come principally because they wanted to make sure that the old fox was truly dead.

She stood beside Beatha, holding her young daughter, Bonduca, in her arms as they watched the bier being carried through the village. All work had stopped for the day. The forges were still, the fishing boats moored, the looms silent. The charcoal burners had left their mounds and the women who boiled bones to make glue had abandoned their cauldrons. All bowed their heads as the procession passed between them on its way to an ancient grove of trees that lay some distance inland from the dead King's broch.

Broichan led the way, his tall, angular frame stiff-legged, his face set hard as stone. His long, grey hair and silvery beard had been combed straight, and across his chest he held a ceremonial staff of dark, polished oak. Behind him came the bier, carried by Crixus, Drust, Eurgain and three chieftains. On the bearskin that had been laid across the wooden frame of the bier lay Coel, crowned by a mass of flowers which served to hide the awful wound on the side of his head, the blow that had killed him when he fell down the dark stairway.

That was the version of events that everyone had been told. Coel had been drunk, they said. He had lost his footing in the darkness and fallen down the stairs. Emmelia, the only person who had been close to him, had kept the truth to herself. She knew that

Coel had collapsed before falling and she was certain that she knew why, but she did not know who to tell.

She had hurried down the stairs, stopping only when the wildly flickering torchlight showed her Coel's battered body lying sprawled on the stone steps.

Men had come crowding behind her, their voices shocked and anxious.

"What happened?" one had asked drunkenly.

"He fell," Emmelia had explained.

"He must have hit his head," another man had said, rather needlessly as far as Emmelia was concerned.

But there was no doubt. Coel was dead.

Not wanting to alarm her friends, she had kept silent, speaking only to Caedmon. He had looked at her with concern etched on his face when he heard her version of what had happened.

"Are you sure he did not simply trip?" he asked. "Could you have been mistaken? It was very dark."

"I know what I saw," she insisted. "What I don't know is whether his heart simply gave out or whether there was more to it."

"You suspect poison?"

"What else could Crixus and Eurgain have been talking about?"

Caedmon had frowned at that.

"I find it hard to believe," he said. "Crixus is a strange fellow but Eurgain always seems so cheerful. At least, he was until Eudaf went away with the others but then, that is often the way with twins."

"How would you know?" Emmelia asked irascibly.

Caedmon was used to her barbed questions, so he simply shrugged. Living with Emmelia had inured him to her quick temper.

He said, "I know a lot of things. It's well known that twins have a bond. Eurgain told me he often knows when something is wrong with Eudaf, even if they are far apart."

"That is beside the point," Emmelia snapped. "I know Eurgain seems like the cheery, simple sort, but I heard what he said. I am convinced he slipped poison into the drink he gave Coel."

"But why would he do that? What does he gain?"

"His father is Coel's elder son. Crixus is likely to become the next King. I'd say that they gain quite a lot."

"It still seems a bit drastic," Caedmon said evenly. "Coel was an old man. I know he was still in good health but nobody lives forever. Crixus would be King in a few years at most, so there is no need for Eurgain to risk being caught trying to speed matters up."

"Perhaps Crixus was fed up waiting," Emmelia suggested.

"Even if you are right, can you prove anything?"

Emmelia shook her head angrily.

"No."

"Then say nothing to anyone," Caedmon advised. "We are still hostages here and you will only make things worse if you go around making accusations you cannot back up."

"But they murdered him!" she exclaimed.

"I believe you. But think about it. There was someone else who could have done it."

Emmelia gave him a sharp look.

"There was? Who?"

Caedmon regarded her apologetically as he said softly, "You were there. If you accuse Eurgain, he will simply blame you. He might say that you pushed Coel down the stairs. Or that you administered poison somehow."

"I was not close enough to push him!" Emmelia protested. "The other men will swear to that."

"They were drunk," Caedmon pointed out. "And Crixus will be their new King. Do you seriously think any of them will speak against him or Eurgain?"

Emmelia lapsed into a pensive silence while she considered Caedmon's advice but he had not finished.

He added quietly, "Do not forget that you have already shown these men that you are skilled in magic. It would not take much for one of them to claim you killed Coel through witchcraft."

Emmelia gave her husband a sharp look but then sighed and nodded her head in understanding.

"You are right," she breathed.

"Then you will keep silent about it?"

"Yes."

"Good."

"But there is something else I have just thought of."

"What is that?"

333

"Do you remember what Coel told us that first evening? Someone tried to poison Tuathal before we got here."

Caedmon nodded, "Another reason for you to say nothing. We might end up eating something unpleasant."

He reached for her hand, squeezing it gently as he pleaded, "Promise me you will not do anything silly. You can tell Calgacus when he gets back but until then, let things take their course."

Emmelia took another deep, calming breath. This was why she needed Caedmon. She prided herself that she was normally confident and capable but sometimes her headstrong streak made her impulsive. Old Myrddin had taught her how to use her mind but there were occasions when her emotions took control. She knew that a sharp temper was a family trait which she had inherited from her mother and which she shared with her uncle, Calgacus. But Caedmon was her balance and she knew that when her emotions clouded her thoughts, she should listen to his gentle promptings. He may not have been a warrior or a craftsman but he understood people and she valued his advice.

"All right," she sighed, her thoughts now more or less under control. "I promise."

Emmelia kept her promise but she did not stop thinking about Coel's death. She watched the faces and movements of Crixus and Eurgain as they helped to carry the old King to his final resting place. As far as she could tell, neither of them betrayed anything except sorrow and a grim determination not to succumb to grief.

Coel was carried to a wide grove where an ancient yew stood in regal isolation as if the surrounding trees were venerating its immense age by maintaining a respectful distance. The trunk of this yew was so thick that four men linking hands could barely reach round its circumference. The tree had stood here for countless generations, its leaves green all year round, marking it as special and sacred. Here, beneath the tree that never died, Coel would be buried.

Broichan directed the burial. Coel was laid in a stone-lined pit that had been dug close to the massive trunk, between the roots. Crixus laid a sword alongside his father while Drust placed a golden torc by Coel's head. Eurgain added a wicker shield which he laid over his grandfather's chest.

Broichan thumped the end of his staff on the ground and stamped his foot to attract the attention of Father Dis, Lord of the

Underworld, alerting the god to the arrival of a famous King into the realm of the dead. Then the druid raised his arms, holding his staff high as he intoned a prayer, asking Dis to care for and reward Coel, the mightiest of kings. That done, he recounted Coel's accomplishments and recited the names of his ancestors, ensuring that there could be no doubt as to the dead King's exalted position.

When the druid finished speaking, the people sang a song of prayer while a heavy stone was placed over the pit and the grave was covered by earth. Most of the onlookers could not see what was happening because the crowd was so great that those at the back were outside the borders of the grove, but once Coel's grave had been covered, Broichan signalled for each member of the crowd to pay their last respects.

Crixus led the way, bowing his head, followed by Drust, whose craggy face was even more haggard than usual. When he moved on, Eurgain took his place, then came the various chieftains. Some spoke aloud, some simply stood in silent contemplation before moving on, while others threw flowers onto the freshly turned earth. Slowly, each member of the crowd filed past the tree before returning to the village in solemn procession.

"What happens now?" Tegan wondered as they made their slow way back to the broch.

"Crixus has arranged a feast," Beatha answered. "After that, the chieftains will meet to decide who the new King will be."

"That should be an interesting discussion," Emmelia commented drily. "Coel disliked Crixus but Drust is a drunkard and Coel's death seems to have hit him hard."

"I don't care," Beatha asserted. "We should keep away from the broch today. I don't want to be anywhere near either of them if I can help it."

It was a fine, warm day, so tables and firepits had been set up outside the broch. Roasted meats, seabirds, eggs, fish, crab, oysters, bread, berries, stewed vegetables and meadow plants were spread out for everyone to help themselves. Great casks of heather ale were broached and left open so that everyone could dip their mug into the dark liquid.

Crixus stood at one end of the spread, welcoming the crowd and inviting them to eat and drink as much as they wished.

Beatha and her companions offered their sympathies although Emmelia received a hostile stare when she looked Crixus in the eye. He said nothing but his expression was dark enough to cause her some concern.

"Beatha's right," she whispered to Caedmon. "Let's stay away from him."

They gathered at the roundhouse that had been set aside for Adelligus and the warriors who had escorted them on the long journey from their home. Despite the fine weather and plentiful food, Runt's son was worried.

"Have you seen how many men Crixus has gathered from his own estates?" he asked.

"There are lots of people here," Beatha replied. "That is natural for such an event as a King's funeral."

"I know," Adelligus frowned. "But there are a lot of big men with swords who are sticking very close to Crixus. My guess is that he has brought in his own enforcers to make sure that he is proclaimed King."

Emmelia said, "He will probably be proclaimed King anyway."

"Whatever happens, it is none of our business," Beatha insisted firmly. "We should keep out of things until Calgacus and Liscus get back. Today we should enjoy the sun and the food that has been provided. Leave Crixus and all the others to themselves."

Following Beatha's advice, they spread cloaks on the ground and laid out the food, waving their arms to ward off the flies which soon buzzed around them. Adelligus was very attentive to Beatha, bringing her a stool and constantly asking whether she needed anything. When she assured him that she was comfortable, he found Emmelia's son, Morcant, and began playing with him, using two short sticks as swords in mock combat. Adelligus, who was renowned as one of the most capable warriors in their village, was defeated several times as he allowed the eight-year-old Morcant to strike him.

"There's a young man in love," Caedmon whispered to Emmelia.

Emmelia gave him an enquiring look.

"What are you talking about?"

Caedmon grinned knowingly and told her, "You really are preoccupied, aren't you? It's not like you to miss things."

"What things?"

"Didn't you notice how attentive he has been to Beatha?"

"Of course. But you are imagining things. She is old enough to be his mother and, in case you hadn't noticed, she has a husband already. Adelligus is just being polite."

Caedmon laughed, "You are so wrapped up in what happened to Coel that you are not paying attention to what is going on around you."

That earned him a frosty look.

"So what have I missed?" Emmelia asked testily.

Caedmon tapped a finger to the side of his nose and leaned close to whisper in her ear, "Adelligus is ignoring Fallar."

Emmelia blinked in surprise. She looked to where Adelligus was now wrestling with her son, letting Morcant straddle him while he lay on the ground. The boy was thumping at Adelligus' chest with his fists while the young warrior pretended to be overwhelmed. When Adelligus at last called out his surrender, he lifted Morcant off, stood and went to pour himself a drink of heather ale. He stood beside Beatha, laughing as he spoke to her.

Fallar was sitting beside her mother, radiant as ever, with her golden hair framing her perfect face. Her large, blue eyes were looking everywhere except at Adelligus and he, in turn, barely seemed to notice her.

Emmelia gave a thin smile.

"I see what you mean," she whispered to Caedmon. "He is trying to gain favour with the mother to impress the daughter. And it seems to be working. Unless I am mistaken, the girl is quite taken with him."

"They more or less grew up together," Caedmon grinned. "But, as I recall, they were usually fighting one another."

"They are no longer children," Emmelia pointed out. "I rather think they enjoy one another's company now."

"Fallar and Tegan have been coming down here quite frequently," Caedmon confided. "Let's hope Calgacus doesn't find out. She is supposed to marry Tuathal, after all."

"She can always change her mind," Emmelia shrugged, remembering the secretive glances the two young women had exchanged.

"And ruin Calgacus' alliance?"

"His alliance may be ruined already," Emmelia said with a frown. "It depends what the new King of the Caledones decides to do. Whoever that King is."

337

Chapter XXXVII

As expected, the chieftains of the Caledones proclaimed Crixus as their new King. He was elected unopposed by an apparently unanimous decision.

"A decision made with swords held to their backs," was Adelligus' wry comment.

Whatever the truth of the matter, Emmelia and the others were untroubled by Crixus because he was fully occupied in negotiations with the other chieftains. For three days there were many meetings and exchanges of gifts. Crixus gave cloaks, swords, jewellery and grants of land to men who pledged their support. In turn, they promised payment of tribute in cattle, sheep, grain or other produce. The broch resounded to the sound of men coming and going. Each day, Crixus dispensed gifts while in the evenings he gave lavish feasts in the great chamber in the centre of the broch, where music played, men and women sang and the young girls danced.

"Crixus isn't only using threats," Emmelia observed sourly. "He's bribed the chieftains into supporting him."

"Of course he did," Caedmon replied. "That's how the world works. What do you expect him to do?"

"I wish you wouldn't be so reasonable," she scowled.

"Unfortunately, young Adelligus was right about something else too," Caedmon continued, ignoring his wife's dark frown. "Crixus has brought in a lot of extra warriors. They are everywhere."

"Yes, and all of Coel's old guards have disappeared."

"You are seeing plots everywhere," Caedmon chided. "A new King will want his own men around him. At least he is leaving us alone."

"So far," Emmelia sighed. "But we are still prisoners and I don't trust him."

She gave Caedmon a worried smile as she added, "I wish Calgacus would come back."

One by one, the visiting chieftains returned to their own homes. Yet even when the last of them had left, Crixus paid no attention to Beatha or any of her companions. For Emmelia, this was almost as bad as if he had forcibly imprisoned them.

"What is he going to do?" she fretted.

Caedmon shrugged, "He is consolidating his power. His thugs are everywhere. Step outside and you'll soon find some of them following you."

Emmelia pulled a face.

"No thanks. I don't think we should draw any more attention to ourselves than we need to."

They waited for two more days; long days that dragged interminably. It seemed to Emmelia that the whole settlement was waiting for something to happen.

Crixus stayed in the broch, an invisible, brooding presence, although his men were everywhere, strutting around and taking pleasure in intimidating the locals. Despite this unwelcome change, the villagers did their best to settle back into a daily routine. Whoever sat in the broch as chieftain, the ordinary folk had no choice except to busy themselves with the tasks of daily life.

The routine was thrown into turmoil when a boat arrived, bringing a messenger who carried the news that Elim mac Conrach had been killed and that Tuathal had been proclaimed High King of Eriu but that the Romans had also landed an army and were attempting to seize control of the island.

Emmelia and Beatha had barely had time to discuss this news when a group of Crixus' warriors stomped their way up the tower to say that the King wished to speak to them. Emmelia's stomach lurched. She knew that this news was what Crixus had been waiting for. Trying to conceal her anxiety, she stood as the warriors' dark shapes filled the doorway.

A broad-shouldered man stabbed his meaty finger at Beatha, Fallar and Emmelia as he snarled, "You three. Nobody else."

His abrupt manner and the menacing presence of the men who backed him made it plain that his instructions were not open to question. This was not an invitation being offered to the King's guests, it was a summons being issued to his prisoners.

"What does he want with us?" Beatha demanded.

She stood proudly, hiding her fear beneath an air of indignation at the peremptory nature of the message.

"How should I know?" the warrior replied with a leer. "But he wants you down there now. So move!"

Tegan clutched baby Sorcha to her while Caedmon placed a protective arm around his terrified children.

"We'll be back soon," Emmelia promised, trying to reassure them.

Little Bonduca began to cry. Caedmon held her tightly, giving Emmelia a wan smile. Then the guards bustled her out of the door and shoved her after Beatha and Fallar.

With their hearts beating rapidly, the three women walked down the winding stair to the main chamber. Above them, Emmelia heard Bonduca's wail of distress, a sound that constricted her chest and made her pulse race even faster. The heavy tramp of the men's feet on the stone steps filled her with dread and brought a memory of the hostile stare that Crixus had given her on the day of Coel's burial. She tried to calm herself but the sound of her daughter's anguish rendered reasoned thought almost impossible.

The warriors ushered the three women into the chamber. As usual, torches burned on brackets set in the stone walls and candles were set on a long table at the far side of the room. Behind the table sat Crixus, a golden torc around his neck. He was smiling fiercely as he watched them cross the rush-strewn, wooden floor towards him but there was no welcome in his smile.

On Crixus' right sat Drust, who seemed to be already more than half drunk, his eyes heavy, his skin blotched and mottled. Emmelia had not seen him since his father's funeral but the old man's death seemed to have hit him hard. He had the look of a man who had lost all hope, as if he could no longer keep up with what was happening around him and had ceased to care. When Emmelia caught his eye, she thought she had rarely seen so much distress in a grown man.

In stark contrast to Drust, Eurgain sat on Crixus' left. As always, the young man was grinning happily, although his expression had an edge to it, as if he knew he was going to enjoy whatever happened next. Instead of the happy expression of the carefree young man they had grown used to, he now wore the manic grin of a bully who was about to inflict unnecessary pain on someone simply because he could. The sight of his face sent a chill down Emmelia's spine.

340

She looked around, seeking some friendly faces but there were none. The guards stood behind them, hard and immovable. Other warriors lined the walls. They were big, brutish men of the sort who always flocked to join a leader who offered the chance to intimidate or bully people who were weaker than themselves. Unkempt and with hungry, hateful eyes, they exuded a menacing air of casual, uncaring violence which terrified Emmelia almost as much as the glint in Crixus' eye.

The only other person in the chamber was Broichan, the druid. He stood behind and to the right of Drust. His face was its usual impassive, disapproving mask as he watched the women approach. Emmelia hurriedly tried to read his mood but it was impossible to tell what he was thinking.

There were no seats available, so they stood in a line facing the new King of the Caledones like supplicants. All three of the women were nervous but Emmelia managed to compose herself enough to conceal it, even though every fibre of her being was wracked by concern.

Beside her, Beatha stood with her head held high. She was a daughter of kings, a chieftain's wife, and she would not give these men the satisfaction of seeing her fear, however nervous she might feel.

On Beatha's left, Fallar did her best to copy her mother's defiance but she could not keep the concern from her face. She was forced to clasp her hands together to prevent them from trembling.

Crixus fixed an iron-hard gaze on Beatha.

"You have heard the news from Eriu?" he snapped.

"Yes."

Crixus' mouth twitched as he rasped, "So it seems my nephew has been successful. Up to a point, anyway. He has been declared High King but now that the Romans have arrived in Eriu, we shall see what happens next. I expect his rule will be short-lived."

Beatha said, "Calgacus will defeat the Romans."

Crixus laughed. It was an unpleasant, chilling sound that echoed malevolently around the chamber. Some of the guards joined in.

Loyal men always laugh when their King is amused, Emmelia thought wryly. She wished that she knew what it was that he found so amusing.

Crixus informed them, "I have bad news for you. Whatever happens in Eriu, Calgacus will not be coming back."

Beatha's entire body froze. Fallar let out a stifled gasp as she gripped her mother's hand, trying to offer some shreds of comfort in the face of Crixus' words which had left little room for any emotions except loss and fear.

"What do you mean?" Emmelia asked, fighting to keep her voice under control so that they would not hear her panic. "What have you heard?"

Crixus' smile was the smile of a man who knew he had won a resounding victory.

He grinned, "I have heard nothing. Yet. But I expect the news will not be long delayed. If the Romans do not kill Calgacus, he will die anyway. It is only a matter of time."

To Emmelia's surprise, it was Broichan who spoke next. The druid took a half pace forwards, his bushy eyebrows furrowed.

"What do you mean?" he demanded.

"Keep out of this, Druid," Crixus warned. "This is none of your concern."

"Of course it is my concern!" Broichan barked. "Calgacus is essential to your father's plans."

Crixus turned in his seat to stare coldly at the tall druid.

"My father is *dead!*" he retorted, slamming his palm on the table to emphasise the final word. "I have plans of my own. If you do not like them, you should sail back to your little island and join all the other pathetic fools who do not know when they are beaten."

Broichan's face grew dark with anger. He drew himself up to his full height as if he were about to unleash a violent outburst but Crixus turned away, ignoring him.

"You must follow the will of the Gods!" Broichan shouted angrily.

Crixus did not look at him. Waving a languid hand, he commanded, "Be silent, Broichan. If you cannot be silent, then leave. The choice is yours."

He looked at the nearest warrior and ordered, "If he speaks again, throw him out."

Broichan was shocked. He did not leave but he took a step back, his face a picture of confusion and outrage. Few men would dare to treat a druid with such contempt but it was evident that Crixus, for so long the butt of his father's scorn, was no longer prepared to remain passive. He radiated certainty and barely-suppressed violence. Beside him, Drust looked down as if the table top in front of him was the most fascinating thing he had ever seen, while Eurgain sat grinning, enjoying every moment of the confrontation as if it had been laid on for his entertainment.

Crixus fixed his eyes on Beatha once again.

"Where was I?" he asked with feigned forgetfulness. He paused theatrically before smirking, "Ah, yes. Calgacus."

"What have you done?" Emmelia asked, her voice scarcely more than a whisper.

Crixus' malevolent leer returned as he surveyed the three women.

"I have decided that the future safety of the Caledones is best served by not opposing Rome," he announced. "To that end, I'm afraid that Calgacus must die. I had hoped that we could present his head to the Romans some time ago but he managed to evade the little trap I set for him."

"You were the false druid who sent those bandits after him!" Broichan raged.

He stepped forwards again but two of the warriors leaped to intercept him. They seized his arms and unceremoniously dragged him towards the door, his feet scrabbling on the floor as he vainly attempted to resist.

"Throw him out!" Crixus cried happily.

"Unhand me!" Broichan yelled, struggling in vain to free himself. "How dare you lay hands on a druid? The gods will strike you down for this insolence."

The two guards paid no attention. The druids had once been all-powerful but their attempts to defeat the Romans had repeatedly failed. Year after year, the sacrifices had been made and still the Romans had conquered. In the eyes of many, the Gods had deserted the Pritani and the druids had lost their long-held status.

Crixus' guards bustled Broichan to the doorway, then roughly pushed him outside. They stood, blocking the door to prevent him returning, impervious to his threats of divine wrath.

Hearing Broichan's furious complaints, Beatha said, "It displeases the Gods to harm a druid."

"He has not been harmed," Crixus shrugged. "Besides, it displeases the Romans to harbour a druid. I have no intention of displeasing the Romans. They have shown that their friends are well rewarded. In fact, I have heard that your own brother has benefited greatly from his alliance with Rome. Is that not so?"

"Cogidubnus is a Roman," Beatha replied scornfully in an attempt to dismiss the jibe.

Yet she knew Crixus was correct. Her older brother was now the virtual ruler of much of the south of Britannia. Supported by Rome, he governed a kingdom that was far greater in extent than anything her father could ever have dreamed of. But Cogidubnus was not the issue for Beatha. Broichan had guessed the truth.

"It was you who tried to kill Calgacus?" she asked in a defiant voice. "Why?"

"For the reward, of course," Crixus explained calmly. "Not only will the Romans be prepared to accept our submission if we have evidence of our loyalty, they will pay handsomely for proof of his death. As they will for your return."

Despite her shock, Beatha frowned in puzzlement.

"What are you talking about?"

"I cannot give them Calgacus' head, but I can give them you," Crixus answered. "It seems your brother, King Cogidubnus, is eager to have you back where you belong."

"That is ridiculous!" Beatha exclaimed. "I have not seen him in thirty years. Why would he want me back?"

"I neither know nor care," Crixus shrugged. "But handing you over to Rome will prove that Calgacus is dead. Moreover, it will ensure that I become their trusted ally."

"You are mad!" Beatha hissed at him.

"On the contrary, I am perfectly sane," he replied coldly. "With Rome's help, the Caledones will become the most powerful tribe in Britannia."

"I will kill myself rather than go back to them," Beatha declared.

Crixus smiled his cold, evil smile as he said, "No, I don't think you will do that. You see, there is more that you need to understand."

He leaned back in his chair, enjoying the moment. Then he went on, "Let me tell you what is going to happen. You will be taken to the Romans and your daughter will become my wife."

"What?" Beatha exploded.

Fallar clutched at her mother, her face contorted with fear and confusion.

Emmelia was frantically looking around, seeking some way of escape but there were too many grinning warriors surrounding them. She briefly considered reaching for the small clasp knife she kept strapped to the inside of her left arm. She was reasonably sure she would be able to reach Crixus before any of his guards could grab her but whether she could kill him was another matter. Even if she could, what would happen then?

She forced herself to clear her mind, to think rationally. Crixus had still not told them everything. She needed to know the full extent of his plans. That should not be difficult because, after so many years in his father's shadow, he seemed more than willing to gloat.

"Fallar will not marry you," Emmelia declared, trying to prompt a response that would explain what he had in mind.

Crixus' eyes turned to her as he stated, "Yes, she will. Both of them will do exactly as I ask or you will be executed."

Emmelia's heart skipped a beat. She gaped at him, scarcely able to believe what she had heard.

Crixus jabbed a finger at her and snarled, "You have confessed to knowing how to perform magic. We have seen you do things in this very hall. How do we know that you did not cast some spell on my father? Perhaps his death was not an accident. Perhaps you were responsible."

Emmelia looked at Eurgain who was grinning more broadly than ever. She saw that the look on his normally open face was one of cruel delight. Like his father, he had unmasked himself. She knew at that moment that he was perfectly capable of killing old Coel.

"It was you!" she shouted, pointing an accusing finger at him.

Eurgain laughed, "I was not even in the room. You were the one who was closest to him when he fell."

Emmelia felt the blood drain from her face. Caedmon had warned her this could happen and now her worst fears were being realised.

Crixus waved a hand, his voice taking on a magnanimous tone as he said, "But we cannot be sure. Perhaps it was an accident. My father was old and he was drunk. I am prepared to be merciful. As long as your friends do as I say, I will keep you alive. You and your children."

"You bastard!" Emmelia hissed. "Calgacus will kill you!"

345

Crixus was not at all concerned by her threat.

"I don't think you were listening to me," he mocked. "Calgacus will soon be dead. Eudaf will see to that."

Emmelia gave a laugh of scorn.

"Eudaf? Calgacus will eat him alive."

"Even the best warrior can fall prey to a knife in the darkness," Crixus reminded her. "Eudaf will succeed soon. If he gets the chance, he will dispose of Tuathal as well."

"What has Tuathal to do with this?" Emmelia wanted to know.

She was still desperately trying to find some way of escaping Crixus' snare but her rational mind was being assailed by waves of fear. The threat to her children had brought her to the verge of panic.

Crixus grinned, "For one thing, his death will mean that young Fallar here will still be in need of a husband. For another, my boys have suffered years of being neglected by their grandfather while he concentrated all his thoughts on helping Tuathal achieve his so-called destiny. Eudaf will enjoy taking his revenge for that. And, of course, it will demonstrate to Rome that we are sincere in our wish to aid them."

"It was you who tried to poison Tuathal," Emmelia realised.

Crixus shrugged.

"It would have suited my plans better if both Tuathal and Calgacus had died before they went to Eriu," he admitted. "But it does not matter. What is important is that my father's plans for an alliance to oppose Rome are dead. There will be no alliance. We will join the Romans."

"Calgacus will come back," Beatha declared defiantly.

"That is most unlikely," Crixus said dismissively. "But even if he escapes the Romans and Eudaf fails to kill him, he will die as soon as he steps ashore here."

The women lapsed into helpless silence in the face of Crixus' certainty. Emmelia felt lost and empty.

It was Beatha who found the strength to shout, "Drust! Will you sit by and let this happen?"

Drust did not look up. His hands rested on the table in front of him, clenched tightly together. His head was bowed, his shoulders slumped in defeat.

346

Grinning, Crixus explained, "My brother is not a great thinker but he knows better than to go against my wishes. Those who support me and my sons will benefit greatly."

Eurgain added, "While those who oppose us will suffer the consequences."

"Indeed," Crixus agreed. "Now, I have many things to do, so I will allow you to return to your chambers. The summer solstice is in five days' time. The hand-fasting will take place then. After that, we will travel to meet the Roman Governor."

He regarded them coldly, adding, "In case you are in any doubt, if you do not do these things willingly, all of your companions will be executed and I will still have my way. I hope I make myself clear."

Fallar was trembling with fear. Beatha's strength had washed away and Emmelia's resolve had been shattered by the thought that her children were in mortal danger. Crixus had indeed made himself clear and she knew beyond all doubt that he would do what he had promised.

With Calgacus doomed, there was no hope left.

Chapter XXXVIII

Calgacus could feel the cold drops of rain pattering against his face. He was glad that he had closed his eyes because it would have been impossible to prevent himself blinking away the drops of water that were striking his face. He was not sure whether the Romans were close enough to have seen such tiny movements but if they were, they would have known he still lived and Scota's deception would have been revealed.

He could hear her now, calling for Amhairgin to bring her the goat. The beast was struggling, alarmed by the smell of blood, but Scota and Amhairgin dragged it close to him, so close that he could smell its musty odour over the stink of the offal that had slopped out from his belly.

He heard Scota give another loud call to the gods to witness what she was about to do. Then he sensed rather than heard her knife expertly slit the goat's throat. Warm wetness sprayed onto his face, the sticky wetness of the luckless beast's lifeblood. Remembering Scota's instructions, he managed to remain still despite the unpleasant addition to the blood and gore that covered him. The goat struggled briefly, its feet scrabbling frantically but soon it too was still. Then he felt its weight on top of his belly.

"Wait," Scota warned him in a fierce whisper.

He lay motionless while she called aloud another prayer. Then she stooped to cut the bonds that had bound his wrists.

"Now it is your turn, Calgacus," she told him. "Stand up. Slowly. Make it look good. Make them believe."

She had coached him in this, told him how to convince the watchers that he had truly been brought back from death, his spirit recalled in exchange for the offering of the goat. Slowly, he twitched his arms and legs before laboriously pushing himself to his feet.

There was a gasp of amazement from the hilltop, a long, drawn-out exclamation of awe that was audible over the sound of the rain that was now falling heavily. Then a great roar swept down the hillside like a physical force as Calgacus drew himself up to his full height and raised his arms to the skies.

He was spattered in blood and gore. His face was sticky with it although the rain was beginning to wash it clean. The great rent in his baggy tunic was wet and heavy with scraps of offal that clung wetly to it. He did not care. The heavy drops of rain felt cool and welcoming, as if he was truly experiencing a re-birth.

Deliberately, he stared at the watching Romans, then he pointed at them before drawing his finger across his throat, a promise of the fate that awaited them. He did not wait for a reaction but turned to look at Scota.

"Let's get away before they send someone to catch us," he said. Then he shot a questioning look at the tall sorceress. "Do you think it worked?"

"They will believe it," she promised.

Runt said, "By Toutatis, I know how it was done and I almost believe it."

Scota had not been happy about revealing the secrets of her magic to Runt but Calgacus had insisted that he be told.

"If you don't show him how it is done, he is likely to try to stop you," he had told her.

So they had shown Runt the leather bag that Calgacus wore over his chest and belly, hung on a cord tied around his neck. The sack contained the innards of one of the mules that had been captured from the Romans. It had become lame and the warriors had already slaughtered it for its tough, stringy meat. Scota had appropriated the guts, being especially sure to place its heart within the sack.

"The robe will hide the bag," Scota had explained. "Especially if we do it early, before it is too light."

"Just don't stab too deep with that knife of yours," Calgacus had warned her.

"That is why you are wearing your leather jerkin underneath," she had joked. At least, he had thought that she was joking.

She had taken a long time over the preparations, checking that he could walk normally and that the sack did not bulge too much under the voluminous robe, then rehearsing their act several times until he assured her he knew what she wanted from him.

"All I need to do is fall down," he told her. "I can manage that."

But there had been more to it than a simple fall. She showed him a tiny bronze box, so small that it was barely large enough to contain a finger ring. She had filled it with a mixture of water and the juice of raspberries. Then she had moved her hand and the box had vanished, as if into thin air. Later, when she had gripped his chin before she pretended to draw the knife across his throat, he had felt the cold metal against his cheek. As she moved the knife, she had also moved her left hand, opening the box to spray the liquid across his throat while he pretended that she was still holding his head. The effect was enough to appear like a spray of blood.

"That is very clever," he said.

"If you do it quickly enough, nobody notices that the knife does not touch the skin," she told him. "That is the trick to most magic. Do it quickly but confidently. Don't give people time to see what you are really doing and always make sure you have distractions to keep their attention away from what really matters."

"That is the trick to winning battles, too," he said with a smile.

Scota had returned his smile with one of her own.

"Just tricks?" she asked. "No magic at all?"

"Only the magic of belief," he told her.

"That is true enough. But, to ensure belief, you must not reveal my secrets. Nobody else must know how this is done."

"I swear it," he promised.

Scota had extracted the same promise from Runt before leading them down the slope to perform their fake sacrifice. Now they were hurrying back up to where their war host chanted and sang their wonder at the feat they had witnessed.

Calgacus hoped the Romans were as impressed as Tuathal's warriors appeared to be because he needed them to be distracted by the performance.

He had done everything he could think of to show how desperate Tuathal was. That was why he had agreed to the night attacks even though he had known they had little chance of success. Despite his warnings, Fiacha Cassan and Sanb had been desperate to take the initiative and eager for the glory of storming the Roman camp but their efforts had soon faltered and Fiacha Cassan had returned nursing a deep gash in his thigh where a *hasta* had sliced across his leg.

"I begin to see what you mean about these Romans," he had muttered to Calgacus as his brother bound the wound.

"Yes, but they are men like us," Calgacus had told him. "And they can be beaten if we do it properly."

Despite the loss of life, the night raids had helped. By now, the Romans would think he had tried every trick he could think of, which would have made Scota's display of magic even more potent. If that did not plant some seeds of fear, he did not know what would. And if the Romans were busy thinking about what they had witnessed, they might not notice his real intentions.

In spite of Scota's warnings to keep her secrets, Calgacus found it difficult not to laugh when he reached the top of the ridge and saw the expressions of Tuathal and their other friends. Young Braine's face was deathly pale, her eyes wide with astonishment. Eudaf looked horrified and even Fiacha Cassan regarded him with an expression of awe.

Calgacus began to appreciate the loneliness that Scota must feel because people once again were wary of being too close to her. Findmall seemed especially reluctant to approach her, as if her display of magic had re-awakened his fear of her dark powers.

Amhairgin helped Calgacus remove the robe, being careful to keep the wet sack well hidden in the tattered and blood-soaked folds.

Calgacus had a worrying thought that somebody would ask why his leather jerkin and his shirt were not ripped, but Scota skilfully diverted everyone's attention away, saying, "Now the Romans have seen my power, they will be terrified of facing us in battle."

"It's a start," Calgacus added. "Now we need to prepare. The soldiers will be frightened but Macrinus won't give them time to sit around and worry. If we are lucky, they will march away. If not, they will attack us soon."

Macrinus could hear the panic spreading through the camp. The men who had stood on the walls had watched the entire scene and had called others to join them. The story swept through the camp like a tidal wave and Macrinus knew that it was already too late to make any attempt to suppress it. The soldiers had seen a man killed, then rise from the dead and it terrified them.

"We must do something," he said urgently. "If we sit here, the men will become too afraid to do anything."

"We should attack," declared Rufus. "The prospect of a fight will stiffen the men's backbones."

"How can we fight such sorcery?" Macer hissed, his eyes wide with fear.

"They are trying to frighten us," Macrinus shot back. "They want to scare us into running away."

Tacitus looked at him, a question on his young face. Macrinus was pleased to see that the shock of witnessing Calgacus' resurrection had not unnerved the young Tribune. Tacitus might be uncertain about what to do but he was not afraid.

"We need to attack now," Macrinus told him. "The longer we wait, the harder it will be to get the men out of the camp."

The harsh light of day had raised more doubts in Tacitus' mind. He frowned, "Are you sure your men can hold the enemy cavalry off? It is not easy to march and fight at the same time, especially when they will need to march sideways if they are to face out to the flanks."

"The lads at the back will need to march backwards," Macrinus replied. "But if anyone can do it, my boys can."

"We will be in serious trouble if they can't," Tacitus observed.

"They know that. Which is why they will do it. Their own lives depend on it."

Macer was still staring out across the rampart, his face taut and strained.

He asked, "What if they use more magic against us?"

"Don't give them the opportunity," Macrinus replied. "We should hit them hard and fast. We need to climb that slope quickly, before their cavalry breaks through our defences."

Rufus grunted his agreement.

"They won't stand when we get in amongst them."

He gave Macer a hard look as he added, "My lads won't let that witchcraft stop them doing their duty."

Macer's face flushed angrily.

"The Ninth can do anything your men can do," he snapped.

"Good," Rufus nodded.

Macrinus interjected, "Remember, if we kill Tuathal, we have won. Press the attack hard."

Tacitus made his decision. In his first months in Britannia he had witnessed the Governor crush a rebellion by launching a bold, decisive attack on a barbarian army that had occupied a hilltop. This situation was the same. The solution would be the same.

"Let us do it!" he decided.

The soldiers were apprehensive. They donned their armour and picked up their weapons but there was a great deal of whispering and grumbling in the ranks.

"Are we really going to attack them, Sir?"

Predictably, the question came from Honorius, a veteran soldier but a habitual complainer.

"Of course we are," Macrinus answered, as if the question was hardly worth considering.

"What about that witch woman?" a voice called from somewhere in the midst of the Cohort.

Murmurs of agreement greeted the question but Macrinus clapped his hands together.

"Enough of that. Are you afraid of a woman?"

He saw from their expressions that they were, so he added, "The only reason she performed that sacrifice was to scare us. She did that because the barbarians know they can't beat us in a fight. They are trying to convince us to give up without a battle."

"But how can we beat them if she brings them back to life after we've killed them?" Honorius asked anxiously.

"We kill them faster than she can resurrect them," Macrinus replied confidently. "Anyway, she is not our problem. All we need to do is keep the cavalry away from the legionary boys while they climb the hill. Let them deal with the witch. We have a nice, simple job. Unless you have all become women yourselves."

He forced a smile as he looked at their worried faces.

"And if you have, you're bloody ugly, especially you, Honorius."

That joke brought laughter and he knew in that instant that they would follow his orders. Despite the rain, despite the unseasonal chill, despite the threat of magic being wielded against them, they prepared to attack.

Macrinus clambered into the saddle. The leather was wet and slippery but the four pommels held him rigidly in place. The rain was hammering down now, drumming on his helmet and armour. As he rode to join Tacitus, the Tribune held out a hand, palm upwards.

"This will make things unpleasant," he observed.

Macrinus recognised that the young Tribune was masking his nervousness by discussing trivial matters.

He said, "It will dampen the barbarians' spirits more than ours. Everything Calgacus has done has been designed to avoid a pitched battle. So let's do what he doesn't want."

Tacitus gave a determined smile.

"Yes. I don't think the Governor would be happy if we retreated without a fight."

"Then perhaps you should order the advance," Macrinus suggested softly.

Smiling grimly, Tacitus raised his arm and pointed to the hilltop where a mob of barbarians waited.

"Forwards!" he called.

The command was acknowledged by the swishing trudge of feet on wet grass and the clink of metal armour as the troops began their advance.

As soon as they left the camp, the two legionary Cohorts deployed into manipular formation. Macer's Ninth were on the right, Rufus' Second on the left. They marched in silence, the standards held high but hanging limp and forlorn under the heavy rain. The fanned plumes of the Centurions' helmets led the way. As in everything the Romans did, the advance was an impressive display of organisation, discipline and power.

"Quickly now!" Tacitus reminded them as he and Macrinus rode after the legionaries.

Macrinus waved a hand to his Auxiliary Cohorts, urging them into place. They hurried into position on the flanks, forming a barricade of spears on either side. Another group of spearmen took up position at the rear of the formation, closing the gap that would be vulnerable to the swift-moving barbarian cavalry.

"Remember, lads. Keep moving!" Macrinus called.

With every unit in position, the Roman formation resembled a box, with walls of armoured spearmen on either flank and at the rear, and the legionaries in the centre. They had deployed quickly but the enemy had reacted almost as rapidly.

"Here they come," Tacitus warned.

Macrinus looked to either side. Chariots and horsemen were already galloping down the slope, charging at the sides of his defensive box. The flanking units performed the drill expertly, turning to face outwards, spears levelled, yet still climbing the hill, stepping awkwardly, slipping and sliding but maintaining their slow advance. Ahead of them, Macer and Rufus slowed the pace of their own march so that the Auxiliaries could keep up.

"That's the stuff, lads!" Macrinus shouted encouragingly. "Keep together!"

"It's working!" Tacitus breathed. "Oh, well done!"

This was in response to a barbarian warrior being skewered by a *hasta* when he dared to come too close to the line of spears.

Frustrated in their first attack, the barbarians wheeled round to the rear but Macrinus turned, signalling to the Centurions who led the rearguard. They deftly turned their men about, shouting at them to keep marching backwards. Some men stumbled but the line held. Barbarians leaped down from chariots to rush at the soldiers but the deadly spears kept them at bay and the inexorable advance continued.

Some men went down, felled by javelins. Macrinus hated seeing that. If a man was unable to keep pace, he was abandoned and would be surrounded by barbarians who would stab and hack until the soldier was dead. Yet only a few men fell and the Roman discipline held. Slowly, they climbed the long slope.

"The barbarians are predictable," Tacitus remarked.

"They only have one tactic," Macrinus agreed. "And it is not working."

With the enemy cavalry nullified, the legionaries soon neared the top of the ridge where the barbarian war host was gathered.

"Now!" Tacitus cried.

As if in answer, the legionaries hurled a volley of *pila* at the barbarians. Three more paces and they threw another volley. The long, heavy javelins caused carnage, killing or wounding scores of warriors. Many who were lucky enough to escape unharmed found their shields had been pierced by the long shafts which had bent when the wooden pins that secured the metal spike to the shaft snapped on impact. The heavy javelins dragged the shields down and rendered them useless.

"Swords!" the voices of the Centurions called in unison, the word sounding clear above the din of battle. "Charge!"

355

Macer and Rufus led their men against the ragged horde of barbarians. The last few paces were covered at a sprint, huge shields used to batter men aside and short, stabbing swords ready to deal death.

The barbarians fought back ferociously, hurling darts and javelins, and stabbing with their own spears. The two lines clashed with a tremendous, ear-splitting cacophony which momentarily drowned out all other sounds. On the long, wet ridge, men fought and died in bloody, hand-to-hand combat.

Macrinus scanned the hilltop. He saw Tuathal, the young High King, on a chariot behind the lines, exhorting his men to throw back the assault. Macrinus sought out Calgacus but he could see no sign of him. Perhaps he was dead already.

On the flanks and at the rear, the enemy cavalry had almost given up their futile attacks. Some had ridden down to plunder the Roman fort but most of them were pulling back, gathering on the flanks to watch the infantry battle. They had failed to halt the advance and now the outcome would be decided by the massed footmen.

Macrinus knew this was the critical moment. He also knew that the heavily armoured legionaries were virtually invincible in these situations.

"Push!" he urged. "Push forwards!"

The legionaries pushed and, almost as if by some unseen signal, the barbarians broke and ran.

"Yes!"

Macrinus could not conceal his elation.

"Now finish it!" he yelled.

"We've won!" Tacitus exclaimed as Rufus and Macer led their men in pursuit of the fleeing enemy.

When he reached the top of the low ridge, Caecilius Macer shouted aloud in delight. He would never admit it to anyone but the sight of Calgacus' resurrection had shocked him. As they had climbed the hill, he had constantly looked for the big warrior but there had been no sign of him. Nor, to Macer's immense relief, was there any hint of the witch-woman casting magic spells. Instead, the barbarians on the hilltop had screeched and yelled defiance while their horsemen and chariots had vainly tried to halt the Roman advance. Macer had doggedly plodded on, snarling at his men to keep moving as he attempted to bury his own fears beneath a fierce mask.

The climb up the wet, slippery slope had seemed to take an age because of the need to slow the advance so that the Auxiliaries could protect the flanks from the barbarian cavalry but gradually, step by step, the distance was closed and Macer could make out individual faces among the wild-haired savages.

"Nearly there!" he shouted in encouragement. "Ready javelins!"

The *pila* flew, then the legionaries drew their swords. Macer pulled his own *gladius* from its sheath at his left side. It was time.

"Charge!"

As the legionaries surged forward, Macer saw that the barbarian line was thinner than it had appeared from the camp. There were fewer of them than he had first thought. He felt a thrill of exhilaration that swept away all his fears.

"Kill them all!" he screamed, determined to punish the savages for having caused him such anxiety. How dare they try to intimidate the soldiers of Rome? Now Macer would show them what real terror was.

He ran with his men, close behind the front rank as the line of shields crashed home. Yells, grunts, shouts and screams of agony filled the morning air, accompanied by the clash of metal striking metal, the dull thud of swords hitting wicker and leather shields, and the unmistakeable sound of blades plunging into flesh. The deadly short swords that had brought the Romans so many victories stabbed and stabbed, and the barbarian line crumpled backwards.

Macer blocked a spear with his shield, stabbed forwards and felt the tip of the wickedly sharp blade sink into exposed flesh. His opponent screamed in pain as Macer drew the blade back, but even as he fell, the wounded barbarian fought on, trying to stab under Macer's shield. Macer kicked the spear aside, crouched down and stabbed again.

Push, block, stab. The familiar routine, the tactics that the legionaries practised day after day. All along the line, they pushed and stabbed in unison. After only a few moments, the crumbling barbarian defence broke.

As they always did when faced by the awesome power of the heavy Roman infantry, the enemy turned and ran.

Macer was not done with them. These men had defied Rome. They had defied *him*. Worse, they had scared him with their ferocious night attacks and their dark magic. Now Macer gave vent to his desire for retribution.

"After them! Kill them all!"

Ahead of him was a broken jumble of land, flanked by trees and scrub, leading down through a maze of rocky hummocks towards a low, marshy plain and a distant lake. Macer knew that it was poor terrain for horses but his men could hunt the fleeing barbarians easily enough. His main fear now was that the enemy would escape.

"Kill them all!" he screamed again. "Don't let them escape!"

Searching for targets, he saw a young man on an ornate chariot. The barbarian wore a golden torc around his neck. The chariot was swaying as its driver tried to steer down the rear slope but the horses were struggling to cope with the uneven ground and the chariot was bouncing alarmingly. It stopped near the trees and both men leaped down, abandoning the vehicle and running for cover.

Macer's heart leaped. They had already achieved victory, now he had a chance to catch one of their chieftains. Perhaps it was the High King himself.

"After them! Kill that one!" he shouted, waving his sword arm to drive his men on.

Scenting a chance for slaughter and plunder, the legionaries charged down the slope, swords eager for blood. They knew that, in spite of the barbarians' ghastly sorcery, they had won this battle and now it was time to seal the victory by slaughtering as many foes as they could.

Chapter XXXIX

Scota sat under a tall birch, draping the hood of her cloak over her head to ward off the drips that fell from the dark canopy of leaves above her. The sound of the rain was loud in the woods, the downpour drumming a tattoo that was almost loud enough to drown out the blares of the carnyx horns that were blasting defiance at the Romans from the top of the ridge.

All around her, huddled down behind trees or among the bushes, concealed in the shadowy gloom of the dull forest, were hundreds of warriors. They sat or crouched in virtual silence, ignoring the rain that soaked them and listening intently to the noise of the battle beyond the edge of the woodland. Scota felt she should say something to encourage them but she could think of nothing to say. She suspected that she would only make things worse. Most of them, even the men of the Scotti who had known her for years, refused to meet her gaze. She had performed her greatest feat of magic in bringing Calgacus back from the dead but now she was paying the price. Nobody wanted to be close to a witch with such dark power. There was a space around her, an almost tangible barrier between her and the others.

She glanced to her left, where Findmall sat beside young Braine. Both of them turned their heads away when they saw her looking at them. Braine, in particular, seemed afraid of her.

Drawing on the habits of a lifetime, Scota withdrew into herself, maintaining an impassive expression on her face. To anyone watching, she would appear calm and relaxed but inside, her mind raced. She closed her eyes as she sought to follow the unseen battle beyond the trees, trying to discern what was happening.

She was distracted by the sound of horses picking a slow way through the trees. She looked up in surprise to see Eudaf approaching, leaning down over the neck of a horse as he ducked beneath the branches. He led a second, riderless horse behind him. He stopped and dismounted, looping the reins over a low-hanging branch, then walked over to Scota.

She looked at him, grateful that at least one person dared to approach her.

"Hello, Eudaf," she said as pleasantly as she could, the words sounding trite while a battle raged only a hundred paces away.

Eudaf tried to smile but she saw that he was not immune to the fear that she inspired. He looked at her anxiously, chewing at his lower lip.

"What is it?" she prompted.

She wanted to concentrate on the battle, wanted to know whether Calgacus' plan was working, but Eudaf demanded her attention.

"I am worried about Tuathal," he said softly, his voice barely audible over the background patter of rain and the cries and clashes of combat. "The Romans are coming and he insists on staying near the fighting. He may be killed."

Scota nodded, "That may happen to any of us. But Fiacha Cassan is with him. He will protect Tuathal with his life."

"That may not be enough," Eudaf objected. "And if Tuathal dies, we are lost."

"The Gods will decide his fate," she told him.

She became aware of Braine edging closer in an attempt to listen to their hushed conversation but she kept her eyes on Eudaf. She did not need her skills at reading people to see his distress. A blind man could have read that the young man was deeply worried.

He blurted, "If he dies, can you bring him back to life? The way you did with Calgacus?"

So that was it. She should have guessed; it was the question that they all wanted to ask but that nobody had dared to voice.

She paused before saying, "There is a big difference between a sacrifice and any other death. What I did this morning was powerful magic, requiring much prayer and preparation. I am afraid that it cannot be done except in very special circumstances."

"So if Tuathal or Calgacus are killed they cannot be brought back?"

Something in his demeanour had changed. She had expected her words to increase his concern but his immediate reaction was quite different. He hid it well but, for an instant, Scota thought she detected a spark of relief in his eyes.

360

She explained, "I am sorry, but I cannot help anyone who dies in the battle today."

Eudaf nodded. The subtle change in his stance puzzled her. She saw that her words had energised him but she was prevented from probing any further by the arrival of Calgacus and Runt who strode through the woods as if they owned them.

Their hair was plastered around their faces, their clothes sodden and dripping but they emanated an aura of supreme confidence. Scota saw the impact their arrival had on the warriors. Men sat up straight, their faces expectant and alive. Calgacus had no need to make speeches. Men knew what he could do. They knew that he had planned Elim's defeat and had seen him kill the old High King. They had seen him die and return to life. What could he not achieve?

"All ready?" he asked. "They will be here soon."

"We are ready," Scota answered calmly.

Calgacus called softly to the men, "Remember to keep out of sight until I give the word."

Nods and the eager raising of weapons in readiness were the reply.

Calgacus gave Eudaf a quizzical look.

"Shouldn't you be with Tuathal?"

Eudaf licked his lips nervously. Tugging the hood of his cloak closer around his face, he explained, "He wants me to look after Braine. I brought a horse for her."

He fluttered a nervous hand to indicate the two horses.

"Good idea," Calgacus nodded.

Braine had edged close. Her expression was still tight with concern, her lips a thin line on her pale, young face but she stated, "I want to watch what happens."

"Watch from horseback," Calgacus told her. "If anything goes wrong, you should be able to get away."

"I thought you said you could beat them," Braine accused.

"Nothing is certain in battle," he shrugged.

She gave him a withering stare as she demanded, "Why did you not simply go to speak to their commander and kill him, the way you killed my father?"

There was a moment's awkward silence before Calgacus replied, "Because Romans do not lose heart over the loss of a leader."

361

His answer did not appear to satisfy the girl who continued to glare at him.

Scota put in, "You cannot change the past, Braine. What is done is done."

Braine gave her a scornful look.

"And it was you who did it!" she snapped. "All of you."

She swept her arm to take in all of them with a single gesture as she cried, "You all betrayed him. And look where it has brought us!"

Tears mingled with the rain on her cheeks as she wailed, "I hate you all!"

Scota made a tentative move towards her but Braine angrily brushed her off.

"Leave me alone! You should worry about yourselves. The Romans will kill you all."

"No," Calgacus responded sharply. "Believe me. We can beat them. We must. It is either that or submit to them. Is that what you would prefer?"

Braine's response was an uncertain shrug as she lowered her head, unable to hold his gaze. Her eyes flickered briefly towards Eudaf but she hurriedly looked away.

Scota felt sorry for her. Braine was young, frightened and confused. Scota suspected that the girl did not truly know what she wanted. Fear of the future, stoked by memories of the violence and bloodshed of the past few days, had overwhelmed Braine's senses.

Calgacus asked, "Did I ever tell you about my sister? She was Queen of a people called the Iceni. They were allies of Rome."

Braine looked up uncertainly as she waited to hear what he had to say.

Calgacus went on, "Bonduca's husband thought he was a friend of Rome but when he died, the Emperor decided he wanted to seize the kingdom for himself. The Iceni were rich, you see. They had good farmland and bred strong horses. The Emperor wanted their wealth, so he sent soldiers to take over, to make the Iceni subjects rather than allies."

Braine refused to look at him, so Scota prompted the story by asking, "What happened?"

"My sister dared to protest. It did no good, of course, because Rome does not tolerate dissent. She was flogged. Her daughters were raped and would have been killed if I had not arrived in time to save their lives. That treatment was too much for the Iceni. They rebelled. They had some success but in the end there was a great battle, just like today."

He shook his head at the memory as he finished, "The Iceni were slaughtered."

"What happened to your sister?" Scota asked even though she knew the answer.

"She died."

He looked at Braine as he added, "Rome does not have friends. That is why we must fight them. If we accepted their false offers of friendship, we would soon be slaves. Do you understand that?"

Grudgingly, Braine meekly nodded her head.

He assured her, "Today it will be us who do the slaughtering. Soon, Tuathal will lead them into our trap. But that does not mean there is no danger, so stay out of sight until the battle is over. Go with Eudaf."

"I want to stay," Braine protested although there was little conviction in her voice.

"This will be no place for you," Calgacus told her. "We all want to know that you are safe from harm."

"What about Scota? She is staying."

"We need her," he said simply.

Runt chipped in, "Listen, that's Sanb leading the cavalry to attack."

Calgacus turned, cocking his head to one side.

"Then we don't have long to wait. Get on the horse."

Reluctantly, Braine allowed Calgacus to lift her up into the saddle.

"Go a bit deeper into the trees," he ordered. "Make sure you keep out of sight until we spring the trap."

Eudaf nodded as he mounted his own horse.

"We will."

He hesitated, looking around, as if waiting for something, but when he saw that Calgacus was still watching him, he eventually turned his horse and led Braine deeper into the woods.

"He's jumpy," Runt commented softly. "It's probably best to keep him out of harm's way."

"He's young," Calgacus said. "Both of them are. The reality of war can frighten people."

"Braine is confused and afraid," Scota agreed. "And Eudaf is worried about Tuathal."

She frowned as she added, "But I think there is something more. He was certainly giving you some strange looks while you were talking to Braine."

Calgacus shrugged, "At least the two of them should be safe. We have other things to worry about at the moment."

He watched until the two riders were swallowed by the wet shadows, then resumed his place by the tree. He was just in time. The sound of the two armies meeting was like a clap of dull thunder that rolled along the hillside. Calgacus reached over his shoulder to draw his sword from his back. He dismissed Braine and Eudaf from his thoughts. There would be time to worry about them after the Romans had been beaten.

"Be ready, lads," he called. "It won't be long now."

The battle raged along the ridge as the Romans pushed forwards, flinging themselves at the men of Eriu. The fighting was furious but it did not last long. There was no need for Tuathal to give a signal because the line broke and men began to run, trying desperately to escape from the deadly Roman swords. In an instant, four thousand warriors were fleeing, leaping over tussocks and dodging around rocks as they tried to escape down the broken ground of the reverse slope.

Fiacha Cassan, sword in hand, bellowed in frustration even though he knew this retreat was essential. He had listened to Calgacus' plan and knew it was a good one but his pride had led him to believe that the warriors of Eriu could defeat the legionaries without the need for Calgacus' stratagem. Now he saw that was a vain hope. The heavily armoured Romans had smashed into the war line and had broken it easily. Fiacha Cassan joined the flight, doing his best to ignore the protests of pain from his injured leg.

He looked for Tuathal and saw the young High King's chariot charging towards the woods. Cursing, Fiacha Cassan raced after him. The chariot careered towards the trees, bouncing wildly. Old Amhairgin hauled it to a stop and Tuathal was out, running for cover. Hundreds of men streamed after him, some of them genuinely terrified by what pursued them.

Amhairgin joined the flight but Tuathal paused at the tree line, turning to look back. Fiacha Cassan ran to him.

"Get into the trees!" the tall warrior shouted.

364

"As soon as I know they are coming for me," Tuathal replied calmly.

"The time is now!" Fiacha Cassan urged.

He grabbed Tuathal's arm and dragged him into the woods. As they fled, he glanced back over his shoulder to watch the Romans. He knew that Calgacus' plan depended on this moment.

Under his breath, he implored, "Chase us, you bastards. Break formation."

"Yes!" Tuathal breathed. "They are coming!"

"Too bloody close," muttered Fiacha Cassan.

They dodged between the trees, Fiacha Cassan limping more heavily with every stride and Tuathal slowed by the pain in his injured side. He was clutching at it, clamping his left hand against his ribs to ease the pain.

"Come on!" yelled Fiacha Cassan as the sound of the pursuit grew louder.

He could not tell how far they had come. Surely it was far enough, but there was no sign of Calgacus' ambush. Ducking and weaving, batting away wet leaves and branches, they struggled through the deeply-shadowed forest.

Then it was too late because the leading Romans had caught up with them. Fiacha Cassan could hear the wet thumps of their footsteps close behind, the jangle and clink of armour and the rasping of laboured breathing. There was no sign of any other warriors; they had all vanished into the woods, leaving Tuathal and him behind.

Swearing, he shoved Tuathal ahead and spun round to face the pursuers.

He was only just in time. Four legionaries, running quickly despite the weight of their armour, were almost on him, their swords glinting dully in the sodden gloom of the woodland.

Fiacha Cassan roared defiance. He leaped to the attack, swinging his great longsword at the first man. The Roman ducked aside, avoiding the blow but Fiacha Cassan swung again, wielding his blade with a speed that caught the legionary by surprise. The edge of the blade smashed into the Roman's helmet, driving the man to the ground.

Fiacha Cassan screamed as he dodged an assault from the second Roman. He bludgeoned the man's shield, smashing shards of wood and paint from the layered wood and forcing the soldier back, but there were two more opponents and more were appearing on the periphery of his vision. His only chance was to use the superior length of his sword to keep the Romans at a distance. Even that was a slim hope because their armour protected them from his wild slashes. Yet he had no choice but to keep flailing at them; once they closed with him, he was doomed.

He danced back, spun, launched a blistering attack, then crouched low to hack at a Roman's legs. His sword bit home, felling the man in a scream of agony.

Fiacha Cassan sprang upright but there were too many opponents. A large shield smashed into his left side, knocking him off balance. He flailed his own sword but could only half block a *gladius* which seared across his right forearm, gouging a splash of bright blood.

Fiacha Cassan staggered back, snarling at his enemies, but more swords were coming for him. He lashed out, catching another Roman on the hand, severing two fingers and forcing the soldier to drop his short sword. But it was not enough. He was hemmed in, backed against a tree and two legionaries were crowding at him, blocking him in with their shields, giving him no room to use his sword. Their blades lunged at him.

Desperately, Fiacha Cassan parried one blow that would have disembowelled him but the second *gladius* drove at his right side, slicing through his leather tunic before glancing from a rib and bringing an involuntary grunt of pain to his throat. He sagged back against the tree, knowing the next blow would kill him.

But the blow did not come. Both Romans were knocked aside as Calgacus leaped into them. As they stumbled backwards, his huge sword flashed, turning one man's face to pulp and crushing the helmet of the second.

All around, the trees were suddenly full of warriors who charged at the Romans, picking them off individually, surrounding them and hacking them down, leaping onto their backs to drag them to the ground to be butchered.

Fiacha Cassan slumped to the wet turf, his back pressed against the trunk of the tree.

"You took your time," he muttered to Calgacus. "I thought I was going to have to kill them all myself."

"We thought you could run a bit faster than you did," Calgacus replied.

"Tuathal?"

"Safe."

Fiacha Cassan nodded contentedly.

"You weren't bad for an old man," he gasped through his pain. "I am glad you arrived when you did. I confess I was in a spot of trouble."

"You weren't bad either," Calgacus returned. "But that makes us even, I think."

Fiacha Cassan nodded wearily.

"Aye, we have saved each other's life. Now we are even. But I'm afraid you will need to kill the rest of them without me."

Calgacus smiled with grim determination.

"Don't worry. We will."

And the men of Eriu swarmed through the trees, hunting their enemies.

Chapter XL

"Kill them all!" roared Caecilius Macer, repeating his mantra.

His men were chasing the barbarians now, cutting down any who were too slow to escape. The Romans were slowed by the weight of their armour but only marginally. Part of the legionary training was to learn to walk, run and jump while wearing full armour. Over a short distance, the heavy equipment was no real impediment.

The barbarians were nimble but there were so many of them trying to flee and the ground on the far side of the ridge was so uneven and wet that many of them slipped or stumbled. The legionaries cut them down with brutal savagery before running after their next quarry.

Macer urged his men on. The fear of magic had affected them all through the long climb up the slope but the knowledge of victory had brought relief from the terror of the barbarians' supernatural power and had transformed their fear into a burning desire for vengeance. Savage blood-lust now gripped the young men of Macer's Cohort as they pursued their fleeing enemy.

Macer himself was not immune to the desire to lash out at the barbarians but he was also desperate to achieve glory. He knew that their objective was to kill the High King and he was convinced that the young man who wore a golden torc and who had abandoned his brightly decorated chariot to seek refuge in the woods was the man they were after.

"Kill that one!" he yelled, pointing with his sword.

The barbarian leader was joined by another warrior, a tall man who carried a long sword. The two of them vanished into the sodden shadows of the woodland with Macer's men in pursuit.

Macer ran towards the trees. He dashed past the abandoned chariot, following the hundreds of barbarians who were already vanishing into the dank shadows of the woods.

The rain seemed to ease as Macer ducked under the overhanging boughs of the first trees. Then he was in the woods, slowed by uneven ground and rain-slick tree roots. He saw one of his men catch a wounded barbarian who had fallen. The short sword jabbed down, the fallen man screamed and the soldier was moving on, using his large shield to push aside the thorny branches of a tangled bush.

Shouts, screams and yells echoed through the forest, muffled and disorienting. The wet sound of heavy footfalls and the metallic jingle of armour and weapons filled Macer's ears but an urgent voice cut through the bedlam.

"Sir!"

Macer turned. It was the *signifer*, still carrying the Cohort's standard, trying to keep the tall flag from catching in the trees.

"What is it?" Macer snapped.

He wanted to continue the chase, wanted to kill the barbarian leader and snatch the golden torc for himself. Already, the man and his companion were out of sight, lost somewhere up ahead. Macer knew that his legionaries were still chasing the High King but he wanted to be there in person. Now the *signifer* was tugging at his arm.

"The Second aren't following, Sir. They've stopped on the ridge."

"Bugger them," Macer rasped. "We can end this war if we kill their King."

"But we can't see a thing in here, Sir," the *signifer* said insistently. "We could be trapped."

"The savages are running," Macer retorted angrily.

Then he swore. He had been a soldier long enough to know that the *signifer* was right. They could not afford to be cut off from the other units. But the barbarians were beaten and Macer's men had a chance to kill more of the savages.

He decided, "We'll pull back as soon as we've killed their King."

The *signifer* looked doubtful but he nodded, "Very good, Sir."

He had barely uttered the words when the world exploded around them.

The screams became a roar, like a gigantic lion bellowing a challenge through the trees. Where there had been only fleeing barbarians, a horde of warriors suddenly leaped into view. They came from behind trees and bushes, they appeared from folds in the ground. Some even dropped down from the branches above the

Romans' heads. Spears and sword glinted dully in the rain-soaked woodland shadows as they swept through the forest, swamping the scattered and isolated Romans.

From the gloom ahead, where the limping High King had disappeared, Macer saw the figure of Calgacus waving his huge sword, commanding the savages to the attack. There was no sign of the legionaries who had charged ahead and Macer's stomach turned to ice as the realisation of what had happened struck him like a hammer blow. There was only one thing to do now.

"Run!" he yelled. "Back to the ridge! Re-form!"

He heard the *signifer* scream. Whirling, he saw that two barbarians had jumped out from nowhere. The *signifer* was writhing helplessly on the ground, blood bright at his throat, and one of the barbarians was lifting the Cohort's standard from the dying man's feeble grip.

Macer shouted a challenge, leaping at the barbarian. He swept his shield forwards, smashing into the man, then stabbed with his sword. The blade missed its target because Macer was forced to block a stunningly fast thrust from the second man's spear. He blocked with his shield, half-crouched, then closed the gap, driving forwards. Knocking the spear upwards with the rim of his shield, he stabbed viciously. The barbarian stumbled back, hitting the trunk of a tree and the sword plunged into his belly.

Macer yelled in delight, twisting the blade and driving it upwards before pulling back and turning to face the first man.

He froze. He was no longer facing one barbarian, he was facing a horde. They came charging towards him, leaping and dodging through the trees, and Macer knew that he had no time to escape.

Among the enemy was Calgacus, his long sword held high in a two-handed grip.

"Time to die, Roman," Calgacus snarled in Latin.

Macrinus and Tacitus galloped to the top of the ridge. On the left, the men of Rufus' Cohort were still formed up, waiting, but on the right, Macer's men were widely scattered as they pursued the fleeing enemy. Some were charging headlong down the far side of the ridge, dodging their way through the broken, marshy ground. Others were in the trees, hunting the barbarians.

Rufus appeared, his dark, swarthy features clouded by anger.

"The bloody fools have left a gap!" he shouted, pointing to the right flank of the ridge.

Tacitus looked right but could see only the leading men of the Auxiliary flank detachment hurrying to the top of the slope.

"The enemy are beaten!" he shouted back. "Pursue them!"

"Not with cavalry threatening our backsides," Rufus growled. After a moment, he added a curt, "Sir."

"He's right," said Macrinus swiftly, allowing Tacitus no time to voice a protest at Rufus' insubordination. "We should form here until we see what their cavalry are going to do."

"Surely they will run," Tacitus insisted.

"Not so far," Macrinus countered, gesturing to where the barbarian horsemen were lurking on the flanks, resting their mounts for what could be a fresh onslaught.

"We must find the High King and kill him," Tacitus declared, trying to re-establish his authority.

"We don't have enough horses," Macrinus replied. "We can't chase them until their cavalry give up the fight."

Tacitus raised his eyes to the leaden sky. He felt as if everything he said was being thwarted by these two rugged soldiers.

"We can at least try," he grumbled testily.

"We should stick to your original plan," Macrinus advised. "Stay together and march to Tara. If we seize that place, we can demand their surrender."

Tacitus frowned uncertainly. His eyes scanned the battlefield, seeking some inspiration.

At that moment they heard the roar from the woodland, a dull, low sound of such ferocity that Tacitus felt a stab of fear in his chest.

"What in Jupiter's name was that?" Rufus asked.

Macrinus whirled in his saddle. Jabbing a finger at one of Tacitus' escort, he shouted, "Get the Auxiliary Cohorts up here. Fast, man! Tell them to form up on the right."

"What is it?" Tacitus demanded.

Rufus let out a groan of despair.

"Jupiter, Juno and Minerva!"

Further down the slope, the enemy army that had been fleeing was suddenly transformed. The thousands who had been chased by a few hundred Romans turned. From behind the rocks, from out of the bushes, from the long grass of the marshland, hundreds more warriors sprang into view, rushing at the scattered Roman soldiers. In the space of two heartbeats, the hunters had become the hunted.

Tacitus gaped, unable to grasp the enormity of what was happening before his eyes.

Rufus summoned one of his men who carried a *buccina*.

"Sound the rally!" he barked.

To the rest of his Cohort, he called, "Stand firm, lads! We hold this ground until the Ninth can re-form alongside us."

"If any of them live long enough to get back to us," Macrinus muttered under his breath.

Tacitus was in a welter of helplessness. Everywhere he looked, barbarians were swarming over the isolated men of the Ninth, dragging them down, slaughtering them. Behind him, Macrinus' two Cohorts were hurrying to reach the top of the ridge but he saw that a horde of enemy cavalry was now galloping from the right, heading into the gap where Macer's Cohort should have stood.

He looked at Macrinus.

"What do we do?" he groaned.

"We fight or we die," Macrinus replied grimly. "You should leave. Take your escort and ride as hard as you can."

Tacitus was appalled at the suggestion.

"Never! I will stay with my men."

Despite the enveloping horror, Macrinus smiled.

"Not the wisest decision you'll ever make," he observed wryly.

"It is the right decision."

"I hope so."

Tacitus pointed to the woods to the right.

"Look, some of Macer's men are escaping."

Legionaries ran from the trees, red-faced, exhausted but pumping their arms and legs as they tried to regain the ridge. Behind them, the dull greens and browns of the woodland became a dark mass as hundreds upon hundreds of barbarians appeared. They stopped at the tree-line, chanting and cheering.

"Calgacus!" Macrinus breathed as he saw the giant warrior step forwards. "But he's too late."

The Auxiliary Cohorts had arrived. They formed up, long spears ready, blocking the approach of the enemy horsemen who swerved aside, unwilling to charge home against such a formidable defence. The men of Macer's Ninth ran towards them, seeking sanctuary in the ranks. There were pitifully few of them. From the open slope below, a handful more managed to run or fight their way back to re-join Rufus' Cohort but Tacitus had lost almost a quarter of his fighting force and the remaining Romans were now seriously outnumbered by a jubilant enemy.

The warriors who pursued the ragged remnants of Macer's Cohort halted fifty paces from the Roman troops, chanting, jeering and yelling taunts.

"What are they waiting for?" Tacitus wondered. "Are they afraid to fight us?"

Another great cheer went up from the barbarians. The Romans turned to see the witch woman step out to stand beside Calgacus. She walked slowly forwards, throwing back her hood to reveal a mane of red hair that was instantly darkened by the heavy rain.

"What now?" Macrinus asked aloud.

Another figure stepped forwards from the crowd. Tuathal Techtmar, High King of Eriu, joined the witch. The two of them stood a few paces ahead of Calgacus.

"That's all we need," Macrinus groaned, more to himself than to anyone else.

The sorceress's hands appeared from under her cloak as she extended her arms in front of her. Then she moved her arms quickly in an intricate pattern, folding, twisting and waving. When she stopped, she held up a trophy in her right hand. It had appeared from nowhere. One instant, she had been moving her arms, the next they were still and the fingers of her right hand were clenched into the hair of a decapitated head.

"Macer!" gasped Tacitus.

Even as they watched, another barbarian held aloft the standard taken from Macer's Cohort and added to the taunting by waving the banner triumphantly.

Tacitus shot an appalled look at Macrinus.

"What do we do?"

"We fall back. A fighting retreat."

"Retreat?"

"If we stay here, they will surround us. We can't hold out forever."

"The camp! We can hold them off if we get back there."

"For how long?" Macrinus challenged dourly. "There is no water and we have precious little in the way of food. Besides, there are already some of their cavalry in the camp."

"Then what are you suggesting?" Tacitus frowned.

"We must fight our way back to Domnan's village. We can be supplied by sea."

"That's a day's march!" Tacitus protested.

"Would you rather die here?" Macrinus asked him. "We must try."

Tacitus hesitated but the decision was made for him when all other sounds were drowned by the roar of the barbarians. Tuathal drew his sword and swept it forwards giving an unmistakable signal, unleashing his army against the Romans.

Macrinus grabbed at Tacitus' arm.

"Get into the middle of the Cohort!"

Tacitus hurried to join Rufus who had returned to the centre of his Cohort, where he stood calling encouragement to his men.

Tacitus flinched as the enemy crashed into the leading ranks of Romans. Men and horses were sweeping round, surrounding the three surviving Cohorts. Tacitus was appalled at how many enemy there were and at the ferocity of their attack. He looked for Macrinus but the Centurion had not followed him. Instead, he had galloped across the thirty paces that separated the nearest Auxiliary maniple from Rufus' men. Ignoring the charging barbarians, Macrinus had skidded to a halt, leaped down from the saddle and pushed into the ranks.

"What is he doing?" Tacitus asked.

He felt bereft without Macrinus beside him.

"Going to die with his own men," Rufus replied grimly. "Can't blame him for that." Scowling fiercely, he went on, "I hope you are on good terms with the Gods. Perhaps you can call in some favours. We are going to need their help to get out of this."

He cupped his hands to shout to his men.

"All right, lads. Let's show these savages what it means to fight real soldiers!"

The rain-soaked hill became a killing ground of mud and blood, and the day had barely begun.

Chapter XLI

As soon as Braine heard the roar from within the woodland she knew that Calgacus had sprung his trap.

Eudaf said, "Listen! It is beginning."

Braine nodded but did not answer. A distant part of her wondered why Eudaf seemed on edge but not excited. He appeared to be preoccupied by some inner conflict. If she had not been so preoccupied herself, she might have registered his reaction more clearly, but she was too confused as she tried to resolve her own internal confusion; confusion that Eudaf himself had sparked when he had suggested what might happen if Tuathal were to die.

The rain gave her an excuse to keep her hood up, wrapping herself in a personal cocoon, a world where she sought to unravel the complex knot of emotions that bound her. Matters had moved so quickly and she had been swept along by events that had been beyond her control.

It all revolved around her father's death. She had not been close to him, nor to her brothers, but she had enjoyed a privileged lifestyle as the daughter of the High King. All her life, people had treated her as special and that was because of her father. Yet there was a price. She had always known that she was destined to marry an important man, a man who would be chosen by her father. That had been her role in life.

Then Tuathal, Scota and Calgacus had changed everything.

Family loyalties and the rules of blood feud demanded that she hate them for killing her father, but Calgacus had broken those same rules by suggesting Tuathal take her as his wife and, perhaps more surprisingly, Tuathal had agreed.

Braine knew that decision had saved her life. Her brief time as a captive of the men of Connacht had shown her what the alternative would have been. She had been truly terrified by their brutish strength and casual violence. She could still recall the rough hands on her, the crude laughter and the leering threats. If Sanb had not recognised her and stopped them, she would have been raped and probably murdered.

The memory made her shiver. She was only fifteen years old and she did not want to die. Was that wrong, she wondered? Everyone said that the Underworld was a place of peace, where she would have joined the spirits of her family again. But what family did she have? Did she want to meet her father again? She knew she did not.

So, when Tuathal made his offer, she had chosen life. It had been her only choice. She had given her vows at the hand-fasting, had shared his bed, joined her body to his, but Tuathal was still something of a stranger to her. She did not love him but was that any different to what would have happened if her father had chosen a husband for her? Love rarely played any part in dynastic marriages.

The difference was that Tuathal had killed her father. But then, her father had killed Tuathal's father. How far back could hatred go?

Tuathal confused her but there were others to consider. Her feelings about Calgacus were also ambivalent. She had watched in horror as he had leaped onto her father's chariot. She had seen the sword swing, had witnessed her father's death. Yet Calgacus had been the one who had saved her from death when he had suggested that she marry Tuathal.

As for Scota, who had pretended to be her father's loyal supporter, her betrayal made it easier to hate her.

And yet, if the Romans had not come, Braine knew that she would probably have come to terms with her new life. She would have been in a position of authority, wife to the most powerful ruler in Eriu. She had almost convinced herself that things had turned out for the best.

But the Romans had come and, as Eudaf had pointed out, their arrival had presented her with a choice.

Intrigued by the prospect of becoming High Queen as a Roman ally, Braine had tried to hate the three people who had changed her life. It should have been easy because there was more than enough justification for hatred. Scota had betrayed her father, Calgacus had killed him and Tuathal had forced her into his marriage bed.

Hatred, though, was not enough. It had taken fear to wring her angry words from her innermost thoughts; fear that all three of them would die anyway and that the Romans would crush their

376

war host. If that happened, she would be alone and vulnerable. Which made Eudaf's suggestion an enticing one.

Then Calgacus had told her the tale about his sister. Braine had instinctively felt the truth in his words. His story had genuinely frightened her. If what he said was true, dealing with the Romans could be a worse fate than a life as Tuathal's Queen.

Braine felt trapped, not knowing what to do for the best. She wished there was someone she could turn to for advice but she was alone, surrounded by strangers who all seemed so sure of themselves. She had nobody to turn to and she was left in a welter of indecision.

She was no closer to a resolution when Eudaf reached across to stop her horse. She realised that they had come to the far end of the trees. Behind them, muffled by distance and by the incessant beat of the rain, they could hear the dreadful sounds of battle.

"Do you really want them to die?" Eudaf asked.

Braine looked at him, blinking in surprise. She was not sure that she had heard him correctly.

"What?"

He seemed eager, his whole body tense, and there was an unusual gleam in his eye. "Tuathal and Calgacus," he said. "Do you really want them to die? You said you hated them."

Her breath caught in her throat. She did not know what to say. She had lashed out in anger but had she meant what she had said? She did not know.

Eudaf took her silence for agreement. His lips curled in a malicious smile as he reminded her, "You heard what Scota said. She cannot bring them back to life if they die."

"The Romans might not kill them," she said weakly, still unable to give an answer to his question.

He leaned towards her, so close that the edges of their hoods brushed together.

"The Romans cannot be defeated," he hissed. "Everyone with any sense knows that. My father has seen their army and it is more powerful than anything you can imagine."

Braine nodded weakly, the urgency in his voice filling her with dread at the prospect of becoming a Roman slave.

Then he whispered, "I will kill them for you."

"What?"

"Tuathal and Calgacus. I will kill them. Then you can become High Queen and join the Romans in an alliance. It is futile to oppose them, so you must seize this opportunity. But Tuathal and Calgacus must die."

"You can kill them?" she gasped, bewildered by the scope of his plan.

Speaking earnestly, he told her, "They escaped me before, but I will be able to get close to them now. Nobody will stop me in the middle of a battle. They will be fighting on foot. I will cut them down and ride away before anyone can catch me."

Braine could scarcely think straight. The malicious venom in his voice both appalled and fascinated her. She put a hand to her forehead, closing her eyes as she struggled for a response.

"But you have been protecting Tuathal. They told me the killer stabbed your arm."

He grinned, "That night on the beach? No, I did that myself, to throw them off the scent. It worked, too. They have never suspected me."

"But the attack in his roundhouse?" she frowned.

"That was me, too," he admitted with a bitter laugh. "I should have killed him then but he woke up in time. Fortunately, I had already given the guards a drink which killed them, so I was able to run outside and pretend I was chasing the assassin."

Braine shook her head in bewilderment.

"But why would you kill him? He is your cousin."

"Because our grandfather always treated him better than he ever treated me or my brother."

His face contorted into a mask of anger. The change from his usual carefree expression was so marked that he seemed like another person.

Bitterly, he went on, "All my life I have heard about Tuathal's great destiny and how my family are second best. That would be reason enough to hate him but if he remains as High King, he could cause problems for my father, so he must die."

With a leer, he added, "And think what we could do without him."

She looked at him blankly, not following his meaning.

He explained, "You and I together, we could rule this place. My father will rule the Caledones as an ally of Rome and we could do the same here."

He stared at her, an intense, frightening stare that chilled her more than the rain.

He stated, "I am going to kill them anyway. Their deaths are necessary."

Her heart missed a beat as understanding came. He would do this thing whether she agreed or not. And what would he do to her if she refused to go along with him?

But did she want to refuse? She was torn by indecision and she needed more time.

Desperately, she asked, "You planned this all along?"

"It is my father's plan," he confirmed.

"But what about your grandfather? Tuathal told me he was a mighty chieftain. What will he do when he hears of this?"

"The old man is probably dead already," Eudaf smirked. "My father is King of the Caledones. I can feel it."

Grinning, he explained the plot to her, telling her how his father would become King of the Caledones and how Calgacus' family would be taken to the Romans as captives, thus ensuring the Governor's friendship.

"But how can you kill Calgacus?" she whispered, terrified that her question might seem like complicity.

Eudaf patted the hilt of his sword.

"This time, he won't even see me coming," he assured her confidently. "He has been lucky so far but I no longer have any need to be stealthy. I can ride up to both of them and kill them before they know they are in danger. I should have killed them before but I will not fail this time."

He sounded confident but she thought she detected a trace of desperation in his stiff posture. The idea of him killing a warrior like Calgacus seemed almost beyond belief. But Calgacus was not the only person who might thwart his plan.

"Scota ..." her words trailed off, fear stifling her thoughts before she could voice them.

Eudaf shrugged, "The Romans will kill her. I will tell them she is a druid. That will be enough to seal her fate."

Braine's mind was in turmoil as she tried to envisage Eudaf carrying out his threat.

"Everyone will see what you have done," she frowned.

"It is better that their deaths are witnessed. When the Romans see Calgacus and Tuathal fall, they will welcome me."

"You will go to the Romans?"

"Of course. I can hardly sit around waiting for Tuathal's guards to cut me to pieces. But I will be on horseback and will ride to the Romans as soon as I have killed the two of them."

"What about me?" she asked uncertainly.

Again he interpreted her question as agreement.

"Stay out of the way," he told her. "Once they are dead and the Romans have won, come to us. The Romans will be only too happy to have you as High Queen."

Braine told herself that this was what she had wanted to hear but something in Eudaf's manner made her skin crawl in revulsion and she felt sick at the thought of his treachery.

But she feared what he might do to her if she refused him and she knew, deep in her soul, that the Romans could not be beaten. Eudaf was presenting her with a way to save her life; just as Tuathal and Calgacus had done.

Yet she could not utter the words. She told herself to emulate her father, to put personal feelings aside and make the decision that would preserve her life and place her as High Queen of Eriu with Roman Legions at her command. She told herself to be strong but all she could do was mutely bow her head.

Once again, Eudaf took this as assent. His face lit up with delight, showing a flash of his former habitual happiness.

"Then wait here and I will complete the task my father set me."

He gave her a final reassuring pat on the arm then heeled his horse into a fast trot, picking a way out of the trees and round the woodland, curving up towards the long, low ridge.

Gripped by indecision, Braine watched him go. Almost without thinking, she nudged her pony into a trot and followed him as he rode along the ridge, heading back towards the battle. She did not know why she did this, only that she wanted to see the outcome of his plot. Whether she wanted him to succeed or fail was still beyond her ability to decide. Part of her prayed for Tuathal to be victorious, to become the High King who would save Eriu, yet another part of her knew this was a false hope and that the Romans would win whatever Eudaf did. And if he succeeded, she would still be High Queen.

She told herself that she could not stop Eudaf even if she wanted to. She had no weapon and she was certainly not strong enough to overpower him. All she could do was allow herself to be carried along by events she still could not control.

Again she wished for more time. She needed time to decide what she wanted and time to ensure that what she wanted was what happened.

But time had run out.

She reached the end of the ridge, climbing with the trees on her right. She turned to look along the top of the slope and saw a mass of swirling men and horses fighting in the downpour, clustering around the hilltop like moths round a candle.

Ahead of her, Eudaf drew his sword. It was a long, heavy cavalry sword with sharp edges and a rounded tip, a weapon that could cause horrendous injury when slashed down with the power of man and horse behind it.

He seemed to hesitate for a moment, as if summoning his courage, then he jabbed his heels into his horse's flanks and rode towards the fighting.

It was only then that Braine realised the combat was slowly moving down the slope. The Romans, she saw, were retreating and Tuathal's warriors were pressing around them, driving them back and attempting to break their formation.

The Romans were retreating!

Her heart leaped with excitement and then she recognised at last what it was she wanted.

Tuathal had brought the various tribes of Eriu together and, together, they were defeating the seemingly invincible Romans. Tuathal's people. Her people.

She had been frightened, alone and confused but the sight of the Romans withdrawing from the scene of the ambush drove away much of her fear and she reached her decision. She saw now that the death of her father and brothers had presented her with an opportunity she would never have found had she been married off to some sub-king or chieftain. Her father had never treated her as anything but a political tool to be used as he saw fit. Her own wishes had never been considered, far less sought. Eudaf had woven a picture of her as ruling as an ally of Rome but she knew enough to recognise she would be little more than a puppet of the Empire. Tuathal represented her chance to be a true High Queen, a person of real power and influence. She did not love him for she barely knew him but that did not matter. He was one of her own, a man of Eriu despite having lived his life in exile.

So Braine reached her decision and then gasped in horror as she watched Eudaf gallop into the fray, his sword held high.

381

She had run out of time and so, she knew, had Tuathal and Calgacus.

Chapter XLII

"We can't break them!" Tuathal shouted to Calgacus, his voice cracking with frustration and exhaustion.

"They'll break," Calgacus yelled back. "All we need to do is keep up the pressure."

Tuathal nodded. The pain in his side was incredible, the stitches of his wound stinging like hot needles. He could see the weariness in Calgacus' face too. The big warrior had already smashed into the Roman lines three times. He had hacked down at least two Romans but had been unable to break through their ranks.

The battered Cohorts were slowly edging down the slope, leaving a trail of dead, wounded and maimed in their wake. Tuathal could not believe that any men could maintain their discipline in the face of the onslaught his warriors were hurling at them. Yet even with one quarter of their force destroyed and the survivors dismayed by the proof of Scota's dark magic, the Roman officers held their men together and tried to force a way out of the trap. Their numbers were being whittled down but the cost to the men of Eriu was high.

Sanb of Connacht was dead. Knowing that horses could never break a solid formation of foot soldiers, he had leaped down from his chariot to lead a furious assault on the legionaries of the Second *Adiutrix* but he had been stabbed in the chest. His men had dragged him away but he had died shortly afterwards, blood bubbling from his lips in a pink froth. Now his chieftains led the men of Connacht but they could not break the Roman defensive formation.

The ground was soaked by rain and blood, churned to mud by feet and by hooves, and still the killing continued.

Tuathal decided, "I will lead the next charge myself."

"No," Calgacus objected. "You need to stay alive. Find your chariot and let the warriors see you, but don't get too close to the Romans."

Tuathal shook his head.

"I have spent too long keeping myself out of danger. What sort of High King would I be if I did not fight for my own kingdom?"

Before Calgacus could argue, Runt called, "Look! There's Scota!"

They turned to see the sorceress on her chariot, her head bared, a sword in her hand. Amhairgin steered a way down the slope, parallel to the Roman Cohorts, while Scota screamed curses at the retreating enemy, pointing and gesturing with her sword.

"By Toutatis," muttered Runt. "I don't know about the Romans, but she scares me."

"They're terrified of her," Calgacus agreed.

Tuathal saw that the big warrior was correct. Scota was doing nothing more than showing herself to the Romans but they had seen her power and they feared her. The nearest Cohort began to lose cohesion as men tried to edge away from an unseen assault of witchcraft.

"That lot don't have a senior officer with them," Calgacus said. "Tacitus is with the legionaries and Macrinus is in the centre Cohort."

Tuathal was not sure how Calgacus could tell who was where. To him, the rain-sodden battlefield was nothing more than screaming men and utter confusion. He could no longer tell where anyone was. But he grasped his own sword, nodded and said, "All right. Scota has given us a chance to destroy them. Now is the time."

Calgacus nodded. He raised his sword, calling to the warriors to summon their energy for another attack.

"For Eriu!" he shouted, pointing his sword at the Romans.

"For Eriu!" Tuathal echoed.

With an ear-splitting yell, they charged at the nearest Cohort. Warriors screamed their war cries and ran with them. Then they were jumping or stumbling over the fallen, trying to avoid discarded spears and shields that littered the muddy ground.

Tuathal vaulted over a dead horse, its lips curled back in a manic grin. He had no idea how his exhausted body found the energy to run and jump but somehow he kept going. Even the pain in his side seemed to have abated slightly. All he knew was that Calgacus was beside him, his warriors were with him and the enemy was retreating from them. Victory was within their grasp. If they could break the Roman formation, that victory would become a massacre.

The Roman shields braced. He could see the small movement as the soldiers prepared to meet the charge, see the blood-caked tips of the swords waiting for him, and the grim faces of the men who gripped those swords.

He screamed a war cry, then saw Calgacus barge into a shield, using his massive frame to push the Roman backwards. A sword licked out but Runt was there, blocking the blade, stabbing back.

Calgacus heaved, swung his huge sword and another Roman stepped backwards. Tuathal leaped into the tiny gap and swung his own sword in a vicious slash, not caring where it struck. He felt it smash into chainmail, heard the grunt of pain and his man was down.

"Camulos!" screamed Calgacus.

His sword lashed out, left and right, driving back the Romans. More warriors were leaping past him, spears jabbing at eyes and legs, seeking vulnerable, unprotected flesh.

Tuathal hacked again. His sword bounced off the curved front of a huge Roman shield but the expected counter-blow did not come because Calgacus' blade had caught the Roman on the back of the neck, just below the rim of the man's helmet.

Without warning, everything changed. The Romans were turning, running away in panic and Tuathal's men were chasing them, charging into the breach in the defence.

His mounted warriors, who had been watching from a distance because their horses would not charge home against well-formed ranks of shields, now seized the opportunity and plunged into the melee, hacking down at fleeing Romans and creating yet more panic and confusion.

Tuathal stopped, gasping for breath, raising his head to the torrential rain, letting it cool his burning face. His legs were weak now and his side was aching again but he found the strength to grin at Calgacus.

The big warrior had planted his sword in the ground and was leaning on it, two-handed, his head bowed, his breath coming in ragged gasps. His long hair had been tied back but the cord was gone, allowing a mass of sodden, tangled hair to fall around his face.

"I'm getting too old for this," he wheezed.

"We did it," Tuathal said. "By the Dagda, we did it."

"Aye, we did," Calgacus agreed. "You did well."

"It is only one Cohort," Runt cautioned. "Macrinus is trying to rescue them."

He too looked pale and exhausted, his eyes like hollow pits in a skull-like face.

Tuathal looked across the field. Many of the Romans had run for protection to their neighbours. Under the stern command of Macrinus, the second Auxiliary Cohort had maintained its formation and was slowly edging towards them. Some of Tuathal's own warriors were now caught between the two groups of Romans and the fight degenerated into a muddy melee. Some of the Romans reached the comparative safety of Macrinus' surviving Cohort but the soldiers who had fled down the hill were being hunted and cut down by the cavalry.

Tuathal was weary beyond belief. He stood, trying to recover while the battle moved on, surging further down the hill as the remaining Roman formations doggedly continued their slow retreat. He had thought the panic created by the breaking of one Cohort would spread but the two other units still maintained their discipline.

He asked, "Should we let them go? We've beaten them."

Calgacus shook his head.

"The Romans don't give up easily. If we want to be sure of driving them out of Eriu, we must chase them all the way back to the sea. It's not over yet."

Tuathal smiled weakly.

"In that case, give me a few moments and we'll finish the rest of them."

Calgacus nodded approvingly.

"You should find a horse or chariot. You have done your share of fighting. Your task now is to stay alive."

Runt, who was standing to Calgacus' right, turned to look back at Tuathal. He was about to say something when his face creased in a puzzled frown.

"Here comes Eudaf," he said. "And Braine is following him."

Tuathal turned. He had time to register only a few brief images. He saw Eudaf, sword in hand, galloping towards them, intent on joining the battle. His face bore an expression of fixed determination as he charged towards them.

Braine was some distance away, her cloak flying out behind her as she galloped towards him, her yellow dress shining like a beacon in a world that was full of green, brown and muddy red. But it was her face that caught his attention. She was waving an arm desperately, shouting something, alarm clear in her expression. Then Eudaf was there, big and tall on his horse, his sword raised high, and Tuathal suddenly understood Braine's warning.

Scarcely believing what was happening, Tuathal threw himself to the side, dropping his sword as he dived to avoid the blow. He landed on a dead Roman, pain lancing into his injured side when he struck the mail-clad body. He rolled, hands and feet scrabbling on the muddy earth.

Groaning with pain, he flopped onto his back in time to see Eudaf guide his mount at Calgacus. The big man was directly in front of the horse, protected from Eudaf's sword but in danger of being trampled. Tuathal yelled a futile warning as he watched, horrified and struggling to comprehend Eudaf's unexpected attack.

Calgacus waited until the last moment, then jumped aside, swinging his sword to catch the horse on the side of the head, then dropping to one knee as Eudaf's blade swept over his head.

Even as Eudaf struck uselessly at Calgacus, the horse screamed in agony, reared, and fell, throwing the young noble from the saddle. Man and beast hit the ground at the same time. But as it fell, one of the dying horse's flailing legs caught Calgacus and sent him sprawling on the wet grass.

Eudaf scrambled to his feet, still clutching his sword but the horse was thrashing its legs, blocking Runt who was trying to reach the young warrior.

Tuathal dragged himself up, grabbing for his sword which was lying on the trampled grass. His fingers curled round the wet hilt just in time to see Calgacus, now on his knees, fend off a furious attack from Eudaf who was screaming incoherently at him.

Tuathal was three paces away. In the time it took him to close the gap, Eudaf had rained four more ferocious blows on Calgacus. The big warrior was too tired to do anything more than block the manic assault. Eudaf was young and fit, unwearied by combat and driven by a blind, furious rage. Tuathal knew it could only be a matter of time before he broke through Calgacus' desperate defence.

387

Tuathal did not give him that time. He raised his sword and cut down, driving the edge of the blade into the side of Eudaf's neck.

Eudaf seemed to take a long time to fall but at last the sword slipped from his fingers and he toppled to the ground, his life ebbing away.

Calgacus looked up from where he knelt, too tired to say anything, only able to nod his thanks. Then Runt was there, ashen-faced and anxious, standing protectively over Calgacus.

Tuathal whirled round at the sound of another horse galloping towards them. It was Braine. She jumped down from the saddle as soon as she had reined in her mount.

"You're alive!" she cried as she ran to Tuathal. Then her mouth went wide with horror. "You are hurt!"

"No," he said. "Just tired."

"You're bleeding," she told him, pointing to his left side.

He looked down. A dark stain was slowly seeping under the links of his mail coat. He shook his head weakly.

"It's the old wound," he assured her.

But he felt faint now and he could not prevent himself from staggering slightly. Braine caught at him but could not hold him. Struggling with his weight, she was able to ease him to the ground where he lay, listening to the distant cries of, "Treachery!" and, "We are betrayed!"

Macrinus could not see what had happened. One moment the barbarians were swarming all around, venting their fury on the soldiers who were trying to escape from the remnants of his shattered Cohort; the next, there was open space and the enemy was falling back in confusion. He wondered whether it was another ploy but he quickly realised that there was genuine fear among the Hibernians. He did not need a second invitation.

"Now's our chance, lads!" he called. "Marching speed! Keep your formation."

He looked across the devastation of the battlefield. Rufus was there, standing in the front rank of his Cohort, his dark face and squat figure easily recognisable. Macrinus pointed southwards and saw the wave of acknowledgement. Then he saw Tacitus, still on horseback, pushing out of the legionary Cohort and riding across to him.

"What's happening?" the Tribune asked. "Why are they falling back?"

"I have no idea," Macrinus answered. "But this is our chance to get away. Let's not waste it."

"All the way back to base?"

"We've lost damn near half our men. We don't have any other choice. Unless you want to throw away the rest of your command in a heroic defeat. The savages may have broken off their attack but there are still thousands of them. They'll be back before too long."

Tacitus shook his head. He looked torn.

"The wounded?" he asked.

"Carry them if we can. Leave them if we can't."

Tacitus nodded his reluctant acceptance as he looked over the battered remnants of his command.

"We have lost so many men," he sighed. "The Governor won't be happy."

"If we get back to face his anger, I'll be delighted," Macrinus replied grimly. "But he's a soldier. He knows things can go wrong."

They were moving now, clear of most of the debris of battle, with Rufus' Cohort close on their heels. A few barbarian horsemen were shadowing them but none of the enemy were making any attempt to stop them.

"Things have gone badly wrong," Tacitus complained miserably.

"It's not your fault," Macrinus told him.

"I am in command. Whose fault is it?"

"Spoken like a true Roman. But if we get away alive, I'll be more than happy to tell the Governor that Macer blundered into the trap."

"We should not speak ill of the dead," Tacitus chided.

"Who is going to argue?" Macrinus retorted. "Macer lost damn near his entire Cohort and left us in an exposed position. Just because he's dead doesn't mean he wasn't a damned idiot."

A wry laugh from the ranks made Macrinus whirl.

"I heard that, Honorius," he snarled. "Punishment duty for you when we get home."

"Does that mean you are going to get us home, Centurion?" came the reply.

389

"Damn right I am," Macrinus vowed. "Now keep moving or I'll send you back as a one-man rearguard."

"Yes, Sir!" Honorius grinned.

Macrinus looked back at the hilltop. A tall figure stood out from the milling crowd of barbarians. It was Calgacus, come to watch them go.

Macrinus raised his sword in salute. He smiled as he saw Calgacus return the gesture, holding his huge sword up in front of his face.

"Time to go home, boys," Macrinus told his troops.

On the hilltop, Calgacus was joined by Runt.

"They are getting away," Calgacus complained.

"They're beaten," Runt observed.

"We need to follow them. Make sure they keep going."

"Tuathal has already ordered the cavalry to do that. We can't do any more at the moment. Everyone is exhausted."

"How is Tuathal?"

Runt shrugged, "Findmall is with him. He'll live."

"Good."

Calgacus paused. Then, still staring into the rain after the retreating Romans, he breathed, "By the gods, I have never felt so tired in all my life."

"I've had better days myself," agreed Runt. "So, what now? You realise what this means? Eudaf, I mean."

Wearily, Calgacus sighed, "It seems Scota was right about him. He did harbour a secret."

"Yes. You heard what Braine said?"

Calgacus nodded. Through tears of relief and regret, Braine had blurted out the story that Eudaf had told her.

"I thought he was mad," she had gasped. "But I could not stop him."

The story had come in disjointed bursts but Calgacus understood what it meant for him.

"We need to get home," he told Runt.

"What about Tuathal? If the Romans stay, he'll need to fight them on his own."

"We've shown him how to do it. He's a bright lad."

"Brave, too," observed Runt.

"He'll make a good High King. He doesn't need us any more."

390

"Home, then?"
"Yes. We have some scores to settle."

Chapter XLIII

Crixus wasted little time in eliminating all opposition to his plans. In the grey light of the early morning following his confrontation with Beatha and Emmelia, he led six of his warriors to the upper floor of the broch. They burst into the sleeping chamber without warning, waking the women with rough shouts.

One of the guards seized Fallar, dragging away the blankets that covered her heather-filled mattress and hauling her to her feet.

Fallar screamed in terror, fighting uselessly to fend the man off but he held her tight, wrapping a burly arm around her waist.

Shocked from her sleep and disoriented by the noise and poor light, Beatha could not tell what was happening. She heard Fallar's scream and sensed the presence of several men. Instinctively, she screamed for help as she, too, lashed out at the shadowy figures looming over her.

"Calm down!" Crixus shouted, his voice cutting across their terror. "I only need to borrow your daughter for a little while. No harm will come to her."

He reached out to grab Fallar's chin, stifling her terrified sobs as he added menacingly, "As long as she does as she is told."

They marched down the stairs, leaving two men to block Beatha's attempts to follow. Emmelia, Caedmon and Tegan, hurrying out to see what had happened, were quickly chased back into their own sleeping chambers by the guards. Alone and helpless, Beatha sat on her mattress and tried to hold back her tears.

Crixus led the others outside where another group of a dozen warriors was waiting. Following Crixus, they marched round the broch, heading across the trampled earth towards the small roundhouse where Adelligus and his warriors slept.

The sun was lightening the sky, illuminating the rugged hills to the east, bringing the promise of another fine day. That promise was broken by the cool breeze from the west and the gathering clouds that blotted the far horizon. For the moment, though, the sun held sway over the broch. Its growing light revealed that Adelligus had posted a man on watch and that he had seen their approach. By the time they reached the roundhouse, Adelligus himself had hurried out of the doorway, a long sword in his right hand. His men quickly fanned out behind him but a signal from Crixus sent his own warriors spreading out to either side, trapping Adelligus against the house.

Adelligus did not waste time with pointless questions. There could be no doubt what Crixus and his men wanted. All he needed to decide was how to react. He and his seven men were hopelessly outnumbered but he was a warrior; he would not surrender without a fight.

Then Crixus gestured to a man behind him. Adelligus' heart fell when he saw Fallar, still dressed in a thin nightshirt, her blonde hair tangled and dishevelled, her eyes red-rimmed and her cheeks stained by tears, being dragged to stand beside the new King of the Caledones.

"Lay down your weapons," Crixus ordered. "I am sure you will not wish to see any harm come to this lovely young creature."

"You bastard!" Adelligus hissed. "Will you hide behind a woman instead of fighting like a man?"

"If it comes to a fight, you will lose," Crixus replied, waving a hand to indicate the men around him. "But you will see her die first. If you lay down your weapons and surrender to me, I swear that you will all live. It is up to you but I suggest that you make up your mind quickly."

Adelligus looked at Fallar. Her eyes were wide with fear but she called out, "Don't listen to him, Adelligus. He will not kill me."

Crixus drew his dagger. Looking at Adelligus, he rasped, "Are you prepared to take that risk? Drop your weapons now or she dies."

Adelligus closed his eyes. With a sigh, he flung his sword down. After a moment's hesitation, his warriors grudgingly discarded their own weapons.

"No!" sobbed Fallar.

Crixus grinned triumphantly.

"Very sensible," he nodded. Signalling to his men, he commanded, "Now put them in chains and keep them well guarded. They will fetch a decent price when we take them to the Romans."

By late morning, the rain had arrived. After so many days of unremitting sunshine, it was welcomed by the farmers, but even they took shelter from the downpour. The rain drove everyone indoors, turning the earth to a sodden quagmire.

Inside the broch's great chamber, Crixus was insulated from the downpour by the massively thick stone walls but the sound of the rain was still distantly audible. Crixus did not care. The unseasonal weather did nothing to dampen his mood. He had enjoyed his triumph over Calgacus' war band and now he had more entertainment planned. Smiling happily, he summoned Broichan to meet him.

The druid was all temper and indignation, glowering at the guards who escorted him into the circular hall. His dark, intense eyes sparked when he saw Crixus but the King silenced him before he could launch into his invective.

"Save your breath, Broichan," Crixus commanded. "I have listened to you these past years and you have nothing new to say to me. I have made up my mind. The Caledones will become allies of Rome. I suggest you leave as soon as you can. I will not harm a druid but Rome will, so it is best that you leave. If you wish to travel by land I will provide a horse. If you would prefer to return to your fellow druids on Iova, I will provide a boat. I really don't care what you do, but be gone from here by tomorrow."

Mustering as much dignity as he could under the eyes of the guards, Broichan retorted, "You are a fool and a godless wretch, Crixus son of Coel. The Gods will have their revenge on you and all your minions."

"Yes, yes," Crixus sighed wearily. "We have heard that before, Broichan. But you are wrong. The Gods side with Rome. Any fool can see that. The old Gods have deserted us. So go. Do you require a horse or a boat?"

"You do not know who you are dealing with," Broichan hissed. "I will return to Iova to inform the druids of your insolence and your blasphemy."

"Good," Crixus said briskly. "Then I will have a boat set aside for your use. It will be ready at first light tomorrow."

394

Crixus waved to the guards, indicating that the audience was over. Broichan shrugged off their hands, glared at Crixus, then turned to stalk haughtily out of the chamber.

"One less problem to worry about," Crixus mused to himself. "This is turning into a very good day."

He called for some food. Eurgain joined him, marching into the chamber with a new-found confidence and arrogance.

"Calgacus' men are all under guard," Eurgain confirmed as he sat at the table. "They won't cause any trouble."

"Neither will Broichan," said Crixus. "He's going back to Iova."

"Let's hope his boat sinks on the way," Eurgain laughed.

Crixus smiled, "That would be convenient but it does not matter. The druids are a spent force. Once we have confirmed our alliance with Rome, I will give them directions as to how to locate Iova. Let them deal with the druids."

Eurgain nodded approvingly.

"All we need now is for Eudaf to succeed."

Crixus lifted a bronze goblet to his lips, sipping at the heather ale.

"He will."

Serving girls delivered food for the King and his bodyguards, and a bard sang while they ate, recounting the story of a hero from the ancient days who had tried to steal a fortune in gold from the fairy folk. It was an old tale, known to everyone, but the bard sang well and added a few bawdy jokes as embellishment. Crixus rewarded him with a silver ring.

When the meal was done, the warriors remained in the warmth of the great chamber because the rain continued to fall. Some of the men played dice, gambling for tiny tokens of carved bone or scraps of silver. Others played the old game of King's Stone, moving the coloured beads around the board in an attempt to capture the central stone. Crixus watched but did not join in. Some people claimed that the game taught players how to wage a war, that the tactics employed in outwitting an opponent on the board could be used in real life. Crixus thought that was nonsense. In life, tactics and plans were far more complex than any two-dimensional game with its fixed rules and pieces that had no free will. It was nothing compared to the great game he had played; the game he had won. There had been setbacks along the way but now, at last, he had almost everything he had dreamed of.

Crixus was a patient man who liked to stick to a plan once he had decided on a course of action. He was content to wait until the solstice before marrying Calgacus' daughter but Eurgain tried to persuade him to act sooner.

"I have a feeling something has gone wrong," he told his father after they had watched Broichan sail away.

"What do you mean?" Crixus demanded, annoyed that his good humour was being tested by Eurgain's pessimism.

"With Eudaf, I mean," Eurgain said earnestly.

Crixus hesitated. He knew that his twin sons had often claimed to have a strange, mystical bond. He had seen for himself how they acted with almost one mind when they were together but they had often insisted that they knew one another so well that they could tell when something was wrong with the other even when they were apart. The boys could not communicate in any meaningful way but at moments of stress for either of them, the other would grow anxious, as if sensing their twin's distress.

Yet Crixus knew that Eurgain's disquiet was probably due to a more mundane worry. It took no supernatural bond to recognise that Eudaf had sent no word of success. Crixus had hoped that his son would kill Calgacus and Tuathal quickly but that hope had failed and the more time that passed with no news of their deaths, the more he worried. Eurgain was obviously suffering from the same anxiety but it seemed to affect him greatly and he had become convinced that something serious had happened to his brother.

"He might have been found out," Eurgain fretted. "He might even be dead."

Father and son looked at one another. Neither of them wished to voice the unthinkable. If Eudaf had been killed, whether by accident or through being caught in his attempt to assassinate Calgacus, their plan was in jeopardy.

"You should marry the girl now," Eurgain urged. "Then we should take the others to the Romans. There is no point in delaying until the solstice."

Crixus frowned, "It would not do to be seen to change my mind for no reason."

"There is a very good reason," Eurgain insisted.

"Not one that I can easily explain. Nobody must learn of our plan. Even if something has happened to Eudaf, that is no reason to rush the arrangements. It would make me look weak and frightened."

"But if Calgacus has learned of our plot ..." Eurgainf objected.

"It makes no difference. The Romans will deal with him. No, we will stick to the plan. There is not long to wait now. Only three more days."

So they waited until midsummer arrived. Crixus had almost persuaded himself that there was nothing to worry about, that Eudaf would soon return, bringing news that Calgacus and Tuathal were both dead. In the meantime, he had a busy day ahead of him.

As they did every year, everyone rose and dressed before dawn, making their way in a firelight procession to a large rock which stood in splendid isolation in the middle of a high meadow. Irregularly shaped, the huge boulder was as tall and broad as a man. All over its rough surface were dozens of small indentations and ring markings that had been gouged into the rock in years long past, sacred symbols made so long ago that nobody could tell how old they were, nor why they had been carved. All they knew was that they marked the stone as special. On midsummer's day, the morning sun would appear in a cleft between two distant hills and rise directly over this rock, a clear sign of the stone's mystical importance. How it had got there, nobody knew because it was far too large to have been moved without the labour of dozens of men. Yet it was there and, each year, the people gathered to celebrate the solstice, the day of Alaunos, the sun god.

Some people carried blazing torches to light their way. Others bore twigs or branches of rowan, elm and elder as totems to bring good luck. Children walked, wide-eyed, or were carried on their parents' shoulders.

It should have been a joyous, carefree occasion, with much good-natured laughter and joking, but this year a nervous pall hung over the procession like a cloud. The people walked in virtual silence, knowing that this year was different. A new King ruled over them but his reign was cause for concern rather than joy. His warriors prowled the settlement, taking whatever they wanted by force. Guests had been imprisoned and rumours said that the girl he was about to marry, the daughter of Calgacus, had been forced into agreeing to the match. A chieftain who would do such things

397

was a man to be feared, so the people did their best to remain quiet and unnoticed.

Crixus appeared to be unaware of the general unease. He led the procession with a carefree step, unaffected by the near silence. Some way behind him came Fallar, walking with her head bowed. Her hair had been combed and a garland of flowers placed on her head but she walked as if going to an execution rather than to her wedding. The armed warriors who walked on either side of her compounded that impression.

Behind her, Beatha, Emmelia and Tegan followed miserably, each of them with two swordsmen watching them closely. Tegan carried her baby and Emmelia held young Bonduca's hand but Caedmon, and eight-year-old Morcant had been taken away in chains. One of the guards had laughingly told Emmelia that they had been placed with Adelligus and the other captives.

"That's to make sure you behave yourself," he had mocked.

Emmelia felt more helpless than at any time in her life. She had been a prisoner before, but never when her family were being held to ensure her compliance. To make things worse, her own life was under threat to compel Fallar to become Crixus' bride. For days, Emmelia had tried to think of a way of escaping their fate but Crixus had kept them apart, preventing them from talking to one another.

Emmelia still had her hidden knife but for all the use it was, she may as well have been defenceless. She knew that there was nothing she could do against so many warriors.

Crixus had come to her chamber the previous night to gloat over what was going to happen.

"Once I am married to young Fallar," he said, "there will be a celebration. Then I shall give you and the other women to my men. It is only fair that they should have some fun on my wedding night, and you may as well get used to such treatment. You will be treated far worse once you are Roman slaves."

Emmelia could find no answer. Bonduca had clung to her, crying, and Emmelia had sat in the cold darkness, vainly trying to think of a way out of their predicament. The only decision she came to was that the first man who came to rape her would die with her knife in his throat. Even that would be a short-lived victory. One way or another, she would soon be dead. She had

398

even considered killing herself before the wedding but, faced with the choices of letting her daughter witness her suicide or of killing Bonduca first, Emmelia could not bring herself to even touch her concealed blade.

Lost in impotence, she trudged across the meadow, hoping for some miracle to save them.

It was a long walk from the broch but for Emmelia it seemed that they arrived too soon. The crowd clustered in the field, everyone trying to obtain the best view of the rock that would soon be lit by the rising sun.

The torches were extinguished and a silence fell over the wide meadow, broken only by the dawn chorus as the birds welcomed the new day. Slowly, the eastern sky grew lighter, becoming tinged with pink fingers of light which gradually transformed into a strong, orange glow and turned the sky above the eastern horizon a glorious shade of blue.

Then, almost without warning, the dazzling brightness of the sun's orb blazed its presence over the top of the great rock, casting long shadows across the earth.

A roar went up from hundreds of throats. Arms were raised as the people welcomed the sun before turning to embrace one another. This was the high point of another year, heralding the arrival of the year's warmest and kindest season.

Crixus walked to stand in front of the giant stone. Beside him stood his brother, Drust, his large frame somehow reduced by the unhappy slump of his shoulders.

Crixus raised his arm, calling for silence.

"My people!" he cried. "This is always a happy day. Now we have another reason to celebrate. I ask you all to witness my marriage to Fallar, daughter of Calgacus."

A respectful hush fell over the crowd. Two burly men ushered Fallar forwards, each of them gripping one of her arms to prevent her making any attempt to escape.

Crixus beamed at her. If she noticed, she did not react, but kept her head bowed. There was some disapproving murmuring from the crowd but Crixus' warriors silenced the dissenters with angry glares and meaningful half-drawn swords.

Seemingly oblivious to the people's mood, Crixus announced, "In this sacred place, we will be united by the traditional hand-fasting of a wedded couple. My brother, Drust, will tie the bonds."

Drust did not look at all happy about his role in the proceedings but he tugged some long ribbons of dyed cloth from his belt pouch.

Emmelia glanced to Beatha but the guards beside her drew their swords, silencing any thoughts that either of them might have of disrupting the ceremony.

Crixus stood beside Fallar, facing Drust who had his back to the stone. Everyone's eyes were on the small group who stood in the shade of the large rock. People shaded their eyes, squinting into the early morning light. They saw Drust look up, hesitate, then stand as still as the rock itself.

Crixus' angry voice carried across the still air.

"Get on with it!" he snapped irritably.

Drust gave a slight shake of his head. He lowered his hands, taking a step backwards so that he was pressed hard against the sacred boulder. His eyes were fixed on something that only he could see.

Crixus turned. Then everyone turned as the crowd parted to reveal more than three dozen armed men striding purposefully towards the rock. Gasps of surprise raced through the crowd as the men marched straight towards Crixus.

Broichan led them, holding a long staff of white, polished ash. Behind him, impossibly, was Adelligus, free of the manacles he had worn for the past few days, wearing his coat of chainmail and holding a sword in his right hand.

And beside him was the giant figure of Calgacus.

Chapter XLIV

Without breaking stride, Broichan jabbed his long staff towards the warriors who held Emmelia, Beatha and Tegan.

"Release the women!" he commanded in a loud, confident voice.

The warriors hesitated. Some looked to Crixus for guidance but the King was transfixed, his mouth gaping.

Calgacus had his massive sword in his hand. He pointed it at the nearest guard.

"You heard the druid," he snarled. "Let them go or I'll slit you from your crotch to your throat."

The man stepped away from Emmelia, lowering his sword, then the warriors who followed Calgacus swarmed around the guards, disarming them and releasing the women. Emmelia felt tears sting her eyes as she saw Caedmon and Morcant following Calgacus' men.

The tension that had gripped the crowd was now mingled with relief tempered by uncertainty. The people watched, fascinated, stepping back slightly to put some space between them and the armed men but remaining close so that they would have a good view of the inevitable confrontation.

Runt was there, pushing through to embrace Tegan and her baby, then Beatha pushed past Emmelia as she rushed to meet Calgacus.

"You're alive!" she exclaimed as she threw her arms around his neck and kissed his face, oblivious to the watching crowd. "Thank the Gods, you are back!"

"Just in time, it seems," he replied, his face a mixture of delight, relief and grim determination.

"But how?"

"Tuathal gave us a boat and a couple of dozen of Coel's men. We were sailing up the coast when we met Broichan going the other way."

Gently, he disentangled himself from her embrace as he promised, "I'll tell you all about it later. Right now, we have some scores to settle."

401

Broichan had marched up to Crixus. Fallar, seizing her opportunity, darted away from the stone, running to Adelligus who wrapped his left arm protectively around her waist. She kissed him on the lips.

"Your father is watching," he warned her.

"I don't care," she said happily.

She kissed him again and this time he responded.

Broichan, ignoring everything that was going on around him, halted in front of Crixus and pointed his staff as if it were a thunderbolt.

"You are a murderer and a traitor to your people!" he declared loudly. "You killed your own father, Coel son of Marduus, and you plotted the death of your nephew, Tuathal, as well as trying to kill Calgacus. You have impersonated a druid for your own selfish ends. You are not fit to be the leader of your people. You have betrayed us all!"

"You lie!" Crixus shouted, although his voice held a tinge of near-hysteria and his eyes darted around wildly.

"I am Broichan. I am a druid. I do not lie."

Before Crixus could voice another protest, Calgacus stepped out from the crowd. "Eudaf told us everything," he told Crixus.

Hefting his sword menacingly, he went on, "I have never killed a defenceless man before but I have a mind to gut you where you stand."

Mention of his son's name jolted Crixus out of his shock.

"Where is Eudaf?" he cried. "What have you done to him?"

Calgacus was a mountain of barely suppressed rage as he growled, "He is dead. Now get yourself a sword or I will cut you down where you stand."

The crowd pressed in, anticipating another spectacle. Some scuffles broke out as people took revenge on Crixus' henchmen, hitting and kicking at them, pushing them to the ground. The warriors who were supposed to be guarding the thugs stood aside, allowing the crowd to have its way. People milled around, some attempting to move away from the violence, others trying to get closer. There was shouting and cursing as all semblance of a peaceful celebration vanished into turmoil.

"Cal! Look out!"

Runt's voice cut across the melee, startling everyone.

But the warning was too late. Eurgain had been lurking in the crowd, trying to remain unseen. Now he shoved his way into the open, sword raised, running towards Calgacus' exposed back. Calgacus was barely three paces away, with no time to turn.

Emmelia reacted before anyone else could move. As Eurgain ran past her, she reached under the sleeve of her dress, turning in one smooth movement to flick open the blade of her clasp knife while she spun on her heel. With a determined slash of her arm, she drove the blade into the back of Eurgain's right shoulder.

The knife did not go deep because Eurgain was moving fast, but he screamed in pain as the unexpected blow cut into him. Staggering, he half-turned towards her. She had lost her grip on the knife which remained embedded in his shoulder but she faced him without fear. Instinctively, she pushed Bonduca behind her as Eurgain stared at her with venomous fury.

Her attack had taken only an instant but it had been long enough. Calgacus swivelled round, sword raised. He cut down, smashing the huge blade into the top of Eurgain's left shoulder at the base of his neck. The heavy sword tore through flesh, muscle and bone, sending a gout of dark blood into the air. There was so much power in the blow that it carved down through Eurgain's torso, almost cutting him in two. The sword jammed in Eurgain's body as he collapsed at Emmelia's feet.

Screams and shouts of shock echoed across the field. People who had been crowding forwards now tried to step away from the mangled, bloody mess that had been Eurgain. Some of Crixus' guards took advantage of the confusion to wrestle their way out of the crowd, creating yet more chaos as they tried to shove their way free.

Almost unseen, Crixus drew his own knife.

Broichan had turned to see what was going on behind him, presenting an easy target for Crixus. But Broichan was a druid and as much as Crixus hated him, he dared not kill a druid. So he threw himself at Calgacus' exposed back.

Calgacus had ruined everything for Crixus. He was the cause of everything that had gone so horribly wrong. Crixus had no thought for his own safety. He knew that he was likely to die but he did not care. He wanted nothing except the satisfaction of killing his enemy before he died.

Again Calgacus was too slow. He heard the movement but his sword was still trapped in Eurgain's corpse. Runt was too far away to help, blocked by the press of people. Calgacus saw Adelligus fling himself forwards but he knew that the distance was too great for the young man to stop the attack in time.

Broichan was closer. He lashed out with his staff, catching Crixus' right arm and knocking the dagger out of the King's hand.

Crixus yelped, spun and dropped to grab for the knife. His fingers closed around the long handle but as he rose, Adelligus swept a frantic blow at him, forcing him to stumble back.

Desperate now, Crixus drew back his arm, preparing to throw the knife at Calgacus. The range was barely five paces. He could not miss. Adelligus would kill him but there was still time for the throw, still time to take his revenge.

Without warning, a huge fist grabbed Crixus' wrist, wrenching his arm. Crixus gasped in pain and surprise as Drust spun him round. Too late, Crixus saw that Drust, too, had a knife.

For all his diffidence and drunkenness, Drust was a big, powerful man. He drove his dagger into Crixus' belly with all the force he could muster.

"Brother!" Crixus gasped as he doubled over.

"You killed our father," Drust hissed. "I hope he is waiting for you in the Underworld."

Chapter XLV

The sacred site had been profaned by the deaths. Broichan spent the remainder of the morning carrying out arcane rites to purify the area around the summer stone. While he worked, the people watched, confused and uncertain.

"I suppose I should thank you," Calgacus grudgingly said to Drust as they stood to one side.

"I thought Crixus was a clever man," Drust said miserably. "I believed him when he told me an alliance with Rome was the best thing for us."

"Just as you believed him when he told you what he wanted to do to my family?"

Drust shrugged, lowering his eyes.

"I did not want that. But Crixus was ..." His voice trailed off uncertainly before he finished, "Well, he was my older brother."

"You did the right thing in the end," Calgacus conceded. "In future, I suggest you listen to Broichan."

Drust nodded weakly. As Coel's only surviving relative, he was likely to find himself elected as the new King, although Calgacus thought he had the air of a beaten man. It was more than likely that other chieftains among the Caledones might soon decide to proclaim themselves King.

Calgacus left Drust to his self-imposed misery. Turning away, he linked arms with Beatha.

As they walked slowly towards their friends and family, she mentioned, "It is not like you to join forces with a druid."

"Needs must," he told her. "Besides, if Drust becomes King of the Caledones, he'll need someone to keep him on the right track."

"You don't want to stay and help guide him?"

He knew she was teasing.

"No. I've had enough of being among strangers."

"What happened to you in Eriu?" she asked. "I was so worried about you."

"I survived."

405

"We heard you defeated the High King."

"I killed him myself."

"And how did you deal with the High King's witch?"

"It turned out she became an ally," he replied flatly. "We parted on good terms."

Beatha gave him an appraising look.

"All right, you can tell me about her later."

Calgacus grunted non-committally. His final parting from Scota had been awkward and strained. He wanted to forget her but somehow he could not dismiss the image of her from his mind.

"I suppose you must go," she had said.

He had read the invitation in her voice but it was not one he would accept.

"Yes," he had replied. "I must. My family and friends are in danger."

"And I will remain here, to help Tuathal and Braine find their way."

"At least your people have a proper home now," he had said, trying to change the subject.

"For the time being," she had shrugged. "Tuathal owes us a debt of gratitude but who knows what may happen in the future? Kings have short memories at the best of times. His sons may have no need of the Scotti. Perhaps one day my people will cross the sea and seek a home among the Pritani."

"I am sure you would be welcome," he had said, knowing it was a lie.

She had shaken her head and given him that strange half-smile.

"I wish you well, Calgacus. If things had been different ..."

"But they are not."

Then she had reached for him, pulling his face close, and she had kissed him. Before he could react, she pulled away, smiled again and said, "Go now. But do not forget me."

Then she had turned and walked away, not looking back.

"What do we do now?" Beatha asked, her words banishing Calgacus' memories.

"We go home," he told her.

"What about Fallar? She is supposed to go to Eriu to marry Tuathal, isn't she?"

"There has been a change of plan," Calgacus informed her.

He looked to where his daughter was sitting arm in arm with Adelligus, their heads together.

He smiled, "Besides, I think she has plans of her own."

Beatha squeezed his arm.

"Then we should get home as soon as we can so that we can have a proper wedding."

"That," Calgacus said decisively, "is the best idea I have heard for a long time."

Epilogue

Gnaeus Julius Agricola, Governor of Britannia, regarded his son-in-law gravely. Cornelius Tacitus was standing stiffly to attention, having delivered his report in a formal tone that invited no sympathy for his failure.

"I am sorry, Sir," Tacitus said when he had finished. "I failed you."

Agricola frowned, then waved towards a stool in front of his desk.

"Sit down, Publius," he ordered.

Tacitus sat stiffly. Holding the Governor's gaze, he said, "I do believe, Sir, that with one Legion we could have defeated the barbarians. We simply did not have enough men or enough horses."

He waved a hand, as if begging a favour.

"I am not seeking to shift the blame, Sir. I was the commander, so the fault was mine. But in the circumstances, I do not think anyone could have done any better."

"Relax, Publius," Agricola replied. "The blame, if any there is, was mine. I allowed myself to be lulled by the chance of a quick victory. You are quite right. I should have given you more men. But there were none to spare. What about our ally there, the boy Domnan?"

"I brought him back with us, Sir. The barbarians were gathering outside his village by the time we were embarking. I assumed that he would have made his peace with the new High King, so I thought it best to keep him as a hostage."

"Well done," Agricola acknowledged. "He will provide us with an excuse when we get round to going back. For the moment, though, Hibernia must wait. We have more than enough to keep us busy here for the next year at least."

"But the Emperor will not be happy when he hears of this," Tacitus reminded him.

"He does not need to hear about it," Agricola confided. "Not in detail anyway."

Tacitus could not mask his surprise.

"You will conceal it from the Emperor?"

Agricola gave him a reassuring smile as he explained, "Of course not. That would be extremely foolish. It is not wise to annoy an Emperor, even one as understanding as Titus appears to be. But there are ways of presenting facts. I will word my next report carefully." He raised a hand, flexing his fingers as he composed a draft of what he could say.

"Let me see. A small scouting force was sent to Hibernia to see whether the natives were amenable to becoming allies of Rome. Unfortunately, our emissaries were forced to withdraw due to the hostile reception they received."

Agricola paused, tapping a fingernail against his teeth, then continued, "At a later point in my report I will say that we had the misfortune to lose a Cohort of the Ninth and some Auxiliary troops who were ambushed by the barbarians led by the notorious Calgacus, but that I fully expect to gain revenge when we resume our advance next year."

He nodded, pleased with himself.

"That will do," he decided. "It is all perfectly true."

"Are you sure, Sir?" Tacitus asked.

Agricola leaned forwards, resting his elbows on the table.

Speaking softly but insistently, he said, "Believe me, Publius, it is better that we forget this whole affair. My aim is to conquer the whole of this island before my term as Governor expires. The last thing I want is for the Emperor to recall me because of some bad news reaching his ear. So, forget Hibernia. It never happened."

Tacitus stared at his father-in-law.

"Very well, Sir. But there were many men there."

"I will speak to the Centurions," Agricola assured him. "They will ensure that no rumours are spread beyond the camp."

The Governor smiled as he went on, "But that is enough of Hibernia. There is something else we must discuss. Some very good news, in fact."

"Good news, Sir? I could do with some of that."

"I am sure you can. And this will certainly please you. My friends in Rome have been working hard on your behalf, Publius. It is time for you to return."

"To Rome?"

Tacitus sat upright, his face eager for details. A chance to return to Rome. Then his face fell.

"Am I to go in disgrace?" he asked.

"On the contrary," Agricola assured him. "I told you, forget Hibernia. I think I can say with a fair degree of certainty that you will be elected quaestor next year. You must get back so that you can be seen by the voters. You will need to don a white toga and gather votes."

Tacitus could scarcely believe what he was hearing.

"Quaestor?"

"That is correct," Agricola said with a benign smile. "So gather your things and set off in the morning. This is the first step on the path to high office, Publius. It is very important for your future career."

"Yes, Sir. I understand. Thank you, Sir."

"There is no need for thanks. I know you will work diligently."

"Yes, Sir."

"But make no mention of Hibernia to anyone," Agricola warned. "For all our sakes."

"Very well, Sir."

"Excellent. We shall celebrate this evening before you leave us."

"Thank you, Sir. It is excellent news. But I will be sorry not to witness your victory next year."

"Don't worry, I will tell you all about it when I return to Rome myself. In fact, I will probably bore you to tears with my tales."

Tacitus smiled dutifully.

"I doubt that, Sir. I shall record every detail for posterity."

He gave a slight frown as he added, "But Calgacus will oppose you. He is formidable."

Agricola's eyes were hard as stone as he said, "So am I, Publius. So am I."

Author's Note and Acknowledgements

Ireland is as rich in myths and legends as any country in the world. One of those legends is the story of Tuathal "Techtmar" ("The Legitimate"), whose mother was forced to flee, with Tuathal either as a baby or an unborn child, when her husband, the High King, was overthrown. Some versions of the legend say that this was the result of a revolt by an alliance of sub-kings led by Elim mac Conrach of Ulster. Tuathal's mother was reputed to be a daughter of the King of Alba, a name usually meaning the land that was to become Scotland. Naturally, the King gave her and her child refuge.

The story says that Tuathal returned to Ireland after twenty years, with an army at his back. With the aid of the brothers Findmall and Fiacha Cassan, he defeated Elim at the Hill of Achall, near Tara, claiming the High Kingship for himself.

There may have been a real character behind the tales of Tuathal but most of the Irish legends were first written down some centuries after the events they describe and there are varying accounts of when he reigned. While Tuathal is often placed in the second Century AD, one version suggests that it took place around 80 AD. When I came across this legend, it was simply too good a story to ignore as it tied in neatly with Calgacus' own timescale.

It has been suggested by some that Tuathal's army was actually obtained from the Romans, although this is not specifically mentioned in the legends and the most obvious assumption is that it was an army provided by his grandfather, the King of Alba. What is recorded by the Roman historian, Tacitus, is that an exiled Irish prince, whose name he does not mention, approached Agricola seeking help to regain his kingdom. This probably took place a year or two later than in my fictional version of the story but Tacitus' account is often less than clear when it comes to the sequence of events, so I felt there was scope to take some leeway with the timing.

Tacitus says that, when presented with this opportunity, Agricola was confident he could conquer the whole of Ireland with a single Legion but that he did not have the time to spare, so the

411

exiled prince was simply given asylum and held in case he might be used as a convenient excuse to invade Ireland at a later date.

According to Tacitus, that expedition never came about and the Irish prince's ultimate fate is not recorded. Readers may therefore justifiably question why my story has Tacitus himself leading an army to Ireland.

Apart from the obvious answer that this is a work of fiction, there is a tantalising reference in a satire by the Roman writer Juvenal, a contemporary of Tacitus, who may have served with the army in Britain at around this time. In an almost throw-away line, Juvenal claims that the Roman army had reached as far as Ireland. Unfortunately, he does not give any details at all in this passing reference, but some Roman artefacts have been found at the fortified promontory of Drumanagh (Droim Meanach in my story), some fifteen miles from present-day Dublin. It has even been suggested that some of the fortifications at this site may be Roman but erosion of the cliffs has removed most of the evidence. So far, there is no conclusive proof as to whether the Roman presence at Drumanagh was military or simply a small trading outpost.

Anyone who has read Tacitus' histories will probably recognise that the fictional conversations I have given him with Calgacus provided the inspiration for some of his later writing. Having brought Tacitus to Britain in an earlier story, I simply could not resist the temptation of having him meet Calgacus. The reality is that there is no evidence that Tacitus ever came to Britain - although there is no evidence that he did not - and he certainly makes no mention of ever having met any barbarian chieftains, let alone the warrior named Calgacus whom he does mention. Fortunately, lack of evidence does not mean it did not happen. In my defence, Tacitus is very reticent about his own life in his writings. He states many things as facts without explaining his sources or whether he had personal experience of the events he describes.

This story of Calgacus' adventures came from putting all these various strands together. Historians will continue to argue over the very sparse evidence but the combination of legend, archaeology and written allusions has at least allowed Calgacus another victory over Rome.

One feature of Irish legend and mythology is that the concept of kingship seems to have become established at a relatively early period. It is, of course, difficult to be certain about this because the written accounts date from several centuries after the Iron Age and may well reflect a backward projection of the political situation at the time the stories were written down. However, many stories do reflect the division of Ireland into four autonomous "kingdoms", with one ruler acknowledged as "High King". According to some legends, it was Tuathal who took land from each of the four kingdoms of Ulster, Leinster, Munster and Connacht to form a fifth, central kingdom known as Meath. Of course, we should be careful of using foundation myths as evidence of ancient political relationships but the legends suggest that the simplified kingship structure outlined in this story was not impossible.

The story of Scota, the Egyptian princess who fled to Ireland, is an old legend, and one that is little known outside of Ireland. She is alleged to be the ancestor of the Scots who, according to the generally accepted history, migrated to mainland Britain in the sixth Century, although they were known to the Romans as raiders from even earlier times.

I must mention that some modern historians and archaeologists have produced compelling evidence to suggest that there was always a Gaelic-speaking people on the western coast of Scotland and the tale of a migration from Ireland is another foundation myth, perhaps reflecting close kin ties between the people who lived on either side of the Irish Sea. While this theory is gaining support, I'm afraid it did not fit with the requirements of my story so I have stuck to the older version of accepted history in order to incorporate the Scota legend and invent a descendant of the same name.

As for the places mentioned, Emain Macha (pronounced, "Owain Maha") is usually known as Navan Fort, near Armagh. Like the more famous Tara, archaeology suggests that it was a place of ritual significance rather than a home, although Irish legends insist that Emain Macha and Tara were the royal seats of the Kings of Ulster and the High King respectively. Emain Macha does have the remains of a large building which seems to have been destroyed by fire shortly after being completed. This was probably a ritual event rather than an accident and it almost certainly took place in the Bronze Age, not in the first Century.

Whatever the true history - and much of it is controversial or open to interpretation where Ireland is concerned - the Romans

413

left no lasting presence in Ireland. Giving Calgacus the credit for that merely adds to the host of wonderful Irish legends. Now that he has achieved that victory, he can turn his attention to halting their northward advance in mainland Britain. Needless to say, he will have more than Agricola to contend with as he attempts to unite the tribes.

My thanks, as always, to those who have helped with the story. Moira Anthony, Stuart Anthony, Stewart Fenton and Liz Wright for reviewing the drafts, and Philip Anthony for designing the cover image.

GA
June 2016

Other Books by Gordon Anthony

All titles are available in e-book format. Titles marked with an asterisk are also available in paperback.

In the Shadow of the Wall*
An Eye For An Eye
Hunting Icarus *

A Walk in the Dark (Charity booklet)

The Calgacus Series:
World's End*
The Centurions*
Queen of Victory*
Druids' Gold*
Blood Ties*

The Constantine Investigates Series:
The Man in the Ironic Mask
The Lady of Shall Not
Gawain and the Green Nightshirt
A Tale of One City

ABOUT THE AUTHOR

Born in Watford, Hertfordshire, in 1957, Gordon's family moved to Broughty Ferry in the early 1960s. Gordon attended Grove Academy, leaving in 1974 to work for Bank of Scotland. After a long but undistinguished career, he retired on medical grounds in 2008 without having received any huge bankers' bonuses.

Registered blind, Gordon had more time on his hands after retiring so, with the aid of special computer software, he returned to his hobby of writing and had his debut novel, "In the Shadow of the Wall" published in 2010. Gordon's books are now being read by a world-wide audience. As well as his historical adventure stories, he has ventured into crime fiction with some spoof murder mysteries in the "Constantine Investigates" series. He is also kept busy with speaking engagements, visiting libraries, schools and community groups to talk about his books.

In addition to his novels, Gordon devotes some of his time to raising funds for the RNIB. As well as visiting schools and social clubs to talk about his sight loss, he has self-published a charity booklet titled, "A Walk in the Dark", a humorous account of his experiences since losing his eyesight. The booklet is available free from Gordon's website www.gordonanthony.net . All Gordon asks is that readers make a donation to RNIB. This booklet can also be purchased from the Amazon Kindle Store. Gordon will donate all author royalties to RNIB.

Now almost completely blind, Gordon continues to write stories and, in his spare time, attempts to play the guitar and keyboard with varying degrees of success.

Gordon is married to Alaine. They have three children. The family lives in Livingston, West Lothian.

You can contact Gordon via his website or by sending an email to ga.author@sky.com

18240179R00232

Printed in Great Britain
by Amazon